The Moon Could Only Weep

By

Rara Hope

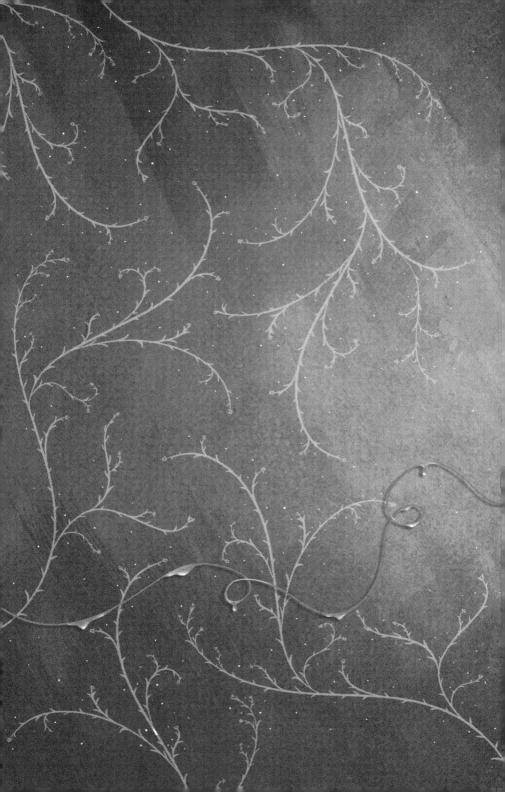

SPENT SPINDLE
STAGE ONE

THE MOON COULD ONLY WEEP

RARA HOPE

Cover art, book design, map, and chapter illustrations by Rena Violet
Act artwork by Brooke Weeks
Edited by Carly Hayward and Jessica Nelson

ISBN (hardback): 978-1-965508-00-8
ISBN (paperback): 978-1-965508-01-5
ISBN (ebook): 978-1-965508-02-2

First edition November 2024
Published by Sterling Page LLC
www.rarapagehope.com

This story involves the following topics: death, grief, violence, suicidal ideation and mention of attempts, infertility, mental health, brain injury, and neurodegenerative disease.
Please read with care.

To your smile when basking in sunlight.
To the most boisterous of your belly laughs.
To the hours spent acting out your favorite movies.
To your inner peace when letting the ocean wash over you.

I promise your story will thrive, so people hear your song.

To Sterling Page Clark.
My little brother.
Our elephant.
Our heart.

Pronunciation Guide

Maijerda: my-djeer-duh

Jeddeith: jed-ee-ith

Lyrian: leer-ee-an

Knax: naks

Wyttrikus: wi-tri-kus

Nadín: nah-deen

Volkari: vole-kar-ee

Denratis: den-rah-tis

Pɛnʌmbrə: pen-uhm-bruh

ælıkar: a-li-kar

ɔpoʊliːn: op-oh-leen

Tiɾın: tier-in

Steslyres: stes-leer-is

Quortense: kor-tense

D'hadian: duh-hade-ian

Ceye: sigh

Hael: hale

Drä: drah

Cë: seh

ɔvrʌ laræk: awv-ruh lar-ak

Roʊzvɛlkə: rose-vel-kuh

Torlen Dovnym: tore-len dov-neem

Torlen Lexnym: tore-len lex-neem

Vythsaden Rosq: vith-say-den row-sk

Dramatis Personae

Maijerda…sailor

Jeddeith…librarian

Wyttrikus…healer

Knax…guardian

Nadín…warrior

Lyrian…sorceress

Denratis…captain

Volkari…necromancer

Act 1

Daemeon's Folly

An excerpt from a faetale detailing the fall of a man to his heart's temptress.
by V. Navanjette
Estimated to be 300 years old

Lilted were her sighs robust with unrequited woe.
Her caress was no less startling than an icy pang to the heart.
Hushed was her song, earnest crescendo before skittering
into dawn.
Her perfume was the humbleness of salt and brightness
of juniper.
Her dance rolled and swelled in fluidly practiced harmony.
She was Daemeon's one true love.
She was the raging sea.

THE WEAVING OF TALES

What brought you to us?
You are hardly a stranger
to our dissonant timbre.

It is embedded in the
shrouds of what has been…

…and the threads of what will be.
Feigning ignorance
will serve no purpose here.

Often we see mortals trudge
From dayspring till gloaming.
Aching and oh, so horridly desperate.

Spent and weary.

It is no marvel to find you here.

Do not burden yourself with
wonderment of our names.

For we are destiny incarnate
and they are not meant for mortal tongues.

You grapple with worry.
I can taste it most poignantly of all.
It is vinegar. And imperishable.

Do you wish to spin
Away your woe?

Will you step up to the task
and hear our song?

To stop living in your reality.

That is what brought you here,
Is it not?
The promise of basking in
the weaving of tales.

Join the fray. Relinquish all
knowledge of your world…

…and step into mine.
Come.

Weave with us.

CHAPTER ONE

STORMS WERE OFTEN UNKIND

FAETALES RARELY LIE.

Maijerda admired them for what they were. Fate-fickle truths ingrained by the inked tongue of books. With the sea vibrant as juniper around her, Maijerda breathed in its salted perfume with a smug grin, the ship bowing before breaking waves. Something about this scene never failed to awaken a mythical hunger for stories and songs that surged in her blood and wandering mind.

Exhaling with the rhythmic sway of the *Norn*, Maijerda didn't bother shielding her eyes from dregs of sunlight illuminating the ship deck; instead she basked in the glow soon to be her spotlight.

She brushed at her collar, freckled fingers adorned with rings, and addressed the crew bribing her to sing. "Aren't you bored with my stories? There'll be plenty more riveting tales to hear tonight in Brine Bend."

A rush of ocean's breath struck Maijerda's garnet curls from her face, reinvigorating her already damp rose-beige skin with sea spray as she lounged against the taffrail.

She kicked her foot to rest on the wall, the Dolzdoem sea at her back. "Surely you don't need *me* to entertain you." Sure, she was searching for compliments. Was that so terrible? Exaggerating her reluctance, she hid a smirk by biting into the last piece of her lokum stash, pomegranate filling melting with the soft crunch of rose petals and pistachios.

A sailor climbing down the mizzen shroud dismissed her guile. "Don't pretend you're not in the mood."

"Yeah, quit stalling!" The handful of them laughed, joining her on the quarter deck.

They knew well and good she couldn't say no to attention. Maijerda? Avoid an opportunity to take center stage? Please. Chuffed with praise, she dusted her hands clean of the lokum. "Come now, your flattery won't be tolerated. Anymore." She winked, thinking of the song she'd picked ages ago.

Fates, it was a damn good one. A song that would have Mother beaming, were she still here... Maijerda tamped the thought clear, denying herself the release of succumbing to the festering hollow of grief. She wasn't without practice.

"Captain won't mind." One man shrugged before knocking back a well-earned swig of tefeuz. The liquor's lush scents of pepper, pine, and coffee roused Maijerda's mind back to her crew. Campfire smoke trailed from the bottle as they passed it along from sailor to sailor.

"Oh I wouldn't be too sure about that." Maijerda leaned in, hand stayed in confidence. "You have actually met him, haven't you?" She swept a tangle of hair over one shoulder. As usual, her frizzed ringlets threatened to swallow up her sea-keen figure. Had she been any shorter, they would have, no matter how diligently she tended to them.

An ıdre woman with ebony skin and pointed ears peeking through cropped lavender hair called to Maijerda as she wound rope. "We've earned it after this trip. What harm is a little song?"

Eyes glossy as opals, with oval irises and pupils, implored her to reconsider with a flirtatious flare.

ιdre were thought to be descendants of fallen starlight from another realm, taking pieces of stone or gems with them. Supposedly this explained the appearance of their eyes, among other aspects.

These particular opal eyes nearly lured her in too, as they often did. Maijerda withheld a flirtatious quip, all but huffing at the irony. What harm, indeed? Especially today of all days. Yet the captain would never understand because he wielded obstinance as his weapon of choice. He'd been a match strike away from banning her storytelling for the last six years, without explanation.

Maijerda sensed fear weeping from him, worsening every Moon. The fear threatened to eat her alive too, but she refused to surrender. One story at a time, she'd choose to fight. If he wanted to flounder in sorrow, so be it. Besides, her stage was set with the *Norn's* patterned sails as her theater curtain and the Dolzdoem her orchestra.

Decision made, Maijerda planted her boot into the deck, grinned at the woman teasingly, and spun to face her crew, hands on hips. He would *not* ruin this. "All right, all right! Hush."

Murmurs and chuckles quieted.

"Fine." She feigned tiring of their coaxing. Eye flutter here, hand toss there, add a shrug. And finally, "You can boast your victory. I'll indulge you."

Everyone cheered as she stacked crates as a makeshift stage. She stepped up and clapped her hands to draw their attention, surveying the crowd for the captain. No sign of him. *Good.* The crew waited for her to begin, hushed and glossy eyed, perhaps leery of missing a single beat. She bit her lip at the memory of her mother spinning this faetale. There was no sense in disappointing them by growing mournful. Mother wouldn't have let it stop her. Maijerda flourished her hands, almost as if creating signs to weave a spell. But there was no such arcana at her fingertips this sunset. Not anymore.

Full of the same spirited gestures, she honored the musicality Mother had used to tell her the story as a child. "Join me then! To honor the Fae Pond in D'hadian. The mythos melded there are a wonder, certainly. In order to make a wish upon its iridescent waters, you must do so on the night of a Dragon's Eye Moon, with your back turned."

Pausing for dramatic effect, she lowered her tone in warning. "You are to walk away, never risking a glance back at the fountain while the Dragon's Eye narrows to watch your every move." Another pause, leaving them hanging before… "If you betray it, the fountain will corrupt your wish." And on that note, she sang.

"Far through dusk I've wandered to find the waning Moon.
With this timeless dance we weave, I tumble in your depths.
In hopes that with my wish, you'll take to conjure bliss.
Your trust is mine for earning. But make no mistake in this give and take.
To chance a glance would spell my undoing…"

She guided each following verse to dance within an eerie lilt. Her chest vibrated with deeper notes before she eased her song to more unusual highs. Hushed in respect for the Fae Pond, she blended the final note with the waves. However, that peace was short-lived.

"What's the meaning of this?" A command layered within the question quenched the crew's flame of excitement.

Maijerda's freckled cheeks burned with retaliation despite the captain's efforts to startle them cold. "Don't be so brash. Care to join us?" She fought his sternness with levity. "It's just a story, after all."

"Attend to your work." He surveyed each crew member too nervous to make a move and follow his orders. *"Now."*

Maijerda's grin pulled to fade but she recovered it to maintain her poise. Their gazes caught and he shook his head pointedly before turning to leave. The nerve of him to show up like this. Stomach swirling uncontrollably, she flinched at a splash of regret and balled her hands into fists, nails stinging her palms. Why was she caving to guilt in the face of his misery? She was allowed to be herself and be happy. So everyone had droned on and on about. It was all a lie.

She rolled her wrist and fumbled to straighten her blouse, the plum linen damp from mist. "You heard the captain. Back to it then." She slid from her perch, wound through the anxiously muttering crowd.

Maijerda marched to the captain's quarters, a lump welling at the base of her throat. Grumbling a few choice swears in A'lorynn cleared it right up. Not bothering to knock, she gripped the door handle and shoved her shoulder forward, smacking into the door. It clunked inside the frame.

"Oh for fuck's sake." She groaned, giving it a swift tug instead.

"Something the matter?" The captain hung his coat, modeled after the latest trends in ælıkar with embossed buttons and embroidered cuffs, on a brass hook.

The matter? Where to begin? She yanked the door closed. "Was that necessary?"

"Please." He ambled to his desk and sat against it with a weary sigh. "Not today."

"When then? You can't run forever."

"I'm not—" He steeled himself, changing to calm. "Your performance caught me off guard." He meant for it to finish the discussion, having used this tone of surrender before.

Leaning on the door, she crossed her arms. "Did it really? That implies you care."

"Maijerda, damn it. Of course I care."

Hah! A bold lie. One she was tired of hearing. "That's rich. You expect me to believe that? You scold every tale I tell. Every song I sing. You claim I'm too old for faetales yet treat me like a child. And—" She ground her heel into the floor. "*You* haven't told a single story, ever since Mother—"

"Don't."

"Why not, Da?" Her incredulity bordered on ridicule; this was far beyond hypocritical. "After all, today marks six years."

He pulled at his graying auburn beard in one exasperated motion. "I'm aware of how many Moons have—"

"Care to lecture me again on how quickly to bury her?" Gesturing openly, she gave a sarcastic twitch of her lip at his reddening complexion.

Silence? What a twist. Da's preferred sedative. There was that fear again. It aged his eyes and rounded his shoulders. She scoffed. "We should honor her with what she loved. There is power in stories."

Da turned to pace from her. "You're speaking out of grief. I'll not argue with you."

Grief, was it? Was grief getting the best of *her* again? She grumbled a throaty chuckle, her words rushing like pelting rain. "We're beyond disagreements. You haven't been the same since Mother died."

He slammed his fist into the desk. "For good reason!"

"Enlighten me then. Don't stow secrets from me. Have I managed to lose your respect?" Standing tall, Maijerda swept her hand from shoulder to waist. These days Da needed reminding she was nearly thirty, no longer an impressionable child.

Da snapped his gaze from the floor, glowering at her. Sun roughened, sand-colored skin, ruddy. Even with their sheen, the moss green of his eyes dulled in comparison to hers. Which was typical for tiraen eye colors, less off putting than idre. He'd struggled for years to look Maijerda in the eyes, painfully similar to Mother's sapphires. Maijerda considered her own emerald gleam a curse bestowed by Mother's ıdre blood. For losing the affection in Da's expression was a curse at best.

He looked to the floor again, his voice a poor show of stability. "Tuft, please. Don't speak like that. We raised you better."

Indeed they had. Maijerda nodded, pressing her lips thin at Da using her childhood nickname. Tuft, as the untamed fur of a fox, mischievous and wild. "You raised me to remain inquisitive and create my own story. Will you ever heed your own words?"

Silence, yet again! She tossed her hands up and moved from the door, accidentally biting her tongue in frustration just as a sailor threw it open in panic, tripping inside. Da should be thankful for the interruption.

"Captain Fenneq!" The sailor tipped his chin respectfully to Maijerda, not forgetting to address her as first officer of the *Norn*.

Her father squeezed at his temples. "What is it?"

"Storm clouds."

Da sighed, urging him to continue.

"They're right close, sir. And Um. They're gaining on us."

Maijerda tilted her head to Da. This hardly seemed important. "We'll arrive in Steslyres by nightfall. We can beat a storm."

Finally, something they could agree on. Da narrowed his eyes at the boy wringing his cap. Poor thing. Always managed to draw the shortest straw. Come to think, maybe that wasn't coincidence.

"I swear, I'm not jesting. Sir. Clouds appeared without warning or wind. Angry as can be. They're moving straight for us. We're being hunted."

STORMS WERE OFTEN unkind. However, this one was an unrivaled menace.

Maijerda hurdled over broken bodies and pieces of her broken ship. Waves pummeled into the *Norn* without care nor a second thought. Her skin stung from the bitterness of cold water. It wouldn't slow her.

Lightning tore apart masses of clouds shrouding the night sky. Shadows and shouts overwhelmed Maijerda's search. Da disappeared on her several times now. Unable to stay put. What she witnessed moments ago as the waves devoured the *Norn* was impossible. Even the most vicious of storms didn't wield claws. Did they? She had to find him.

Maijerda nearly lost her footing as the ship rolled to one side. Thunder rumbled in her bones. Lunging for a mast to cling to, her matted curls pulled free from her skin in the gale.

"Hard to starboard!" She called to those nearest fighting to keep the ship upright.

As soon as the deck leveled, she anchored on the planks and charged forward. Scorched salt tinged the air, no longer pleasant and peaceful. Her tongue was ripe with an acrid burning.

She ducked as the next bolt struck far too close for comfort, nearly blinding her. Maijerda gruffly wiped away rain with her laced sleeve to clear aching eyes. At last he was plainly in view, assisting sailors who were ill-equipped for such devastation.

They were severely outmatched. A mage versed in storm arcana would understand how to counter the damage, but none among their merchant crew were advanced tapestry weavers or casters. Back-splintering efforts were their only hope.

Maijerda urged him away. "Da, listen!" A roar of thunder pounded and she fought to clamp her hands over her ears. "Someone's following us." Another boom sounded.

"We need help!"

He began to usher her to the heart of the struggling crew, she gripped his shoulders and leveled him to face her. "I saw another ship."

"Then signal for help!"

He tried to jerk away and she grabbed a handful of his shirt, the cotton soaked through. "No. They're tracking us." Apparently this wasn't enough. She didn't have time to explain her instincts. Something wasn't right. "Untouched by the storm."

Why wasn't he responding? Now was not the time for silence. "Da, listen to me. I— I swear the storm is alive, with claws and fangs. It's a creature." The words tasted odd.

A whip of lightning harrowed his frown. "Show me the ship."

There wasn't a moment to spare. Time didn't make exceptions for those in need. Without another word Maijerda bolted to the other side of the ship, obligating him to follow. "I don't recognize their colors." She handed him her spyglass, the metal etched with a blessing for a sailor's watchful eye. "Do you?"

Even as he peered through the spyglass, Maijerda couldn't take her eyes off the swirling fog. Within, there was a second ship barreling for them, uncannily steadfast.

While the *Norn's* sails were shredded beyond repair, this phantom ship appeared unscathed and calm.

"Impossible." He lowered the spyglass.

"Apparently not." Maijerda snatched it back and forced it into the cuff of her boot, beside a dagger. His lackluster response warmed Maijerda's ears, all the way to their pointed tips, despite the rain biting her skin.

With authoritative fervor she begged of him to break his silence, just this once. "Da, what are we going to do?"

He turned to her, his jaw slack. "Pray."

"Pray?" Maijerda's eyes widened as she stretched to meet his height as much as possible. "We can't abandon them on a wish." She gestured vehemently to the dispersed crew. "They're family!"

"Maijerda. I'm out of time." He sprinted from her as if she were a demon unleashed from its prison.

Without hesitation she chased after him. "What're you doing? Wait! Da. Stop. Tell me what you saw! Don't be a coward."

He rounded on her, seething. "What has gotten into y—?" He gawked over Maijerda's shoulder in utter disbelief.

She turned on his cue. A tidal wave brewed ahead, aiming for the heart of their ship and growing in height with deliberate force. Maijerda lost precious seconds, hypnotized by the layers in the ocean. It was similar to fantasizing shapes in the clouds as a flash of lightning painted the impression of a snarling creature within the head of the wave.

She could have sworn it was real, a sea monster incarnate and skulking in the waves themselves. After she succumbed to blinking at the battering rain, it vanished. What she may or may not have seen was irrelevant. Options were running thin and she was searching for him yet again. Perhaps this made her selfish, but there wasn't another choice.

She couldn't bear the blame for his death too.

True pandemonium spread as wildfire and he was engulfed in chaos. She shoved, she pushed, she leapt through the crowd, willing herself to move faster. Faster. And faster.

It was then a torrent of arrows ambushed the ship. Maijerda dove for cover and braced herself before they struck. The crew's dying cries were deafening, more so than thunder. Clambering to continue her hunt, she faltered at the sight of him. A numbness in her ears swelled and muffled the screams.

She skidded in a pool of blood that was too deep to have drained from one person. Maijerda crawled to him, her hands slick with blood. His blood? She spit a glob of it that had splashed into her mouth.

This can't be real. This can't be— Her heart beat to escape agony's drooling maw. Fates, it should've known better. There was no escaping this.

"Da. I—"

Her fingers trembled around an arrow of decayed coral and barnacles buried in his throat with his last words. It may as well have stolen hers. There were no words capable of binding her stress into something tangible. Maijerda grimaced and grunted around the fire consuming her voice, ravenous for grief. What more could it possibly want from her? Da was dead.

And… he was clutching a leather book, drowned in rain and blood. She struggled to breathe, ears ringing at a noxious pitch. Her vision blurred with panic as the wave reached a monstrous height and descended upon the ship.

"I'm sorry." Without thinking, Maijerda grabbed the book and tore through the wreckage. She leapt over the *Norn's* edge, into the mouth of the wave.

Into the deep beneath. Into the darkness of the sea.

CHAPTER TWO

DESTRUCTION WAS DELECTABLE

ABOARD THE BLACKENED DECK OF THE *Oracle Rift*,
Lyrian flooded with primordial rage. Her opaline skin
bore veins pulsing as rivers on maps, coming alive in
the night.

"Trust me when I say it is in your best interest to bring me
something more palatable." Lyrian raised her voice, her whole
body shaking with fury. "Where is the book?" She chastised the
scum of a crew as they cowered and hissed.

Let them tremble. If they wished for wounds to lick, she'd
gladly oblige.

A tiraen with scars crisscrossing up her olive arms cawed at
her companion's cowardice. This quickly earned her a side eyed
glance from three sun-tanned ıdre adorned in faded tattoos from
pointed ears to muscled forearms.

Sparks of Lyrian's arcane lightning quivered at her wrists. It
didn't require much thought to tap into this aspect of the tapestry.
Not with the bonds she possessed. Not with the aftermath of the
storm she'd conjured, wild inside her. "Silence is the best gift you
have to offer? Pathetic."

She pinned her arms at her side, burrowing them within free-flowing silks and chiffons, fingers aching to weave another tempest to wipe these imbeciles from her sight. Frustrated at her weak tethers to arcana, she curled her lip. Conjuring the storm to strike down the *Norn* had depleted most of her arcana. But not *all*.

Lyrian dared anyone to argue she didn't reflect the wickedness of her beloved sea, commanding the ocean to rumble, as did the sky. She didn't remember what it meant to be tiraen. She had no desire to remember. All quieted, rocking to maintain balance as the ship swayed.

"Best to not see to our untimely demise." Denratis quelled behind the helm. Fathom-deep-green sails bowed and blew taut above him, darkening his brown skin. "We still have use of them." Stiff in posture, he gestured to his crew.

"Perhaps you do." She spat, loosening her grip on the ocean, pushing past two gray-skinned ersul-bloods. The thundering ceased. "They're little more than scavenged corpses to me." She turned her full, berating attention to the crew. "The *Norn* was subdued so you may board without altercations. I will not be forced to tend to you as babes."

"Not that I would ever doubt your prowess." Denratis countered by stepping beside her. "What are the odds any survived?"

Lyrian's eyes flared. She had scraps of patience left. Awfully pompous of him to suggest someone slipped through her fingers.

The captain raised his hands confidently, yet defensively. "I mean to say there's a possibility the book was taken."

His arrogance was tiresome and transparent, no matter how well he believed he wore his disguise. She knew the truth of it. However, never in her twelve hundred years had Lyrian imagined a time in which a tiraen might be right. Breathing through clenched teeth, she entertained him. "You seem full of suggestions. Ripe with ideas. Go on then."

He motioned toward the crew. "We could send a party on land, ask locals for word of shipwreck survivors. Townsfolk grow chatty if it means a chance in the spotlight with liquor in hand."

"What if this rouses suspicion before we've had the chance to strike?"

Denratis loosened the collar of his sailor's coat, the stitching near seamless with the night. "A fair point—"

Lyrian cut him off with a twist of her hand. She couldn't risk leaving any stone unturned. She didn't need Denratis providing insight. Of all the lunacies. It was painful enough that she couldn't search the shore herself, reliant on being near the ocean to sustain her arcana at such strength.

"Wait for me to return. There will be no rest until we find that book." Without another disgusted word she drifted to quarters below deck.

Upon entering her chambers, the air groaned and morphed into something personified. Where others might breathe deeply to test the weight and strain of the air, Lyrian breathed indulgently. As a nezdrade, she did so to honor her elemental tapestry connection to both sea and tempest. From fire, earth, water, and wind, to elements of legend, elemental bonds manifested based on each nezdrade's innate, arcane strengths.

She maintained her spectral poise as she unpinned the side of her aquamarine-stained silver hair. It caressed the angles of her features, reaching her lean waist. She removed a blue leather pouch from her sash, locking it inside a trunk with an arcane glyph for good measure. It had taken her years to collect each morsel of stone inside. That was an ordeal she couldn't embark on a second time. Without them, obtaining the book might mean little on its own. She wouldn't fall short in her endeavors, no matter how her… *mistress*, Volkari, reveled in lessons warning of overlooking details.

Unclasping a pewter brooch, her sea-foam wraps and green scaled-leather robe slid to the floor, leaving her body free to collect dew from the dampness. Thin, reddish scars of spell glyphs marring her body remained dull in the candlelight. Unlatching the window, she sat, swinging her legs to the tide. Her gaze fixated on the storm-weary sea to mimic each ripple.

Lyrian rotated an intricate chain draped around her neck, as metallic as her hair. The end nestled against her breastbone, a tiny tentacle wrapped on the end of the chain emitted a muted teal.

Using a focus, or talisman, aided her in channeling arcana within the tapestry as well as within her god's influence. Before she'd become nezdrade and pledged to intertwine with the elements, her deity, Othesk, taught her of the beauty in harnessing freedom and consequence. Though not all elementals required or preferred a god to enhance their connection to the elements, Lyrian resonated with Othesk and their divine teachings unconditionally. How solemn she was, to have not heard their voice in nine hundred years.

Her arcane bonds were strongest at sea as a nezdrade. Even so, she would need to harness her arcana carefully for what remained of the night so as to not waste it. These years weren't bountiful for her when it came to weaving. The world wasn't alone in suffocating under that wretched Veil. She could hardly spare the notion a thought, ill with contempt. Now she must labor for abilities, earning few as boons from Othesk. It was their gifts that granted her strength to create the storm which destroyed the *Norn*. A rise in power, brief.

Rhythmically she spoke with words made of the sounds of storms long since passed. She encouraged the ocean to want her. To *need* her. To care for her at her demand. Waves crested and crawled for her as though vines starving for sun. Higher they climbed, embracing her waist and limbs. The weight of the enchantment pulled her from the sill, merging her with the unpredictability of the tide.

A RING OF fog encompassed the *Norn*, guising the massacre from potential passersby at Lyrian's behest. Once she removed herself from the water and regained her bare form, Lyrian glided through the carnage, chin held high.

Destruction was delectable, wasn't it?

Lyrian puffed her chest, heart beating to fill the space, smug with victory. An obscene passing of Moons, from Dawning to Bitter, for nine hundred years had waxed and waned from Pɛnʌmbrə since Lyrian last bore the freedom to unleash her true self. Pɛnʌmbrə, meanwhile, had been oblivious to her sequestered state over the centuries.

Tonight heralded her dedication to the renewed vigor of self-importance. This realm would never be so naive as to smother and forget her ever again.

She investigated with deadly silence, not bothering to sidestep slicks of blood. Smirking, she cocked her head at the sight of the captain of the *Norn*. Beaten and battered. Her arrow was embedded in his neck as a harbinger of mortality.

"Aw, Theo." She raised her eyebrows, the scent of his blood fresh and mingling with the sea's ferocity. "I do hope your reunion with Relona is pleasant. You should be grateful I bothered reuniting you."

Lyrian lowered to the deck and scavenged his body for the book. When this proved worthless, she conjured five featureless sprites composed of water and lightning to scour for signs of forgotten life. None returned with word of the book. They confided in her that they couldn't find it under fractured bone or spilt blood. Nor was it tucked under splinters of masts or tattered sails.

Lyrian dismissed them without a word, an unusual heat flushing her face. How insulting. And infuriating. Denratis' lackeys hadn't weaved a web of lies from languidness or perpetual fear. The book managed to escape. But how?

The ocean was attentive to her curses, feeding off rage and thinning patience. Cracking her fingers, she plucked a sailor's knife from a corpse and strode to the railing. Without a quiver, she carved three vertical lines of varied lengths into each forearm, twisting the blade. She chose a patch of skin unmarked by glyphic scars, despite her desire to strip them from her flesh. Given her arcana was as stifled as it was, the cost of this spell was greater than it would have been during Volkari's reign.

She cracked her neck, her jaw twitching, and stretched her palms toward the sea. Lyrian began to weave. Using the arcane dialect of her ocean's song, her voice mimicked and melded with the sounds of the waves. Pulling her consciousness and desire with each measure, she searched via the ocean's guidance to find her mark. Murky blue blood pulsed from her forearms and spattered into the water obediently to strengthen the spell.

Her enchantment's strength increased tenfold, responding to the demand by creating a wall of water before her, streaked with blood. She ceased the incantation as the wall rippled with the visage of a gaunt woman, her lips keen on devouring pride.

Lyrian lowered her hands and brought her left palm to rest at the base of her neck. It was a well-rehearsed sign of admiration and supposed obedience. In turn, she left a smearing of blood behind. She refused to reveal symptoms of fear. What was fear but a disease?

"Mistress." Lyrian bowed her head. "I come to you out of respect and in confidence."

No response came. Volkari drolly spun a luminescent etheric thistle stem between her fingers.

Lyrian withheld a scoff. How unsurprising. Volkari was continuously tempted by possibility, never bold enough to act. A bird with clipped wings. Her arcana was weaker than Lyrian's and more challenging to access. There was also the matter of Volkari being denied use of their era's foundational arcane language, ɔvrʌ laræk. Lyrian, among others, utilized different dialects to weave spells. It was how she spoke the same tongue as the sea.

Lyrian held a rigid posture. "The book has disappeared. We need— I need, your guidance."

"Does he still draw breath?" Volkari's voice was unnervingly smooth. The tone alone could stir the dead from long-awaited slumber. It raised hairs on the back of necks, made people question their faith, and sent them to an early grave.

Save for Lyrian. Volkari's hollow resilience wore her nerves by the day.

"No Mistress, his body is spent."

Volkari brought the thistle to her lips, her head turned from Lyrian. "Is it help you're asking for?"

The manifestation of this request was no comfort. Regardless, agreement was the only choice. Lyrian drank the chill of the night with a sharp inhale. "Yes. The book has escaped our grasp. He must have discarded it before I killed him."

"Did you search the sea? Call upon your blood?"

"I did. No reply came from the waves. They're just as bewildered as I am."

No response.

The top of Lyrian's spine sparked, fully aware her suggestion would condemn her to return to Volkari's fortress. "Perhaps the seer can rifle through her whispers in the fated dark. And tell us what's become of the book."

It was true, Volkari placed far too much faith in her prisoner. The seer was a tiresome and miserable waste of efforts but had proved useful these recent Moons. The prophecy she offered Lyrian being one reason to keep her alive, if that was what she could be called. And her insight into hidden arcane ley lines and nexus points, another.

"Somber suggestion to use her divinations." Volkari laid the thistle on a table, the left side of her mouth twitching upward. "You must be desperate."

Lyrian sharpened her stare and tightened her jaw as the ship buckled. Desperation was beneath her. They *both* were reliant on discovering the book's secrets and its inevitable destruction. Success in this search was no solitary deed. Without it they would fail to complete their ritual. The fate of the realm was dependent on it.

Volkari tilted to cross her legs, her cadaverous complexion enhanced by burn scars stretching across her neck and fingers. "What of the seer's prophecy you pretend to not cling to? Have you seen signs of someone who will fulfill it?"

"Nothing. Mistress."

In time with a dissatisfied bend of her neck, a glow refracted an intensity of green painted at the fringed tips of her obsidian hair. "Your failures are vast, Lyrian Llach. Be grateful for my sympathies. Now, the captain and I have much to discuss. Take your place."

Lyrian mustered a show of submission, bowing again. She positioned the knife and engraved a rune in her chest. Breathing into the seeping pain, she braced against the ship, shoving aside what delight Volkari must have in watching Lyrian bleed for her.

In the water's image, Volkari rested her head on a slab of slate stone the shade of bruising. Her ears, drawn into a point typically seen with ıdre bloodlines, peeked through her hair.

Her eyes rolled until a gloss replaced the oval pools of deadened gray-pearl irises.

Lyrian's body convulsed and contracted in response to the cold emanating from the glyphic wound and when she raised her head, her eyes weren't her own. Instead an overturned green film vicariously savored the bloodshed.

Entranced as a conduit, Lyrian returned to the captain's corpse, knelt on one knee, and rested her fingertips on his forehead. Together the women summoned an arcane path and sympathetic balance to contact the soon-to-be-forgotten dead.

It was an inherent consequence of dying, being forgotten. Loved ones are the worst offenders, as they strive to forget their dead to lessen the suffering. However, the world still remembered him. For now.

Maintaining this bond in the tapestry at such a distance diminished the efficiency of their already strained arcana. They extracted tatters of Theo's emotional flares with respectable force.

Adrenaline fueled thrills, terror, and loss. Embedded within the final surge rested a conflicted void desperate to remain hidden. There was a piece of him that was incomprehensibly still alive. Could it mean unfinished business? Hardly. It wasn't his soul lingering before passing. No, this was different. Familiar. Gentle, young, and loved. And very much alive.

Together, the women breathed deep and spoke in dissonant unison. "Who are you holding close?"

They were met with defiance. Pathetic.

"Show me. Who is it? Friend? Mother." The ship creaked. "Father. Brother. Sister." Even the wind listened with bated breath. "Daughter?"

Theo cowered. A pulse within the disarray.

Was this to mean a figurative tether? Tiraens were unnecessarily complex. The concrete significance of this particular affection was a spark reeking with protective urgency.

The kind brought on by kin. Tiraens, fortunately were tactlessly obvious and sentimental. Their binding shattered precisely at that moment, the arcana unreliably taxing for them both.

Volkari awakened in her own skin, no longer occupying Lyrian. Her discoveries rang through the mirage in a struggle to catch her breath. "Did you feel his affection? He has a child. He must. There's worry resonating within him, that he will not abdicate." She reached with a crooked finger in his direction. "He's protecting someone."

Lyrian rose to her feet, her sight watery and legs thudding through numbness. "A child?" Depraved pleasure formed a thin line from her dour expression. "From what I recall, Relona was more intelligent than that."

"Once upon a time, she was." Volkari was twisting the thistle again to mask her tremors. "Even I won't speak ill of the dead. She did us a great favor with her death. One I will not forget."

Lyrian didn't appreciate people attempting to toy with her confidence. Leave it to Volkari to thank the dead instead of the woman before her. The woman responsible for finding a way to free Volkari from banishment in the first place, by tearing the Veil ever so slightly with Relona's demise.

"Nor I." Lyrian played along.

"Ah, but I forget myself in reminiscence." Volkari waved memories aside. "Send Denratis into the city to investigate."

"Denratis? Mistress, he—"

"Send... Denratis. Are you not reliant on the sea for your arcana?"

As though Volkari didn't have her own limitations? This weaving to fuse herself to Lyrian was risky. She'd be weak for days if not a full Moon cycle.

Yes, Lyrian's arcana was restrained too. Yes, she would overcome this and thrive again. Lyrian swallowed hard, blood pulsing as cold sap. "Yes, Mistress. Which proves why I must also continue pursuit of this prophecy. To find another with nezdrade threads to aid in destroying the Veil."

Ignoring Lyrian's concerns, Volkari set the thistle aside. "In four weeks you are to return to my side. Your talents are needed here, in Gazdeq."

"Mistress," Lyrian protested, her disdain increasingly difficult to swallow.

"Do you despise my company so terribly? Lyrian. We must continue preparing for the ritual. Your leave was temporary, do not pretend to believe otherwise. Until then, spare nothing in hunting the child down. Seize the book and bring them to me." A flurry of pure detestation leapt across her face. "Should you fail to find them before the next Moon, task Denratis with continuing the search. You will return to Gazdeq."

With such a delicate relationship to maintain, there would be no arguing tonight. Choose your battles, so mortals say. Lyrian strained her oath. "Very well Mistress. I swear it will be done." With a murmur and flourish of gestures, Lyrian dismissed the spell, granting the water permission to rest.

So, they were to chase down a child? So be it. She'd confronted far more dangerous creatures in her time. Lyrian spared the *Norn* a sigh and sneer, before balancing on the railing. She'd destroy it tomorrow when she was stronger. For now, no one would see through her arcane fog. Lyrian called upon the ocean, using every last thread of herself to meld with its form. Rest was needed before charting their fresh course. One which smelled deliciously akin to hunting Relona's blood those paltry years prior. What pleasure it would bring to soak her hands in the blood of Relona's child.

CHAPTER THREE

Halcyon's Warm End

A RAW, ABRASIVE ACHE OF SALT ON Maijerda's lips paired inharmoniously with the rustle of cresting waves. The salt was also a paralytic, refusing to wake her limbs, ravaging her sight. Ears ringing, body stiff, somehow she wasn't a corpse. She'd survived the battle to swim for shore, the ocean storm no longer attempting to drown her. Shoving a brittle limb into sand, Maijerda pressed to roll to her stomach, shaking and soaked with a death-foreboding chill.

The pitch of night lessened to blurred glimpses of a fog-laden beach. With sight came merciless reality. She called for Da, or at least she tried. Water convulsed from her stomach and up her throat, sending her coughing and sputtering.

A gurgle, an incoherent shout. Then another, until… "Da!"

Stumbling to unsteady feet, Maijerda blinked in the blur of city lights both arcane and flame behind her. The city of Steslyres perched in a crescent of coast, harbors full of docked vessels. Across the ocean, the hope of finding the *Norn* or the phantom ship was oppressed by darkness and fog, eluding her entirely. Even the lighthouse down shore wasn't visible. To be left in such darkness was dreadful. Frantically, Maijerda sought her one constant companion in this life, someone she could trust with her worry. But the Moon and her guardians were smothered by storm clouds.

Maijerda's chest tightened at the stretch of beach littered with rocks and shells. The brimming truth taunted her, surreal and intolerable. She couldn't be alone. Others must have survived the wreck. Sole survivors were for faetales, not whatever this nightmare could be called.

A vile burn raked through her chest, splotched her skin with rash, and struck her eyes. Her throat tensed with efforts to stifle tears. Unable to hold on any longer, she rocked as she knelt, bursting at the seams. Sand and kelp falling from her ringlets of garnet and red wine.

Maijerda scratched and tugged at her blouse, stretching the torn fabric, grazing sandy, bloody wounds. Why was it so tight around her chest? Making every nerve burn! Everything pressed on her, everything wanted to consume her. There was no one to turn to. "I'm sorry Da, I—" Her words cracked into a moan. "I'm so sorry. Please. I didn't mean to abandon you. I didn't—"

This was *impossible*. To be eviscerated from the inside out again, after Mother. "Please come back. I want him back. This can't be real! This isn't real." Her body shuddered with an incredible howl of pain, forcing her pleas to choke. An awful pitch. Fog rushed clear of the space immediately around her. As she bellowed, for there was nothing left to do, Maijerda retched on the spot.

She wiped the sick from her chin while staving off rolling surges of nausea. Sinking deeper into sand, she recoiled as her stinging palm met with something cold and sharp. Maijerda dug into the sand, finding the metal corner of the book she had taken from Da. Of all things to have in that moment. A book she'd never seen before.

She pulled it free, dusting the hardened cover as best she could. It was inexplicably dry. Hadn't it been doused in Da's blood? She'd never know it now, pristine as it was. With a tug, she secured it under her belt to ensure it wouldn't stray from her side. Illogical thoughts, sure. But what if it did? It was all she had left of him. One thing at a time. This was too much.

She needed help. Judging by where she landed on the coast, the Smithies wasn't far. Liam and Selene would know what to do. This time of night? Wytt should be there too, studying. At a dead run she stormed from the beach to the streets of her home and sanctuary, instinctively forging a path through the city to Brine Bend.

On any other night, Maijerda would've indulged in the sweet perfume of the wisteria vines decorating the woodwork frame of the Smithies. It didn't matter what time of year she returned from a trip, she relied on their calming blooms. Tonight deemed such pleasantries utter nonsense.

She ran up the steps and burst through the robust doors darting her gaze to find her friend. Not that it was difficult. He was the only varlodeth in the tavern. Candlelight flickered off Wytt's pink and mauve mottled skin. His opaque golden eyes startled from the books he was studying and landed on her, beaming. "You're back!" He flung his pen aside, papers fluttering from his table to the scuffed wooden floor.

Before Maijerda could react, Wytt wrapped her in a hug, one of his twisted black horns gently pressing into her jaw. He pulled back, frowning at her weak return. Waves of Wytt's alabaster hair fell into his eyes with his frown. He rubbed her arms. "You're soaked to the b-bone. Mmmaijerda, what happened?"

"I don't know what to do."

"About w-what?" Wytt steadied her as she swayed, flicking his tail to her waist to help. Panic set in again, just as it had on the beach, her chest constricted, her mouth watered, and her breathing strained rapidly in and out.

"Hey. Hey. Maijerda. Stay with me."

She struggled for focus, panic consuming her breath, her pulse, her hearing. Everything. Even the neutral hues of Wytt's clothes overwhelmed her vision.

"Breathe w-with mme. Hey. Sssh. Sh. Sh." Wytt held onto her shoulders, exaggerating his slowed breaths for her to imitate, well practiced in guiding her to calm.

When she could speak again, she grimaced. "I'm sorry."

"What? D-don't apologize." He pulled her in for another hug, more gently. "Tuvon's breath. You're bleeding." Her plum-colored blood coated his hands, speckled with sand. His demeanor switched ever so slightly to the attentiveness taught to healers, searching for her wounds.

Motherly urgency ushered Maijerda to rest. "Come, sit down."

Maijerda blinked at the salt and tears in her eyes, struggling to see clearly. Maijerda's breath quickened at the sound of Selene's voice and her hand joining Wytt's to guide her to a chair. "No. No. I can't just sit down. I can't."

The graying and finely wrinkled woman's grin fell, her tanned skin flushing, expression worried. "Talk to us. Tell us what happened."

"I-I-I don't know what to do." Damn words. There were a thousand ways to say—Fates, scream—about what happened. Yet she couldn't. Wasn't it obvious? She was beaten, bloodied, and bruised, soaked through. Did she have to say it?

Wytt squeezed her forearms, pleading with his gaze for her to speak. "We're rrrrright here. Y-you're sssafe."

Selene cupped her cheek. "Don't know what to do about what, love?"

"The storm. Our ship. It—" Maijerda's words hung in the air with a snap of a tear-streaked breath. People turned to localize her cry, glancing between mismatched lanterns and candles propped on the tables.

Liam lumbered through the kitchen doorway then, ash-blond hair damp with sweat, his brow furrowed. "Selene what's the matter?"

"She's just stumbled in. Looking as if—"

Selene's words were garbled in the return of the ringing in Maijerda's ears. Her vision watered again. A brisk cold from Wytt's nimble fingers brought her back as he gripped her arms harder.

Liam stood behind Wytt, lowering his voice. "What storm? Where's Theo?"

Barks grumbled from the kitchen as Morel squeezed past Liam, his black and gold fur glossy from rain.

"The *Norn* is gone. My father is... I-I found him. Dead." What a heartless way to break the news to them. There was no other way. "The others, I don't know."

The dog skidded to her, promptly sniffing and licking her boots.

Wytt gently scratched Morel's neck, his hands practically disappearing in fur. "Hey buddy, not now, all right? Rest."

Morel sat at the command and whined, his nose still twitching.

With a stiffness in attempt to steel herself, she said, "I survived. There must be others."

Wytt nodded and looked to Liam to make the call.

Liam's baritone demanded his patrons' attention. "Anyone who is able and willing to search, be ready in ten minutes."

A beat of silence was all that breathed before every guest checked the clock on the mantle and shouted to each other to meet at the docks with plenty of lanterns and blankets.

Wytt unwound his patchwork cowl from around his neck and settled it around her neck and shoulders. "Your wounds need t-tending," he stated to try and sway her from arguing.

"Wyttrikus. I can't sit here wondering."

"I understand th-that, but you've p-prrrobably lost more blood than you r-realize."

"I'm fine. Promise. I need to go with you."

Wytt huffed and sighed. "I know. Let's g-go. When we get b-b-back, I'm patching you up."

She settled for a nod and went to the door. Morel whimpered and groaned into another bark, making Maijerda jump.

"Rel. Fates, I'm sorry. You stay. Please. I don't want you getting hurt."

Rel cocked his head at her, acting as if he didn't understand.

"Don't give me that. Stay. Rest." She swallowed hard, signaling with her hand for him to be calm. "Good boy."

He paced and yawned by the fireplace as she and Wytt stepped outside to wait for the others.

It proved to be more hopeless than she wanted to believe more quickly than she'd expected. Collectively the search party returned their rowboats to the dock with the extra weight of their hardened souls. Everyone parted ways after providing words of comfort and condolence to Maijerda, hats in hand. Promises of company, prepared meals to come, and an endless string of "sorry for your loss."

As the last woman released Maijerda from an embrace, Liam stood beside her. "I'm sorry, hon. I know you've heard it a thousand times already. But I am, I'm so sorry." He cleared his throat and tried to wipe his tears with his wrist so as to not draw attention to it.

"Thank you for trying." She sniffed, nose dripping. "Da knows you tried. You should go back with the others."

"You best not be far behind."

"I won't be."

Liam gripped her tightly in an embrace of solemn love. "Watch yourselves out here. We'll see you soon." He took Selene under his arm and together they walked away.

Wytt blinked rapidly at her, likely fighting to keep from crying too. If he started crying because she was already in tears, it would worsen hers. They both knew that. "I-I-I'll walk with you home."

"Home? You make it sound simple."

"It d-does sound w-weirdly easy, doesn't it?" Wytt's tail drooped to the sand. "You shouldn't be out here a-alone."

Maijerda waved the sentiment away, drawn to the monotony of the waves, her skin numb to the cuts and abrasions on her limbs. "I'm not ready."

Wytt closed his eyes, their golden hue dimmed by the midnight sky. "You're not abandoning him. This isn't y-your fault."

If that were true, why was guilt all she knew? Her back stiffened and she pressed a fist into her thigh. She could never abandon him. Not like Mother. Not again. "Don't wait up for me." She produced her most convincing smile. It was horrendously draining.

He gave her a prolonged once over and sighed. "I-I'll leave you b-b-be. I won't rest till you get back and we bandage you u-up."

"Deal."

He lingered a moment longer before returning to the city proper. Relieved, she settled onto a boulder and began her vigil. Staring into sand she mindlessly grazed her fingers along the floral tattoo twisting down her left arm to the top of her hand.

The pebble and ash-colored swirls of the sand were hypnotic in the way they organized her sorrows within the patterns. Something to dissolve into.

But where to begin when coping with death? How to manage it all? It should be easier by now. She wept. Would it ever feel less poisonous? Most people are flesh and bone. Maijerda was beginning to feel made of failure and blame.

First, Mama. Now Da? She'd failed him. "I'm so sorry Mama," she whimpered. "I promised you both I'd protect you and I... I didn't."

Fog crept to her, growing ghoulish. It taunted her hopes for there being time to spare, time for others to flounder from the wreck. The fact the wreckage was out of sight throughout the entire search, that planted a doubtful, rotting seed within her.

In that promise of time, Maijerda worked up the means to sing. At first she considered the melody she affectionately called her "lullaby." It'd been with her for as long as she could remember. Wordless and without an identifiable origin, it was something she alone knew. Mama and Da had never heard it before in their lives. Calling her talented and wistful for having created it. Which she hadn't. It stuck in her mind like a catchy tune from a show. For whatever reason, she couldn't bring herself to sing it now, compromising with herself to sing a funeral song meant for those taken in soul and body by the sea. Usually hopeful in its mourning, Maijerda's unfiltered upset changed its key to accompany the fog.

Bereft of key, bargain or plea,
My mind aches for a voice departed.
Peace tethered to withering flame,
Time comes for souls to sway.

A song forged in silence, hushed evermore.

A winged stillness upon a setting sea,
Wondering why each thrum hurts to breathe.
Your memory cast to drifting glass.

Maijerda paused where she shouldn't when performing this verse, senses wary. Was that a voice on the waves? Others joining her, as if called forth from her sadness? It couldn't be true. She was hearing what she hoped… what she wanted, but it wasn't real. On she carried, using the sea as her metronome.

On the rush of waves lulling salted bones kept as sand,
Journey well and turn to glass at long, long last.
Until the Norn do weave the coming of my tide
Guiding my threads to the edge of the sea.
Our memories cast to drifting glass.

She pushed from her rock, searching for him. There was another singing with her again for the final phrase, only one this time, as opposed to many. Da? Singing with her? Against every odd buried and burned. He was here with her, in wish, not flesh. There was no sign of him and there was no helping it. He was gone.

Even hearing his voice was a figment of her somber imagination and therefore a lie she wouldn't believe. There was no comfort in it.

Maijerda resumed her vigil until the tide changed its tune and the air was sick with a mixture of Halcyon's warm end and a humid crispness.

Finally, the waning Tempest Moon and her three celestial stone guardians reappeared through cloud cover, their auras robust. Two of the guardians, adjacent from one another, crossing diagonally around her swollen belly. The third wound a more central course at the Moon's middle.

Maijerda sobbed at their appearance, pleading with the Moon to share in her mourning. "I've been lost without you tonight. I don't know if you saw the storm. It has taken more from me than I can spare." She poured her sorrow for losing Da into the Moon, for she was stoic enough to hold onto it. It couldn't be hidden and Maijerda could not bear this alone. The Moon was there for her when Mama was kill— When Mama died, she forced to correct herself. As close a friend as Wytt. She was grateful for the Moon's empathy, holding her together as she let herself fall apart.

When the Moon and her guardians trailed in the sky toward dawn, they encompassed Maijerda in stiff numbness as she willed her body to tread the path home to the Smithies, her mind nowhere near.

CHAPTER FOUR

A MASK OF VALIANCE

THE SEA RELUCTANTLY RELEASED LYRIAN INTO her chambers aboard the *Oracle Rift,* to Denratis staring at his bare chest in her speck-stained mirror. Lit cigarette in hand, he brought it to his lips and puffed the smoke to obscure his reflection.

Brooding while she was gone? How fitting. He did not shift his gaze in awareness when she stepped to him. "Feeling sentimental?" She grazed a hand down his honed shoulder, giving him the attention he ceaselessly craved. "I'll never forget the night I found you shipwrecked, drowned to death." His silvering brown hair was coarse between her fingers. She twisted a lock of it and whispered, "Convenient for us both, was it not?"

Denratis shivered, her sea-glass stare reflecting ahead of him. "I wouldn't dare take your generosity in reviving me for granted." He reached for her hand, giving it a light kiss, and leaned on the dresser to face her.

His efforts to don a mask of valiance were weak. She couldn't let him on to the fact she was quite aware of his apprehensions. He was a tool to be kept sharp for her use and he would be worthless to her if he was privy to her insight. No matter how badly he wanted to leave her, he never would. Because he couldn't.

"Do you still question my right in resurrecting you?"

"Never."

He was lying. Adorable. It wasn't necessary to expose him in this moment. "Hm. Good. You were resurrected with the life water brings, not necromantic bidding." Lyrian bunched his linen shirt in her hand, tracing a path along his breastbone to admire her craftsmanship. "Never dismiss that force."

His wound was everlasting, exposing several ribs. An eel slithered around his heart, coursing currents of energy in a steady tide to pump his blood. What bone was visible among the jagged tears of his body was engraved with runes she carved to enact the ritual. It'd taken days to complete, but it was well worth it.

"What became of your search?" Denratis posed, holding her hand to his deeply brown and tanned chest, though out of reach of his heart, taking a long drag of his cigarette.

As if distance could thwart her?

She grinned before pursing her lips. "Unfortunately, they spoke the truth. The book is no longer in his possession. However, I have reason to believe the captain has a child." She slid from him, donning her silks without replacing the sea creature brooch, so as to accent her figure. He played into her game, lust overtaking his eyes.

"We have four weeks until I am to return to Gazdeq, per Volkari's demands." She hadn't intended to pause, though the looming sacrifices tied to her return to that wretched island gouged a hole in her stomach, pulling to her throat.

Forever persevering through her loathing, she continued. "Admittedly, I must rest at sea. You will…" Oh, how best to feed his ego in giving this task? Lyrian added a touch of gravity to her sultry inflection. "…you will spare nothing to search Steslyres for Relona's child. This is your task to oversee; Volkari can think of no one better to see it through." Lyrian certainly could. He didn't need to hear that from her. "Bear in mind, they should be no younger than six years old. It's on your head to reveal the truth, and I expect you'll report to me when you do." Predictably, he held his chin aloft, sternly taking the direction.

"Understood. We'll reroute the ship to take cover from lighthouses watching the coast."

"See to it that our company is informed." She sauntered to him, tempting his will to slip with her touch, for the need of feeling wanted.

He smirked, his icy blue eyes eager for the bait. "Come morning?" Denratis shrugged to remove his shirt.

"We're nearly there as it is. The Moon is tiring." She forced blinking with coy invitation, stroking him from neck to chest. "Though I can't say the same." Tilting her neck to catch the Moonlight and to invite his touch, she gave him his cue to take action. Lyrian needed him to feel in charge.

Denratis spun her aggressively, pressing her body tightly to his as though she would slip free. One day she would. Til then, this would satisfy. They collided into the dresser and he raised her up by the waist until she was perched on its marble counter. Her silks, soft against her skin as Denratis brushed them to her thigh and leaned in for a kiss. The fabrics sent a tingling pulse through her that even Lyrian wouldn't ignore. They breathed through the kiss in unison, Lyrian brushing her lips to his ear. Then her tongue along his neck. He shuddered just as she planned and pulled her close by the small of her back, arching his hips. Always wanting more. He'd have to earn it. As he kissed her from collar bone to navel, Lyrian leaned back so he could better reach all of her.

She made sure to pleasure him in ways which sent him to the edge and kept him wanting more. A decade had been plenty for her to learn the truth of passion for Denratis. It was not romance he craved, but to devour and to be devoured. Lyrian discovered this early in their partnership because she longed for it too. This was among the myriad of secrets he remained oblivious to under her control. Famished, they enveloped each other in animalistic fury, the eel writhing around Denratis' heart with each ravenous kiss.

CHAPTER FIVE

SOLACE

OREL WHIMPERED AND LICKED THE SIDE of Maijerda's face, waking her from an excruciatingly vivid nightmare of—well, of... she couldn't think on it.

"Rel..." She wiped slobber from her chin with a bandaged hand, hardly sober from sleep. Midday already? Delightful.

Rel jumped off the bed and pawed at the door.

"Yes, yes. I know." She rolled off the bed, groaning at the aches from peeling wounds and scrapes from the wreck. The salve Wytt used to numb them had worn off by early morning. Wrappings likely needed replacing too. Rel squeezed between her legs, barely fitting, and raced downstairs so quickly she grabbed the door to keep from toppling over.

"I'm not awake enough for this." She rubbed her eyes, resigning to the one thing left to do. Ready for the day.

Choosing from her worldwide collection of salts, herbs, and oils she prepared a bath. She brewed a blend of dried chamomile, jasmine oil, and rosemary freshly picked from her sill garden Wytt helped maintain when she was working at sea. Once she gingerly settled in the bath, each ingredient worked to soothe her battered body until the water ran cold.

Down two flights of stairs, Maijerda took her usual spot at the bar nearest the kitchen, Wytt eagerly waiting for her, his leg bouncing.

With an exaggerated double take, Wytt closed the notebook he was pretending to study. His rose skin was the faintest more purple beneath his puffy eyes. "Did y-you sssleep?"

"I gave it my best. I see you didn't."

Wytt widened his eyes with a perkiness she'd seen before when he'd drunk far too much coffee. "W-what? Of course I did." With a swoosh of his tail, he tried to hold his ground.

"Lies, Wyttrikus? Really?"

"Well, I-I was worried about you."

Liam lumbered from the kitchen, as he often did, with a display of fresh herbed biscuits and jam. "Stayed up all night, he did. He's just as stubborn as you."

"Fates know why you put up with us."

"I may never know." He spared a wink in the name of levity before bracing himself on the bar. "Probably get me nowhere by asking, but what can we do? Would it help to talk about… about it? Tell us what happened?"

Confrontation lurched in her and she dug her nails in the worn woodgrain countertop. Without any real purpose other than avoidance, Maijerda stared at the mugs and steins hooked along the arches above the bar. No, talking about it sounded less than desirable.

"You don't have to. T-tell us. If it's too ssssoon. We want to understand. No one here will force you."

Tears ebbed in her eyes when she turned to Wytt, his face softened by his white waves framing mauve cheeks. Wytt's tone had a way of bringing her from the pit of nerves. "I know." She gripped his forearm, the fabric of his pine green shirt chill between her fingers. "And thank you for that. I'll talk about it sooner or later. Right now everything feels disjointed. Like I'm not grounded."

"We could take Rel for a walk? D-doubt he'd say no to that. He misses you when you're gone, you know."

"Oh, it's not me he misses. It's the scraps I sneak him." She tried to smile, struggling to muster it.

Liam busied himself in their silence by scrubbing a spot on the bar they all knew was imprinted in the wood and couldn't be cleaned. "Wisteria sure could use some attention. Might help to spend the morning in the garden? Like it did me years ago, when I needed a clear head—"

This was a tale she knew well, given how often Liam told it. She took the liberty of finishing, warm hearted. "You labored for days planting the vines and had them enchanted on a new Moon. Ever since, they bloom unhindered and bless your patrons with serenity." She grinned, finally looking him in the eye. "Your very own faetale. I remember."

He'd been successful too. Their vines were indeed charmed to bloom throughout all seasons. From the budding season of Aurora, through the heat of Halcyon, enduring Undern, and through the harshness of Eventide at year's end. "Maybe later? If that's all right?"

He grunted and turned his attention to cleaning casks of mead and ale behind the counter. "I-uh. I heard there's to be a ceremony. Er, a service soon. They're building a memorial."

"We could all g-go together, if you want to visit?"

A memorial? Not exactly something she wanted to remember, regardless if the efforts were supposedly well intentioned. As they were for every service following a tragedy at sea. Steslyres, being the port city it was, was accustomed to these instances. She didn't care for talking about death, fearing her views and values were too dark for most people, save for Wytt. His academic pursuits

39

of healing and the study of diseases groomed his opinions to be more open minded. "I'm not sure I can handle that. As it is, I can hardly keep my thoughts together. Honestly, I could do with a cup of tea."

"And pro-probably something to keep your energy up," Wytt reminded with a knowing raise of his brow. "With all this stress, you're bound to have more troubles than usual."

He was right, unfortunately. Stress heightened her struggles with concentration, amplified her fatigue. Not to mention her anxiety.

Liam's eyes lit up. "Sounds like you need to fill your belly." He tucked the cleaning cloth in his apron. "I know just the thing." The relaxation in his shoulders indicated that by all means, he was thankful for the prompt.

Before she could argue he bustled to the kitchen with renewed purpose, returning several minutes later with bowls brimming with stew and rosemary sourdough. Her favorite of his breads. For a retired blacksmith, he was a remarkably good cook. Shortly after leaving these, he brought figs and apricots along with her favorite mug full of a Halcyon white tea. Floral with a touch of peaches and oranges. It was refreshingly sweet compared to the smoky black tea she'd run through on the *Norn*.

The cream stew was plump with vegetables ripe with Halcyon's end. Potatoes, celery, carrots, tomatoes, and zucchini. Sliced on top was an apple sausage. As far as Halcyon meals were concerned, this ranked high on her list, largely due to the fact it signaled that the warmer days of Halcyon were coming to a halt. Ultimately making way for the changing leaves of Undern.

Wytt didn't counter her silence, devouring his bowl so quickly it was a wonder he tasted it. Drool dripped on her knee, followed by the scuffle of paws. Rel licked his snout and gazed at her longingly for a scrap. She slipped him slices of sausage and savored her meal by the spoonful, intentionally procrastinating the impending hassle of handling emotions.

Such fussy creatures too, emotions. Wasn't there another way to care for them? Why couldn't they be like Rel? Feed them scraps from your plate and they're content. But no, emotions hungered for more than scraps.

She'd missed how the carvings in the clay and hourglass curve of her mug had felt nestled in her hand. Brewing more tea would soon be in order. A rose blend perhaps? Or a smoky, mint might be better. Ah, Fates, she was getting distracted. Again.

Liam stayed near them as they finished, no patrons having wandered in just yet, and busied himself with unnecessarily polishing flatware.

"I was hoping you both might be able to help."

He plinked utensils into place. "What's on your mind?"

"Did... did Da ever show you a book?"

"You might need to be more specific." An aching fondness from Liam.

"I know Liam knew him long before mmme, but you know as well as I d-do your dad was hard pressed to g-glance at a book after Relona... after your mom died."

"Right." Wytt wasn't wrong. Da had abandoned stories pretty much the night Mother passed. He avoided explanation, rationalization, pretended it was normal. Which was far beyond the truth. Her parents had been keen storytellers when she was growing up. Always sharing faetales and histories with a flare of arcana from Mama to enhance the experience. Characters traveling through an orange grove? Maijerda could smell the very same citrus in the comfort of their living room. The sting of blades slicing the air clamored in their kitchen as Mama and Da regaled her with the tale of an ancient war. To go from that to Da cursing songs and faetales? Not understanding why would haunt her until the day she died.

Wytt and Liam stared at her, waiting for her to elaborate. She could run upstairs and grab the book to show them. Visualizing holding it made her queasy. "It's green. Stiff bindings, silver border. There's a silver glyph down the front and a metal latch. Sound familiar?"

"A glyph?" Piqued academic interest lit up Wytt's tired eyes genuinely this time.

"Yes, I don't recognize it, but that's no surprise." She wasn't the academic sort. Her arcane knowledge was inherited from her mother's teachings, nothing formal.

Liam squinted and added a spoon to the pile. "Can't say that rings any bells. Why do you ask?"

She hadn't expected this part, explaining herself. She wasn't ready to delve quite so far. "Um. It's probably nothing, I found it in, in Da's quarters before the storm overtook our ship." Swallowing hard, she stuffed another piece of bread in her mouth and cracked her left wrist. She wasn't planning on lying to them, for now it seemed the safer route to take.

"Mm. Have you looked inside?"

Fervidly, she shook her head. "Can't." Bread stuck to her gums. "Can't bring myself to."

"If you ask me, I don't see a point in rushing and poking around your da's things. Nothing wrong with waiting." He took her hand and squeezed it, giving it a few taps before continuing his work. She tore at what scraps of bread remained.

Disappointed, Wytt tried to remain supportive, rolling his slumped shoulders straight. "Y-yes. Waiting, we could wait. For as long as you need. A glyph though? On a book your father had in his cabin?"

"Yes. Strange isn't it?"

"D-definitely."

"Perhaps we shouldn't harp on it just yet," Maijerda suggested, noting Liam's frown. Remember, he had lost a dear,

dear friend. "Liam, can we be of any help today? Sort things out for the evening? Course I shouldn't speak for Wytt. I'm sure you have studying to do."

"N-nah, they can wait a day. I already told Xander I wouldn't be in the shop today. There's no lectures in town. Steslyres will go on for a day without my b-being there to remedy people."

"If you're up for it, I'd love your company. Grab your aprons and we'll whip up tarts for week's end."

There was solace to be found within the kitchen's hearth and each seasoned pot. It was in the softness of leaves in the herb garden, the open brick oven swelling with freshly baked bread. And even the kettle, hanging at the ready near a copper stew pot.

During each holiday taken in Steslyres, working here was soothing and provided creative space for revisiting routines. She'd work in the kitchen and Wytt would visit frequently from his apartment to study. Always studying, Wytt was determined to complete the prerequisites and gain experience he needed to apply for a position at the medical university in D'hadian. He'd make it in one year, but Fates, he'd have to actually apply first. Excuses were rife with him, second-guessing his skills. She feared his involvement when Mother was ill tethered him to doubt. She'd tried to soothe him, since he never did forgive himself.

As much as she wanted to respect her mother's passing, there was no room for it today. She tuned her mind back into the present. Maijerda fell into a rhythm with the sway of chopping vegetables, slicing hunks of meat, mixing brine, and molding dough for Liam's city-famous honey and fig tarts.

As she pressed the dough into the tart molds, the butter melted with each indent. The predictability was satisfying. It was silent confirmation she was making an impact on a simple something. Even if it was a small thing as pastry crust.

The metallic clang of a falling copper pot stole her focus, Wytt struggling to gather it from the floor. "Tuvon's breath! S-s-sorry Liam."

Not resisting a slight grin, Maijerda embraced spending the day with her closest friends. Maybe today wasn't the day to conquer emotions. Impulsivity had a habit of besting her. In all actuality, today would be better suited for rest and acceptance. There was no hurry to make herself ill over prying inside that dreadful book.

Nor was there a rush to research the baffling nature of a seemingly sentient storm. No matter how strongly she wanted to. Truthfully, she wouldn't accomplish much tonight. It was sundown and the escapades of last night weighed on her heavily as waterlogged lungs. She paused and wiped floured hands on her apron. Not that it was doing much. Both her high-waisted, gray trousers and embroidered navy blouse were quite filthy with flour and butter.

Starting to drift into sorrow, Maijerda offered to light the candles around the pub as a means of distracting herself. Liam agreed, so long as she promised to do so properly. "None of that tapestry flame. Save it for the fancy businesses and the magistrate. Any other color than what I'd find in a forge is plain unnatural."

"Think I know better by now." She took a jar of matches from him, grinning.

"You've been away so long this trip, I wasn't sure if you remembered an old man's whims."

Stretching on her tip toes, she kissed him on the cheek and went to the main room. Maijerda waved politely to two tiraen girls and a varlodeth with skin pocked from the troubles of growing older. They returned the gesture and continued arguing among themselves as she lit each bulky chandelier.

"Oh come off it! Dwymers and vetalas? Those are stories your mum spat when you were a tit-suckling babe."

Their friend rolled her eyes. "What of dhampirs? Harpies? I heard…" She leaned over the table. "South of here, they spotted a nest of harpies singing for the flesh of sailors. What does the Bramble Guard do about it? Nothing!"

"You're working yourself up over nothing. What're you going to fuss about tomorrow? Vampires and lycans? Strzygas? Kloidach? Demons too?"

Sheesh, kids these days. Maijerda hovered to eavesdrop, admittedly entertained.

"Strzygas and lycans *are* real. So are harpies. And selkies! You've just moved to the coast, what do you know?" She folded her arms, pouting.

"There hasn't been a strzyga documented in decades! The Rivyn Borne—"

"What about the Rivyn? The Wrought, they call themselves. Traitors, the lot of them, summoning demons back into the world," she said in a rush. "Suddenly you've read all there is in the Toll have you? And the Menagerie? Hm? Thought not. Besides, they don't want us to know."

"Who doesn't?"

She gestured as if accusing those in the Smithies. "Anyone. The lords of the capitals, the elders of the Pearl, the vizier in Zefk, our magistrate!"

"Oh piss off."

"Fine. I will!" She slammed her palms on the table and made a dramatic exit.

Maijerda snickered while the friends ran after her. Despite her exuberance, the poor thing wasn't too far off. Many creatures were rumored to be hidden around the world. What anyone believed depended on how much faith they placed in such stories. Including rumors of the Rivyn Borne, cursed monster hunters most of them. Others were a range of academics who dabbled too closely in unusual arcana and politics. She didn't know much of their downfall, other than it had happened a not-so-distant decade or so before.

Her thoughts wandered with each candle wick, her impulsiveness for action depleting. She apologized for interrupting a conversation in a sign language between two patrons sitting in plush arm chairs near the fireplace and lit the last of the lanterns. Maijerda knew some signs in Tirin sign language, having taught them to her crew to use at sea.

Da prefers to sit by the hearth. Or rather, he did. He does. He did? Fates. What if she couldn't go through this again? With Mother's murder—no. No. She wasn't murdered. Da would be bitter, livid if he heard her. *Enough floundering, little Tuft,* he'd say. But he couldn't hear her, could he?

Between Mother's... passing and a worsening daily struggle with a medical condition that disrupted how Maijerda's body handled fatigue, cognition, emotional health, and most notably, her bleeding cycle, she had learned balance. These days she was working on mastering the art of setting aside what the world wanted and focused efforts on self-betterment. In whatever way she could handle.

Whether that meant sleeping longer than usual, journaling, singing, crafting medicinal teas with Wytt to ease symptoms, screaming into the wind, baking, or setting flame to candle wick, the time would come to step forward to grander paths. The moment never failed to make an entrance. But it is a choice to accept the invitation.

INTERLUDE:

The Harrowing's Plight

Are you acquainted
with the Harrowing?
Your world refers to it differently.

Most often do.

The Witching Hour,
I've heard it named.

Our Harrowing
is responsible for many
fiendish speculations.

Some preach it is
when damnation ventures
freely among mortals.

Others warn that
belief in such fantasies
feed their existence.

When the hour grows late,
minds risk being led
astray by their
own thoughts.

Stray thoughts threaten
to reach the
cataclysmic point…

…of no longer differentiating
between reality
and a tired imagination.

It is an hour
when superstitious
beliefs are challenged.

Sometimes to the grave.

What about being
lovingly enraptured
by the night,

Asleep and unaware
in your bed?

        Is it possible
      to be vulnerable
      to the Harrowing's
      plight even then?

                Of course it is.

How naive
to believe otherwise.

      What other explanation
      would you have for
      the birth of nightmares?

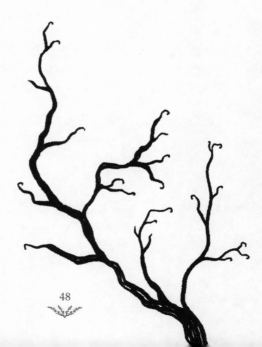

CHAPTER SIX

THE REQUIEM TOLL

IN THE DAYS which groaned by after the attack on the *Norn*, Maijerda battled what was merely the beginning of her grief. It burgeoned from her refusal to open the book. Not out of stubbornness, but disbelief. What good could it possibly bring? Answers? Potentially, however unlikely.

And so, in the Harrowing hours she fought what she imagined would be classified as a demonic reincarnation of denial, burying it in sand with resolve and the tip of an unnamed blade. It tore through the earth, undead and starved for her flesh. She screamed into the aging night on the beach until her voice was swollen and sore. She begged Wytt to help bend fate to bring her family back. Her freckles, from wrist to brow, had blended with the heat in her cheeks and she dissolved into unintelligible sobbing within his arms.

This morning helplessness anchored her thoughts and seeped into joints to slow her steps into a mixed stage. Ah yes, defiant determination. This she was familiar with. Wytt had offered to join her today, but she needed to start this search alone.

Seeing as the season of Undern had begun with the blessing of a new Moon on the rise, this was her opportunity to harness new endeavors and renewal for personal betterment. Today, on the first of Tawny Moon, fresh air and indulging in the city's melody would do nicely. The new Moon would take Maijerda under the wing of her blessings and show her what it was to focus on this task. Steslyres was a unique beast, and it would be good to move with its sultry heartbeat again.

Maijerda relished in the chaos of people weaving in and out of booths and shops for anything from sailing supplies to arcane trinkets and spell components. She guided her fingers along rivers of sturdy fabrics and stopped to smell baskets of tea leaves brought in from Neseth. Mounds of bottles casting dancing fae lights on the cobbles brought a gift of peace to her step.

She appreciated the city's renewed sense of normalcy with every open window and coastal frayed door. It was most evident in the hollering of merchants, echoing as she wandered in the sunshine filtered by ruggedly handsome buildings of earth and sea paints. Given the customary rainy lull, it wasn't often the wet put a hold on the city's bustle. However, when the sun did care to shine, it provided a refreshing gusto to the meandering streets, even to locals.

She avoided taking the route of any tunnels or closes, not wanting to rile up the day by taking the wrong stairwell and emerging on the opposite hill. Instead she took her time to visit each ward, steadily making her way to the library in Token Row.

In Cove Side, the sheer number of fellow sailors lounging about taverns careened her ease. Da would have been among them, laughing and gambling the afternoon away. It wasn't the same without him.

Her throat tensed and she wiped at tears sliding down her cheeks. Bleeding piss, how did she have any tears left to shed? She rushed by the rickety Flagon and Fleet, wringing her hands as sailors worked to impress with storytelling or to out-gamble their best mate in a game of dice, cards, or rune stones.

As their cheers quieted, she was careful not to run into a group of children as they raced by. She then ducked and swiveled to mind the mongers and their display of fish tossing to wrangle in a crowd. It was hardly a hassle and she regained feeling in her tongue enough to bid the mongers a good day.

Maijerda turned the corner. Her pace and breath hitched. Damn it. She meant to avoid this. Just as Liam mentioned, there was the temporary memorial layered with papers, trinkets, and incense in remembrance of the lost *Norn* and her crew. Though the magistrate, lord, and patrons of Steslyres had concluded the incident was attributed to nothing but an unfortunate accident, it was a polite gesture.

There was no need to argue their stance. And she didn't need to go around challenging the magistrate again. She wasn't in the mood. Maijerda kept quiet to pass the display, not wanting to pry open scabbing wounds. Unfortunately her appearance didn't go unnoticed and she was forced to wave awkwardly at acquaintances and consoling faces.

Most were frequent patrons of the Smithies or shop owners she and Da conducted business with. Fewer were an unfamiliar gathering of sailors grumbling amongst themselves, skin burnt and flaking. She told those who asked a tale depicting Da's passing with the ship. The truth that she found him struck by a hailstorm of arrows loosed from a ghost ship didn't coincide with their theory.

And so she kept this secret. Uncovering the truth and reason for the attack was for her alone. As it should be. As a straeldan man no taller than her waist, with deep grooves of wrinkles pooling at his jowls, preached to Maijerda about the sea's volatility, one man in particular snatched her drifting eye.

His dusky brown skin was slick from mugginess. He was craning up at the monument, appearing to search through the parchments for a treasure he hoped wasn't buried in the ocean floor. He reached near the top and held a paper still, his ink-dark coat striking upward in a gust. The gray at his temples amplified his anxious mien as he searched the opposite side of the memorial.

Maijerda motioned to approach him, but couldn't form the words to ask which of her crew he sought. What was there to say? Hello, I was the first mate of the *Norn*, which of your family did I fail? Or... I'm sorry? She was. Though it would never be enough. Abandoning the effort altogether, she left before anyone else could stop her.

Blanketed condolences and painful reminders weren't the attention she needed, but there was reassurance to be found in song. Yes, music was faithful to her, as it had been since childhood. A song of a poet becoming king came to mind and Maijerda strode to the tower library, humming to herself.

Once she left Brine Bend, the musical whims of pipes and strings raised her spirits with a much different faetale. The word faetale, being nearly interchangeable for songs or stories, encompassed the meaning and power of tales in a single word that promised much more.

She hadn't heard this one in ages. Each lyric came to her as easily as sailing the Query and Dolzdoem Seas. She tossed the bards spare bronze seeds for their gifts.

Eventually the Requiem Toll loomed in the northeast corner of Token Row. Covered with coastal stone and vines, its grandeur beckoned her to take comfort within its spires. Typically the roof of the Toll was cloaked with fog. Today's clear sky made an exception. Near the towers, so very determined to touch the sky, were stone gargoyles perched and protecting Steslyres with eternally distant countenance.

It didn't matter how often she visited the Toll, she regarded the library's doors as nothing short of a living piece of history themselves. Magnificent stained-glass panels showered her in color at the top steps.

Each panel told the story of the city's evolution from fishing village to war trade center to famed, grand port city. Steslyres was built for those who don't find the desire to settle in their bones. These days, Maijerda didn't care much for the idea of laying roots.

Maijerda pushed open the doors to an all-encompassing calm and one of her most cherished fragrances in the whole world. A blend of ink, leather, tea leaves, and parchment. Rows of wooden tables with arcane lanterns and shelves of books adorned the bottom floor, but choosing a perch here was far too exposed. Besides, it was unlikely anything useful would be on this introductory level.

She nodded politely to the librarian watching her at his desk. The tiraen adjusted his glasses and gave a curt smile as she darted to a spiral staircase. The Toll didn't require a strict ledger of those who entered but she was fairly certain the same couldn't be said for the university's Menagerie in D'hadian. One day, she'd make sure to find out for herself and pay it a visit.

She skipped her hand along the stone and ironwork banister of the staircase. Each floor landing, though home to differing subjects and muses, was similar in structure. The landings opened to spaces akin to that of a balcony providing options to step into the floor proper or continue upward. From each balcony, bookshelves stretched underneath stained-glass arches, depicting the theme of the floor. She refused many offerings of epic battles reincarnate through the color and caress of the glass. She dismissed wildlife, astrological depictions, history of sorcery, and the tapestry. Visualizations of music, famous artists and the growing pains which served as their muse? All useless. Creatures both of factual and mythical origins all fell by the wayside.

None of these would do. None seemed fitting, so she kept her head low and scurried upstairs, through a connecting corridor to the southernmost tower. It took great restraint to avoid veering into the play scripts section and abandoning her mission. She'd been trying to get her hands on a copy of *The Rose and the Wyrm* since the Vernal Moon. Best to check the bookstore down the road later on.

It wasn't until the ninth floor that she found the perfect nook. It was rather wide, carved into the wall, and plush with overused pillows. Ah yes, this would do nicely. Quiet and empty. Maijerda sat and rearranged the cushions. Upending her bag on the wooden table, she organized her research tools. Torn parchment, broken quill, drying ink, and *the book*. Da's book.

Fates be damned. She still hadn't opened it.

Her anxiety rose in anticipation, about to curdle into anger. She'd battled anxiety her entire life; it was more than nervousness. It had snatched time and opportunity from her. Now it was ten times as vicious with Da's death at stake.

Fates, Wytt was right. She should've brought a snack and finished her morning tonic. Energy fading and replaced with a pounding headache, she shouldn't be this damned tired so early in the day. Yet it wasn't the first time she'd felt laden limbs and hollowness straight after waking. And presumably it wouldn't be the last.

Back to this moment, trying to suppress her frustrations with her body, she imagined her final moments on the *Norn*. Da ran from her when they should've worked together and escaped. Why would he risk his life for this book? With all the love books gifted her over the years, never had one betrayed her before. And yet... it was an uncomfortable realization at best.

It was also illogical. A book wasn't capable of betrayal. It wasn't alive. But anxiety is a dreadful thing, even in the strangest of circumstances. Whatever was inside this book, had better been worth sacrificing a life. It had better have an explanation for his death or a murderer to blame.

Holding it was the first step.

The spine was slender, though sturdy. Tarnished and decorated silver clamped at the cover's edges, matching the metal latch sealing the book shut. Most notably, the green leather was engraved with glyphs.

Whether historical or arcane in nature, she was unfamiliar with them. She ran ringed fingers along the geometric grooves as if trying to use touch to attune to their meaning. Mindlessly she scratched at the back of her neck with her other hand. With a sigh, Maijerda pried the book open to the first page. It was time to unmask the villain who murdered Da.

Before she could lift the guise, a slip of paper stuck to the inner cover. It was crinkled, as though soaked through and now dried with sea salt. The ink, a rushed black, bled until it was more of a thin blue in illegible splotches. The sole part of this book that showed signs of wear from being nearly drowned in the sea. On the surface at least, the rest of the book was unscathed.

She squinted and held the paper at odd angles trying to get a better read of what was written there, to no avail. A problem for another time. For at hand was the book itself and the arduous task of diving in to see what it had to say for itself.

A blank first page, of course. On to the second.

Also blank. The third? Empty. The Fates were mocking her, certainly. She narrowed her eyes and she flipped through the rest. Not a single word. Not one mark. Not one ink splat. Or smudge. Nothing. Absolutely *nothing*. Animosity raged from deep within her belly, rising up to her jaw. This was a cruel jest. Even for death. Oh the absurdity of it all!

"This is your fault, you know. *You* did this." She scowled at the book as if it were Morel when he chewed her boots as a puppy.

She began to laugh, which blossomed into a cackle. Her hands trembled as if she was kneeling in the pool of blood beside Da. First a wailing storm, then a ghost ship on their heels, Da's death, and now this? An empty handed, good for nothing book. Which he, for some godsforsaken reason, found necessary to abandon her for? And now she was talking to it? No, this was ludicrous.

With the declaration screeching in her mind, she forced the book shut. Maijerda stared at the cover until she could string thoughts together. It was quite the scramble, mentally grasping for a sequence to follow. The glyph burned into her with eyes it clearly didn't possess.

A book with eyes to see her thoughts? Not a chance. She leaned back, scoffing to the ceiling. Whispers of air stroked her wrists. Maijerda whirled around, the tips of her ears turning cold. The chill stretched to her spine and she rubbed her neck.

Was that… voices? But there was no-one near. Turning to the book, she tapped her fingers at the stiff leather, itching for more. There was more to this than she knew, wasn't there? For Da to die for it, there must be. Maijerda huffed and snatched the book as she stood to wander the shelves. "Don't disappoint me," she grumbled to it.

Research it was then. Blank pages wouldn't stop her from seeking answers. She would work with what she had, and that was the glyph. Without much to go on, it was a struggle to pinpoint what she expected to happen.

Maybe a siren song would lure her. Perhaps it would simply be a gut feeling, which would beckon to her. Love at first sight? Hah! Ridiculous, honestly. What was the probability of the symbols suddenly communicating with her? She glared at the book, folded her arms, her boot heels keeping time of her rhythmic search.

She pulled her tongue across her teeth. If only she were in D'hadian with the Fae Pond near. "What I'd do for a wish."

MAIJERDA'S ENTIRE PLAN for the day changed. She was moving far too quickly, her mind whirring. Nerves rattled her deeply, causing her hands to shake. Nauseated, she abandoned the Toll, promising herself she'd return tomorrow with a new approach in hand. She needed a timeline; without it she might fixate here for ages.

If in two weeks there was nothing to be found, maybe the answers were outside of Steslyres. The Menagerie was said to be one of the most comprehensive libraries in Penʌmbrə. There might be useful information there. In the meantime, the distraction of errands would suffice.

First was a shop not far from the Smithies, aptly titled Eye of the Needle. She replenished her wardrobe with the latest fashions from all over the realm. Sashes were apparently the rage as well as vests. Which was good, as she preferred those regardless. Maijerda enjoyed keeping up to date with the trends in fashion and makeup, but sailing most of the Moons in the year made that a challenge.

Returning to the Smithies her boxes were piled high, filled with clothes in plums, burgundies, olives, blues, blacks, and grays. The tailor had insisted on a thick brocade scarf, a coat, cardigans, sweaters, and a pair of leather, fingerless gloves. Best to be prepared for the elements if she was anticipating leaving Steslyres.

Inside, a couple of gentlemen were clearly cheating in a game of bone might with a scraggly looking person. She flashed a smile to them, walking to Selene filling Maijerda's mug with a fruity Halcyon wine with an iridescent green shimmer.

In turn, Maijerda plucked a bouquet from her stash. "I couldn't resist."

"How stunning. Thank you, love."

Maijerda gave her jars of nettle thyme, curry, and uttorôn spice for Liam as well. Selene was gentle in her conversation, following Maijerda's lead and not poking at the obvious sadness encompassing them all. At that point Selene insisted she share a meal of peppered-garlic eggs, goat cheese, and dark sourdough bread.

Maijerda embraced the tranquility Selene left behind as she retreated upstairs. She applied a brown-red lip stain before writing in her leather journal. Her fondness for cosmetics having returned since her return home. Equipped with a new metal-tipped pen and burgundy ink, she let her consciousness flow. From research, songs, and memories of her parents, she worked until evening, attempting to sketch and dictate thoughts on paper. Lastly, she tackled the glyph from Da's book, though it hurt to hold it. Line by line, curve by curve, she recreated the glyph and spoke silently to the Moon for gifts of stability, thoughtfulness, and hope. It was just as she finished the final diamond-like symbol on the bottom that Maijerda noticed someone tiptoeing to her.

"Is-is that the glyph you mentioned?" Wytt settled his bag, weighted with books, on the counter and shook the rain out of his hair, scratching at the base of a horn.

"Oh, yes. Thought maybe if I drew it, something would spark," she replied with a defeated air.

"Mmay I?" He reached, still wearing his fingerless gloves.

She nodded, afraid that if she spoke her mind would change in an instant. At first she considered handing him the journal; instead she handed him the book.

Wytt cradled the book in his hand as if it was an act of honor.

"Hm. Iiiii have no idea. I know I haven't been through schooling yet, but I thought maybe I could at least determine th-their o-origin. These are completely foreign. Did you open it at the Toll?" Wytt lowered his voice, softening his already gentle pitch.

She should've known she'd have to answer to this. "I did."

"A-and?"

"Nothing."

"Not the answers you hoped for, you mean."

"I wish. But no. I mean, there's nothing."

Quizzically he frowned and opened the book at her behest. Slowly he flipped through the first few pages and then fluttered through the rest. "Blank. It's entirely blank."

"Sure is. And I haven't a clue of what to make of that."

"Me neither. Maybe tomorrow we go together, see what we can find."

It took a deep breath to force her agreement ahead of guilt. "I'd appreciate that."

"Deal then. Oh! I nearly forgot." Wytt scrambled to rifle through his bag, with a struggle. "I-it's in h-here I ssswear. Oh come on. Ah, here we are." He pulled free a black and gold box sealed with a matching wax stamp and slid it in front of her. "Happy birthday."

"That's not for over a week."

"I th-think you've earned an early birthday gift, Maijerda. Go on, o-open it."

He'd been holding onto this one for a while. Tail swishing, hands at his breastbone, eagerly waiting for her to open it. So she did. Atop a nest of green velvet was a brass colored chain, knitted to resemble rope, holding onto a roughly cut rust, gray, and amber crystal. The colors swirled with one another and collided in a solid mist. Latching the stone to the chain, a fixture of a bird talon. Raven? No. Too small. Blackbird, more likely.

Chomping at the bit to explain, Wytt freed it from the box and held it to the light. "It's qu'stite. I've enchanted it. To sssupport your c-c-concentration by warding off stress and improving emotional balance. Might even bring you a bit of luck. I've been wanting to craft this ever since we started to treat your symptoms." He pointed out runes engraved in the stone. "I thought, if weavers can use embroidery stitched in clothes to enchant them, I could give jewelry a shot, es-especially if it's related to health and wellness, so to ssspeak."

Of course he would. Damn him and his thoughtfulness. Donning the necklace, she spun it, thinking of balance and acceptance. "It's absolutely lovely. Thank you, Wytt." She wrapped him up in a hug and kissed his temple. "You've been too good to me. I don't know why you stick around after all we've been through."

"Y-you're practically family. I'd never abandon you."

"I wouldn't dare dream of it." She pulled him in again tightly, regretting it as she shivered. He was chill as packed snow. "Fates, aren't you cold? Have some tea would you?"

"You know I don't feel it. I can't help what tapestry threads come naturally."

"Still. It can't hurt to warm you up." Maijerda hopped on top of the bar, swinging around and plopping on the other side to make some tea for them both. "Have you learned anything new lately? About why you seem to favor arcana related to Eventide?"

"No, nothing new. Maybe if I make it to D'hadian—"

"When."

"Wh-what?"

"*When* you make it to D'hadian."

"Wheeeeen I go, there might be somebody who can help. It can't be that unusual. Can it?"

"Honestly I couldn't say. Maybe in other countries. Not something I see regularly weaved in Steslyres. Most people practice simple sorcery here, or storm arcana for work aboard ships. Usually I'm not in any port long enough to notice. We'll figure it out."

"We-we always do."

"Exactly." Maijerda punctuated her agreement by handing him a mug of warm, spiced milk tea. "Cheers to that."

"Ch-cheers."

From around behind them, Rel gave a bark and pranced to lie down at their feet. Given the chaos, it was a pleasant scene. Tea and friendship. Promises of progress. A simple moment free from anxiousness, a moment that Maijerda promised herself she'd treasure and be sure to thank the Moon for next time they spoke.

CHAPTER SEVEN

BLANK IN DESPAIR

NINE DAYS. NINE! AND NOT A damned thing to be found. The exception being Maijerda now knew the beshin working the front desk with the tiraen librarian she'd greeted on day one, enjoyed filling dull hours by flirting with him. Ms. Banderson was gray and shriveled in every meaning of the word. She required a stool to reach the top of the desk, greeting visitors with a dried, tulip-pink painted smile.

Maijerda hadn't caught the man's name. But his two-toned eyes never ceased to stoically stare, ignoring the beshin's advances. Unlike any day previous, his gaze followed her up the spiral stairs leading to the bridge that would take her to the southernmost tower.

"Has she always been that forward?" Maijerda whispered to Wytt.

"Oh yes, with-without a doubt. She's d-definitely the lonely sort."

"And what of him?"

"He's more the quiet sssort."

"How boring," Maijerda quipped as she skipped steps up ahead of Wytt, passing a handful of characters. A plump-cheeked tiraen, two chittering beshin, no taller than her thigh, and an idre with golden peach hair. Pastel hair shades were becoming quite popular in other continents. They must be visiting. Or maybe they were an exchange student.

Up the last flight she went, fiddling with the crystal swaying at her breastbone.

"Wait up, Tuvon's breath." Wytt panted up the last step.

"Don't you study here?"

"Yes, but, I don't run about like it's a shipdeck."

Maijerda shrugged and led him to nestle in her preferred nook. "Ssso, where did you leave off?"

"Yesterday I decided to go on a whim and tried using arcane fire to reveal invisible ink, but the book was blank as ever."

Wytt looked all around them for listeners, harshly whispering. "You didn't weave a spell in *here*, did you?"

"Using arcane fire is hardly tapestry weaving."

"Maijerda!" He squeaked. "Th-that's prohibited in the Toll. Just as true flame, it's forbidden for the protection of the books!"

"Oh hush. I wasn't casting it on a Toll book, it's my own. What does it matter?"

"Something could've gone wrong. You rarely practice arcana."

"Anymore," she corrected.

"You could've ruined something ancient!"

"Da left a blank book that we know nothing about, but my weaving a spell, that's what's got you in a twist?"

Wytt huffed and sat down, not realizing he'd stood from his seat to lean forward. "S-sorry. Don't want to get banned is a-all."

"We won't. Or if we do I'll make sure it's just me and not you. Fair?"

"F-fair."

"All right, today I'm thinking..."

Together they decided to focus on sifting through the more unique books she'd set aside, configured in shapes from triangles to hexagons. More than she expected were folded in clever patterns with pockets to hold tidbits of information, creased precisely so the reader would replace the pages correctly.

Fascinating, but an empty trail nonetheless. And what of the chapters in ıdre infinity tomes? Bound in circular forms to be free from decisive beginnings and ends, they dared review what was known of the hells, their associated leaders, devil types, and societies. Given devils didn't roam freely in this world, most writings were pure speculation. Even the oxymoron of a hell, frozen over with a hatred so penetratingly cold. The infinity tomes even challenged fate, discussing that with no apparent end, the most important aspect of time was the experience of *now*.

A frustrating number of books required a codex to decipher them. Maijerda didn't mind, but she was jittery and it was difficult to divide attention between codex and text. Wytt paid close attention to that pile. Though it couldn't be conquered in a day, he searched for similarities in the codex to the book's glyph. Others were enchanted with distinct smells to accompany context, for the sake of impression or discerning scents of poisons, plants, or even creatures that lurked in the world beyond the port city. Wytt pointed out runes embroidered in the thinnest of threads on the pages. A more permanent binding in the tapestry than using ink for the enchantment.

What were the chances of a smell connecting to the glyph?

Couldn't hurt to keep it in mind. Much as another volume Maijerda pulled, though it was common knowledge for the bookish sort, the guidance it offered on the language of the land, potentially imperative. Unfortunately, even now in the year 3046, the language of the land was often misconstrued and butchered. Likely misunderstood too.

The book was of quaint, rectangular design, meant to be flipped lengthwise and read horizontally. The bindings were crafted of a parchment-thin metal, embossed with inscriptions. She flipped through few sheets of parchment describing the runes and orthography used in conjunction to define the land's language.

Derived from the influence of each of the four elements in weaving arcana, this language was used to describe three concepts. The realm defined as actuality, continents, and four celestial phenomena. Regarding these with respect, despite the lack of concrete definition, ensures these spellings and pronunciations are undisturbed and the elements' homages sacred.

Elements were wild and unpredictable. While it is perfectly acceptable for tapestry weavers to include them as companions in spell craft, it is generally frowned upon and even feared if a caster manipulates and commands them. Fire, earth, wind, and water deserved more than to be treated as slaves. They are the core of existence. Bearing in mind there may be more elements, or so the faetales say. But none were openly discussed.

Scholars and those without inclination for academics alike are confident in the use of the language of the land. Though no one could explain why. It's uncommon for someone to take pause and consider the why of it. Not that it swayed Maijerda. Much like anyone who chose to ponder, it often felt as if she misplaced the notion in a long since visited port. It simply was.

Regardless, few examples of pronunciations were transcribed:

Pɛnʌmbrə.../pen-um-bruh/

ælɪkar.../al-i-kar/

ɔpoʊlin.../op-oh-leen/

Tirɪn.../teer-in/

Roʊzvɛlkə.../rose-vel-kuh/

Maijerda slid the book off to the side, open to an entry on Roʊzvɛlkə. Words were powerful bastards. This one muddied bliss with woe.

Roʊzvɛlkə, a time-honored celebration marking four events throughout the year. The shortest day with the longest night, and the shortest night with the longest day. The other two celebrate days when the sun and Moon share equal reign over the sky. Each is revered as a time of augury, transition, and change.

For Maijerda, the upcoming Roʊzvɛlkə Eventide not only warned that there was one full Moon until the seasons shifted, it was a season to reflect on changes made and those to come. These practices were hallmarked by mulling wine with citrus and warm spices as a blessing for the future. The other three Roʊzvɛlkəs had differing customs, appropriate for each season. Maijerda treasured each in their own right.

Sighing at the unruliness of fate, she set this aside too. And what about this other book? Poems and nursery rhymes. She was thoughtlessly drawn to it repeatedly. She propped it open to one piece in particular.

OF WISPS
A children's rhyme
Believed to be derived from an essay penned by Illruth Tin
Original document, safeguarded in the Menagerie

She scanned the piece, playfully admiring the wandering fae energy known as wisps. Supposedly they sought to help people find something dear to them. The final stanza read:

A finding will never render them shy.
Eternally bound and so they'll pry,
in search of the something of you.

Say you harmed the wisp? Well, the lore said it would turn to coal. A story for children. She clutched Da's book in her hands, for fear it might run off at her sullied accusations.

What if it did? What did she care if it disappeared and faded away? Maybe there was peace in being left alone to cope with guilt and death. But no, it lived on, forcing her to persist.

The grains of an endless sea of pages stung her eyes. Each second brought her nearer to creeping into starry-eyed madness. Her eyes twitched and pulsed as her mind drifted, losing thoughts and motivation. It was incredibly difficult to think clearly. She should give it a rest.

No. If she abandoned the book, she abandoned Da. There must be a direction to follow. If she could craft someway to— Wait. That was it! Perhaps she could.

"I've got it." Maijerda slammed her hands on the table and rushed to her feet.

Wytt startled at her exclamation. "You found something?"

"Not exactly. Why haven't we tried a truth spell?" Maijerda dug into her past, desperate for answer. It would be worth trying to weave this spell and tap into that side of herself.

"Another spell? Nooo, no no, Maijerda. I am not en-enabling this. If that's what you want to try, we can go to the Smithies. I'll help you."

"Why? We can do it now, no one ever comes up here. It's why I picked this spot."

The clock on the opposite side of the room struck six tolls.

"Well, would you l-look at that?" Wytt slid off the cushioned benches, bag in hand, expression anything but sly. "Turns out I have to be going anyway. Late night project in the observatory with Xander."

"Astronomy? You, a healer-to-be, are using astronomy as an excuse to leave?"

"I-I've told you before—the Moon, her guardians, the stars all can intertwine with any tapestry threads. Especially depending on the weaver. It's not an excuse. It's an experiment."

Suspicious behavior, even for Wytt. She crossed her arms. "That you're just now telling me?"

"Couldn't have w-w-warned you about what I nearly forgot, could I?"

"Sure, Wytt," she smirked. "Whatever you say. I'll find you when I'm done."

"You better. No getting into t-trouble."

She laughed and shrugged innocently. "Promise."

"Agh." Wytt sighed and trudged out the stained-glass doors to the pseudo balcony. "I'll never believe that."

Over a brief minute, Maijerda watched him leave until his tail was out of view down the curved staircase. For someone five years younger than her, he sure acted the older brother sometimes. Regardless, this spell truly was nagging at her. She had to try.

Using what she had on hand, she constructed a color arcana altar on the floor near the table. Slate gray inkwell for unraveling mystery. Earthen brown snacking chestnuts for grounding the elusive nature of a blank book. And an olive-green handkerchief for enticing the manifestation of an abundant wealth of information.

Arcana was inherently sympathetic, often requiring connections between object and desire. This could be interpreted literally or symbolically depending on the weaver, their intentions, and how they bonded to the tapestry. Especially when delving into sortilege of this type. Convincing an object to disregard the coveted nature of well-kept secrets was no easy task.

Taking a piece from her box of colored casting chalk, Maijerda sketched a symbol from memory. Black would suit the nature of mystery and shadow, precisely what she wished to remove from the book. Truth or revelation spells were fickle, no matter how you chose to weave, and it had been seven years since she'd cast one.

In that span, her relationship with arcana ebbed and flowed as any living thing, her trust in its gifts and her own arcana never quite the same since Mother—

No. Not. Now.

Maijerda scraped the chalk on the floor, surpassing paranoia, and sketched a rune circle around the objects, placing the book and the ink-splotched piece of paper in the center. She tapped her foot and surveyed her makeshift altar, wishing she had wisteria petals to symbolize clarity.

She popped an entire dried mushroom cap in her mouth from a bundle of snacks Wytt had packed. She chewed, mindfully centering around the ability to regenerate and the cycle of death in procreation. Sure, it was likely a stretch, but it would simply have to do given limited resources.

Picking the last morsel out of her teeth, she noticed a vase of gardenias, petals white. Perhaps these for purifying the mystery of this Fates-damned book. She sprinkled the gardenia petals in the circle. The petals' perfume coated her fingers and followed her as she plucked a candle meant for tapestry flame from her table and sat at the northern side of the triangle.

North, for the grounding properties of the earth. The candle she placed opposite to her, at the southern edge of the altar, and struck to life with a match from her satchel. No one had entered the room, thank Fates. She was in the clear.

The true flame flicked and danced with a wild air. She inhaled the smoke with intent. Integrating sensory aspects into her tapestry weaving was a practice Maijerda preferred and resonated with ever since she was a child when Mother began teaching her. Targeting your senses inarguably enhanced the experience.

She straightened her back and began her incantation. May Da's death not be in vain. For whatever reason. "For refuge in my altar, reveal the deep-seated truth."

It was more of an improvised poem. Some incantations were dedicated, others required weavers to create their own. She closed her eyes, swiping her right hand over the circumference of the altar, followed by the left circling to rest fingertips under her right wrist. She slid her left hand upward until her thumb and first fingers crossed into place, forming a triangle.

Hand gestures were another component to some arcane abilities Maijerda gravitated toward. It could add a layer of exactness yet artistic flair, like a choreographed dance. "These pages blank in despair, I beg of you to repair."

Counting silently to nine, she waited with cold, bated breath. Nine to represent completion and new beginnings. New beginnings? Undeserved and built out of bloodshed.

Shit. She was getting distracted. Focus. Harness the sensation of it all. The flame, the floral perfume. Anything but her teetering emotional upheaval.

Focus.

The petals levitated over her offerings, the candle flame split in two. However, they wrinkled as if diseased, turning a noxious red. Each twisted and curled in pain. Maijerda knew their suffering to be true by the way they crescendoed in anguish. Uncomforted, the petals melted into gunk that wept to the floor.

Careful to avoid touching it, she grabbed the book and unlatched it, fanning through the pages. Nothing had changed.

"What is the matter with you?" Shockingly enough, the book didn't reply. "Don't you trust me?"

Just like Da, it chose silence. Her heart beat faster with the flush in her cheeks. She didn't want to cave to bitterness. This was a whole level of vexation she was clueless to face.

Fates be fickle. She shoved the blank tome into the altar, scattering the components and spewing a stream of A'lorynn curses until she resolved to try the spell again. Flustered by her failure, she hadn't regarded the slip of paper. Assuming it was just as much of a lost cause as her nerves. But… the message it bore was proof the spell had worked in some way. And would surely have her shedding even more tears than had been wrenched from her these days.

Tuft,
I never wanted this for you.
Da

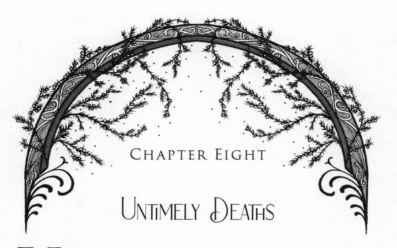

CHAPTER EIGHT

UNTIMELY DEATHS

K LOIDACH.

Untimely deaths. Typically female. Specters cursed to…

Cursed to…?

Repeat a loop of events for eternity. Bound to the site of their death by a body part. Usually.

That was why it was better to burn the dead. Err on the side of caution.

Yes, that was the textbook definition of kloidach. Jeddeith was confident in that. Which was… agitating.

Jeddeith grunted to himself, adjusted his glasses, and closed his ledger. He nodded to a varlodeth patron scampering to leave the Toll, his mind distant as ever. It needed to be wrangled in.

Vythsaden rosq.

The phrase came unobstructed. He was trained for it to. A reminder to root yourself in the situation. Assess what you know. And what you don't. What you see. And what you don't. Be on your guard. Be aware of, not just see the bigger picture.

Ignoring signs got you killed.

Signs of a kloidach haunting. He challenged himself to recall the details.

Something on disease and illness affecting those who witnessed a kloidach. Targeted victims. Versus random hauntings or killings. Retaining his education on monsters readily as he did likely had some idiotic, philosophical meaning. It deserved to be ignored.

What he didn't turn his back to was the kloidach haunting his library for the ninth day in a row. Every morning she dashed past his desk and upstairs toward the southern tower. Satchel in tow. She wasn't actually a specter, but her repetitious behaviors were on par for the damned things. She was likely in her late twenties, maybe early thirties. ıdre heritage judging by her features.

ıdre…

Thought to be evolved from fallen starlight. Not of this realm, but any other. Taking pieces of stones or gems with them to tie a source of arcana to their home. This was said to explain the crystal-like appearance of their eyes.

Between her freckles and posture, the calluses on her hands, sailor seemed apt. Or at least she traveled for work. Unfortunately, seeing familiar faces in the Toll wasn't unusual. He dreaded that aspect of his work. The social part in remembering people and their interests. Problem was, far too many people thought highly of themselves.

Kloidach or no, he sought to investigate. Say she needed help in freeing herself from this place. Jeddeith had met both optimists and theologists who believed kindness was all it took to help kloidach break their bonds. He'd also encountered a kloidach or two.

Intentions were moot. From what he remembered.

Jeddeith stood from his desk. Just when he moved beyond the edge, Ms. Banderson was a knuckle width from his side. The elderly beshin leaned close. "Abandoning your duties again?"

She peered up at every bit of him, craning her head up from her short stature. Unfortunately enticed by his two-toned eyes.

Most were put off by the amber and gray hues against his warm, sandy and olive skin. Banderson here was an odd exception.

He sighed. Don't chide her. She'd never look him in the eye again. And that'd make for bad working company. "I would never, Ms. Banderson. Expanding on them actually." He clasped his hands at his lower back and rocked on his heels.

Raising an eyebrow, she shimmied lopsided shoulders. Broad, hooked ears wriggling. "I do wind up feeling so dreadfully bored minding our desk. Can I be of any… use?"

"No." More certain than ever.

Ms. Banderson's smile, uncanny and crooked, huffed into a frown. "Very well. Perhaps next time." She sauntered, or tried to, away.

Jeddeith made for the staircase, mumbling. "As if there was a first?"

His specter was long gone. There were no forest grounds to track her steps in either. But the forest floor wasn't the only place to track someone. This wouldn't be difficult. He imagined how the tapping of his specter's footsteps might've sounded these last nine days.

Vythsaden rosq.

The stone of the Toll remembered her. Her pattern lay underneath his steps. Her rhythm reflected here, at the ninth floor. Hardly anyone ventured to the southern tower. If anyone at all.

The stained-glass display in front of him was chaotic between symbols and archaic writings entwined with each other. Both enemies and lovers. Some rumors declared them to be from a more ancient source of arcana. The oratory nature of storytelling was the reason for these rumors.

Most people didn't realize they were true. And it wasn't meant for common knowledge. Jeddeith meanwhile, had grown intimate with the concept in ɔpoʊlin. Another truth he could recall. Much else around it was unclear. How had he gotten there? When did he begin training? Who were his companions? What was his role? His duties? All of it, muddied as a bog.

What wasn't unclear, least now, was his pull to a glyph in the glass. He shouldn't feed it. Shouldn't let it steal his gaze. Don't fall for tricks. Or goading.

He smirked. Fixed his glasses.

A lacking threat. Glass shouldn't be feared.

Usually.

He turned his shoulder to the glass to enter the wing and examine. Corner table, splayed books. The woman's satchel, strewn. Scuffed leather. Patchwork scarf tied at the base of the strap. Must've taken it on her travels. Well worn. Cared for.

More importantly. There she was, the kloidach.

Sitting on the floor with her back to him, unaware of his presence. Surrounded by spell components, all destroyed, melted, and abandoned. But she was distracted. Gripping a piece of parchment in her fist.

He cleared his throat, folded his arms over his velvet vest, sleeves secured to his wrists with cufflinks. Another means of erring on the side of caution. Couldn't have strangers recognizing his marks, it'd give him away. He'd be forced to flee the city. If he weren't caught first. A risk he'd successfully managed since living in Steslyres. "Spell weaving, are we?"

It could've been dismissed, unnoticed by another. But Jeddeith caught the twitch in her back.

"Is that illegal?" The woman stood, tugging on her cream silk shirt, half-tucked into burgundy trousers. Flushed cheeks. Stained with tears. Eyes irritated and makeup running. Blood-red lipstick, smudged. Sleeves rolled to the elbow, exposing freckled skin inked with floral tattoos. Her copper hair, frizzed. Curls stretched, presumably from fidgeting. Her jeweled irises were softened and rounded in shape.

"Won't get you arrested, but it might ban you from these grounds."

"I wouldn't dream of harming a book." Again a subtlety an untrained eye would wave off. Not him. He noted the glance she gave the book opened on the floor in her altar.

Regarding the altar. Color arcana. Melted petals. An unguided candle flame. North facing arrangements. Chalk on the floor? Gods in shadow. What was so important she chose to pursue it here? "If you're resorting to truth spells…" Intentionally leaving her room for interpretation, he analyzed her reaction.

She blinked and swallowed, briskly extinguishing the candle and cleaning her piles of research. Frustration honed her movements. Avoiding his eye? So it seemed she was seeking some hidden truth and was masking her own.

"…perhaps I can help?" He grinned, forcibly beneath, radiant on the surface.

"I'm perfectly fine."

Insistent. Nervously she pulled her curls into a twist. Her jewelry, now exposed, might give clues to her culture or heritage. A cuff, pierced high on her ear. A chain to a circular piece nested inside. Connecting to one of two earrings pierced in her lobe. The opposite ear was pierced with two jewels and a hoop in the center. A thin hoop of warm gold, snug on the right side of her nose. No ceremonial or cultural significance from what he could tell. No signs of mourning. Marriage. Or political status. Tips of her ears not quite drawn to a sharp point. Ah… that explained her eyes. Not *full*-blooded ıdre then.

"You're certain?" He slid his glasses from the tip of his nose, folding and placing them in his vest pocket. A single wave of umber-brown hair drooped out of place.

The woman, bound to her task, continued organizing her table. "Positive." She slammed a book closed and a torn parchment fluttered to him from between the pages. She rolled her wrist, cracking it.

An old injury? Also an interesting tell for a supposedly innocent lie.

Her stare held unspoken words to challenge him.

She reached for the torn paper but he intercepted. The edges were questionably near crumbling to ash. Knitting her brows, she tensed as he read.

...souls were forfeit. Hypotheses are generally classified as rumors meant to startle and daze the enemy, as opposed to surrendering truth. If a soul wanders frequently in shadow, their aura wanes and withers. It is coined as poisoned. The Rivyn Borne did not heed such warnings. They must agree to forfeit protection and devotion from divine...

Jeddeith cleared his throat to ignore the stabbing at his breastbone. "Refreshing teachings on the Rivyn." She snatched the parchment from him as he offered it.

"Not particularly. Rivyn articles are difficult to find."

"As they should be."

"I'm exploring ideas as they come. A society of people destroyed? Forgive my curiosity."

He clasped his hands behind his back, at full attention. "Tread carefully."

"Not my style." Smirking, she picked another book up off the floor to bring it to the table. She snapped it shut, signaling him to leave with her stance. Hands braced on either side of the book. Leaning over it. A stone necklace dangling. Eyes wide.

Intimidating to the *right* people. But the book beneath her? A curious book. Not one he'd seen here in the Toll before. He should know.

Green leather. Silver trim. Etchings on the cover. A glyph.

A glyph which looked like… no. It couldn't be.

His jaw tensed, gut wrenched.

They'd gone six years without warning. Why now? The possibilities alone were slim. And yet…

She cocked her head to catch his gaze. "Do you rec—?"

He raised one eyebrow and rocked on his heels. Forcefully diluted response on the surface. A surge to react, beneath. She'd never see through it. "Should you change your mind, I'll be at the main desk. Don't… hesitate to find me."

"I won't." She cracked her wrist.

What are you hiding? He studied her one last time. "It would be a welcome change of pace." He bowed his head and made for the stairs.

A nebulous probability, firm as steel before his very eyes. The markings on that book were unmistakable.

Unmistakable as the fact he needed to act first and keep this woman from destroying Pɛnʌmbrə.

Chapter Nine

The Librarian

NEVER WANTED... WHAT?

Since finding the note from Da, Maijerda was fed up with researching in the Toll. Fed up with prying eyes. Fed up with finding more questions than answers.

She left her nook by nightfall. Stark quiet cascaded with no one tending to the ground floor. Not even the scruffy librarian from earlier. He'd been odd. Polished with his vest and cufflinks. Polite in a way. Judgmental though, too nosy for her taste.

Ready to crawl into bed, she headed into Undern's embrace. A persistent drizzle of rain greeted her, and for the first time in days she cracked a smile. The Moon watched over Steslyres proudly, merely five nights from being plump in the sky for the first of three full Moons of Undern. The waxing Tawny Moon.

Her three guardians shone reverently with hues of orange, purple, and green. Three guardians, forever faithful by her side. The loyalty of Hael, Drä, and Cë was admirable. Even more so because each was named for one of the three Fates. Not that the Fates confined themselves to one or even two names. Of course not. They were known by many names and more to come.

Cë remembered the past. Serene as carnelian.

Hael wove the present. Inspiring as amethyst.

Drä pondered the future. Harmonious as verdite.

Valuable reminders to keep close these days. With the waxing Tawny, what arcana practices would be strongest— Maijerda collided into a complete stranger with tousled, graying hair. His midnight-dark sailor's coat whipped in front of her as he flicked his cigarette in an inexplicable hurry. He was out of sight before she could apologize. But not before he sneered at her. Icy eyes narrowed.

The carelessness of some people, honestly.

Miffed, she twisted her satchel strap, the book's presence weighing on her. "Oh stop it." It didn't have a presence. It had physical weight, weighing down her bag. "You're wandering for the stars, Maijerda." Quit personifying the Fates-damned thing.

Onward she went. Threaded beats hummed by until Maijerda's skin no longer crawled and her cheeks softened with the blossom of a smile. Her sigh carried her into Token Row. Shop windows dull, while pubs bristled with guests. Laughter sung above all else, even the rhythm of the tide. There was something missing from this symphony accompanying her stroll.

She knew exactly which song she wanted to sing. Could she let herself revel in the sweetness of it? Closing her eyes helped to harness her attention to the echo of her boot heels. Tempo. The rumble of cheerful cacophony in the pubs. Pitch. Her lullaby was waiting for her, hopeful to be shared with the Moon as a practice of patience and reminiscence.

Maijerda hummed her lullaby, slowing the tempo and keeping it close to her chest. It was a bittersweet communion. Hopefully the Moon was enjoying the lullaby's company too.

About halfway through her route, near a print shop, unease slunk in the air. She stopped humming, cutting her lullaby short. The hair raised on the back of her neck and her ears pricked up for sounds reeking of something untrustworthy. Even though no one else was around, she wasn't willing to bet she was so denotatively alone.

A black cat sprung from a muddled shadow, hunkering atop a barrel near baskets of bread in the bakery window. Yellow eyes wide, fixated perfectly still, it stared over Maijerda's shoulder. Far too focused. Someone was there, keeping the cat on edge.

Quickening her pace wouldn't be wise and so she avoided doing so blatantly. If someone was watching, rather, following her, best to not let them know she was on guard.

She changed course after another city block, casually as possible, through a less traveled passageway. A shadow swelled. Which could be explained by any number of lights flickering in the windows. A flutter of cloth caught in the corner of her eye. "Scalded piss."

Someone was molded in the shadows, tracing her every step. She rushed for an alleyway and reached for her dagger belted to her thigh. The blade itself was slender and steel. Brass and black accents were melded at the pommel and hilt, tailored to her palm and no one else's, as a gift from Mother.

"Predictable," the shadow jeered.

The reply which came was from a single thunderous beat of her heart.

She darted her gaze upward and sideways, mind shifting to Mother's lessons in defensive strategy. There must be an escape.

They continued, "I wouldn't draw your blade. It seems we share a common interest."

The edge of his cadence gnawed at her, urging her to turn. It would've been wiser to bolt for a head start. Curiosity, as it had the cat, persuaded her.

"Is there a reason you're following me?" On an impulsive whim, she pivoted to him, his tone recognizable. "As I recall, your help was unwanted."

The Fates must've been grinning in agreement. She was right. It was the librarian, now wearing a hooded brown coat over his oxblood waistcoat. His facial scruff obscured his features even more in the dark. Moonlight shone on the flecks of gray in his hair. "Sure are a persistent bunch, you librarians. What do you want?"

"Your book."

Maijerda furrowed her brow, held up a hand. "Fates. Straight to it then? I was expecting a bit more banter from you. I've no idea what you're talking about."

The librarian smirked and pressed, urgently though hushed. "As for your research. End it."

Maijerda started talking over him, incredulous. "What I'm researching is my own business. Don't make a fool of yourself." Quite finished, she whipped around to leave. A decisive grip ushered Maijerda back around. "Piss off!" She shoved his hand.

He tilted his head to the side. "Apologies. You really should consider my bluntness a favor. Your book is a bad omen."

She scoffed. "It's not *my* boo—. Absolutely not. My endeavors don't concern you."

"Trust me, I'd rather they didn't. Unfortunately, I must insist you come with me."

Souring her inflection, she swung her arms in mocking resignation. "Oh? You insist, do you? Well, let me throw caution to the wind! Would you care to grab a pint first?"

His smile was wry, not the least bit frustrated. And every bit closer to her. "Come back with me to the Toll. We can discuss matters there. You can trust me."

"Trust you? Should I be flattered you've stalked me through the streets?" There were few words left to describe her distaste. This was outrageous, truly. "I'll have the magistrate see to your behavior. Give him something useful to do for a change."

Decidedly she feigned stepping away, unsheathing her dagger with intent to strike.

However, another blade was poised against her ribs.

The librarian's bargaining changed to disapproving resolve. "If you won't agree, I've no choice than to assume your intentions are questionable."

"My intentions?" Maijerda blurted at the accusation. "What the hells are you on about?"

"This is your last chance. Come with me to the Toll."

"I'd really rather not." She tried to shift, but he pressed the dagger more firmly, though without breaking fabric or skin.

"Be it on your head. In future, do remember I approached you with courtesy."

Fuck this prick. In a single step Maijerda shifted and pushed his blade to the side, bringing her own to his torso. She wasn't quick enough and was whirled out of control by the wrist. She collided onto the cobblestones, landing awkwardly on her left arm. The bastard twisted and pinned her right arm before she could roll over and punch him.

He dug his knee into her lower back as Maijerda seethed trying to break his grip. Panic set in and adrenaline bent aggressively in her favor.

She twitched just so, finding leverage, and pushed him off kilter by kicking his chest. Sitting up, Maijerda struck him right under the eye with her elbow, sending him reeling. She scrambled upright and readied for another round.

Blade in hand, she aimed low for his thigh, hoping he wouldn't deflect it. Damn it! He did and punched her while she was reconfiguring her approach. She never was the best at sparring, but in a pinch...

She snarled and swung right back in retaliation as he ducked, gliding to grapple her. They hit the ground and jostled each other beat by beat, each shifting for dominance. Maijerda managed to land on top but he rolled her right back down, sending her dagger clattering. She bit his hand pinned to her shoulder.

He retracted reflexively, without making a sound. Using the distraction, she wrapped her legs around his right and twisted to flip and use his weight as a counterbalance to stand. Ready to regain the upper hand, it was the most peculiar thing.

Odd how she fumbled at the bidding of spiraling vertigo. Growing closer to the cobbles with each slowing breath. Slowing? Her heart was pounding with the fight, until now. Her sight dimmed with invasive tides of gray. Her limbs, laden with sand. With a final attempt to stretch upright, she rapidly lost control and fell face first. Dazed, she inspected her shoulder. A syringe? Completely drained.

Fan-bloody-tastic.

"As impressed as I am, I'm sorry to do this." The librarian knelt beside her and wiped blood from below his eye.

She curled her lip and slurred, "Fuck you—" Darkness consumed her.

CHAPTER TEN

FORGOTTEN KNELL

MAIJERDA JOLTED AWAKE. BEHIND HER EYES throbbed with a headache piercing through to the base of her skull. She rolled her head from side to side on the back of a chair to relieve a knotted strain, groaning at stiffness.

Her vision adjusted to a familiar light alive with heartbeats. Moonlight? Faint, floating orbs emitted a glow to envy the clearest of Blue Moons. The Moonlight bathed the den, a creature looming in front of her. Perched atop a silky marble table, it bored through her defenses.

Maijerda recoiled, gritting under a weight digging into her chest and limbs. There were no physical bonds to be seen, yet she was lashed to this chair. Struggling pressed her shoulder blades into carvings in the wood.

Words composed with the ring and crunch of gnashing pebbles sounded. "You've nothing to fear, Maijerda."

The forthrightness of her name tumbling down a hill of rocks paused her struggles out of pure, unadulterated fear setting every bone on edge, drawing beads of sweat. Her tongue was scaly, stuck to the roof of her mouth. "What in the bleeding piss are you? Something from the Harrowing? Devil? Demon? Or worse?"

What was worse than a demon? She couldn't say. Demons supposedly hadn't been seen in centuries, but there were rumors. Always. Some might've managed to leak through to this realm. Summoned by cults, fallen from dying stars, born from rotten trees, cursed souls sent back as punishment... the list goes on. From what Maijerda knew, sightings had increased, though she'd never witnessed one.

The creature stretched his back, his stone skin etched with cracks alluding to muscles and veins. He leapt to the floor with unorthodox grace, his wings breathed behind him. With his clawed steps, the pulsing cloak of trickster Moonlight accentuated the artistry of his prominent brow, maw, and twisted horns.

Fascination overtook her wholly. "You're one of the stone? A gargoyle? Impossible. I've only ever heard of your kind in play scripts."

"Impossible as I may be, my name is Knax. I apologize on behalf of the librarian who brought you to me. You have my word when I say Jeddeith is a trusted friend. We mean to help you."

Maijerda raised an eyebrow and belittled this unwelcome decree. "I beg to differ." She indicated the unseen restraints.

The gargoyle gestured solemnly and tilted his head. "I am sorry for the extremes. Jeddeith deemed it a necessary precaution. Trust it was not backed by malicious intent."

"Then what was it backed by?" As if on cue, the librarian trotted down several steps into the room, a bundle of herbs, crystals, and incense in hand. "Speak of the bastard." She radiated hatred at him, livid and distrusting.

A mark was forming under his eye. At least she'd gotten in decent hits. Maijerda didn't bother suppressing a smirk. He ignored her, setting the burgundy-veined crystals along the eastern edge of the table. East, to best represent knowledge?

The gargoyle spoke imploringly. "I do wish the conditions of our meeting were different."

Maijerda cut her cackle in half. "As if you have no part in this?"

The creature stretched his wings, contemplating. "My part in this is curious indeed. You see, I was crafted by someone who left me here to care for the Requiem Toll, secretly of course." His words ended with indications of forlorn remembrance, his shoulders hunching under unseen burden.

"You're prolonging the inevitable," Jeddeith interrupted, aggressively hushed. He gripped Knax's shoulder. "She is not your forgotten knell. Be done with it and free her to live on as she pleases." His agitation was evident as snow on a grassy knoll as he slammed the incense on the table.

She pulled her arms taut, fruitlessly demanding their attention. "Knell? What are you talking about?"

Knax didn't stray from Jeddeith. "How can you be sure?"

Jeddeith left him unanswered and distanced himself from the spell components, obscuring her view of the table with his lean muscled form. The velvet of his waistcoat was a stark contrast to the intensity in his jaw. Not to mention that scowl. His eyes set his overall expression on edge. His left eye pooled with a bright golden honey, sharply offset by his mahogany hair. The other, a smoky gray. Their colors deepened, contrasting with the faintly warm olive of his skin.

Two could play at this game. "You obviously know more about this book than I do. Tell me what you know."

"It won't matter when we're finished."

Fates, he was smug. As if what he said was final and nothing else mattered. "Finished with what exactly?"

"Once we remove all semblance of this—" He revealed Da's book. "—from your mind. Then, you'll no longer be in danger."

Nothing made sense. Was she sure she wasn't still unconscious in the alley? Dreaming. "I'm not in danger. Thanks for your concern, I suppose." Knax lit a match. What was it being set to? Jeddeith remained the part of a heavy theater curtain, blocking her view. Incense settling in the air robust as cedar answered her distress. Spell-work? Fuck. "Let me go."

"Not an option."

Genuinely baffled, Maijerda asked, "Why are you doing this?"

"To protect Pɛnʌmbrə."

"What is *that* supposed to mean? I'm not a villain." What was this? A play she'd somehow never read?

"Neither am I." Jeddeith began carving a rune into a teal candle with a bronze casting needle.

The way these two were twisting everything. She wasn't trying to destroy the world. Nor was she trying to save it. From what? All she wanted was proof Da and… and even Mother were murdered.

Knax uttered the beginning of an incantation several times over and traced arcane symbols in the air with the incense, putting the spell to work.

"Don't do this."

He paused, seeming to gather himself. Grimly he continued, the design settling at eye level, more permanently than if they hadn't been meant for casting. Was he hesitating? It wasn't clear. If he was, maybe his spell would fail.

Opportunity was slipping like sand. Maijerda sputtered and ground her teeth, testing the invisible restraints. "You bastard. So much for discussion."

Against better judgement, she inhaled while she strained to free herself and practically drank the incense. Her eyes started to burn, growing glossy. Her breathing heaved with vengeance that she struggled to spit from the churning in her lungs. No one would take this from her. The Fates may have stolen her parents, but they couldn't claim her need for vindication. Riddled with desperation, words contorted in her mind as she pulled against the arcane cording. She started questioning things she knew the answer to mere moments prior.

Why was she struggling? Why was she sitting? What time was it? How did she get here? Where was *here*? Shit. Her mind was starting to grow unsure. The book! She couldn't let go of it. She pictured it in her mind, held onto its image. It may be the source and target of her vexation these days, but it was hers to hate. They couldn't wipe it clean from her memory!

"Stop! Please. I mean no harm by having that book. It's all I have left of my father. Don't take my memories."

Knax stayed his claw after lighting the candle, his stone straining to wrinkle. "Your father, is he—?"

"Dead." She stared him down. The word an anchor, taunting her will to live through this sea of guilt. "Our ship was attacked by a storm, a creature. And my father died holding this Fates' forsaken book." Saliva slung from her tongue in hatred. "I need to know *why*." Her voice raised in pitch, sweat beaded and stung her eyes, from tensing the bonds.

Jeddeith clenched and stretched unsteady hands. His gaze shifted from her to a singular ring banded around his first finger of his right hand, made of roughened charcoal gray and antiqued pressed gold. "This is to protect you and our world."

Unwanted tears scorched from cracks in her emotional barricade. He wasn't making any sense. Didn't they understand her distress? "I've searched for days for answers with nothing to show for it." She pressed her fists into the chair. "My revealing spell was unanswered. There's nothing in that damn library about sentient storms. Nothing regarding this symbol. I've been repeatedly disappointed by every. Fucking. Blank. Page. In that book."

She shot her glare between Knax and Jeddeith. See reason, *please*.

"You would have us believe you haven't seen a single mark in this book?" Jeddeith's tone was difficult to place. Condescending and somehow, amused?

Of course the damned thing was empty. Why did they care? "Yes."

Knax reached for Jeddeith to give him the book. "You're positive?"

"I swear on the Moon's guardians."

Knax gradually shut his eyes. "What was your mother's name?"

Maijerda shook her head, half smirking, miffed and resigned to her despair for him to not finish his spell work and take her memory. It sent her skin sickly cold. "Relona."

If stone could pale in color, Knax would've been the softened gray of river pebbles. Wings solemn, he reached for the teal candle.

She lunged as much as possible, curls falling over her shoulders, hairpins falling with them. "I offered the truth!"

Knax picked up the candle.

"She died six years ago."

And brought it to eye level.

"I'm begging you. Have mercy. Please!"

"I'm sorry." Knax blew out the candle.

And dismissed the spell entirely. Her galloping heart refused to believe the nightmare had ended.

"We were both quite mistaken, Jeddeith. She may not be my knell exactly. But she is the daughter of one."

Panting, Maijerda raised her voice, demanding. "Tell me what the fuck is going on."

At the corner of the table was a journal the color of stardust, dwarfed by Knax's hand. He opened its hardened spine, flipping through pages. "When did you say your mother passed?"

Maijerda's ears rang as blood pumped in them. The room tilted as if the *Norn* was rolling beneath her. "It's been six years, as of a couple weeks ago."

Without explanation Knax freed her of the restraints with a wave of his hand. Impulsivity hollered at her to bolt past Jeddeith, find her way out. The unhealed morsels of her that longed to see and hear of Mother had her heatedly demanding information, compensating for dread. "How do you know of her?"

"The power of names run deep." Knax closed his eyes, brought his claws to his chest. "I wouldn't blame you for refusing. I suggest we all have a discussion."

Jeddeith turned his shoulder to her and interjected. "You're certain she can be trusted?"

Maijerda latched onto him with a snap of her head. "You might want to rethink that question. You're the one who kidnapped me, remember?"

Knax calmed them both with a sigh and tired expression. "The choice is yours."

Maijerda rubbed clammy palms on her thighs. It would be careless to trust. What had these two done to earn hers? She needed answers if she was to avenge Mother and Da. Even after all these years, there must be more to her death than illness. No matter who disagreed. Even if that person had been Da. She closed her eyes, staving off reminders of their arguments over the years. What if their deaths were connected? What were the chances?

"If either of you cross me, I *will* defend myself."

"Understood." Knax nodded.

"Good. And I'd like my daggers back. Now." She opened her palm to Jeddeith and raised an eyebrow.

"Say please."

"Fuck off."

Jeddeith removed them from his belt and tossed them to her.

"I'll fetch some tea, yes?" Knax didn't wait for their response, heading out the door and upstairs. His gait was stoic and rigid, yet graceful. It'd be a wonder if he could maintain balance on a ship. Oh Fates, not important. Maijerda sighed, annoyed at her nerves finding holds in other, more comforting topics.

Awkward silence ensued, Maijerda and Jeddeith sizing one another up for the entirety of Knax's absence while she sheathed her blades. One strapped to her thigh, the other in a sheath hidden by her boot. When he returned, Knax formed a pattern with his claws. He muttered an arcane word or two and four orbs of the very same Moonlight twinkled into being.

She turned her focus to the arcane light. "Moonlight's rarely so clear with tapestry weaving." The trails of periwinkle orbs soaring apart to light the room were stunning, as if he'd borrowed pieces of the Moon herself.

"The art of Moonlight weaving was taught to me as a means of forming a bond. It is my creator's signature, should we ever need to ensure the other wasn't an imposter."

As Knax spooned loose leaves inside a cast iron kettle, he handled the tea as delicately as stone claws would allow. Knax laid a marbled claw on the kettles' rounded side and called upon a small favor from the tapestry. He didn't need components or runes, the hand gesture enough for his castings. Orange heat radiated from the kettle and boiled the water.

Jeddeith was being awfully quiet at the opposite side of the table, arms crossed. Likely waiting for her to reveal her evil plot. Fates, he was broody. Probably had trouble sleeping and thought himself the dark, handsome, misunderstood type.

Knax nudged a lavender mug closer to her. "Please help yourself. I understand tea is a creature comfort. I don't require nourishment. It brings me joy to share with guests when I'm able. Please." He gestured again to the tea.

He was the most endearing gargoyle she'd ever met. Granted, the only one, but still. "Have you ever had guests?"

"Come to think, no I haven't. Disregarding this one." He referenced Jeddeith, who didn't ease at the quip.

Maijerda grinned at the good-natured revelation before addressing Jeddeith. "You first." She nodded.

Without visible irritation, he poured his tea and sipped. "You might want to take another look at this." The book seemed to greedily pull itself across the table with Jeddeith's guiding push. Like Rel scooting closer for attention.

She grimaced, swallowing a spitefully frequent twinge, chasing it with a sip of earthy, mint tea. The bile percolated again, restraining her will to speak. One more sip of tea to shoo it down and with a solid thud she placed her cup on the table, dragging her hand to the book's edge.

Her breath stiffened, resulting in quick and shallow efforts. With it came a faint lull, encroaching around her with a hum. Shaking her head, she hoped to toss it from her ears and mind. She fiddled with the latch a handful of times, resenting touching it. Nervousness rendered her fingertips tingling and helpless. After a split second, she opened it.

Maijerda's sense of betrayal for this book was unmatched as it now, after all this time, beamed at her arrogantly with the strangest of markings. Splats of ink were scattered on the first few pages, faint as the earliest memory a babe can bear. Enough to know it's tangible. Yet the story it was attempting to tell, elusive.

Her expression hardened in calculation as she traced the markings with her fingers. The pages were dry, it couldn't have been a trick. She turned the page.

Whispers of black ink scrolled along in a linear fashion. Prose? It seemed likely, but the scribbles were unceremonious.

She flipped to the next page. A variety of colors were blurred and lost within the paper. One more page turned and she took to mindlessly rubbing the back of her neck, elbow digging into the table.

"I've never seen these markings before." She bounced between the pages flabbergasted, daring the book to alter its appearance for her to witness personally. The colors and black lines refused, steadfast as a seaside cliff.

Jeddeith and Knax shared a look of reproachfulness.

"I believe you." Knax spoke first. "Just as I believe you are a muse."

"I couldn't possibly. Muses are not an entity or being. The term is conceptual at most." Maijerda, rarely lost in words, was floundering in their purpose. "How do you mean?"

"What proof is there to show muses are not quite real? Legend says, for every knell there is a muse. And for every muse there is song. Muses are born in response to a knell's energy as means of balance. Similar to the phrase *dreams the sun, so dawns the Moon.* A muse is not meant to nullify negativity from a knell, but complement it.

"Plainly speaking, muses are a rarity that offer arcane inspiration to people, nature, and items alike. There are some enchanted items that require convincing before sharing their treasures or histories. No trigger is alike, from what I gather. It's been ages since a muse has been documented. Research most notably poses not all muses are people. That being said, I suspect you inspired this book to begin painting its pages."

"I haven't the slightest idea how." Maijerda unintentionally whispered, her intended confidence overshadowed by dismay. "This doesn't explain how my father came to possess this. Our bloodline is of no significance. How do you know about this?" She closed the cover to expose the symbol.

"Truthfully, I didn't know of the book's existence. Nor did my creator. Nadín. I was crafted to help watch for signs of the glyph. She didn't know how it would manifest, or what it would foretell. She feared its appearance and what may follow. When she left Steslyres, she instructed me to be wary for its return. If I encountered the glyph in any capacity, I was to prevent it from being exposed completely and if need be, from falling into the wrong hands." He sunk a claw tip into the glyph's grooves on the book. Stone brows knitted, concern etching his jaw, he seemed hesitant to share more of what he was withholding. "As for your mother…"

"What part did she have in this? Did Nadín know her?" Mother certainly never mentioned the name Nadín before but Maijerda feared she knew the answer.

"I assume so. However, all Nadín shared was that Relona's involvement or appearance was that of a requiem knell."

The ache in Maijerda's eyes, swaying her to laugh? Or to cry? Maybe one and then the other. "My mother was a bad omen? I'm sorry, you're mistaken. If anything she's the true muse. If you knew her, you'd understand."

"I wish that were true. Nadín was insistent with her worry. I know this is the sign, the tapestry threads I've—" He stopped himself and eyed Jeddeith. "We've been tasked with searching for."

"Yet you were oblivious of this book for over a week?"

"Odd isn't it? I have my suspicions. It wasn't until Jeddeith came to me after your meeting that I learned its existence managed to escape me. As caretaker of the Toll I'm sensitive to those coming and going through pages, resonating with their true intentions as they consume ink. My conclusion is the book was not ready to say anything. But just before Jeddeith brought you here, when I awoke for the night, I could feel my body-stone fester with acidic alarm. Once we opened the book a flood of warning washed over me, like wormwood and poppies. This is what I was meant to find. I could taste the foulness of its potential."

His volume diminished by the end of his monologue. Knax beckoned an orb of light hovering at Jeddeith's shoulder to come closer but he plucked the light before it flew past. The orb beat slowly, as if savoring Jeddeith's attention and painted itself a soft, intimate lavender for no more than a prolonged sigh.

He looked to Knax questioningly. Just as he released it, the orb resumed the Moonlight hue before reaching Maijerda's hand.

"Nadín left me with the mark in a manner that surpasses ink and parchment. I would like to show you. I owe you that respect and trust."

Without forewarning his bottom jaw stretched with unconventional ease and Knax tilted his head back. She held the orb aloft, peering inside the gargoyle's maw. His tongue was sculpted with precision, as if to better equip him for speech. His teeth, imposing with their sharp tips and rounded roots. In the smooth surface of his palate was an engraving of the symbol haunting the cover of Da's book.

She retracted, overcome by a quickening heart. There was that damned pit in her stomach again too. She was growing weary of its return.

Don't spiral. Don't lose hold.

She leaned in for a second inspection.

There it was, plain as day. She couldn't convince herself otherwise. Each angle, each line identical.

Knax rested his jaw. "I believe this is to blame for your parents' deaths." He motioned to the book. "Now that we've found both the glyph and blood of Nadín's knell, we should leave Steslyres and consult with her. I assume you were attacked at sea and those responsible seek this book's secrets."

Jeddeith set his tea down, firmly. "We don't know that."

"I can taste it. It's brimstone and bile. Warning us that our lifelines are bound to stakes atop pyres. You've trusted me faithfully for six years. Ever since you appeared at my doorstep. What causes you to waver?"

Jeddeith sucked in a cheek and folded his arms again. "We'd be sending ourselves on a crusade and eventually what, a battle between light and dark? All over a book which unveils its pages when it chooses to? It's a tale fit for children. This is our reality, not a faetale."

He was so arrogant and fickle, with no place in this. "No one is asking for your help," Maijerda tossed at him.

"This *is* our reality and it's our obligation to protect it. We cannot do so without Maijerda. I suspect there's more to this than Nadín anticipated. Don't forsake responsibility. Nadín instructed that she be contacted when the glyph or Relona emerged. I must follow through with my oath."

"We learned of this book *today*. We don't know what we're getting ourselves into." Jeddeith leaned across the table. "If you're eager to defend it, what exactly are we protecting it from?" There was worry in his face, mixed with the red-veined distress of someone who'd recently lost a decent night's sleep.

Knax's wings tensed.

"This isn't worth the risk. Send Maijerda on her way and we'll find Nadín on our own."

"You can't dismiss m—"

"You may keep your reservations close to your chest. She deserves to know, as my muse." Knax addressed her, stone eyes furrowed. "Have you ever entertained the theory of the Spent Spindle?"

Maijerda's eyes fluttered in search of resonance with the idea, but none surfaced. "No? Can't say I have."

She chanced a sidelong look at Jeddeith. It was strange, his defenses appeared to slip at the mention.

"We shouldn't discuss the Spindle."

"And why not?"

"I've spent half my life— I can't stop you. I just don't agree."

Maijerda suppressed a snicker. What *did* he agree with? Fates. "I for one would like to hear more about it," she remarked with a flick of her hand.

Knax nodded, rustling parchment and three books bound in loose leathers. "The Spent Spindle is a theory of global misrepresentation, hastily set aside by the majority of academics. Supposedly, there is reason to believe Pɛnʌmbrə is not in an untampered, natural state."

"I—I don't follow. Natural state? How do you mean?"

Knax unfurled the parchment to reveal an essay penned in minuscule script. "This offers some details on the matter. The author treads so terribly careful, I can't discern if they did so in fear or if they didn't have the ability to fully draw upon their thoughts on the matter."

Maijerda surveyed line by curved line, as Knax furthered his explanation, tapping at her temple.

"Pɛnʌmbrə may have not been harmonious in the dawning age. What we see and experience daily is quite real, but it may be a repercussion from altering the bindings of this realm's existence. The Spent Spindle, refers to the emptiness of the world's original state. Spent and bare, bereft of goodness and purpose, a new spindle is said to have been spun to remake the world anew. To allow a second chance at arcana and life."

The parchment crinkled in Maijerda's sweaty palms. She quickly released it and smoothed the wrinkles. "What we see today, isn't how the world is meant to be?"

"Not necessarily. It may very well be how Pɛnʌmbrə is tended to flourish. It also may not be how it was birthed. Things which survived the transition to a new representation of threads may have been forced to lose pieces of themselves in the process."

Maijerda stared at the book, nervous to touch it. So it was more than it seemed, if this were true.

Knax lined up an array of open books. "Art from unknown time periods, books written in dead languages—"

"The language of the land?" The revelation poured from her.

"I believe so. Maps of supposedly uncharted lands." He handed her a map of an island, scratchily labeled, *Gazdeq*.

She furrowed her brow, checking the landmarks. "I've sailed by here countless times. There's no island there." Sarcastically she cocked her head. "Whichever cartographer drafted this must've been drunk or dreamed it for a faetale. I've never heard of Gazdeq before."

"None have. It's remained undiscovered for centuries. Supposedly its wilds mimic tunnels found across the seas fit for a slew of subterranean creatures. Proof of the Spindle doesn't end there. Haven't you heard bards mention songs lacking the plainness of words and manifest as poetry within the walls of your mind?

"There's documentation of creatures never seen, nor tamed. Mention of nexus points or leylines filled with elemental arcana. Shifting and befalling around and between reality. Elemental creatures, called nezdrade. Which of course are a myth. Some texts speak as if they're quite real.

"There's languages misused. Unfounded linguistic features. Empty hourglasses which must adhere to specific times and places before they can be used…"

"Books which keep silent?" Maijerda's fingers slipped from Da's book.

"Indeed." The rocks in his throat ground and consoled her with imperfections. "It stands to reason, that an artifact from another time, another spool long since spent, would struggle to be heard in a new reality that inherently smothers its roots."

"Which is why you suspected there was a trigger? A grounding conduit to aid it?"

"Yes. Do you believe in fate?"

"Fate is as mischievous as time. I can't decide if it exists or if we create it for our own comforts. If it were true, wouldn't she have shared that with me? Or Da? Wouldn't he have warned me of this after her death?"

Tears immediately glossed at the stabbing mention of death. Gnawed stone resurfaced in her mental dissonance.

"I wouldn't fault him for it. He may not have known any more about this book than we do. He may have been protecting you."

From what? From Mother? The truth? This all was about to send her anxiety to the brink. All she could picture in her mind was the note from Da.

Tuft, I never wanted this for you.

Maijerda pressed her hands into the table and bit her rolled lip. "If what this book holds is as dangerous as you've made it out to be, why are we playing with fire?"

"Per Nadín, encountering this glyph or Relona indicates we may not have the luxury of secrecy. The attack on your ship proves that, I fear."

Staring at him with aching eyes, Maijerda sighed to fend off a tearful collapse of wits.

Knax frowned. "I am sorry to share this burden with you so suddenly. But, I do believe we must help the book find a voice to better understand what is at stake. The decision is yours."

Maijerda nodded, wiping tears with her sleeve. "In both name and blood. I'll do what it takes."

Jeddeith cleared his throat, testing her patience. "I'd advise against getting involved."

"Don't speak to me like you... like you know... as if there—" Agh! Fates, she was losing words off the tip of her tongue, shrouded in tiredness and stress. It was so endlessly frustrating not being able to say what she could picture in her mind. Fuck this. Pinching the bridge of her nose, she tried again. "Don't pretend we're friends. If it means my parents' deaths will not be in vain, I will hear what the book has to say. I'll take the risk."

Jeddeith's voice grew louder. "You don't at all find that self-absorbed? Risking devastation all because you're grieving your parents?"

Her cheeks burned with rage and she stood to challenge him. Grief bore many shapes. "Yes. And?"

Jeddeith scoffed but she cut in. "I'd risk the state of the world for answers. To find my father's murderer. To know how and why my mother died. The unknown is worse than the end. Clearly you've never lost anyone."

His jaw was so still, he could've been a stone likeness atop a tomb.

"Are you quite finished? I don't need you two at each other's throats, and we need to figure out what triggered this book to begin communicating."

Maijerda shrunk back at the disappointment and frustration in Knax's tone. Oddly, so did Jeddeith.

Knax slid books and parchments toward them both. "If you'd be so kind. This stack isn't going to research itself."

Maijerda reached for a purple damask fabric book, while Knax arched a brow at Jeddeith.

He drug his boots off the table and begrudgingly took a blue scroll of parchment with catching crunches. What a poor job he did too, hiding his distaste for Maijerda and disagreement with Knax behind the parchment.

Chapter Eleven

A Sweetness
Not Meant to be Tasted

SEVERAL POTS OF A BRIGHT, LAVENDER Earl Grey tea were brewed throughout the evening and handfuls of exasperated sighs interjected the crumple of turning pages.

At least two hours in, Maijerda pinned her hair using a filigreed comb. It was petty, stray strands tested her nerves if she was already set on edge. Unfortunately her mindless fidgeting set fly-away hairs and several curls free from the comb. She grumbled and looked up from her book. Jeddeith was peering at her from over the edge of his glasses.

Oh the subtlety of men. She sighed and worked to keep from rolling her eyes.

"Are there more where this came from?" Maijerda didn't care if she was breaking tension. The tea was a temporary fix for her lethargy and being in one spot too long made her antsy. Especially with someone who evidently didn't trust her as far as he could throw her. What gall he had to judge *her*.

"Mmm, down the hall to a modest left. If you reach the harp room, you've swung too far." Knax didn't come close to relaxing his clutch on his map, studying the inscription along the border.

She excused herself to the library, making sure to keep her left turn as modest as possible. The study was unlike any personal collection she'd ever perused, invited or otherwise.

Luminescent rust draperies, some with elaborate needlework, others with sheer inlays, were hung along what little of the walls remained free from bookshelves. Fabrics laced the ceiling in swags, eliciting a carnival-tent atmosphere.

She veered to the right and assumed the awkward bent neck posture that comes from browsing shelves. Where there wasn't a book tucked away on the shelf, knick-knacks filled the vacancy. Crystal orbs on clawed stands, telescopes, and music boxes. Boxes of wax sealing stamps, collections of figurines, gaming boards, and puzzle cubes. Maijerda picked up a brass bell, but no ring sang from it. She tilted an hourglass, assuming sand would trickle from the ether. Oddly, it was empty.

Maijerda traced the spines of the books once she reached the third shelf, willing herself to pick up the pace, choose one, and get back to the den. Fabrics and leathers reached her fingertips, then— She stopped short and backtracked a few spines.

Wood?

She knelt to inspect it more intently, sliding it gently from the shelf. If there was a trap or secret door to be sprung, it wouldn't be all that surprising. This book was crafted and painted to mimic a leather-bound tome. In reality… she rapped her knuckles on it.

Yes. Solid wood.

She hugged it closely and sat on the floor, legs crossed. She thumbed through thick pages, quickly dissatisfied with the botanical drawings inside. Replacing it on the shelf, she resumed searching for the impossible among so many books.

Endless books. What used to be a comfort was starting to become overwhelming. Though inked pages were one of her many loves, music being among them. And so, for the sake of change, she gravitated to a music box for a chance to bathe in melody. Maijerda turned the silver key and opened the lid to drink in the song. The mechanisms within creaked into motion and fondly sang a rhyme Maijerda recognized by the fifth note. The lyrics sung of children chasing wisps of fae arcana bundled into tufts of mirthful light.

The music box slowed to a finish and she replaced it on the shelf, immediately setting her eyes on another. Hungrily, she picked it up, leaned her back against the bookshelf, and twisted the key until met with resistance. Beneath the octagonal lid a needle lay on a pillow of fabric. Cogs clicked inside, but no music arose.

She wound the key a second and third time, still no music played. Should she speak to it? Fates knew why. It seemed... right?

Say this little needle was simply longing for company after being lost and forgotten on a shelf. Maijerda brought the box up to her nose for a closer look at the sewing needle. "Feeling a little tired are we? I'm sorry to hear that. How difficult it can be to sing when you're feeling bogged down by it all." Cogs finished whirring and she turned the key. "Torlen lexnym. I understand, truly I do."

The needle performed the most strange flourish. Strange because there was no weaver around to command it to move at their arcane will. Maijerda sat taller, taking in the moment as it floated up from the pillow and righted itself. The music box sprang into a song for the needle to dance to. Maijerda's heart lingered in dissonance with the tone as the needle was busy at courtly work above the pillow. It moved as though an unseen hand was guiding it to stitch on a canvas stretched in a hoop.

Her skin flushed itself of the peach warmth in her cheeks. Intuition striking her before cognizant recognition. Fates be fickle. There was no possibility in all the hells. There wasn't even the slightest chance! Was there? It—it couldn't be.

The music box clicked on, longer than before, singing a song never sung by another that Maijerda had met before. Which meant her instincts were right.

It *could* be.

She gasped and bolted for the den.

A chorus of muffled clicks and snaps rumbled from within the box, her heartbeat knocking against the wood to be let in. She skidded inside, set the box on the table between the other two. "Listen!" Maijerda was frantic, grinning ear to ear, nervous to believe what she was hearing.

The clicks and metallic snags interlocked in a staccato dance. Fragmented and almost unrecognizable, another more lyrical tune layered with the hymn. The most enticing lullaby eased into the air one note at a time. Far from any ordinary lullaby. It was hers.

Enamored by the peculiarity, Maijerda nearly missed Knax leaning over the box beside her. "This box has never played a song before."

"What?" She attempted to pull herself from observing the music box. "Impossible."

"Is it?"

"The Spent Spindle." Muttering her thought pattern, Maijerda's fingers went numb, the pit in her stomach fluttering with brittle hope.

Knax smiled softly, placing a hand on her shoulder to guide her gaze to Da's book. "Reminds me of a tale I once read of a mythical flower. No one knows the name, but it blooms only when sung to. Ah, it appears somebody has something to say."

The book, closed, vibrated so pronouncedly it was practically a hum, as though it also was searching for the right note. The silver of the glyph was fluid like a river, the green leather blurring. When Maijerda picked it up, her skin prickled in response, her heart beating as if she'd sprinted through Brine Bend. It was Fates-awful work to push Jeddeith and Knax's presence aside. She wanted to focus her mind on the book and her lullaby, trusting a flow of consciousness modeling after a poet drafting long into the Harrowing.

Maijerda homed in on the fragmented measures of her lullaby to find the right note to fill in the gaps. Honeyed trinkets flitted to her. Each longing to be understood. And that was just the thing, wasn't it? Knax mentioned the book was trying to speak with them. They just needed to listen.

A rhythm seduced her senses and stitched to the parts of her intimate with the tapestry. It was inexplicable. And yet, simple as song.

Maijerda sang. It wasn't a decision. It was a compulsion, completely overtaken by her lullaby. It was greater than any arcana she'd ever woven. She sang with drawn, waiting vocalizations. She paused for the music box melody to swoop in with feathered wings, and then eased into another formless measure. This verse dipped low and lulled her music to tiptoe cautiously, reaching for the stars and the unknown curiosities beyond them.

The entire experience created a lullaby for the senses.

The sound of it was lovingly eerie.

The taste of it…did she dare risk a taste?

Or was it taboo? A sweetness not meant to be tasted.

She couldn't resist temptation. It tasted of… what else? Sweet, like honey.

To touch it was to caress velvet.

Even the smell of it was that of fading fires, ocean brine, meadow dew, and pirouetting flora.

To witness sight of it was to imagine a chaotic web of veins surging anywhere and everywhere granting the gift of living redefined.

Tumultuous was the ending, diving off seaside cliffs into the unknown.

She didn't want it to end. Potential for an infinity of cycles reflected in the resonance of the final measure coming to a reluctant close. Yet both she and the music box drifted off, longing to persevere.

Silence soothed in return. Trust.

The hush was pithy, as the music box crackled an instant before combusting into white hot flames. The fire was wild as ever, consuming the box with impossible hunger.

Jeddeith reached for it in an attempt to suffocate the flames; however, they retaliated in response and grew more feral. Singed, he retracted his hand. A piece of the fire broke off and unleashed its wrath by catching a nearby parchment on fire. Knax lunged for his map in a moment of delayed panic. It didn't stop there. This fire was starved for something to fill a swollen, malnourished gut.

One sprite of flame leapt from the music box. It arched dramatically and latched onto Da's book. Defiantly, the book deflected the predator with a wave of dull blue energy and remained unscathed in every way. The flames subsided. Trepidation took hold. All three looked vastly uneasy between one another and the pile of ash.

"Someone care to explain?" Jeddeith remarked defensively, while Knax could barely conjure a shake of his head.

Without directly responding to him, Maijerda picked up the book. Had it actually released that arcana? On its own? "That song, I know it as if it's a part of me. Ever since I was little, except I never knew where I learned it. I call it my 'lullaby'. My parents never had the faintest idea of what I was talking about."

Jeddeith, for the first time, seemed vaguely interested. Arms no longer folded and standoffish. "What of the lyrics?"

"There aren't any. As far as I know." Her hold on the book tensed, as it writhed with longing. A puppy wanting attention, nipping at her. Except it nipped at her instincts, not her scarves like Rel once did. She tried to ignore it but it kept at it.

Wait, what was it doing? No, it couldn't *do* anything. Could it? Something tugged at her to goad her uncertainty and Maijerda opened the book. What little breath she had left escaped in an incredulous gasp.

Each page was boldly expressive with watercolor paintings and prose scrolled along the side in a thin black ink. Complete and waiting to be read. She flipped through it several times over to make sure she wasn't hallucinating. Apparently it wasn't a figment of her imagination or wishful thinking. She leveled her hold on the book, flummoxed.

"Maijerda." Knax's voice was gentle, as if trying to quietly wake her from a nightmare. "Have you ever cast song arcana before?"

"Song arcana?" What was the meaning of this? A prank? She silently accused the book. "No, of course not. Is that even possible?"

"I don't see why not."

"I think you're digging too deep, Knax. The book was responding to a trigger. Just like you mentioned. A key unlocking a door. I didn't weave a spell."

The expression on his face read *are you so sure?* Well, no. She wasn't. Was that relevant right now? Reeling from the epiphany, she moved stiffly to a chair, book clutched to her chest. "Before you stopped me in the alley, I was singing that song, or at least, a part of it." She waved her hand and brushed stray strands of hair before motioning to the ashes. "Fickleness of Fates. What am I supposed to make of this?"

"For every knell there is a muse. And for every muse there is a—"

"Song," Maijerda finished, staring at him.

"As I suspected, you possess the innate arcana of a muse, born unto a knell. I may be a gargoyle who's grown complacent with his perch and getting ahead with theories, but I do think regardless of how this book's pages came to be—" He paused, holding his claws behind his back. "Might I suggest you read what it has to say?"

Why hadn't she dove into its pages? After spending days and days trying to reveal its secrets with blood, sweat, and tears, all she could do was stare at it. "Oh," she half muttered, half sighed. "Right."

Hesitating, should it lash out against her, Maijerda placed the book in her lap. Fear thudding in her chest and ears was contrary to what she'd expected to feel when this all came to be. Why was she frightened of what was written inside? Seemed counterintuitive at this point.

Drumming her fingers on the latch, she abruptly clicked it open. What harm could a book possibly bring? This is what she wanted, more than anything in all the tapestry. Wasn't it?

Chapter Twelve

The Spark

Night after quilted night,
the Moon longed to frolic among the tapestry threads bathing
in her light.
So it began, a Spark of Moonlight grew restless.
The Moon's curiosity burned inside the Spark. Knowing no
other passion but that to explore.
She pulled, she stretched, and she dreamed until she tore free
from the Moon.
Renewed, the Spark drifted to weave within the tapestry
and discover what there was to be seen.

She entwined with tapestry threads and they carried her to
their raveling depths.
Three voices spoke to her, harmonious in their song welcoming
her to their home.
She illuminated the weave with her thrill, but they hushed her
to heed their cautionary tales.
Warning of misunderstandings? Of eagerness bolstering her too
far? Of disappointment?

The Spark found it all terribly troublesome to believe.

Exploring the tapestry was supposed to be full of wonder and song,
not consequence and omens plenty.
The Spark apologized to the voices three for intruding.
Oh, how they insisted she wasn't an unexpected guest.
The Spark was baffled by the madness here, her brightness muddled by these threads and their bewildering words.

With the three bidding her farewell, she continued to soar.
At dawn, the Spark found a creature waning in a language new.
It drew her in with sensations she'd never experienced before.
Each as fleeting as the next. But no less extraordinary.

Wrapped in an embrace, the Spark knew true warmth for the first time.
She then was overtaken by the perfume of petals.
The decadent shades of forest and sea.
The soothing pitch of falling rain.
The silky sweetness of nectar.
There was tapestry in each of these, longing to be spindle spun and needle threaded.
The pinnacle of creating experience, unmatched by any other.

The creature waited, expectant of a gracious reply. To which the Spark gave none.
She meant no ill will.
Though she sung, the Spark was disheartened when they didn't understand the melody.
The creature insisted she was mocking them by muttering nonsense.

Saddened by their bitterness, the Spark departed, her glow a melancholy hue.

At midday, she dove below.
Here she was approached by an unveiling force.
Fire did spark, water did burble, earth did grind, and wind did whisper.
The Spark whipped to and fro, searching for what seemed ages when it struck her, and her light gleamed. This song was all around her.

Rather abruptly, the elements lashed out with their power, displaying to the Spark what glory it was to be the very veins of the realm.
Boastful and pompous, they tousled the Spark about, ruffling her nonexistent feathers.
She was agitated, not knowing how to respond.
Even the elements demand to be heard, and they would have no more of her silence.
Through with being ignored, the elements used their threads to send the Spark far away.
For in their eyes, she did not belong among them.

At unfading dusk, the Spark sputtered, surging with the inner workings of a rattled mind.
She recognized nothing of the tapestry's melodies.
Did they not all sing? Did they not all wish to be heard and understood?
Perhaps those three voices were right in their warnings.
The Spark did not want to believe.

Her brightness ached, straining with confusion.
How lonely a thing it was to know despair.

Rage colored her distress, until she was scorched.

She was completely overwhelmed without a song to sing.
Betrayed by wanderlust.
The Spark abandoned all without regard for which direction
she soared in the tapestry.
Fleeing deep into the Harrowing, she could no longer endure
the pain.
She used her devastation to rip threads to shreds, dooming
herself to burst.

She shattered into fragments of her untold woe, stories to
dream, and muses to wonder.
Each tattered morsel of the Spark interlaced with the tapestry,
creating a lullaby.

Oh, how the Moon mourned her light, extinguished in agony.
She yearned to comfort her little tuft of a Spark.
To hold her tight and sing the song she once loved.
Never had the Moon shed tears.
But on that night, burdened by grief, the Moon could
only weep.

From that moment, the Moon swore she would not let this
piece of herself be forgotten.
Promising to sing her Spark's lullaby until the end of each
night, for all the tapestry to glean.
After all, being rendered silent is wildly different from having
no story to tell.

ACT II

EEL HEART

Chorus from a Boendean sea shanty
Tells a cautionary story about a captain who had
her heart ripped from her chest by the siren
she claimed to be her lover.

Started in 3036

Shipwrecked at sea, not a star to be seen.

Clear the deck there's a storm on the rise.

Swear upon the eye, oh the eel heart's eye.

And trust she won't sentence you to die.

Chapter Thirteen

Something Worth Vindicating

"A FAETALE?" What was she to make of this? A horridly contrived prank? A misguided lapse of Da's judgement? Maijerda silently accused the book.

Jeddeith added to her confusion as if stacking lopsided dishes in need of washing. "Not what you were expecting?"

"Hardly. I thought it might be a relic or spell book. Fates, maybe a journal. Not a faetale I've never heard before. As much as I adore them. I was hoping for something more tangible." Tapping the book, she followed her thoughts aloud. "The lullaby. I can hardly believe it. Of all the impossible…"

She was reeling from the truth. Good thing she was already sitting. "Before you stopped me in the alley, I was singing that song, or at least, a part of it." She waved her hand and brushed stray strands of hair before motioning to the ashes. "Fickleness of Fates."

Knax nodded, eyeing her with a tilted gaze.

"I know what you're going to say. Evidence of muses and knells and the Spent Spindle. How it was all laid out before me."

With a twitch of his snout into a smile, Knax said, "Never would I prove a point simply to say, 'I told you so'. It wouldn't be fair. What I would like is for the three of us to agree we should find Nadín. I've never heard of a faetale such as this either. Jeddeith?"

Without taking his eyes off the book, arms folded, Jeddeith shook his head.

"Then it should be brought to her attention. Nadín will know what to do next."

"And where is she?"

Knax shuffled through parchment and uncovered a map buried beneath an anatomical sketch elaborating on the transition to lycanthropy during the full Moon. Below, notes explained key differences which occur during the Curor Moon of Undern, red as freshly let blood.

Using books, Knax weighed the corner to prevent it from rolling shut. "This time of year? Let's see. Her troupe should be in D'hadian."

"Troupe?"

"When she left me in charge of guarding the Toll, she joined a theater troupe, thinking it an inconspicuous way to travel the world while having access to multitudes of people and places at a time so she could better sense for signs of Relona or the glyph."

An interesting choice. Weirdly, it made for good strategy. Unless Maijerda's bias for the theater was playing into her appreciation for Nadín's plan. "The sooner we find her, the better." Her leg started to bounce, proving troublesome to force still. Her nerves were trickling into unwanted focus. Questions were rolling in. How would Nadín react to seeing her? Did she know her mother? Were they once friends? Lovers? Why had Maijerda never been introduced to her?

Maijerda pursed her lips as Knax traced a route to D'hadian on the map. Not now. Later was for breaking down and crumbling. Here she needed to remain whole.

D'hadian was situated far beyond the edge of Scorn Wood and Lake Levondún. Probably a decent two weeks of travel. Maijerda's guess wasn't the most reliable, being more accustomed to sailing.

"D'hadian it is then." All these days without direction and now that she had one, Maijerda loathed the sense of disbelief pitted in her gut.

"While we're in D'hadian we should take advantage of exploring the Menagerie." Wanderlust illuminated Knax's eyes. "The largest library in all the continent? It would be an honor to witness its halls. Though it will have to be in secret. I fear my very existence may give people quite the fright." He sighed, looking to the stone carved ceiling. "Never thought I'd see the day I'd leave the Toll. If I may say so without sounding selfish, we should leave for D'hadian within the next day."

"We?" Jeddeith's judgmental terseness interrupted Knax's declaration.

However, Knax assured in earnest. "You don't think I'd send my muse alone in this endeavor, do you?"

Jeddeith, disturbingly contemplative, frowned. "No. You're a much better man than I."

"My dear friend. That is further from the truth than you will ever believe."

Eyes fluttering, jaw tense, Jeddeith seemed to have a retort, but he remained silent.

"Tomorrow, then." Maijerda clutched the book, ravenous for answers.

"Not until nightfall," Jeddeith said as an odd reminder to Knax, one brow raised.

Knax was cheerful in admitting his forgetfulness. "Ahead of myself as usual. During the day I am without the arcana that brings me life and am still as my stone kin atop the Toll."

"So the stories are true."

"Some. I've an enchanted astrolabe I can use to scry on your whereabouts. I'll keep pace with you as best I can at night. Do try to pretend you don't despise each other, would you?"

Maijerda's face warmed and she eyed Jeddeith, who shifted his gaze from her just in time to do a poor job of hiding it.

"Tomorrow evening then, so we may all leave together. Maijerda, we'll meet you at the northern wall of the Toll. Plan to leave quietly."

"Understood."

Jeddeith clasped his hands behind his back and rocked on his heels. "If that's decided, I'll see myself out." Without waiting he bowed his head with the slightest air of snark and left the room.

"Wonderful conversationalist, isn't he?" Maijerda stared down the hall after him.

"He has his moments." Knax cleared the table and handed her Da's book. "He'll come around. He needs time. I'm sure he'll spend the rest of the night tending to the Toll to clear his head among the books."

Maijerda didn't want to admit that was something she could understand, needing time among pages and ink.

Knax lead her to a hallway, lit with arcane Moonlight nested in glass lanterns. It was a dead end, with the exception of a stained-glass window shining as if sunlight frolicked behind it. Given the hour, that was impossible. It stretched from ceiling to floor and was wide as outstretched arms.

A gargoyle was depicted on a stone perch, not unlike those situated on the parapets. Crystalized water poured from the gargoyle's mouth, feeding the glass greenery framing him. At first it appeared to be flora, but upon closer inspection, she smiled at the symbolic trinkets taking place of traditional root and stem. Each represented some aspect of knowledge and study.

Knax positioned himself dead center of the window and closed his eyes while murmuring an incantation.

The language he so carefully enunciated was vaguely familiar. Augv'k? No, not quite as guttural as that. Xeskos? Or a dialect of? Possibly.

With a final whisper in the ear of the glass gargoyle, Knax blew on the window as if it was a fire in need of stoking. From the center on outwards the glass rippled as the surface of a pond. With each wave, components of the glasswork sprung to subtle life. Water poured from the gargoyle's maw and plants quivered in response to an invisible breeze.

"See that plum flower there?" He pointed to a high corner. "Take it, walk through the glass. Replace the flower to seal the portal. You'll find your way home from there."

Reaching for the bloom, she stopped. "Thank you, Knax, I don't know what else to say."

"Sometimes words are overwrought." He grinned.

Maijerda dazed both Knax and herself with an embrace, accepting companionship in this endeavor. "Thank you."

"Of course. Now go rest. Gather yourself. The Moon wanes."

Walking back down the hall, he left her to pluck the plum flower constructed from feathers with leaf-like veins. She pinched the delicate stem and pulled a glass replica free from the window between her fingers. Never had she seen such artistic arcana outside of theatrics. Mages go on about the tricks up their sleeves, but this was a darling beauty even Wytt would struggle to believe.

Taking a deep breath, she plunged inside the window. The glass licked through her sleeves with an icicle smoothness. Colors from the stained-glass gathered her in a bouquet of wonderment, tempting her to play among the flowers. Turning down their offer, she emerged into a stone corridor, the glass releasing her to a room subject to devouring darkness.

Quick so as to not disrupt the arcana of the portal, she reminded herself to replace the flower. It absorbed into the window as if she'd never disturbed it.

Clever of Knax to hide in plain sight. What a delight it would have been to tell Mama and Da of the secret gargoyle protecting the Toll. No matter how much he would've denied it, Da would have been thrilled.

Maijerda thought on little else as she left what turned out to be the thirteenth floor of the Toll, trekking to the Smithies. Conflicted, hurt, and confused. What if this wasn't the right decision? What if it led her nowhere? The spiraling nerves she'd been wishing would leave her be encroached on her step by step. Why was breathing painfully difficult? How were tears so quick to brim?

Before she could go home, she needed to speak with the one true companion she'd had since she was a babe toddling about Da's ship. She wouldn't find her with such a city-obscured view of the sky. Decisively, Maijerda cut through a close and hurried down a curving staircase, veering from Brine Bend.

A PRESSURE UNDER her ribs dug as if she were scrounging at the bottom of the barrel for options. She needed guidance. If she allowed herself the decency of self reflection, it appeared she was blindly following suggestions because it was the first semblance of progress. Perhaps there was some truth in that.

However, there was truth in admitting she wasn't bothered by clinging to this hope. This may very well be her one opportunity to uncover more details and meet someone who might've known Mother. It would be careless to not at least entertain the idea.

Cautiously, of course. Da had instilled the importance of caution in curious matters.

Maijerda altered course to an abandoned watch tower, seeking reprieve in this spot her parents often brought her to as a child when docking in Steslyres. Shouldering open the door to the rooftop, Maijerda removed her satchel, tossing it to the floor. The clock tower in Cove Side chimed. Near midnight already?

A sea-salt breeze and Undern rain soothed her skin. A storm was on the rise. She stretched and took in the rambunctious skyline of Steslyres. Though the sea was an enchantress in her own right, nothing compared to the wiles of the Moon and her guardians. The Tawny Moon's parchment brilliance poured over coast and hearth. It twinkled in bowed windows and in puddles gathered on the cobbled streets, gleaming to ease Maijerda's sorrows. Her guardians were equally as boastful as clouds curtsied for their queen.

Unable to withstand the calamity of death any longer, she sank below the surface of acceptance. Maijerda dropped to her knees, the stone gritty through her clothes. The Moon would understand her distress, she would offer comfort. Maijerda needed to stop questioning herself and let her emotions free. Stop chastising them for existing. She was allowed to feel.

Breathing for a count of three, Maijerda closed her eyes and soaked in the Moon's light.

"I'm grateful you're here. I can't help thinking you must think less of me by the day. Falling apart at the reminder of death. I don't know how much more I can bear. Mama and Da deserved peace. And that was taken from them."

Every heated tear was loathsome, but she was unable to prevent their coming.

"I keep telling myself none of this is true. That this isn't *real*, but the pain from the hole in my chest tells me differently. It doesn't just tell me, it screams it at me every night when I wish to be free of nightmares and every day I curse waking for one more sunrise they don't see."

Damn it all to the hells, she was a mess of an unstoppable rant as she trembled. "I know children are meant to see their parents buried, but not like this. Not like this."

She needed to keep on, to let the Moon in on her secret. The Moon wouldn't judge her as others might. "I don't think I can do this. And I don't want it. Any of it. I don't want to be consoled. To be told this will make me stronger. I don't want pity. Or a riddle to solve. I wanted to be wrong and to be told you can't predict fate, that accidents happen. I don't want any of this to be real. I want to mourn and rest before I learn what it means to pick myself back up again. Fates fucking forbid that ever be! It doesn't matter what I want, does it?"

She paused, as if the Moon would reply. In her mysteriously fickle way, she did. In that Maijerda's frustrations released their grip over her throat, easing her voice and assuring her it was all right to let herself unleash the most honest of her thoughts. She let herself heave with sobs, without care.

"No. Of course not. Because that would be reasonable. That's the real faetale isn't it? Peace, love, harmony, and everything in between. Their importance is dependent on them being stricken from you. A cruel joke. And I will never forgive the Gods for it." Maijerda's tears made a sloppy mess of her, nose dripping. She stretched over her knees, pressing her hands into the slippery stone until edges punctured her palms. Just to feel something other than useless. "Am I senseless to believe there is something worth vindicating?"

The Moon's light brightened as the rain slowed to mist. It was a sign of regretful agreement.

"If you're right, then I won't be daunted by theories. I'll seek the truth. Even if it's beyond the stars where madness waits. For their sake. Torlen dovnym, Mama. Da. I hear you. I only wish I understood." Tears warmed her lips. "Torlen lexnym."

Maijerda offered an A'lorynn hymn of gratitude and praise to the Moon. With each note, it was as if Theo and Relona knelt at either side of her, no longer inhibited by death and the spilling of their blood. The song washed over the dead of night, numbing her sobs.

She really should go. The others... oh shit. The others at the Smithies would be worried.

"Mai-maijerda?"

Speaking of. Maijerda winced and turned around to find Wytt ducking under the arch open to the rooftop. "Thought I might find you here. Is e-e-everything all right?" As soon as he asked, his expression was empathetic.

Maijerda wasn't proud of how well he recognized that she'd been crying, but they'd known each other too long for it to be different.

Without a second thought or digging for answers, he sat next to her and pulled her against his chest, resting his head atop hers. "I'm so sorry, my friend. I will always be sorry."

"It's not your fault."

Wytt huffed a, "Hm."

"You know it's not. You did what you could for her."

He adjusted his hold of her and sniffed. "Your Da would disagree in a heartbeat."

"Well, he was a stubborn bastard after she died. Her death was not your fault."

The notable lack of response, as it did every conversation they shared about Mama's death, meant Wytt still didn't believe her. She pushed up to look at him. "Promise me you still don't believe what he said."

"I can't promise you th-that. And we both know I'm a ter-terrible liar."

Unable to keep from chuckling she nudged him with her shoulder. "You really are."

Stillness encompassed them while they sat, Wytt patient as ever. The clock tower sounded again. Midnight. "Wytt, I need to tell you something."

"Anything."

"You're probably going to regret that." Maijerda turned to sit across from him and his confused but lighthearted countenance. "I haven't been up here all night. A whole mess of things happened since you left the Toll."

"Th-that can't be good." Wytt joked, laughing until he realized she was deadly serious.

She told him everything from start to finish. Every detail from the attack on the *Norn* through the conversation with Knax and Jeddeith. They trusted each other and that was a trust she'd never let break. Not once did he interrupt. Fates, he hardly blinked. Absorbing it all extremely... well?

"Are you listening? Wytt?" She leaned forward. "Wyttrikus, say something please."

"A gargoyle?"

Not the detail she'd expected him to be shocked by, but all right. "Yes."

He was processing it all in fragments, tasting bits of the truth. "A storm attacked the *Norn*? It wasn't bad luck at a-a-all. A-and your lullaby—"

"Is the key to unlocking a once-blank book? Also yes."

"Who wrote the faetale?"

"No idea."

"Tuvon's breath. This is in—"

Oh, she knew exactly what this was. "Insane?"

"I was going to ssssay incredible. Sure. We can go with insane."

"We should get going."

"P-probably," Wytt agreed as he stood, extending a hand to help her up. "Wouldn't want to worry Liam more than usssual. Besides. You didn't finish your tonic this mmmorning."

"True." When did she start getting so stiff? Must be getting old. She stretched and cracked her back.

"Plus it is your—" Abruptly with a pointed finger and snap of his jaw, Wytt stopped himself.

"What was that?"

"N-nothing."

"Remember what we said about you being a terrible liar?"

"Y-yes but, that's neither here n-nor there."

He was lucky she was so exhausted she was about to fall flat on her face and was in no mood to counter. "Fine, fine."

Once they reached the base of the tower, Maijerda stopped Wytt from leading the way back to the Smithies. "Thank you."

"For what?"

"Being there. For listening and not judging me."

"Always. You know you're family to me."

"And you know I feel the same." It was true for them both. He was practically her little brother, enamored by life and tiresomely cheerful when he wanted to be. "Still, I shouldn't be your burden."

"You're not a burden. Torlen dovnym?" He prompted her response with the question meaning, *to be heard.* A hard to believe sentiment these Moons, but if she were to make it through, she'd have to.

She'd taught the phrase to Wytt after Mother died, sharing their secret exchange with him. She'd never heard anyone use it before, not in all her travels. It brought her to her childhood, learning to listen and understand the realm as wholly as she could muster through her use of the tapestry.

That last nib of her tension faded reflecting on those experiences. "Torlen lexnym." *To be understood.*

It remained subsided as they walked to the Smithies, Wytt asking questions for her to clarify the strangest parts of her storybook adventure of an evening. Difficult to choose which aspect was the most ridiculous, really. Thank the Fates the chaos was over. She could let it all go for the rest of the evening, find a stiff drink, and be done with the unthinkable. At least until she left for D'hadian.

CHAPTER FOURTEEN

A TERRIBLE COINCIDENCE

A STRIKING GUST OF RAIN DISRUPTED THE pleasantries within the Smithies for a split second. Maijerda waved apologetically at the sparse crowd, gray-laced boots clicking as she and Wytt marched to the counter. The wind was quite rambunctious tonight with the storm right on top of them.

"Oof! And hello to you too, Rel." He jumped to lick her cheek and she scratched his ears.

She hadn't been gone *that* long. Then again, he was an eager pup. Not a second was wasted as Rel begged Wytt for his share of scratches.

"Shouldn't you be going home?"

"I-I think I'll stay here tonight. Liam won't mind." Wytt shrugged her off. "There's loads I-I c-could be studying."

"This late?"

Wytt backed away from her, already opening his bag and pulling out a book.

She saluted to him playfully. "Best of luck."

Torn between the two as they parted, Rel decided to follow her to the bar, scurrying to his water bowl. She went to sit at her preferred spot near the kitchen, but some sailor currently rolling a cigarette had beat her to it. Just as well.

Maijerda plopped a couple of stools from him, noting the curved sword and pistol resting on his belt. Firearms were spotty in their existence. Particularly in ælıkar. From what she knew, most fired one to five shots before they required reloading. A time-consuming process. Even for protection against pirates. It was why Da was never keen on the idea.

Liam set aside a wine bottle. "Evening treat you well enough?"

"Yes." She cracked her wrist. "It's lovely out. At least before the wind blew in, in a hurry. Undern has certainly made its arrival." Gathering her scarf more tightly, she sipped at her mug of amber ale Liam slid over. She eyed the sailor as he raised his drink in greeting.

"Well good, I'm glad you took a moment for yourself, hon. After all, it is your birthday."

Maijerda immediately perked up. Fates! That's what Wytt was on about on the rooftop. She'd nearly forgotten, having wanted to in the first place. It wasn't fair that she should be a year older when Mama and Da… well. Would never—

"I know you don't want to make a fuss of it. Happy thirtieth, hon. It's an important milestone."

"Not for ıdre."

"Still, you're half-ıdre."

"Fair enough."

Liam smiled as she sipped. "Er, well. Um. If you want to celebrate, let us know."

"I will." It wouldn't feel right, but she appreciated the offer.

Clearing his throat, Liam gestured with his thumb. "This man here just joined us after a lengthy trip at sea. You've been traveling… how long did you say?" He braced himself on the counter and raised his voice to the sailor with salt and pepper hair.

"Since the Meadow Moon." He tapped his cigarette ash into a clay dish and smoothed his dark coat, as if trying to impress her.

"He's new to the area. Maybe he could use local insight on where to go around here? Eh, Maijerda?"

Maijerda nearly inhaled her ale and grunted to cough.

Social niceties? Now? Oh Liam. Sweet, dear Liam. Even so, how could she disappoint him?

She swiveled to the stranger. "I'm not sure how much insight I can provide."

He seemed vaguely familiar, but with as many people as there were in Steslyres, all faces sparked murky recollection eventually. Her mind refused to disregard his sailor's coat and the acrid sting of his cigarette smoke.

The man offered his hand and Maijerda withheld a twitch of her upper lip as she shook firmly with him, promptly unimpressed by the way he carried himself.

Fates let this encounter be swift.

"My deepest condolences, Maijerda."

Liam half-smiled in apology and took her mug to top it off.

Not something she wanted to share. "Thanks."

Rel started to trot around the corner of the bar, then he stopped and sniffed the air, ears perked.

Maijerda whistled softly to him. "Come here, boy."

Rel backed away and sat in front of the kitchen door, staring and panting.

The man scratched at his chest. "Heart wrenching. Horrifying. I hope you don't mind, I was discussing the tragedy of your father's passing with your friend here. I must say, what a terrible coincidence." His melodramatic gestures and head shake were rife with sympathetic heartache, making her cringe.

She did mind, though Liam hadn't shared spitefully. He could do with easing up a bit with the melodramatics. Sure, this sailor was attractive. So was the woman two tables behind them. Maijerda romantically and sexually appreciated people of all sorts. All were deserving of fun and love. Regardless, Maijerda wasn't in her usual flirtatious mood. Grief having muffled it these weeks.

She fiddled with her mug, rubbing at spots of copper glaze. "Have you ever endured a sinking ship?"

"Actually yes. Gods know how many Moons ago. I managed to survive, same as you."

"What a terrible coincidence." Her smile was pained.

He gave a somber chuckle. "Indeed. I know they say a captain must go down with his ship, but in the right circumstances, I'd argue."

Maijerda's back teeth gnashed as the man simply wouldn't shut it. Was the circumstance ever "right?"

She took another repressive sip of ale.

"…an arrow to the neck? That's…"

She nearly spat out her drink. All chatter dulled. With a flip, her stomach fell into that dreaded pit, while her blood crystalized.

An arrow? How did he—? That detail was hers and hers alone. No one was the wiser about *how* Da died, except Wytt. And especially not Liam.

She shook her curls to subside the ringing in her ears, fighting for composure. Stay even keeled. Don't panic. How could he possibly have known? There was but one explanation. "Something I try fervently to forget." She slid a finger to the ring on her thumb, slowly spinning it to keep from falling into this apparent trap.

Seemingly casual, she reached for the satchel still slung across her chest.

A hungry glint devoured her movement. "I meant no disrespect." He seemed genuinely worried to have caused her pain.

Actually, genuinely was quite the stretch.

"We've just met. I would hate to startle you by my leaping several pages ahead of friendly introduction. Forgive my misstep. Best to go by the book…" He took a sip. "As they say."

"No offense taken." She downed what little ale swished in her mug. "I'd prefer not to discuss the matter. You understand."

"I do." He bowed his head and rose with her, offering his hand again. She went rigid. She would *not* play the doomed part of a cornered animal.

Suavely arrogant, he kissed her hand, left arm placed behind his back for show. The act was ridiculously elaborate and when he still grasped oddly possessive, peering into her eyes, she snatched her hand free. He was still taking her in.

She swiftly adjusted her hair. "Pleasure meeting you…" Her show of etiquette didn't sound convincing. Maijerda backed away with her inquiry. "I must have missed your name?"

"Denratis." He straightened his shoulders. "The pleasure was all mine, Maijerda…?" Her name lingered as it drifted from his tongue, which may as well have been forked.

From the far corner of the bar top, Liam nonchalantly checked in with a thumbs up. She meant to grin to insist all was well, but it came off as more of a rictus. "Fenneq. I appreciate your understanding, Denratis." She put her own theatrics to the test, covering her heart and blinking at fake tears and weariness. "The pain of it all has been so draining, and the hour is late. I should rest." She mustered a pitiful countenance, sulking for the stairs, holding her bag pinned closely and trying to subtly catch Wytt's attention. It took a second before he did a double take and questioned her with a look. She rolled her gaze to indicate Wytt should meet her outside.

"Rest well." Denratis clasped his hands. "Til our next meeting."

The moment her boot touched the second landing, Maijerda broke into a run.

Terrible coincidence indeed.

Shit.

MAIJERDA CURSED UNDER her breath and locked her bedroom door. So it was true. That damn storm had attacked the *Norn*. Worse yet, their pursuers were here.

Jarred, she grabbed her leather pack from under her bed and stowed belongings for whatever may lay ahead. What that was, Fates be damned for keeping her oblivious.

There was no waiting until tomorrow.

A knock rattled her door. She stopped mid shove and let go of her pack, unsheathed her brass inlaid dagger, and leaned into the door.

"It's me," Liam fessed, much to her relief, and stiffly she unlocked the door.

Eyeing her weapon, he stepped inside. "Hon, you haven't been acting like yourself, is everything all right?"

"I don't know the answer to that anymore. Please hear me when I say I must leave. Tonight."

"What happened to maybe needing 'time away', you said. What aren't you telling me?"

Her back was to him as she rolled clothes into her pack. "Please. Trust me. I know you have given me everything. And I hate to ask this of you, this might be the most crucial favor I ever ask."

"If you can't share your burden... I trust you." Liam shrugged, crossing his burly arms, still hardened from years spent blacksmithing.

She stuffed one final trinket in a side pocket and buckled the pack slinging it over her shoulder. "Thank you. I love you."

"And I you, hon." Liam wrapped worriedly around her.

"I miss him," she mumbled into his hearth perfumed shirt. "I don't want to let him down."

He sniffed and held her by the shoulders, hunkering to eye level. "I miss him too. You could never disappoint him. Don't get in your own head. You'll be your own worst enemy. Give yourself grace."

She dabbed at her nose. "I'll fix this and everything will be all right."

Liam kept a hold of her shoulders until Maijerda kissed his cheek. "I'll be home before you know it."

She glided out the door to the hallway to find Selene. If she looked back now, she may never leave. Thankfully, she found Selene fussing with dishes in the kitchen.

"Psst. Selene."

She jumped and muttered an endearing curse. "What are you doing? Is that... are you leaving?"

"I came to say goodbye. For now," she added.

Selene set a plate onto the counter, nearly missing the edge. "In the dead of night?"

"I know. I'm sorry, I can't say more." She was desperate for Selene's understanding.

"How long will you be gone?"

"I don't know."

Another difficult to endure embrace came.

"I understand," Selene whispered in her hair.

Maijerda struggled to let go of Selene's hand, her legs hollow and rotten. She cracked her left wrist. "I'll send word. Keep your distance from the sailor at the counter."

Selene set her expression and nodded. "Be careful."

With a faint creak of the door, Maijerda slipped out the back.

CHAPTER FIFTEEN

INDIFFERENCE IN DEATH

MAIJERDA HUGGED THE BRICK WALLS OF the Smithies, keeping hidden and keen. Her pulse thundered, rowdy as the brewing storm.

She rushed by the windows, with the hood of her cowl fending off the brutal rain. She needed to make absolute certain Denratis was still at the bar. Reaching a front paned window, she peered inside, cautiously.

Denratis was gone. And where was Wytt? He should be out here waiting.

Crouching on the other side of the window, she readjusted her pack, readying to say goodbye to Wytt. Something warm brushed against her leg, claws quickly pounding into her thigh.

"Agh!" She spun around. "Rel?"

The rain darkened the white fur on his chest. His eyes, round and ever so worried, yet excited. If only she could find excitement in all this and be none the wiser.

"Rel, I'm sorry. You have to stay."

He whined and pawed at her. Fates this was terrible. Between tears and the chill from rain, she wiped at her drippy nose and knelt to hug him. "I'm so sorry. Liam, Selene, Wytt, they need you. You have to protect them while I'm gone."

Rel stopped whimpering.

"Please. Go rest."

He ruffled her hair with his nose and she squeezed him close. "I'll come home. Promise."

Rel licked her cheek and pranced away in a flash of lightning, ducking around to the back of the tavern. Leaving the four of them behind was for the best. They would be safer this way.

Now where the fuck was Wytt? She spun round and checked the perimeter for him. He was nowhere to be found. "Damn it, Wytt. Honestly."

With a heavy thud, someone pushed through the Smithies' front doors. She pressed against the wall to hide, waiting to get a better view of who it was. Horns covered by a cowl, rosy fingers clad in fingerless gloves, and... a bag in tow?

"Wytt, what the bleeding piss are you doing?"

He startled and stumbled to turn to her. "Don't d-do that! I swear." Trotting down the steps as if this was perfectly normal, he pulled on his pack, checked if his satchel was closed. "E-everything's in order. Where are we-we going?"

Mouth agape, Maijerda shook her head. "No, you're not coming with me."

"You said to meet you outside!"

"Yes, to say goodbye, not to secretly whisk you away!" She motioned to his pack. "What, were you expecting this?"

"N-not exactly, but I had a feeling you'd leave the city soon and you sh-shouldn't go alone."

How could she argue? "We have no idea what we're in for."

"Do we ever have that handled?"

"Wytt, be serious."

"I-I am! Especially after I heard what he said. Denratis?"

At least she didn't have to relay what happened, Wytt was tracking her same theory. "What if he was on the ship that attacked ours?"

"I-I was thinking the sssame th-thing. He disappeared quicker than I did."

"Shit." Somehow that was worse than knowing he was in there. "We need the others." Options were slim.

Wytt's eyes, golden discs in the night, widened with wonder. "Does this mean I get to meet the gargoyle?"

Leave it to Wytt to find joy in this. "Oh for fuck's sake, come on." She made to sprint before changing her mind.

With each city block the storm crept closer, the lightning bolder and brighter. Typically the Toll didn't close its doors, no matter the hour. Allowing for apprentices, historians, clerics, casters, and insomniacs alike to indulge at their leisure. The occasional celebration or holiday kept the librarians from their duties.

Halfway there.

She used the bolts to aid in her watchfulness for anyone who might be following. No out of the ordinary shadows yet. With the Toll in view she nearly spun out of control. She hadn't thought this plan through, not knowing the incantation for passage into Knax's keep. But someone else did.

Bounding up the steps of the Toll, she skidded around the doorjamb. The elderly beshin woman with frayed curls and glasses perched on her nose glanced up, scolding her for the racket.

"Sorry. The storm, is uh, well— you know." She attempted to appear carefree.

Wytt didn't stop short in time and bumped into her. "Oo, s-s-sorry."

The beshin waited tersely for them to elaborate, wide ears flattening more so.

"Is Jeddeith still loitering about by chance?" Maijerda chuffed the question up to one of friendly inquiry. "He... uh. He promised he'd meet me tonight."

The librarian's drollness evolved from quizzically annoyed to entertained. "He's upstairs. Northern tower, third floor."

An enormous weight lifted from Maijerda's chest and she exhaled. "Thank you!"

"Not a problem dear. Good luck!" She giggled.

Maijerda bounded to the third floor, praying he would still be there. Ten more steps... five... three... onto the balcony, into the room she spun. Just to career right into Jeddeith.

He lost hold on the books in his arms. "Gods in shadow. Dare I ask why you're here? And who is this?" In mocking interest, he flattened his lips to disappear in his facial scruff.

Wytt peaked out from behind Maijerda, waving. "Hello, I'm Wyttrikus." He offered to shake Jeddeith's hand and was left awkwardly ignored.

Maijerda bent to help him gather books. "There's been a wrench in our plans. Maybe we should." She tipped her head away from the few onlookers gawking.

He dropped the books on a table and went to the stairwell, propping against the banister, seemingly bored. "What is it?"

"I met someone at the inn who knew *exactly* how my father died. You, Wytt, and Knax are the only ones I told about the assault. But *how* he died? I've only told Wytt. His name is Denratis. He must've been on the ship that attacked mine." She searched for reactions in Jeddeith's expression. "Jeddeith, we need to go. Now." It took every ounce of her patience to maintain a hushed tone. "If you're too bloody selfish to give a damn, at least get me through the portal so I can speak to someone who does!"

"All right."

"All right? Wha—?" She was cut off as he grabbed her wrist and pulled her up the stairs behind him, Wytt keeping pace.

He didn't let go, even through bridges and corridors. Running onto the thirteenth floor, Jeddeith recited the incantation. Maijerda dug her own coin out of a side pocket in her pack.

Through the window they went, Wytt gawking the entire time. Jeddeith swiveled to replace the plum flower to seal the entrance. Moonlit lanterns lined the corridor, swaying as they bolted through.

"Knax!" Their shouts came in turn.

"How did w-we do that? Will you teach me that spell?" Wytt asked Jeddeith, who was stone faced as ever.

"No."

"W-well never mind then." Wytt leaned to Maijerda and whispered, "Touchy, that one."

"Oh you have no idea," she said indifferently. By all means, let Jeddeith overhear.

Knax lumbered from the study, meeting them on the landing. "What is it? And who is this?" Juxtaposing Jeddeith, he smiled at Wytt.

"Name's Wyttrikus. I-uh-I…" His eagerness was supplanted by being struck with disbelief at Knax.

"Pleasure is mine."

"Save the introductions. Steslyres is no longer safe," Jeddeith warned. "Someone knows details of how her father died."

"You were right to fear the worst. They're pursuing the book. And Denratis knows I have it."

Knax's seriousness was quick to rise. "Let us leave for D'hadian. Is your friend joining?"

Wytt was nodding before Knax finished. "A mysterious faetale? Arcane song? A sentient storm? With Maijerda at the center of it all? I wouldn't miss it for the world."

There it was, his ability to see the silver lining. "Great. Off we go then." Maijerda sighed.

No one, not even Jeddeith quarreled as they readied and scurried out a hidden door at the base of Knax's keep. From building to shadow to alleyway they sprinted in a stealth-driven fury. Still, no sign of anyone following in their wake came about. Though with the downpour, an error in judgement would prove fatal.

Jeddeith motioned with a dagger, puncturing thin, for them to stop. They gathered underneath an enclosed archway bridging the council and magistrate's headquarters. His second blade was lithe as a shamshir. The hilt crafted with accents of bloodstone, unusual for weapons in ælıkar.

Maijerda's self-doubt latched onto her eagerly as a leech once they halted. "Did you see someone? Should we turn back?"

Jeddeith shook his head and peered around a stone column. A perfectly timed clap of thunder punctuated his movement. The city's edge was near. Around half a league stood between them and the gates. A vast, clear courtyard covered the expanse, leaving few options for stealth. The surrounding watchtowers mirrored the barren courtyard.

Jeddeith fixed his hood and adjusted his bow around his leather pack. "Stay close. After we pass through the gates, make for the Scorn Wood."

Knax, Wytt, and Maijerda readied themselves as he counted down wordlessly to them. *Three. Two. One.*

In unison they braved the storm. Bolts struck with their pulsing run, Jeddeith leading the way. One crooked branch of lightning framed the towers to their right. Another crackled behind them, exposing the entirety of the courtyard. Another sprawled ahead, stretching a claw in their direction. A fourth to their left.

A booming echo of crumbling and crashing stone. Heaps of debris from a tower sent Maijerda and Knax lunging for safety. Jeddeith was at her side instantly, lending a hand. Shoving through rubble, Knax heaved himself upright with Wytt's aid and pointed to the source of chaos.

A thin illusion of a zuihl with misty-gray, scaled skin, and the head of a reptile snarled to bare dagger-sharp teeth. Remnants of the arcana he cast on the watchtower were crackling around his clawed fingertips. He was dressed in heavy sailor's clothes befitting a pirate of the Solemn Sea.

Jeddeith freed his bow, the wood stained a rich cherry, and loosed an arrow. The arrow struck the reptilian weaver in the side. Without hesitation, he yanked it free by the tawny feathered end, ripping a patch of scales. Slowly, he bit his skin from the tip before tossing it and disappearing into smoke.

Knax reached for Maijerda to usher her back to the gates. Leaping over rubble, the four resumed their sprint. Circles of gray and blue smoke materialized. The smoke snapped at them until they stood with their backs to each other, surrounded.

As the smoke dissipated, it revealed multiple illusions of the mage, each a convincing facade indiscernible from truth. Maijerda ran her fingers to the dagger sheathed on her thigh.

Jeddeith pressed into her back. "Stand your ground."

Seven or so silhouettes emerged from the rain beneath the archway, no less savagely than a pack of wolves.

Maijerda's lip curled in disgust. "That's him. Denratis."

Jeddeith twisted around, arrow notched and at the ready.

"Don't be foolish." Denratis raised his voice to counter the cacophony of the persisting storm. "Although, that would simplify matters."

He stopped his advance and the rest of his crew stepped to replace each of the mage's illusions. The facades evaporated, leaving the zuihl's true form to stand at Denratis' right hand side.

A forked tongue whipped from his teeth at Maijerda and she gripped her blade in such a way that the hilt's etchings dug at her palm, urging her to react first and think later.

"Come, come now, let's not tear each other apart yet. We've just met." Denratis focused his irksome suaveness solely on Maijerda. "I'll speak plainly. Hand over the book and your companions will live, as I can't guarantee mercy for you. Cliche, you might say. However, this is your opportunity to adopt the role of a martyr. Save your companions. Be noble and surrender to me."

"I doubt you need us to spell out our answer." Knax's tenor, forever the gnashing of pebbles, traveled under the pitch of rain with resolve. He opened his wings defensively.

Maijerda spun her dagger. Never would she cave to this prick. "You'll have to do better."

"I was hoping to avoid conflict." His sigh was unsurprisingly drawn out and dramatic. "A shame too, I'm fond of Liam and what was her name again? Selene? Not mention that sweet dog of theirs."

Even if Maijerda possessed the will of the gods and Fates combined, there was no masking fear. It showed between layers of budding rage.

She separated herself from Wytt, who was holding onto her forearm, to close in on Denratis. The rain deepened the wine of her curls draping her shoulders and provided her overall demeanor with a fierceness she dreamt was worthy of song.

Gesturing with her dagger, she warned, "Harm them and I'll make certain you're incapable of pleading for mercy. No matter how much you beg."

Denratis didn't retreat, nor did he speak. He only smiled.

Maijerda didn't have the measure of control to not reach out and punch the smile clean off his face. She lunged, seizing the chance to punch his jaw. He sprung up to grab her wrist and prevent her blade from slashing him as an aftershock.

She caught a blow to the abdomen as Denratis gripped her hand high. All control over her breath evaporated and she collapsed to the slick cobblestones on her knees. Her cheek burned from a blooming wound and she bit through the ache.

Denratis' lip sported a brilliant split from her hit. They locked glances as he wiped blood from his chin and unsheathed his blade. A dao? So she thought it was called. The end, bluntly forged and bearing scalloped edges for tearing and hacking. Maijerda tossed a soaking wet rope of hair out of her face and lashed out again.

Flanking Denratis, Jeddeith drew an elegantly thin blade, curved to be a cross between a rapier and scimitar. Denratis parried her thrust and swerved to counter Jeddeith.

Steel sparked in the courtyard, their exchange of parries building on top of the echo. Jeddeith crouched low, swiping with his dagger when able and throwing Denratis off kilter with his sword. Both men were unyielding, using any means possible to prove being a step ahead.

Maijerda sliced wide in controlled panic and Denratis groaned and grabbed his side. Retaliating, he hollered and swung to cleave through her ribs. Jeddeith countered, ducked, and placed himself behind Denratis, kicking him in the back. Even though Denratis appeared to be ungracefully losing, the encircling crew stood at ease. Zealously, Maijerda deflected several blows from Denratis before landing another punch along his temple and spinning to knock him off balance.

A thrum in her arm threatened to throw her focus as Denratis cut deep into her with his dao. Her blood, a melancholy purple, dripped from his blade. As she reeled from the force of his attack, clutching the wound, an outcry from Jeddeith overpowered her own. He was flung arcanely back to the feet of the pirates who stood behind Knax. A handful of the crew grabbed and restrained both Jeddeith and Maijerda, extending her arms painfully stiff.

Wytt started to run for her but Knax held him back, noting the weavers targeting them with spells ready.

"I won't let you get away with this." Maijerda spit through blood.

"Aw, why so quiet? Speak so we can all hear!"

She cleared the gob of blood from her tongue, glaring. "Piss off to the abyss you crawled from."

Denratis clicked his tongue condescendingly sharp. "So crass. Didn't your mother raise you better?"

"Fuck you!" She jolted to break free, hungry to rip his throat out. The pirates yanked her back, gripping her tight as shackles.

Wytt, without warning, roared in anger Maijerda hadn't seen in years. He sprinted for Denratis, hands forming a sign to weave a spell. He was blasted back much like Jeddeith earlier, skidding on the cobbles.

Maijerda shouted for him, queasy at how still he was. "Wytt!"

He stirred, groaning and holding his head in his palm as Knax helped him stand.

Denratis, unfazed, ambled to her, sheathing his sword. The mocking pity on his face was insulting as he peeled away hairs plastered along her jaw. Fresh raindrops lined her lips, which Denratis wiped with his thumb, rolling over her bottom lip indulgently.

"You sadistic bastard." She returned the favor and spit in his eyes.

His face lit up in response, jerking her chin.

"And you are as fiery as all the hells combined. I'll give you that. To think, we were looking for a child... it's almost disappointing to have to kill you. I respect your lust for vengeance."

The obsidian-skinned ıdre with scarred arms restraining her chuckled. The one on her left shoved their nose in her hair. "You can smell it in her blood. Let's spill it!"

She tried yanking free, stopped by the woman jabbing her wound. Stunned, Maijerda groaned hoarsely.

Jeddeith managed to drag his captors forward. "Don't you dare harm her!"

Maijerda forced herself to look at Jeddeith. Honestly baffled by his distress and threatening tone. Did he actually care? Not about her, but about the book?

"Making promises runs too sentimental for my taste. And, I'm sorry. I don't think we've had the pleasure. Who are you?" He moved to address Jeddeith. "My guess is no one of real consequence." Just as he did Maijerda, Denratis tilted Jeddeith's chin up, studying his eyes. Denratis stepped back, curiously slow. "I'm willing to be proven wrong."

"Who I am won't make a damn difference once I'm through with you."

"Oh, you've struck me to the core." Denratis mocked, clutching his coat lapel. The crew crooned again as he stood between his two captives. "I came here with two goals. Capture you. And…"

The pirates holding Maijerda kicked her to kneel, while the crowd bellowed in unison. Denratis rummaged through her satchel.

"Don't you fucking touch it!" She tried to twist free, desperate to protect Da's book.

"Aaah, yes." He admired, lost in congratulatory thought as he held the book. "Lyrian will be pleased."

His whisper of devotion was almost too quiet to catch in the rainfall. Maijerda however, savored every single syllable.

"I'll treasure the instant hope leaves your eyes. Failure will suit your spite much better. Because you have, Maijerda, failed miserably. Just as your mother failed. And soon you are to follow in her same cursed footsteps. Dying to protect a cause that would inevitably betray you."

Maijerda fought with toppling and faulty puzzle pieces that didn't fit together. What cause? "My mother was ill. She died because her *mind* betrayed her." The statement flowed from her obediently, having been conditioned well those six years to convince herself of this.

"Is that so?"

Maijerda was at a loss. Every cleric, every mage, every physician had told them it was nothing more malicious than pestilence. Yet here stood this prick, confirming her gut instinct.

Murder.

"Was it you?" She spit the words vehemently, locking onto his blue leer. She wanted the gnarled truth of it while there was still a chance.

Denratis arched his eyebrows, cockily. "As much as it would please me to take full credit for such a feat, I cannot bring myself to lie to you. Even so near your soon to be found indifference in death. Take comfort in that." He demeaned her by posing a frown reeking with satisfaction.

Denratis took hold of the book's cover and pried it open.

A sickeningly garish and ghoulish hand sprung from the book and thrust into Denratis' chest with a force which defied all logic of the material world. Forced to his knees, he sputtered and clawed at his chest.

The tattered claw tethered Denratis to the cobbles. He embodied the most putrid of dread, gasping and cursing as he gripped the wrist to break it, but it wasn't so fragile.

Several screeches and grunts pulled Maijerda from the spectacle. Jeddeith had seized the moment and took his captors by surprise. He yanked one of their arms and pinned it to the ground. With impeccable pace and elegance, he recovered his knife and sunk it into the ersul's hand.

He removed it just as quickly, the blade a blur as he took his opponent's head and thrust his knee directly into her nose with crushing force. A garbled shriek of pain came from the woman. Her blackened blood splotching her dark green and brown skin.

The other to his left was readying a crude mace to clobber Jeddeith on the side of the head. His movements were obtuse, giving Jeddeith the upper hand. His coat whirled as he positioned his left arm to block the blow, driving his knife deep under the ersul's jaw and ripping into the roof his mouth. Stunned, they retained an arched stance mid-attack before crumbling when Jeddeith removed his blade.

Inspired, Maijerda kicked her foot and used the weight of her captors against them. She shoved and knelt to the ground, slicing at their heels with her second dagger. A third brute of a tiraen charged at her and she veered, cutting a massive gash diagonally from jaw to temple.

Knax and Wytt were taking on three others. Knax hurling gusts of blue arcana to knock them off balance while Wytt was throwing arrow thin spikes of ice conjured from the air. Rain froze around his outreached hands for each bolt. Since when had Wytt learned offensive arcana? Suppose now really wasn't the time to question it.

With them taken care of, Maijerda rushed Denratis to rescue the book. He wasn't going to get away. Not if she had anything to say about it.

Denratis coughed up a muck of purple and brown, staining his teeth and chin as he frothed. Seemingly content with his predicament, the ghoul's hand withered in Denratis' grip.

Unfortunately, he was free to move and he fumbled to draw his pistol, eyeing Maijerda. That wicked grin returned with a flick of his tongue to the corner of his lips. Denratis aimed his pistol at Wytt. Her heart clawed to her throat. Lightning flashed and Maijerda rushed Denratis, swift as she could manage. She'd be damned if she lost Wytt too.

His pistol sounded, cracking in the air and vibrating Maijerda's bones. She grappled Denratis to the ground, rendering the courtyard brawl a blur as they tousled. Ears ringing from the shot, she had no indication if Wytt was safe. All she had was hope, spread thin as it was.

Denratis flipped and straddled Maijerda, pinning her firmly. With his pistol out of reach, he pried her dagger from her hand and struck the cold edge against her throat. He forced his weight on her and snarled into her ear, the purple stains on his lips smeared deviously to his neck. An open wound oozed from the tear in his shirt. It could have been a trick of the surrounding lightning, she could've sworn light flickered from inside his chest.

"Enough parlor tricks!" The edge of her own blade nicked her jaw.

She wrestled and scratched his hands to find leverage and shove him off. He didn't budge. In synchrony with another garble of thunder, Jeddeith barreled into Denratis and tackled him off of her, narrowly dodging bolts of sizzling red.

The stone behind him crashed and added to the remains of the watchtowers. Maijerda had barely regained focus on the book and scrambled for it when the warlock plucked a bottle of gelatinous liquid from his belt and launched it.

She slapped her palm on the book and pulled it to her chest, rolling out of range with a split second to spare. Ice collided with the bottle, tossing it far from her and splatting gurgling acid on stone.

Panting, she glanced behind her. Wytt was stumbling to her, arms stretched and arcana fading from his fingers. Thank Fates, he was safe. She heaved and stood with the book in hand, daring the warlock to try again.

He growled at her, acknowledged Denratis in his overpowered state, and disappeared in a cloud of smoke.

Denratis roared at this turn of events mid scuffle with Jeddeith, earning him another punch. He coughed into an arc of maniacal laughter, while Jeddeith locked him upright on his knees.

Denratis fought Jeddeith's hold. "Go on, Maijerda. I know you're hungry for blood and vengeance. Neither is a temptress you'll deny."

She stood still as stone, wrath spilling into her thoughts, tainting her spirit. She needed to know who murdered Mother. This wasn't finished.

Maijerda recovered her dagger.

"W-wait. You d-don't—" She cut herself off from Wytt's reasoning.

"What is there to lose? End this!" Denratis' enabling, echoed in the courtyard, strained.

She grabbed Denratis' shoulder and positioned the blade at the base of his neck, heaving. "This is your one chance for redemption. Who killed her?"

Denratis choked and laughed.

The satisfaction that came with punching the bastard was worth everything she had left. "Tell me! Who murdered my mother?"

Wytt grabbed her shoulder, his touch more frigid than usual. She shoved him off. He had nearly died. Didn't Wytt understand what was at stake?

Blood splattered the ground and her boots as Denratis spat.

Dagger anchored to strike, she demanded of him. "Who was it?"

He tutted at her. "You'll learn. When she's ready."

The inside of her cheek split open as she fumed and clocked him again.

No. She wasn't going to wait. He *would* tell her. "Don't patronize me! Tell me who killed her."

He scraped his tongue to lick poison and bile from his teeth. "Do you want to know what I heard?"

Nostrils flaring, the pelting rain beating into her wounds, Maijerda's wrist was so tight it could snap. The tip of her dagger angled upward.

"I heard your mother tried to kill you. Her own daughter. She did attack you, didn't she? Clawing and shrieking at you. Like a demon." He gurgled and coughed. "I heard... she didn't even know your name when she died."

Guttural and rivaling a banshee, Maijerda screamed a harrowing war cry. A single, isolated sound pumped to enshroud her. It was her heartbeat. And nothing else.

Hand shaking, her blade lurched.

A release of breath warmed her rain-specked skin.

Confidence retreated from Denratis' eyes, replaced with the recognition of failure. His body caved and crumpled from her dagger. The bloodied dagger tumbled from her grip and she fell to her knees.

He was dead.

She didn't mean— She wouldn't— He *knew*. He knew about mother. He—

Maijerda braced on all fours, as her stomach melted and compelled her to retch. Her lungs quivered. Her legs faltered. Her tongue tingled with cracks.

She was lying on her stomach, face pressed into the grit of cold stone. Shuddering, the courtyard vanished except for Denratis' stiff glower. And a pool of blood.

A voice, so very far away, rang above her. She rolled onto her back.

"Maijerda. Maijerda!" Jeddeith was shaking her by the shoulders, Knax behind him. "We have to leave. Now."

She shoved him off and sat up, heaving. What was even left to vomit, she didn't know.

Wytt coaxed her to stand while Jeddeith retrieved her dagger.

"We're wasting time, there might be more of them. We need to leave."

Dragging her wrist along her chin, she nodded to Jeddeith. At least she thought she did. All about her body, numb.

Wytt swooped in front of her, blocking her view of Denratis. "Stay with me. K-k-keeping moving forward." He settled her arm around his shoulders, aiding her to limp away from the scene behind Jeddeith and Knax.

Was this what the Fates planned? Of all their spools of prismatic threads, they chose this? Without a second glance, they made their way for the Scorn Wood, leaving Steslyres behind to bathe in blood.

CHAPTER SIXTEEN

GODS IN SHADOW

THE SCORN WOOD WAS MONOTONOUS. A trap. To those careless with their surroundings. Jeddeith was not among those people. Even though he'd never traveled here before, he didn't let his uncertainty show. Ironically, what he was vastly uncertain about, was whether he actually hadn't been here. Maybe he had.

Moot either way.

Needles under his boots. Moist from constant rainfall. Rocks sinking underfoot. Fern beds, a decent mask for their footprints.

Good. One less thing to worry about. Even so, he should root himself to better be on guard.

Vythsaden rosq.

Flora. Choked tree roots. Humidity fed this place. Jeddeith maneuvered over a log camouflaged with a blanket of mushrooms and moss. Maijerda lumbered in the path he led, silently.

Stoic silence. A battered shield to wield.

Maijerda hadn't uttered a single word since the skirmish in the courtyard several hours ago. Wytt's consoling efforts were lost on her. Too stunned by her first kill. Granted, she hadn't specified this. Jeddeith didn't need her to.

He adjusted his cowl around his neck and shoulders as a breeze rushed them. Knax raised his hand to halt them, moving ahead and listening.

Jeddeith might be trained to root himself in his surroundings. To merge his consciousness with the tapestry when he had the right tools. But gods in shadow, Knax's hearing was uncannily better than his. Arcane influences and all. Wytt stumbled over a log, trying to stealthily linger in Knax's shadow. That one was going to be trouble. No doubt about it.

Maijerda sniffed behind him and Jeddeith turned to her. The color drained from her complexion and the cold wasn't to blame. Her leaf green stare was disconnected. He had plenty to say on the matter. Comforting though, it wouldn't be. So he stayed quiet.

A league or so ago, she refused to take her dagger back. Jeddeith had tucked it into his belt. She'd want it eventually. Or need it. Whichever came first.

Knax returned. "All's well. Truly was just the wind."

They trudged forward. Jeddeith and Maijerda in the lead. He held a curtain of moss at bay, waiting for her. "We need to press on. Can you handle that?"

Marching by him, she kept her eyes forward. "Yes."

At long last, a response. He cocked his head and resumed the lead. If something was sneaking about, she was far from being able to notice. Neither would Knax. It wasn't his fault per se; he wasn't the adventuring type. And Wytt? Well. Who could say what his experience was. Though from the weight of books in his pack, Jeddeith assumed it was academic in nature.

Once the Moon was high in the sky, he suggested they stop for the night at a pocket of trees, bound and twisted together.

The result was a bent half circle, mimicking a tent. Violet flowers dangled from branches layered with moss and fungi.

"Get some rest." He dropped his pack at the roots of a tree and searched for his tobacco pipe. "We'll need to quicken our pace tomorrow."

"All right."

Gods in shadow, she'd best not sulk for the entire journey.

"Will you sleep?"

She was sitting on a blanket, knees hugged into her chest. For the first time since the courtyard she looked at him in the eye. "You ask a lot of questions."

"Try. It's near sunrise." He left her to wallow with Wytt as he fussed over her, finding a place to take watch with Knax outside of the pocket. Knax didn't have much longer before he would be confined to stone for the day.

Several boulders and a fallen tree served as a much needed sanctuary. Much needed, indeed. He ran his hands through his hair and rubbed at his temples before preparing his tobacco pipe.

The leaves he chose were blended with honey and the full-bodied warmth of spiced nuts. He loosely tamped the first pinch into the bowl, layering the rest more tightly. Engraved along the sides, this pipe bore runes in Xeskos, which spoke of a travelers' well wish. He lit the leaves with a match and rested his forearms on his thighs. He needed to mull over the details of this day. Such an arduous day.

The runes glowed as embers of a fading fire with each puff. A branch above him bore purple and blue bell shaped flowers. He couldn't recall their actual name. Lunar blooms of some kind. There were several left on the stems to blossom this night with the Moon.

What chaos. Even compared to life prior to living in ælikar. Then again, life had been equally chaotic in drastically different ways. From what he'd pieced together in memory. Those limits were something he pushed, cautiously.

"You should be the one sleeping, friend." Knax often spoke as a character in a faetale. Offering wisdom, warnings, and poetic cadence.

"I know."

Stone on stone, Knax sat on the boulder next to him, stretching his wings. "What is it you want to ask?"

Jeddeith puffed on his pipe, stalling with shaping the smoke. Knax was far more insightful than a creature made of myth and stone should be. "That obvious?"

His chuckle was throaty, cavernous. "Since the day you appeared on my doorstep, stripped of memories."

That day seemed distant. But how distant? "Five years ago?"

"Six."

"Gods in shadow." Thinking on it, it seemed absurd. Knax had taken him in. Treated him as family. Helped him try to uncover what had been happening to him his entire life. Moments of time... gone.

He'd woken up in random places before then. Alcohol was never to blame. It just... happened. Maybe alcohol was to blame, once. He'd been eighteen years old then. When he was still living in...

He couldn't remember. Couldn't even picture the damn place. He filled his frustration with another puff of smoke.

"Have these leaves helped expand your memories?"

"Too soon to tell, I bought them yesterday." It was an experiment Knax had created and convinced him to trial. By variegating the flavors of tobacco he used, the hope was he would tap into the shrouded parts of his mind. University research published journals detailing strong links between memories associated with smells. Knax was optimistic in his approach.

Confident that different types would recover more memories. So far, it hadn't.

"I'll be curious to see if that's changed by the time we make camp next."

"Mm." Jeddeith grunted. "What do you make of her?"

"That is your question?"

"She did push into our lives. Her and that godsforsaken book."

With the tone of a lecturer at the Pearl in D'hadian, Knax said, "She can't be blamed for the weight it carries. Nadín will guide us."

"Assuming she wants to be found."

"Of course she does. She didn't abandon me. This was her intention."

That wasn't the point. The point was something he couldn't bring himself to confess. Even though he'd sworn to Knax he'd aid him in this endeavor to watch for signs of Nadín's knell, he'd never truly believed anything would come of it. He lowered his voice, speaking around the truth. "I wanted peace, Knax. Not to get run out of town."

"Ah, it isn't your past that brings you to these woods."

"No. But it is insultingly sardonic. Steslyres was just beginning to feel like home. Nearly let my guard down."

"Steslyres will always be your home. We'll return, when this is through."

One could hope. That was a feat Knax wielded with more skill than any blade Jeddeith was proficient with. "Gods willing. Maybe then I'll find peace."

Indicating their sleeping companions, his only true friend dared refute Jeddeith's pessimism. "You might find it here."

"Hah! You've read far too many stories, Knax."

"And you, too few."

Well if that were true, Jeddeith wouldn't recall, would he? Finished with his pipe, Jeddeith prepped his bedroll for sleep.

"You haven't mentioned anything of your dreams in several weeks. Have they spoken to you at all?"

Jeddeith gave a curt, "No. They're vacant and silent as always. I don't see that changing." Another reason Knax took to conducting arcane experiments for Jeddeith's cause. He hadn't endured a single dream since waking in Steslyres.

They say you don't remember all you dream each night. Jeddeith was intimate enough with his mind to know the difference between losing the details and never having them to begin with.

"A shame. I long to know what it is like to dream."

"I don't think we're missing much excitement. Dreaming inherently risks nightmares. Seems a waste of energy, fearing darkness you've crafted yourself."

"Or a great feat of self recognition."

"You are wiser than I am, dear friend."

Knax laughed. "Then heed me when I say you should rest."

"We'll wait for you in D'hadian. Fly well."

As if he needed the reminder, Knax bade him to promise. "Keep them safe."

"Til my dawn fades." Jeddeith pledged.

Nodding in contentment, Knax took watch a few paces outside their camp, finding shelter for when he'd turn to stone at dawn. This left Jeddeith to fight sleep. A not-so-foreign battle.

He stared blankly in the depths of a patch of silver leaves and golden poppies tucked under the fallen tree beside him. Nettled at the wormwood and poppies, he mumbled to himself as he lost his battle with sleep. "An omen, are you? We're beyond prophecies of caution." He rolled over. If he ignored them, he could readily deny their foreboding and guard himself from misfortune a little while longer.

CHAPTER SEVENTEEN

UNDYING LOYALTY

LYRIAN EXTINGUISHED THE LAST OF THE oil lamps, engulfing the *Oracle Rift* in pitch. and strode over singed corpses. She'd slain the cowards where they dared grovel before they could relay much. Save the warlock. Unfortunately she needed him, not necessarily unscathed.

The others? Worthless.

The crack of a whip sounded from below deck, followed by a yelp swallowed into a groan. Pity it did nothing to ease her agitation.

Crackles of lightning circled her wrists as she paced. Denratis would return to her any moment, as always. The sniveling fool.

Right on cue, oars dipping into the ocean drew her ire. The rope ladder clattered on the ship's hull.

"Tread carefully." She taunted with the waves.

Beaten and bloodied, Denratis knelt to one knee and clasped his fist across his chest to rest in partially dried vomit.

"What lies did they feed you?" He eyed his fallen crew.

In the budding Moonlight, his marked veins commemorated this new encounter with death. Not all marred his skin. Those that did? Memorable as the new tracks of deep claret and algae stretched on his weathered skin.

"They fed me nothing, as I do not hunger for foolery. They told me how you disgraced our cause. Of how she managed to best you. Kill you. And seize the book from you. Is there something I missed?"

Lyrian's veins pulsed and her necklace glowed as she imagined gouging his flesh. Weaving arcana while recovering from the tempest would be costly and regress her recovery, wounding her. Pain, she could handle. It would be worth the price to hear him scream.

"Without that book, my world will be lost forever. Do you understand what you've done?" She plunged her hand forward and retracted it to her chest, no longer saving it for imagination. Using her arcane focus simplified the spell, allowing her to react rapidly. No excess components. No verbal incantation. Just rage and will to push her limits.

Denratis lost his balance, barely catching himself with one hand while the other reached for his heart. She constricted her grip without an ounce of mercy. He was undeserving.

Denratis howled with dissonance. She supposed it was rife with resentment, but his suffering brought pleasure in the face of adversity. The toll came for her, splitting the skin on her hands, the pain of raking coals on her bones. The sensation of a nail being hammered into the base of her skull. Lyrian was running dry of tapestry threads. She needed to free her spools of arcana from that damn Veil.

With a flick of her quivering wrist she dismissed her hold, letting the eel resume its labor around Denratis' heart. Best to pace herself, seeing as she alone could grant him solace in death. Her word would be the last.

"Lyrian, there— "

She wasn't through. Lyrian thrust her hand in the dark and he was cursing again. Lightning skittered off his skin, charring his clothes.

Another flick and she stopped. Waves lapped with increased precision as Lyrian's impatience swelled.

Denratis' excuse dragged itself weakly from his chest. "I was attacked. By the book." He scratched at the sporadic branches reaching from his collar bone to the left side of his neck, dying off before reaching his unshaven face.

"What did you just whimper?" She arched her fingers for the third time, nostrils flaring.

"A hand materialized from the book and latched onto my heart. It poisoned me."

"Poisoned you?" She craned her neck in search of the lie. She'd assumed he'd been struck with a coated blade.

"Yes," he spat at her as he slicked his hair, matted with rain and grime.

"You're certain it was an enchantment?"

He slung his hand inside his partially unbuttoned shirt, applying pressure to his chest. "More than certain. After poisoning me, it vanished."

Relona and her tricks. She should have suspected. "An illusionary ghoul? How quaint. If our hand is forced to stay the blade I would very much like to hold to her throat, maybe Relona's daughter can be manipulated to our advantage."

"She's clever, determined. And wasn't alone. She was accompanied by a gargoyle, a varlodeth weaver, and a man with two different colored eyes. I believe he is the one you've been searching for. I could sense a connection to him, as if we shared common ground."

Lyrian's entire demeanor went rigid and she gripped the pouch of stones on her hip. Was it true? Her prophecy come alive? Othesk, grant this clarity.

"What were his eyes?" Lyrian didn't compose her eagerness for the answer.

"One amber. One gray."

She rushed forward and grabbed his coat, needing to know his name. She would be able to taste his name if he were the true prophecy. Othesk had sworn it. "Swear on what you claim as life." Spots fluttered around Denratis' shock and her stomach surged with forbidden warmth. "Tell me his name."

Denratis leaned from her as much as she'd allow. "Jeddeith."

The name left Denratis and latched to her arcane thread, ever present. It was him. She *finally* found him. The man to be reborn, lighting his own pyre. The man she would sacrifice in her stead and who would subsequently aid in the return of the nezdrade.

Victory was sweet, but it wasn't over. She laughed, riled with the taste of his name. An ashen tempest, a lightning strike upon a vast darkness void of breath. "Of all the people in this city she could have intertwined herself with on this idiotic quest."

Her untamed expression widened. "The answer was there, ever so patient. I should have known the tapestry would weave his threads closely with the book's. After all these years of searching, praying, and trifling with prophecy... I almost don't believe you."

Denratis was near pouting, his eyes flitting between the deck and her. "Believe me or don't. It's your arcana at stake." He massaged one of many majestic sores. Oh how she wanted to rip it open and curse him for his quick tongue. She eyed her split skin, her blue blood trickling, spine needling hollow. She couldn't bear the surge. Which escalated her resentment.

"We mustn't stop hunting them. In the meantime, Jeddeith might prove obliviously useful."

"You'd best hope he's a fool," Denratis replied.

"Say he is. She seems no better by the sounds of it."

"If you crave him, why not murder and resurrect him as you did me? Would you not acquire the same control?"

Was that jealousy seeping through? How adorable.

"That won't suffice. He needs to claim his tapestry threads so I may take them from him. If he dies before then, I'll be forced to do as Volkari bids and I'll—" No, she couldn't confront it. Not aloud. Denratis mustn't see her weak, mustn't see how she feared what this ritual would take from her. Trade the grief, her misery, and transform it to wrath. "I've already been betrayed, used by Relona and Nadín. I will not stand to forfeit my arcana to tear it down. Not when I can use his."

"If you insist." Denratis pressed his hand on a bloodied slit at the base of his neck, reflecting on the fight no doubt. "Maijerda assumed I killed her mother."

"What did you tell her?" Lyrian's lips parted, curling her hand in preparation to strike.

"The truth. That I couldn't take credit. I would never…" He accented the denial with a confident gesture of his free hand. "… ever take ownership of your credibility, Lyrian."

She couldn't resist exposing a crooked smirk. Winning control of Relona's mind had been a satisfying feat. It was a shame she wouldn't have the same opportunity to kill Nadín herself. She hadn't survived the creation of the Veil. In the thirty years since Lyrian's return to Penʌmbrə, she'd seen no sign of her. Even to this day, the comfort of Relona's demise deflected Volkari's ungratefulness and jealousy.

"Will you poison her mind as you did Relona?"

Lyrian sunk and bit her cheeks, loathing being questioned. "Without a bond there's nothing for me to grasp within the tapestry. As for Jeddeith…" Othesk, that name was true glory on her tongue. Jeddeith. "We share a unique connection. I will mold his dreams, infiltrate his mind, and guide him through the dark. Water has shared arcane influences over dreams since the dawning of the tapestry. Not even the Veil can ruin that."

Lyrian placed her hand over his everlasting wound, short of remorseful. That quality was lost to her centuries ago after Relona sacrificed her to fuel the ritual and create the Veil. Self-serving bitch. May Relona burn in hell. Swallowing the soreness in her throat, Lyrian blinked away a rapid blur in her sight. She mustn't grow distracted.

"I admire your undying loyalty, Denratis." The hint of irony was delectable. "As much as I'd relish hunting Maijerda myself, I must heed Volkari's demand and return to Gazdeq." Lyrian gritted firmness into her voice, her silks oddly unnerving against her skin. "This is where we part ways. Follow their trail. Send me word and I will return to you as soon as I'm able." She handed him a glass bottle with three strips of parchment and a vial of her blood tied to it. "I'll receive your message, but you must write it in my blood. Place the parchment in the bottle and fill it with ocean water to send it to me."

"Your will be done." Denratis bowed again, accepting the enchanted bottle.

Lyrian addressed his appearance with judgmental cadence. "As pleased as I am to see the eel has fulfilled its duties… I have business to tend to in conjuring nightmares. Besides, you're an absolute disaster. Clean yourself up before coming to bed. We'll part at dawn."

She stormed to her chambers, not wanting to squander nightfall. Even without the book, she was one step closer to Jeddeith. His name was a golden thread to add to her tapestry. Greater still would be the day they were at last united as one. The first step, as it should, would begin with the sea.

The next would require her to entrance herself to lucid dream. Here she would set the stage for his nightmares and the show would unfold. Lyrian gathered her scrying basin in her chambers, full of ocean's blood, and rested it in her lap. After signing casting sigils, she began chanting to the sway of the ship. Letting herself drift with the water in search of him, mentally floating to the place of dreams. Incantation rolling on her tongue. One name echoing in her mind.

Jeddeith.

CHAPTER EIGHTEEN

PEACE IS A LIE

ROOT YOURSELF AMONG THE TREES. GROUND your mind. Vythsaden rosq.

Jeddeith dug the heels of his palms into his eyes to alleviate the sting. Disoriented. Senses overloaded. A glimpse of surroundings was all he needed. So then, what could he rely on other than sight?

There was the rush of a river. Faint but near.

He blinked at the Moonlight. Bright and stormy blue. How? The Tempest Moon had since past, Tawny Moon should be out tonight. Something wasn't coming together. He needed more. More notes for mental calibration.

Which forest was this? Not the Scorn Wood. Hells if he knew. Even if he'd been here before, he wouldn't remember it. Jeddeith approached the river. But stopped at the scent.

Salt? That shouldn't be. Was he near the sea? And which sea? Dolzdoem? Wrent? Query? Pausing, he knelt to inspect the earth for clues. The Solemn Sea.

The stones. Polished white. Specks of green. Little to no moss. No leaves. No needles. It was clean. Too clean.

He peered at the sparse tree tops. The trees were nearly dead.

If this was the Tempest Moon, the forest should be healthy, not bare like in Eventide Moons. Jeddeith rubbed the soil in his fingers and tasted it. Everything about it was dry and grainy, not the softened earth he expected. Jeddeith rose and continued to walk to the river.

Search for more clues. Fish, flowers, herbs. If he was near the sea, vesper moss might be around. Or findrel. An herb used to prevent wounds from rotting.

Good. He remembered these aspects effortlessly.

Odd. Who was this? Jeddeith stopped and reached for his belt. There was a woman standing waist deep in the river.

Damn. No weapons.

Her robed form shimmered and he swallowed his unfounded anticipation.

Where had she been? He jogged to meet her. He'd left her here? Waiting. How could he've broken his oath? After he promised he'd never forget, after they agreed—

It'd been too long since he'd seen her. It'd been ages since—

Jeddeith reached her side. Gripped her arm in apology. He was sorry for all his wrongs. She didn't move. Or acknowledge him at all. Something grazed the back of his leg and he looked down. Plush golden poppies and wormwood entwined with river pebbles at his feet.

"Peaceful, isn't it? Pushing forward no matter the obstacle. Inspiring really."

He snapped his gaze to her.

That voice. He didn't recognize it. Ethereal. Feminine. Which begged the question, why was he treating her as an old friend?

She hummed and her fluid form blurred, shrouded in mist. She had no true features, hints of an expression beneath watery shapes and mist. As if a nymph. Nymphs. Creatures born around natural sites of arcana that began to have their own thoughts and imaginations. Similar to Oagbain.

"Rivers can't choose their path. Unless dammed. There isn't anything inspiring about being stripped of autonomy."

"Is that what peace means to you?"

"Yes." Jeddeith nudged a rock into the poppies. "Peace is a lie."

"What if I told you this river could bestow upon you the very solace you crave. Would it be a lie then?"

It would always be a lie. He had never earned the luxury of peace or forgiveness. Therefore it could never be true.

Jeddeith looked to answer her but was met with unexpected cruelty. Watery fingers carved through his muscle. The nymph stretched her grip around his throat. His grunts gurgled and roiled as he fought to speak his mind. He needed to free himself to survive.

She transformed from nymph to sea witch, hellbent on his demise. "Dive, my sweet."

Simultaneously Jeddeith was lifted off the ground and submerged in water. He thrashed to pry her fingers free. Before he could unsheath his bloodstone-hilted dagger, he realized it wasn't here to begin with. Her grip was deadly. Constricting every second.

She vanished without warning. He'd lost track of how much air he'd lost. The shock and force from her assault was replaced. An overpowering cold. Icy tendrils sunk through his clothes and scratched his body as he was dragged into fathoms deep. His lungs cried out. Tricking him into gasping for air, flooding his lungs. A trick he shouldn't have fallen for. Unless he'd subconsciously wanted to.

The water encasing him was dense; an arm's length was too far to see clearly. The intense cold spoke to him. Burbling nonsense. Jeddeith's efforts to question it stole more of his breath.

The sea witch urged, her words reverberating. "It offers you peace, do not ignore it."

Peace was another ploy. One he wouldn't be cowed by. Not ever again.

Jeddeith kicked to swim and break the seaweed winding around his limbs to his torso.

"Save yourself! You've buried your past, don't light your future's pyre."

The weeds tightened and strangled around his neck. If this was peace, then he was right. It was a lie and he'd lived his life plenty.

Regarding fate with placidity, he refused to entertain her.

The water absorbed him. Body and soul.

JEDDEITH TORE ASIDE his coat as if it were seaweed. He threw himself over the edge of the fallen log he'd fallen asleep against. If he didn't vomit now, he'd never clear his lungs.

"Jeddeith, what's happened?" Knax came to him, wings unfurled and tense.

Jeddeith stumbled from the log and kneeled on a bed of ferns, forcing himself to retch the salt water scalding his insides. Skin aching, he shook.

Sand and salt water poured from his mouth. As if his body had swelled with the ocean in his sleep. Every muscle was strained, his ears ringing for as long as it took to rid himself. Sand grated in his teeth. This was miserable. All his days spent wandering between realms never left a visceral impression. What brought this on?

That wasn't the question he should be asking. He actually, for the first time in… "Knax." Attentive, his friend was kneeling next to him, waiting for explanations. "A nightmare."

Knax leaned back, prying into Jeddeith's eyes with emotions he wasn't expecting. After all the work they'd done, Knax likely thought he'd be thrilled at the revelation of dreams. Concern subdued Knax's enthusiasm. "Nightmare? Since the day we met, you've struck me as a man who'd not use that word lightly."

Groaning, Jeddeith unbuttoned his sleeves and stared at patterns of runes and glyphs tattooed in white ink on his arms. Wouldn't cause any harm to show them here with the others asleep.

He'd chosen each so diligently back when… well. He wasn't sure. He did know that he had intentionally crafted them to support his arcane practices.

Vythsaden rosq, you old bastard. No changes in the tattoos. They were dull, no arcana lighting them.

Rain tapped through the forest canopy and he rolled to sit, cradling his head. "Think nothing of it."

Rain. And thunder. A loyal companion.

"Nothing of it? Jeddeith, this is what we've been hoping for."

"Not exactly. We were hoping for reminders of my past. Not nightmares."

"True, but perhaps we've opened a door. With all that's happened today, maybe your mind is stirring with possibility."

It wasn't so implausible in the scheme of things. This entire evening was brought on by Maijerda's tale. A storm accosting her ship. Her father dead. Unanswered was identifying the nymph. A sea nymph. He could practically smell the storm on her. It wasn't Maijerda. Definitely not tiresome enough to be her. The pull he felt to the nymph was unmistakably familiar. Odd. The sense of companionship, as if he'd known her and possibly even loved her. Which he didn't.

"I'd very much like to close it. If death is where it leads."

Knax nodded his head. "I'm listening. Should you wish to share."

Jeddeith fiddled with the metal band on his finger. Before he changed his mind, he confided in Knax each detail. He was unpracticed with the skill. Relaying dreams. Never would he have realized this beforehand. As he finished, dawn started to pry into the forest.

"I'm sorry to hear this. What I regret more is having no idea what it might mean. If it were one nightmare among many, I'd say there's nothing to fear. But your first in six years…"

"At least six years." Jeddeith clarified. "Given the nature of my past, this could be the start of something dangerous."

"Cause for concern, I'm afraid."

Jeddeith pushed himself to stand. No use in sleeping any longer. "As ominous as it may be, it can wait another day. There's nothing I can do now. Save reflect on it."

"I've one question."

Jeddeith took a shallow, strained breath, posture taut with his back to Knax.

"Did you want to believe her?"

"Did I want to believe she could lead me to peace?"

There wasn't a need for Knax to confirm.

Maybe there wasn't a need for Jeddeith to lie to his closest companion. But he did. "No."

For a beat, he waited, before turning to Knax, expectant of his tacit gaze. By the time he turned, a patch of sun warmed his skin and Knax was peacefully wrought from solid stone. Asleep until dusk.

Just as well. Best return to camp and cover his tattoos first. Before the others caught glimpses and grew suspicious. It wasn't enough to be run out of every city he tried to lay roots in or to risk being turned in to authorities, captured and experimented on by Zefk's arbiter? Now he had to fear the return of nightmares. What else would cross his path? Test his limits.

Gods in shadow.

He could try tricking his mind. Declare the nightmare wasn't real. The nymph, also imaginary. Along with the longing he felt for her. All equally as false as the faint ache in his throat.

CHAPTER NINETEEN

A Choice

S UN SLIPPED THROUGH THE PINES AS if the Scorn Wood
didn't want to rudely wake visitors. As Maijerda's skin grew
warm to the touch, she stirred upright, clearing the sleep
in her eyes.

Fates, nightmares were exhausting. How was it past morning?

Jeddeith was next to her, picking at a bundle of brambleberries
in his lap. He mixed them with nuts and bits of chocolate and
offered her a handful with a plate of bacon, beans, sweet potatoes,
and tomatoes. Surely this was Wytt's doing.

His expression made it seem like an obligation instead
of politeness.

She took it, curtly. "Why didn't you wake me? We shouldn't
have wasted the morning."

"Oh, I tried. Several times. You nearly clawed my eyes out
an hour ago, half asleep. To be fair, Wytt did warn me."

Swallowing a berry, she grimaced. "Ah." Right. The
nightmares. "Where is he?"

"Foraging for herbs. Says he didn't pack as much as he
should have. He should be back soon. Sleep well?"

"No." How could she? The night had been a bloodied blur. She raked through her curls to untangle stray bits of leaves and moss.

"Mmm." He tossed a berry, catching it in his mouth. "He was your first kill."

Freezing before dropping a leaf, she looked at him. The nerve to state fact as if he knew her, as if he understood. Her dagger was still on his belt, the one that had kill—

She hadn't been able to touch it the entire night, unable to fathom holding it again. Apparently they were going to discuss this? How could he think she'd want to? Heartless bastard.

"Yes. And I shouldn't have. I didn't— I didn't mean to."

"Not from what I saw."

"How can you say that?" Finding it difficult to breathe, her lips parted.

"You had every right. Wytt was in danger. He was going to take you captive. You'd've been killed eventually."

She pressed her palms into her knees. "I'm aware. Wytt shouldn't even be here, it's too dangerous. He shouldn't be risking his life for me. I would do anything to protect him. "

"Then why punish yourself?"

Didn't he see she crossed a line? "Denratis was already poisoned! I should've left him. I shouldn't have reacted."

"So, if you left him to die from poison, your hands would be clean?"

"Well— yes— I mean… I don't know!"

"I think you do."

"He was goading me about my mother. Hearing him talk about what she was like before she died. I don't understand how he knew." Damned tears were starting to blur the forest. "I wasn't thinking. Next I knew he was dead. I didn't mean to." The claim was vacant and distant.

"As I said. You had every right."

She did not want to discuss this. Say anything! Anything to shut him up. "If you say so. Doesn't make it easier."

His tone deepened, gaze drifting from her to the forest floor. "No, I don't believe it would."

"Then why do you keep insisting?" Her hands shook from his prodding. The coffee pot brewing on the campfire mirrored her roiling frustration.

"Because it's the truth." Jeddeith folded his empty cloth and tucked it into his pack. His honeyed eye was strikingly golden when he turned back to her. "And if you hadn't, I would've. Because that's what *needed* to be done."

"You speak like it's nothing. I did take that life. Why are you indifferent to death?" His disregard was provoking her blood to boil.

"I understand how to act when faced with choice. Especially when confronted with disagreement."

A choice, it always comes down to a choice, doesn't it?

Drying her eyes, she ran a hand in the dirt, to help ground her. "And what of peace?"

"Peace is a lie."

"You don't believe that," she accused.

He didn't reply, donning his coat with finality.

A stubborn frizzy curl loosened from her bun as she stood and approached him. "You wouldn't be helping us if you did."

He flipped his coat collar and snapped at her, his hand raised. "Stop. Where do you get off on scrutinizing me? You have no idea who I am. What I've seen. What I've done. This is not up for discussion."

She pushed her sleeves up, the green nearly blending with the forest, and splayed a hand on her chest sardonically. So it was within his right to decide what was worth discussing? Absolutely not. "Is that a request? Or a demand?"

Scoffing, he shook his head and shoved belongings into his leather pack.

Apparently his conversational skills hadn't improved overnight. His gall was something else. Licking her lips, she pulled a loose curl from her lashes. "You've been dismissive, uncooperative, and selfish since we met."

Jeddeith straightened his back, standing his full several inches taller than her. Agitation poignantly brought him so near her face, pipe tobacco overpowered the thyme rich, forest dampness as she stood her ground.

"Selfish?" Jeddeith flattened his dark waves with dew. "Are you confident in abusing that word, Maijerda?"

"So says the pot."

Jeddeith leaned even closer to her. "You claim to care for your friends' well-being. Selfish was you manipulating Knax's intellect and naive desires to drag him into your nonsensical scheme! If he had listened—"

"Nonsensical scheme?" She tensed and it read in shrillness. "After barely escaping Denratis how, how in all that is good in this world, could you possibly believe I'm conjuring this in my imagination? That's absurd! And for what? Attention? Glory? Pity?

"Jeddeith, I haven't the faintest idea of what's happening. I have nothing left except this fates-ruined faetale! Knax could've seen his spell through and taken my memories. Left me behind to find Nadín. He gave me a choice and a chance to pursue something, to avenge my family. He chose to trust me. Why won't you?"

"You didn't need Knax's permission for revenge. You granted it yourself by killing Denratis." He sheathed and belted his sword. "I will not coddle your guilt." Jeddeith concluded his diatribe with one last look of distrust.

"If that's how you feel…" Branches and ferns snapped on the ground with her quick to spill wrath. "…then why the fuck…" She forced him against a tree, pressing her forearm into his collar bone. "…did you bother coming with us?" Her eyes furiously darted between his of molten gold and somber graying sky.

Without holding back in the slightest, he shoved her off his chest and spun her into the same tree before she could retaliate.

"As I said. Selfish."

Maijerda revved up for another attack, but he cut her off. "I never involved myself in this for you. My loyalty is to Knax."

She lowered her voice, leaning into his arm pressed against her chest. "You've made your point. You've sworn no oath to me. For someone who insisted I had a choice during our little confrontation, it's strange you're acting like you don't have one now."

Releasing his hold on her, he scoffed. "There's always a choice. Whether we like it or not. What I choose is to not sacrifice my loyalty."

He tugged at his cowl and pushed his tongue into his cheek, exhaling. He spun his hand to reveal her dagger.

She did her damnedest to not show she was shaking, gripping the hilt and making no other move to belt it.

"You might need it." His gaze shifted about her, from hair to wrist.

The hilt was unnervingly warm. She couldn't bear to look at it.

Choking her grip, she thrust it into her bag as words grew foggy. She was losing her focus and handle on them, wanting to throw them all as daggers. But they weren't sharp enough. If she weren't so pissed at him, she'd be able to find the right words and give him a real piece of her mind.

Challenging each other with stern stares, Jeddeith backed away.

Loyalty, was it? He could lie to her all he wanted. She didn't believe it for a second, not if her life depended on it.

Wytt's footsteps sounded behind Knax's dormant form. It would take getting used to traveling with a gargoyle. No number of play scripts or stories could've prepared her for the reality of it. "Wh-what'd I miss? S-sorry if I kept you waiting."

Against every bit of desire to lash out at Jeddeith again, she smiled to assure Wytt he hadn't done anything of the sort. "No, you're fine. We should get going though. Tell me, what'd you find? Actually before you do. When did you start practicing arcana outside of healing?" She brushed by Jeddeith as she ignored him, intentionally ramming her shoulder into his.

"Oh! Xander thought I should expand my horizons. I can't do much. And I-I rely on what's a-around mmme as a jumping off point, but I'm working on it. Guess it's good he suggested I practice. Who knew we'd be off on a quest?"

Wytt had quite the bundle of herbs, rattling on their healing properties and setting aside those he gathered for Maijerda to make into tea to help keep her mind sharp and physical energy level. Her frustrations softened for the time being, grateful for a true friend at her side.

Deeper into the Scorn Wood they traveled. Not a grunt or murmur sounded from Jeddeith for hours bereft of eye contact. Fuck it for all she cared. So long as she accepted he was a selfish bastard, there would be no leeway for disappointment.

THE REALITY OF DEMONS

A thought occurred to us.

On demons.

We have not had the pleasure
of discussing their true nature.

Not that we'll divulge
all their secrets.

Where's the joy in that?

Unfading as their presence is.

It is crucial you consider

their potential.

Extinction can never
truly become them.

For even a fleeting

thought,

is existence enough.

Demons are rife

with lust for fear and trickery.

They want you to question

if you've dared cross paths.

The demons know.

They've taken diabolical delight…

…in toying with emotions.

Leaving you wondering…

…while they revel

in the knowledge of *knowing*.

It would be foolish to not entertain

the reality of demons.

Civilizations have shriveled

dry for assuming less.

Rest assured…

...they are alive and unwell.

Watching.

Waiting.

And wanting.

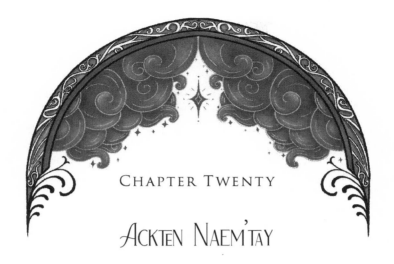

CHAPTER TWENTY

ACKTEN NAEM'TAY

UNWANTED ADRENALINE COMPELLED THE TRIO FOR three more days with individual retrospection. Darkness swayed them to consider slowing for camp. By then the Scorn Wood merged into a lullaby of inky green with trees clustered as looming silhouettes.

Lullaby? Maijerda hadn't entertained it since leaving Steslyres. She owed it overdue attention and gratitude. She started humming a random measure of her lullaby and stretched her hand, abruptly aware of how white her knuckles were from clenching her satchel. Scratching at the back of her neck, she gingerly removed the book from her bag and unwrapped her scarf from around it. Hopefully it wasn't too cold. Or too lonely in there. She wasn't trying to ignore it, but her relationship with the faetale was, let's say, tenuous. After so few nights with it, was there another way to be?

Without her needing to ask, Wytt wove a white and purple flame for her to use as a light to read. He smiled at her nod of thanks and went to pester Jeddeith about some plant he saw a few paces back. Maijerda meanwhile, let them traipse ahead and read silently while continuing to hum. She didn't want to feel this way, wanting to trust the faetale and for it to trust her in return. Could it trust? Ridiculous, surely. It didn't have trust issues. Or feelings? Thoughts?

It did have defenses though, that much it proved in the brawl with Denratis. The back of her throat diffused tension, her chin quivered. She cleared her throat and masked it as singing off key.

Branches crunched in moss under their boots and a breeze stirred to howl. An owl hooted, a living timepiece. Nature alone pierced the night's rigid silence when they came upon a glade abruptly devoid of trees, marked with jagged stones at least three times Jeddeith's height. Structured like grave markers, they weren't of the earth, not in the strictest sense.

The page she was reading, where the three voices spoke to the Spark, rippled. The texture of the paper, the watercolor inks, tearing to reveal a glow the color of stardust.

What the fuck? This was... new. Maijerda ceased her song and fumbled to not drop the damn thing. In her scuffle to catch it, she tripped over the forest floor and entered the glade. A mirror image of the tear, gleaming with a pulse of determination was centered among the stones. She paused, holding out her hand. "Hold on, something isn't right. Are you seeing this?"

"Seeing what?" Jeddeith asked, hardly looking her way.

"The curtain. A..." Was it too bold to say? "A rift. Between the stones." This was, oddly familiar. Mother's stories. Something about a demon rising from graves, keen for a hunt.

"I-I don't see anything." Wytt scanned the glade, shrugging.

Memories of Mother's faetales were devoured by wolves unleashing a wave of bellowing.

Wytt flinched, the howls fading. "That, I heard."

Maijerda, baffled, urged them to look more closely and gestured to the tear floating between the stones. "You honestly don't see that?"

"A rift in what Maijerda? There's nothing."

"Don't chastise me. It looks like this." She shoved the faetale into his hands to show him the altered illustration.

Jeddeith's judgement ebbed while he examined the page, lips pursed. "How? You shouldn't be able to see that," he said, genuinely perplexed it seemed.

She was just as confused, if for different reasons. "And why not?"

"Not to int-interrupt. W-We all see that, rrright?" Walking backward, Wytt stopped at Maijerda's side.

Body tensed in concentration, Jeddeith unsheathed his blade, promptly trained on two massive dire wolves emerging from the rift, flanking a horseman. Anchored upon a bulky steed macabre as the pit of a freshly dug grave, its mane was coarse and swooped low along one side. The horse's eyes were an impenetrable milky white, swirling like mist. With a heavy and muddied hoof the horse pawed at the ground, tossing its head and dispersing fog.

The horseman tightened his claws, bruise-hued and scaly, on the reins. His jacket was torn, suggesting it had fought battles against both steel and age. Globs of ichor pooled around his collar and crept down the horseman's chest until it was lost in the fabric of his clothes.

There was no mistaking it. Mother had warned her of these creatures. She'd woven tales of reanimated corpses of fallen knights who betrayed an oath. Turned into demons, wielding weapons crafted from the spines of victims.

Demons.

She'd never seen one before, despite worried whispers of increased sights. What other explanation was there for this dullahan?

The horse reared on its hind legs and released a piercing bray as the dullahan's form was wreathed in a billowing cloak of smoke and flame.

"Keep him busy!" Maijerda ran for the nearest tree, unsheathing her dagger.

Jeddeith cut in front of Wytt, the horseman drawing nearer. "I plan to."

She paid no mind to their clashing steel, not wanting to lose sight of her plan. Carving a rune into the trunk, bark chipped away and her intentions were unorganized. Riffling through her unease with arcana, missing the practice of weaving thread, needing to trust in the abilities she'd learned with Mother.

She risked a glance, and her stomach plummeted. With deadly intent, the dullahan was within a single sword's swing of Jeddeith, taking a great swipe at his neck with a relic of a broadsword. Jeddeith dodged, the horseman's flames scorching his back.

"Come on, Maijerda. Focus." What was it about time ticking by that made things that much more difficult? Think on the binding. The incantation. There was a binding in A'lorynn. Which naturally there was, when A'lorynn is meant for spell weaving. What was it? Fates! Forgetfulness wasn't becoming. Fumbling through iterations, all of which were wrong, Maijerda landed on one, hoping for the best. Was it gold dullahans were afraid of? Well, not fear but weakness? Was it metal or gold floss she needed? Neither? Fuck it.

Removing one of her gold rings to amplify the spell, she pressed her palm into the rune. "Ackten naem'tay."

Traces of white and orange sparked in the rune, the incantation taking hold. Gearing up for another attack, the horseman ripped a whip of rusted vertebrae from his belt and sent it cracking for him.

Thunder lashed around them, though no lightning came before it and the ground rolled. Jeddeith lost his balance and deep wounds split the earth. The beasts crowed and the horseman charged for Jeddeith with hardly a flinch, snapping his whip again. Wytt swooped in and sent an icy gust to wrap around the whip and yanked it from the dullahan's hand.

Seizing the chance for escape, Jeddeith leapt out of the way and sprinted to Maijerda with Wytt. Sweat trickled down her temple and panic collided her words into one another. "I'm making no promises this will work."

"No gold floss?"

What? How did he—? "Nope, fresh out."

The horseman reached the perimeter of the gravestones, brandishing his broadsword. Maijerda remained immovable, her expression taunting. This *had* to work.

He thrust the sword at Maijerda's neck. Wytt shouted for her to move, but she shouldn't if this was to work. She'd have to risk herself to satisfy the spell. Translucent gold shuttered into view and severed his strike, sparks flying. Maijerda's smirk widened into a victorious smile. The tip of the blade was seared, leaving behind a white hot, broken end.

The dire wolves were no match for animalistic pride. They charged sidelong into the golden barrier, visible as a cage that melted through muscle and exposing bone. Smoking fur saturated the air.

Jeddeith raised his bow and in one movement shot an arrow straight for an exposed eye. Convulsing, the wolf whimpered, eyes rolling back, and collapsed in a lump. Without warning the second wolf stood still, grunts and howls trailing into the night before he too crumpled into a pile of exposed flesh and bone.

The horseman flexed his claws around the hilt. In one fell swoop he drove the sword into the ground as if marking an impromptu grave. The dullahan paced the length of the thread, cracking his whip of bone nearest Maijerda each passing.

"He should be imprisoned until sunrise." Jeddeith said, stowing his bow and retrieving his blade. "Ackten naem'tay, yes? It should hold."

Maijerda eyed him, unsure if she should be thrown by him knowing the exact phrase, so readily. The world was full of tapestry weavers, it shouldn't bother her. Yet something about it did. "We should go." She turned her shoulder on Jeddeith and the horseman.

Panting with hands on his thighs, Wytt called for them to stop. "Demons? H-here?"

He had a point. A demon appearing out of nowhere. Or could it have been intentional? She placed her hand on her bag and whispered to the book lowly, to keep them from noticing. As odd as it may be, the book had shown her the rift before it appeared in the forest. Had it shown her? Or caused it? She certainly didn't conjure it. "You can't go about summoning demons." Unless it hadn't. "Unless you didn't. Then I'm sorry to accuse you. Fates, don't do that again."

Maijerda's mind continued theorizing to comfort herself that it wasn't the book, but Jeddeith interrupted. He always had something to say. "Seen demons before, have you?" There was a struggle for levity in his question. His wide eyes spoke to his interest and his concern from before.

She halted her trudging, the horseman behind them. "I've read of them plenty. Haven't you read of dullahans in the Toll?"

"That doesn't explain your intuition. What are you hiding?"

"*Nothing.*" She rolled her wrist and gave Wytt a look to signal he should keep his knowledge close to his chest.

"Bullshit." Frustrated, Jeddeith gestured at her to accentuate his point.

"If you insist. Are we going to argue or carry on?"

"People don't read about demons for fun. If they did, they'd end up—"

Maijerda started pacing, shaking her head and grumbling. "They do if their mother insists. Let's say her bedtime stories were... different."

Jeddeith folded his arms. "How do they trap victims?" He asked this of her sternly, as if a professor testing a student.

"Dullahans manipulate their victim's perception of their territory to keep them pinned until they rise from the grave at nightfall."

"How do they choose prey?"

"Myth says they're attracted to people who are missing parts of their soul, but that is colorful speculation."

"Th-that and those who wander. It's vague, really. Not entirely sure what that means. I've ssseen it in a few books."

Jeddeith sighed, shoulders relaxing, blinking at last.

"Is there a reason? For the school lesson?"

"I'm sorry. I needed—" Jeddeith slicked his hair back with sweat. "I needed to hear *why* you knew as much as you did."

How did he mean? "Fair enough. I suppose."

"What of the rift? Untrained weavers can't see—" flustered he hesitated. "Traditionally weavers need spellcraft to allow themselves to see..." trailing off again he widened his stance and placed his hands on his belt. "Physically recognizing changes in the environment or atmosphere requires spellwork. Yet I didn't see you cast a damn word. Nor gesture. How did you see the rift?"

Protecting the book from his shooting stare with her hand of all things wasn't going to do much. The truth might though. She shouldn't hide what she saw, especially without knowing if it was real. "It matched what I showed you in the faetale exactly. I'm not sure how I saw it. Or how it was there." There was no room to question her verity.

Barely nodding, Jeddeith ran his tongue along his teeth and lips. "I believe you. You don't need to know the answer. I assume the dullahan emerged from the rift you saw. A tear in reality. But I wasn't sure how the rift manifested."

Maijerda scoffed, seeing Wytt crack a smirk. "No idea. Sounds eerily familiar to the whispers I've heard of Rivyn Borne claiming demons were returning through disruptions in reality."

"Accounts began, twenty-five?" Wytt peered up to the fir tree tops. "N-no, thirty years ago? But as she s-said. Whispers."

"Whispers or not, what we witnessed was no trick. Keep an eye on that book of yours. We all saw what it unleashed on Denratis."

"He's—it's not causing problems, Jeddeith. It's a book. My father's book." She reminded curtly.

Graceless silence, their usual order of things today. Jeddeith walked closer to her, frowning. "I'm sorry. I shouldn't have spoken to you the way I did the other day."

She planted squarely to stare at him, her nostrils flared. "In hindsight I find it hilarious how comparatively charming you were when we met in the Toll. But then you attacked me. Poisoned me. And Fates, what else am I forgetting? Oh yes. You kidnapped me. You entangled yourself in this mess, yet blame me. And I do not deserve to be treated that way."

"No, you don't."

Arms crossed, she twisted the ball of her boot into the forest mulch. "I'm sorry I took my guilt out on you and pretended to know your motivations."

"Likewise. I'm also sorry for our... convoluted introduction. Hopefully we can find a rhythm in trusting each other. Promise I'm not always an ass, if that's difficult to believe."

"Extremely difficult. But I agree. Trust would be a comforting change." What to make of apologies eluded Maijerda, much as her childhood misunderstanding of how Da navigated the seas by starlight. Something tangible, yet elusive. The best she could offer was tilting her chin in thanks and turning to lead the way through the forest.

"I have one favor to ask of you."

"That's all I'll give at this rate." She turned to Jeddeith, hands on her belt.

"I need you to answer one question."

"That'll be?"

"Why are you pursuing this?"

Had she missed something that was unclear? She and Wytt exchanged a similarly colored look. "How do you mean? Knax set us on this path."

"He did. Is that the only reason you're here? Because he gave you direction in grief? Or is there something more?"

Of course there was more, there always was. Maijerda relaxed her arms at her side and closed her eyes before meeting his. "My parents lost their lives for this book. I need to risk deciphering what's inside to understand why. And to understand why this Nadín saw my mother equally as foreboding as wormwood and poppies. I want answers. And if I can help in fulfilling your oath by doing so, then I want to see that through."

"My oath?"

"To protect Pɛnʌmbrə and mind your knell. It would be cowardly to hide or force ignorance. I want peace. That's why."

Drawing a thin breath, Jeddeith grinned numbly, facial scruff scrunching. "Peace. Peace is difficult to come by. I can respect that."

She nodded solemnly. "Thank you."

When he reached her to continue on the path, she didn't berate him, letting him lead in silence, abandoning the horsemen entirely. Seeing she was still frazzled and battling sequencing her thoughts, Wytt offered her a bag of mixed nuts, seeds, fruit, and chocolate. He'd taken to noticing that foods such as meats, nuts, seeds, eggs, and cheese helped the most. Damn him, it worked, as his snacks often did to keep herself balanced and less jittery.

If maps and Wytt's bookish memory were to be trusted as often as she did, they were close to the next town. The next bout of travel lacked threats of pending doom, comprised of efforts to tend the invisible wounds between them which desperately warranted healing.

CHAPTER TWENTY-ONE

ETHERIC THISTLE

UPON ARRIVING TO THE ISLAND OF Gazdeq after weeks of sailing the seas, the messenger greeted Lyrian at the door with a hunched flourish, bow, and deceitful drool. His wide zuihl eyes, with narrow pupils built for prowling, met her own. Wringing his hands, he brought his broken nose to the floor near Lyrian's feet.

His mocking was glaringly obvious. He wasn't worth the energy to reprimand.

"Our Mistress waits, wayward tide." His ash green skin, akin to ersul bloods, was wrinkled and spotted with warts. He grinned at her, lips lilted with zuihl fangs.

"I'm aware."

Patches of black hair flopped on the servant's lump of a skull as he hopped, clapping his hands. "Mistress says to meet her below."

Without thanking him, Lyrian bustled through double doors guarded by two barbaric creatures clothed in knotted leather armor spiked maces at the ready. Volkari was waiting, as Lyrian had already informed her of Denratis' mistakes and she wasn't pleased. When she told Volkari of Relona's daughter, she was seething. And when she learned of her name, Maijerda, she laughed, calling Relona egotistical. They agreed on few things. That notion happened to be *one*.

Lyrian traveled deeper into the fortress, the halls moaning in submission. At the entrance to the catacombs, Volkari waited. A reaper atop a tomb, refusing to make eye contact in her usual display of power. Her hair caught in the green haze of arcane orbs floating above iron pedestals framing a gate in the crook of an alcove. The train of her tailored black gown split at her abdomen and trailed behind her. The leather pants she wore underneath the train suggested she would have no issues acting on the call of battle.

Before the Veil, Volkari upheld that image. However, it was doubtful this rang true now. It hadn't since she'd returned to this realm when Lyrian took Relona's last breath. What differed today?

"Is this absolutely necessary?" Lyrian interrupted her brooding, impatient with Volkari's silent manipulation of the situation.

"What is causing you such distress? She relies on you to live. And we need her insights. Do you resent your responsibility?"

"No." Lyrian sighed, jaw clenched to bite her tongue. It wasn't responsibility she loathed, being a prideful woman. It was being manipulated and drained for her arcana as a spell component that made her eyes and throat sting. "I'm honored to serve."

Volkari raised her chin, tugging at her pointed cuffs. "Better."

Removing a ring from her hand, she placed it in her palm. A black metal scarab beetle fluttered alive with her curt incantation. It flew to the winged keyhole in the gate, clicking flush into place. Both the ring and the keyhole vibrated with a magenta flare. The hinges ached as Volkari extended her hand and the beetle assumed the inconspicuous pretense of jewelry.

They continued down a stone stairwell, diving beneath the stronghold to a labyrinth of catacombs. Given the fortress was situated on a coastal cliff, Lyrian's veins sparked at being nearer her lifeblood. The taste was crisp.

Stairs led into the rotund entrance of the tombs, their steps echoing among skulls and misshapen skeletons to emphasize the enormity of it all. No torches were lit and so the iron cages for these lost amenities were filled with spiders' webs. Primal symbols carved into the stonework were a language even Lyrian didn't understand. But their macabre sentiment of roaming among the "unseen" was clear.

Passing several archways, they reached the seer's prison. Lyrian moved to barge inside first, interrupted by Volkari pushing by with calm. Lyrian tilted her head and cracked her neck, subduing the arcana bustling to appear at her fingers.

The seer's hardened skin cracked as she woke from a trance at their arrival. She greeted them with a hiss and jagged sneer. Her etheric thistle roots tensed and her floral imprisoned limbs quaked. "What brings you to my resting place? Ah. The skeptic too? This is a treat. I am parched."

The seer's eyes were wide and hateful. Solid red blinked and shifted constantly searching for visions of the corporeal world she would never again witness. There was a price to pay when overindulging in etheric thistle. You lost sight of the material world, bound to the etheric instead. The mind is a fragile thing.

Her brackish red vines slithered among metal chains and collar, thirsting for someone to latch onto. Not *anyone* of course; Lyrian alone could satiate her thirst.

Volkari rested her hands at her waist, muted in voice, commanding in figure. Lyrian gnashed her back teeth and retrieved her knife from a slender sheath at her waist. All Volkari wanted from her was blood, but she wouldn't dream of spilling it all. Because then she'd lose her precious store of ocean's blood.

Relona hadn't just used Lyrian to feed the Veil's creation, she'd ensured Lyrian was primed as an arcane resource to be consumed for as long as she lived. As if it wasn't enough to be betrayed once, eternal ruin was her future if she didn't bend Jeddeith's will.

Rigid, Lyrian tried relieving the ache in her jaw by grinding her teeth harder and before she spoke out of turn, slashed her arm in a spot not still healing from letting wounds. Chains sounded as the seer lurched for blood. Lyrian smiled, tilting her head to savor the seer squirming and drooling for her. There was some benefit to this, controlling the seer's satiation before quenching her thirst. The seer would never be allowed simple enlightenment from natural water. Lyrian let her murky blue blood trickle down her arm.

The seer's slithering vines slowed. "I need water."

"No." Lyrian corrected. "You don't."

Offended and bitter, the seer hissed with the moist friction of winding vines, beholden to impart the sooth connecting her to Lyrian. "Blood of the sea, a curse strung in life's thrum, for you to bleed and mine to need."

Pleased with the seer's admission of life-dependent subservience, Lyrian presented her arm. The red tint to her runic scars, marred by her blood, gave an involuntary, faint glow. "I hear accepting your flaws is quite the undertaking. I'm proud of you."

Thirst dominated the seer's temptation to argue, hatred fleeting. Lyrian braced for the vines lashing around her wrist, resisting slightly to cause the seer primal panic. She stepped to her, vines still lashed, and let the seer drink from her arm. Torn between pleasure at the seer relying on her and hatred that Relona was the reason her blood sustained these qualities to begin with. If Othesk had granted it to her, she'd be honored to bear the arcane properties of the ocean's blood as her own. Relona's selfishness being the cause fueled her loathing.

Blood smeared around the seer's cracked lips, darkening and mixing with the etheric thistle tinge to her skin. Vampiric in her hunger, the seer would have drank her fill. Lyrian didn't allow it. "You've had plenty," she said as she opposed the seer's hold. "You should have no trouble weaving your fates' threads. You'll live a little longer yet."

Volkari dismissed the seer's attempts to refute. "Much has changed this Moon. We've lost the book. Learned Relona's blood still lives. Without that book we are doomed to fail in understanding how Relona crafted her ritual. We risk its existence acting as a seal for the Veil. I need to know what will become of our hunt."

"The gods refuse gifting that knowledge to any soul. Not even what remains of mine."

The seer was likely bereft of a soul completely. She had died centuries prior, there wasn't much left to restore when Volkari resurrected her. Volkari lacked the necromantic strength to sustain her, yet another reason she relied on Lyrian's arcana.

"Will we destroy the Veil?" Volkari was steadfast and fierce, stepping within reach of her prisoner.

The seer brushed her fingertips on Volkari's face, winding vines onto the side of her temple. Fanged teeth split the cracks in her face. She was still. "Four siblings stray from hearth and hock. The fifth lost in grains of sand, abounds in curious lark. Bleak as ink, darkness bends in will to follow."

A riddle? Proof this creature didn't know the answer.

"Bends? In success or failure?"

She guided a vine to Volkari's chin and tilted it upward. "The Fates do not thread that needle before my eyes."

"Riddles are tiresome. And evasive." Lyrian glided next to Volkari, her tone tightening with the tingling in her arms and ears. Let this creature prove her worth. "Will that poor excuse of a daughter die?"

"Her kin?" Vines creaked and entwined with Volkari's hair, caressing her temple. "Maijerda?" Her red eyes brightened as a pool of blood with divine recognition as she searched the ether.

"She is no family of mine," Volkari rebuked.

Such riposte. Was it worth the lie? Admitting to familial ties didn't obligate compassion, nor mercy. It was a tool.

"Your denial, an exquisite facade. You should know better. You cannot conceal truth from my sight." Her black and red spotted tongue slithered to lick her lips.

"The filthy wretch is of no consequence to me. I will use her to my benefit. Should she die in the process, I'll be sure to prepare myself to cope with loss." She forced her wrists to her hips, sarcasm twisting her sneer.

The seer choked on a chuckle garbled by decay and sighed. "I'm tempted to believe you." Her free hand rested on Volkari's collar bone. "Tell me, in your ravaged heart, what would you sacrifice for the sake of knowledge?"

"I've sacrificed plenty. Being banished from my home for nine hundred years. Being trapped here!" Her despondence rang in the cavern, her whole body trembling. "When will I leave this wretched island behind?"

"You've burdened me with this question before." The seer turned her head, the collar shifting and cinching at her neck. "Time. Ruthless time. So rude to elude us."

"I'm no stranger to its demands. After all, I spent weeks resurrecting you. The one bond we share is understanding the passing of time. How long then, until the book is ours?"

The seer's eyes became horrifically wild and bulged.

"Blood is a promise, made to keep. Shadows of doubt burrow within and without."

Was she speaking of blood arcana now? Would they need Maijerda's blood for their ritual? The way she referenced shadows placated Volkari's concerns. Lyrian was through with this nonsense. "You couldn't possibly know the truth of it."

"No? Does it bother you that the lost one refused to abide by you in your dream? Do you fear being discarded again?"

Lyrian's fingertips sparked, her breathing quickened, and her veins brightened. "Jeddeith is no longer lost to me. Did you miss that in your augury? He needs time to learn who he is."

"So I understand. I did tell you of his existence after all."

"Othesk promised him to me long before you relayed prophecy."

"A prophecy you've latched onto for years." Her pause was dramatic and unwarranted. "As does another, weeping from negligence. Bound in parchment, it breaks. Bearing burdens no living thing is expected to understand. With a soul to claim it shall tremble under your reign." With each verse her voice sacrificed robustness for the far-removed mundaneness of breathing.

Negligence? It was under Maijerda's care, so to speak. Did this imply uncertainty on her end?

"You've done well," Volkari congratulated.

The vines retracted and the seer's face fell in dreaded anticipation of what was forthcoming. What was left of her knee suddenly burst in a tangle of thistle vines, weaving like a blunt needle. She cried an ear-piercing shriek the could have awoken the encompassing dead.

Volkari grimaced sullenly with the most forced of sympathies. "Your sacrifice is much appreciated. You will be rewarded."

"Beware the day you will be forced to pay for your vices, as I paid for mine." Spewing venom, her advice fell on deaf ears.

Volkari adjusted her scarab ring. "You were dead for centuries. I suggest you don't stray outside the boundaries of your destiny. You most of all, should know better than to test those limits."

An indignant hiss came from the mutant ensnared in her prison as they left her without further conversation. Orbs of bottled, corrosive green fog and lightning crackled awake at their arrival to Volkari's study. The mausoleum housed several marble tables displaying various instruments, components, and contraptions.

Volkari tended to a bronze cauldron with clawed feet, filled to the brim with the potion she relied on to stay alive and attached to this realm. An unfortunate residual effect of being banished in the first place. Lyrian did not envy her. As strenuous as it was, being bound as one with the ocean for nine hundred years was preferable.

Mixing morels for regeneration, Volkari awoke the ladle with a nonchalant wave of her fingers. Pine oil flourished in the air as it began stirring. First to the east for twenty three counts and then ninety times to the west. Intermittently, the ladle scraped the natural grain of quiet.

Lyrian rested on the divan as she worked, mindlessly fidgeting with her talisman, plotting her course of action to craft Jeddeith's next nightmare.

Rudely interrupting, Volkari expressed the obvious. "We must fulfill this prophecy, no matter the cost. Maijerda cannot be allowed to repair the Veil."

"Naturally, Mistress. The book's soul will meet a much-deserved end."

"Can you imagine Relona's rage if she were alive? Seeing her Veil destroyed?"

"Everyday."

"We've waited long enough. I will not be denied this victory."

Always thinking of herself. Was it acceptable then for Lyrian to be denied?

Lyrian cleared her throat of an encroaching heat. "Blasphemy, Mistress. The sky has never denied the rain to fall. Trees shed their leaves to bear anew. Hawks prey on the weak. An empress protects her throne from all manner of disloyalty. Your reign will come again."

"It will. I will be unmatched." Volkari went to a table covered in an eclectic collection of papers.

Fingers spread wide, she crossed her wrists in front of her eyes and pulled her hands swiftly apart. Obediently the papers rose from the table. She rearranged them in the air, guiding each with broad gestures.

Several scrolls unfurled into maps Lyrian either acquired or had drawn from memory with Volkari. The ones she painstakingly drew were of places and landmarks conceivably irrelevant or invisible to the people and creatures of Pɛnʌmbrə. A world swallowed in myth.

There were others scribbled with attempts at recalling the syllabic runes of ɔvrʌ laræk, the spell casting language Volkari once used to weave her spells. The Veil had cut her off completely, since being banished, from connecting with and using her once-beloved tongue. This complicated her spell weaving, forcing her hand to rely on components more than she had before. Lyrian, however, remained connected with her own water bound dialect of ɔvrʌ laræk.

What remained of this tongue had become known as the "language of the land" in this version of the world. One new language used to weave was called A'lorynn. A horrific insult. Lyrian learned this studying the new world, ensuring she grasped what changed. This was before she had the arcane strength to kill Relona and weaken the Veil, allowing Volkari passage to return. It was then Lyrian learned of this book and the secrets it selfishly kept.

"What has become of your prophecy, Lyrian?"

Lyrian debated keeping this to herself, understanding the importance of delegating information, especially when his existence guaranteed her survival. "Jeddeith. The man who protected Maijerda when Denratis confronted her. He is who I've been searching for. His name called to me through the tapestry."

"You mean to use his threads to keep from sacrificing your own when we complete the ritual to destroy the Veil?"

"Yes." She'd answered this question a thousand times before. Volkari didn't trust using dormant tapestry potential, nor did she believe Lyrian would be able to succeed in swaying Jeddeith to join their cause. "I was able to craft one dream, there will be more to come. I will trick him into using his arcana, unleashing his elemental potential. His true allegiances evade the both of us, so I will try each of the four. I'm certain it's a matter of time before we have our answer."

"You best hope he'll cave under your will."

"Yes, Mistress."

Volkari gestured to bring a parchment closer and plucked it from the air as though it were secured with a pin. Lyrian went to her and clawed her fingers into her still folded forearms. "I don't understand why you hold onto her. Her treason was unforgivable."

Sketched in thin grays was a portrait of a woman, her hair cascading around chiseled features with hints of ruthlessness seconds from being summoned if needed. The oval of her irises, cunning and keen.

"That is precisely why. So I may never forget Relona had no qualms belittling and betraying me."

She slammed the portrait onto the table, crinkling the parchment.

"Careful. Sentiment is a vicious distraction."

Shoving the portrait, Volkari turned from the table. "And a deadly one at that. We aren't victims of affection."

"No Mistress, we are not. Nor will we fall prey to her enchantments. Clearly she's used blood arcana to protect the book by giving it a soul." Lyrian's ears pulsed with the swiftness of her rushing blood.

"All the better that we ensure we're prepared. You are to remain at my side until you hear from Denratis. Continue to rebuild your arcana. You must have strength to resume engraving the incantation for our ritual. I've waited long enough for you to return. Finish it before you abandon me again."

Abandon her? How ironic. Volkari wanted to pretend she was choosing to command Lyrian. In reality she wasn't capable of inscribing the stone, because of her disconnection to ɔvrʌ laræk. Volkari needed her and she'd never admit it. "As you command, Mistress," Lyrian managed without visible spite.

She flexed her hands in her silks. They needed that cursed book, or else it may be the end of them in Maijerda's hands. Relona's death was but the first step in ending the Veil by destroying arcana tied to its' creation. There was still work to be done.

"Next I pry into Jeddeith's mind, I will seduce him to slip and show me where they've run to so I may inform Denratis. Gods know he could use the help."

Volkari brushed Lyrian's cheek, her fingers rigid and cold as a corpse. "My wayward tide."

Lyrian's upper lip twitched. She belonged to no one.

"I am pleased your journey to Steslyres wasn't entirely worthless. You demolished the *Norn* and killed Relona's husband, as planned. A great feat. How difficult can it be to recover a book? I'm sure you'll do better." Volkari's sallowness contradicted her bloodlust. "Manipulate this *child* and her companions as you see fit. We will succeed in rebuilding our tapestry and in resurrecting our home. We will free Pɛnʌmbrə of all its faults."

"Praise fortune. Bleed victory." Lyrian pledged as they had in Volkari's reign.

She eyed Relona's portrait, appreciative for the lessons of fortitude bestowed by those who betrayed her. However, she was less convinced it ever struck true for Volkari.

Time would tell.

CHAPTER TWENTY-TWO

BOG BERRIES

AVING LEFT THE SCORN WOOD AND acquired horses in the quaint town of Quortense, travel was for once peaceful. They rode hard, the wind whipping Maijerda's hair and growing more chilled the nearer to D'hadian they traveled.

After several days, they happened upon a berry bog surrounded by a forest of birch and turning Undern leaves. With the top of the bog simmering with fog, it was a picturesque scene to honor the full Reaping Moon.

They stopped to water the horses and Maijerda took the opportunity to wade into the burgundies of bobbing berries and commune in silence with the Moon's boastfulness.

Reinvigorated, the bite of the water dampened her worry. Worry for the danger she put Wytt in by confiding in him. Worry for Jeddeith's role in this quest. Worry for the truth to come. Worry she'd never earn the truth. Deftly she collected a spare linen cloth's worth of bog berries while Jeddeith sat, smoking his pipe.

That evening, Maijerda boiled the berries with freshly harvested thyme and served it with a seeded bread she purchased in Quortense with cubes of salami, a thick, spongy cheese meant for frying, and root vegetables roasted on the fire.

"Where'd you learn this?" Jeddeith munched on his piece of compote-soaked bread.

Maijerda sighed heavily and avoided Wytt's uneasy stare. "It was a tradition my mother started when I was young."

Quiet blossomed between them before Jeddeith set his meal down and sat up earnestly. "I am sorry about your parents. I realize burying your parents is expected, but this seems cruel."

"Funnily enough, I said the same thing." She set her own bread aside, unable to stomach it. Jeddeith had been more personable since the dullahan, but even so she was still wary. Trusting him would be too easy. Fighting it was exhausting and stubborn, she could admit. Maybe this was a moment to kindle friendship.

"Thank you. I suppose. I still can't wrap my mind around how Denratis knew." Her curls were shaking and she closed her eyes briefly, the heat of his final breath haunting her. Reaching for her necklace, she palmed the crystal and steadied herself.

In and out. In and out. Wytt placed a hand on her back. She opened her eyes and licked her lips. Had they always been so dry?

"Back in the courtyard you mentioned she was ill. You don't believe that, do you?"

After what Denratis said, no. She didn't. Maijerda pulled on her coat and scarf to bundle up, wrapping her arms around her knees.

Wytt started to speak and hesitated before explaining his theory. "Technically she *was* ill. B-but the more time I spent in h-helping care for her, the more I speculated it was incited by a darker side of the tapestry."

Confused, Jeddeith narrowed his eyes for them to elaborate. So, Maijerda did. "We met Wytt when we were seeking advice from clerics in Neseth. He was a ward of their temple—"

"I was nobody, really. Th-they never w-w-anted to hear what I had to say."

"Fools, all of them. He was the only one who offered to help. It was odd how she changed. At first she was forgetful. Until it became so she forgot not day-to-day tasks, but misplaced who she was.

"A year in, violence overwhelmed her and she lashed out at us. Me in particular. Unintentional outbursts expressing her anger and frustration. Eventually she was too great a liability to herself and others. I told Da I couldn't sail with him anymore and I stayed home to care for her. I refused to send her anywhere with strangers. I couldn't have done it without Wytt."

Maijerda had fooled herself into thinking she could recount the events without growing emotional. She teared up and grimaced, gripping Wytt's hand for stability. He'd been there for every worsening change and for every breakdown after. "She lost her ability to speak and eat. Or it could have been her awareness and will, we were never concrete in our understanding. We tried everything. Healers, surgeons, potions, amulets, prayers. Every night I sat by her side, my prayers empty.

"Eventually, Da begged me to join him on a trip to recover a cure. Said he couldn't make this trip alone. His despair wore on me and I agreed. Wytt was kind enough to take on caring for her while we are gone. For which we are still grateful." She tried to look him in the eye, to squeeze his hand in comfort.

Wytt was staring at the ground, jaw clenched, unblinking, tears streaking his face. Fates, his blame would haunt him forever. She wished she could relieve him of it. He didn't deserve to bear that pain. It wasn't and never would be his fault.

Pushing through a streak of warbling sadness, Maijerda continued. "We returned empty-handed from Ceye after ten weeks. Wytt was waiting for us at the docks in Hostlen, having just laid her down to rest for the afternoon. But when we returned, she was dead."

There was no bouncing cadence or joy in Wytt's words. It pained Maijerda to hear him like this. "She w-w-was fine when I left. Stable. Quiet. Peaceful. I wouldn't have left her alone if she hadn't been. I may not be a trained physician, I knew well enough then what to look for and recognize if she were close to death. I-I don't know what happened but she didn't die peacefully in her sleep."

"When I went upstairs to see her, she was twisted on the floor, the dresser mirror shattered around her with her blood. She was clutching clumps of her own hair. Jagged marks of blue and green were around her eyes, and they were—" Fates, it was grotesque to remember. "Her eyes were partially... melted? I don't know how to explain it."

Jeddeith repressed an exhale. "Gods in shadow. Was it a demon? I know they," he emphasized, "say they're not allowed in our world. I assure you, sightings began some thirty years ago. Whether people want to believe it or not. Perhaps the dullahan wasn't your first."

"As far as I can tell it was no demon. But Father wasn't keen on my researching to rule that out."

"Then a disease ravaged her mind? Function by function. Did anyone rule out a brain bleed? Heart dysfunction?"

Wytt nodded. "I-I specifically requested an autopsy. They found nothing."

"This is where Da and I disagreed, the more I learned what I could about medicine with Wytt's help. We've since heard of similar cases in homes for the elderly. Most people there suffer from dementia. It doesn't add up."

Maijerda swallowed a nasty lump welling in her throat. "Her death screamed murder to me. My father and I argued for weeks until I realized I was causing him more stress than it was worth. So I stopped searching for a monster to blame. Apparently, they may be more real than I ever imagined."

"This was six years ago?"

"Her death? Yes. But her... illness stretched across almost two years."

"Hmm. Six years." He watched her with thoughtful countenance, genuinely even. "What are your opinions on coincidences?"

"If you're referring to creature comforts we pretend are tangible when we don't want to accept hardened truth, my opinions are brash. I've seen plenty to convince me otherwise."

He chuckled. It was strangely comforting? Assuring? Fates no, not that. It was simply *new*.

Jeddeith placed his fingers on the cuff of his shirt and pulled at it. And then after a breath, he unpacked his pipe, tamped it with a flourish of orange peel and honey from the leaves, and settled. "I used to feel the same."

"Not anymore?"

He struck a match and lit his pipe, looking her dead in the eye after he blew it out. "When I saw you with that book, I thought you capable of destroying everything."

Having dried his tears, Wytt chuckled, to which she glowered at him before asking Jeddeith. "Do you still believe that?"

"That you're capable of ruining the world?" Another puff, and the runes of his pipe glowed.

"Yes?"

"I mean no offense, but no."

"Well, that's certainly a relief." She rubbed her arms and dodged his glance by studying the curling bark of a birch tree.

"After what happened in the courtyard, I'm not sure what I'm capable of anymore."

He released a puff a smoke. "No one does, not until we're faced with—"

"A choice?"

"Your words, not mine."

Wytt, his seriousness returning, said hopefully. "You didn't intend to k-kil him, r-r-right?"

"What would it mean if she did?"

A throbbing twitch pulsed in her eye and she pressed against it with her fingertips. "I don't know, Wytt. What I do know is that he almost killed you. And in my nightmares my dagger melts into his skin effortlessly. I feel his breath. I smell the vomit and the poison and it's awful.

"It's odd. I've spent six years battling nightmares of my mother's decline and demise, yet I am unfit to battle these. It's as though I'm being punished."

"You probably are."

What was *that* supposed to mean? She was at a loss for a reply. Two steps forward, one step back with this man, honestly.

"But you're punishing yourself."

She scoffed, wrinkling her nose. "Hardly."

"You're so sure?"

"Well. No. But—"

Wytt interjected, "Give yourself grace."

"I was impulsive."

"Is that wrong?" Jeddeith countered.

"I don't know. I didn't that night, and I don't now."

Jeddeith scowled at the ground, his baritone deepening with sincerity. "Being intimate with death more than most colors perspective, in my experience. I respect what you did."

What an uncomfortable notion. Was it because he was surrounded by misfortune? Or because he caused it? "Maybe one day I'll understand."

"Maybe."

This was all too much. She needed space. Clearing her throat, she stood awkwardly and grabbed her journal along with Da's book. She wouldn't last long with the aches making her skin crawl and the incomprehensible need to sleep. Exhaustion was overcoming her the last few nights. Determinedly she tried to ignore it to tend to the faetale. After so much time in her bag, it needed some air, stretch its— well it didn't have legs, but still. "I'll take first watch."

"Wake one of us when you're ready." He didn't look at her as she walked away, staring into his pipe smoke as though it were a scrying basin.

He was hiding something, she could tell from his tone more than his calculated body language. It didn't feel malicious. Fates knew she was the last person to judge someone for keeping secrets.

Journal in hand, she wrote every detail she could recall from the courtyard. Whether she believed it to be coincidence or not. Including that name Denratis whispered in worship before the book attacked him.

Lyrian. Whoever that may be.

CHAPTER TWENTY-THREE

NICK OF THYME

IT WAS THE GRAND SILHOUETTE OF D'hadian on the nineteenth of Reaping Moon that spurred the nervousness of Maijerda eating a raw bog berry, favoring its bitterness. The nearer they drew to the city gates the more her anxiety rose, and so the snap of the bog berry numbed brimming doubt. Asking for stability from the invisible Moon, she asked they find success and for the trouble they were sure to encounter to be worth the strife.

Farmlands awaiting the peak of harvest cradled D'hadian in quilted patches for several leagues. Beyond these, the outermost plains catered to renowned fields of wheat. Rows of tress, plump with the fruits of their labor, shuddered under the weight. Rolling vines covered knobby-necked gourds and pumpkins aplenty. D'hadian was in no short supply for the coming Festival of Embers. In several weeks, celebrations and parades would arise during the Cruor Moon, to commemorate the tale of Undern and Eventide battling for reign of Pɛnʌmbrə. It was a toast to wily nature and her deities.

Riding up to the mosaic and stone melded gates, a distant clock tower tolled and the armor-clad sentries welcomed them as enthusiastically as the city itself. Their horses' hooves clopped on the meticulously cobbled streets of D'hadian as they joined the afternoon bustle. It was more than Maijerda had imagined, gazing up at the many-storied buildings with stained-glass or oxidizing metal rooftops. Some curved to cast a ripple like peacock feathers across the surface. After a stableboy was quick in offering to settle their horses, they agreed on finding beds and much needed baths. Wytt's complaints of the dirt caked in his hair weren't exactly unsubstantiated; they were all quite the mess.

Carriages adorned with markings dictating their route whisked by each other, well rehearsed in their paths and crossings. There were toy vendors, dedicated to the craft of cultivating cheer, crates of wildflowers fresh from picking, and bundles of culinary herbs. Maijerda insisted they stop at a bath shop for fresh bars of soap. Fates knew her hair would need a bar of its own to freshen it up from travel.

Potters' shop windows were overrun with wares. The robustness of leather came through on a gale from open doors of several workshops with a range of wares. Maijerda's nose warmed with pulses of heat from glass blowing shops.

Once in the neighborhood of Tarot Root, they chose an inn, its sign engraved in distressed blue-painted wood. The Nick of Thyme. She and Wytt chuckled at the pun, but Jeddeith wasn't keen on word play. Odd for a librarian, Maijerda decided.

They spent seven jade to book two rooms. The straelden proprietor, bulky with muscle and standing just at bar height, was quick to pocket the triangular, arcanely embossed jade quills when Maijerda offered them to ensure good service.

The three agreed to freshen up before meeting for dinner and by that time, Maijerda had chosen a table near a window, the gold in the curtains' designs glimmering in the sunset. Scrubbed clean from stem to stern, Maijerda took to people watching, waiting for Wytt and Jeddeith.

A tiraen woman, no more than twenty, scurried by Maijerda, fighting to keep pace with the packed dinner crowd. The smile she wore spoke of unraveling nerves. After one lap, she hung over the lip of the split kitchen door, shouting to her brother, and came to take Maijerda's requests.

She ordered supper for all three of them. The special, pork and ginger soup dumplings with vinegared cucumbers, and two stouts and a peppercorn ale for Wytt. Once the stouts arrived, she sipped while writing in her journal. The stout was bold, layered with unsweetened chocolate.

Maijerda scrawled the date in her journal and it dawned on her. Tonight was the Dragon's Eye Moon. For Fate's sake, this was an opportunity not to be missed. Surely someone could point her in the direction of the fountain. Childish excitement had her jittery with anticipation. She jotted the lyrics from the song in her journal, occupying her wait and humming to herself. Her fingertips pricked as she did, buzzing with her love for the tune.

She meant what she said to Jeddeith after encountering the dullahan. She didn't intend on betraying her vow in seeking the truth of this faetale, buried as it was. And she didn't expect Jeddeith to continue at their side much longer. Even if she wanted—

She peered up from her journal at the figure in front of her. "Well hello again." She stoppered her ink bottle and fidgeted with her embroidered collar. The ornate black leather belt cinching her waist tightened with her nervousness.

Jeddeith's hair was damp, scented with pine from his soap. His peppered facial scruff cleansed from the dust and clinging dry grass from travel.

"Better?"

A dagger hilt caught her eye as he sat. It seemed to be smithed from iron with an obsidian shine and oil slickness. That would've been more than strange if it were. He hadn't wielded that before, had he?

"Much actually." Jeddeith shifted his coat, covering his belt, and took a long swig of stout.

"Supper's on the way. Figured we could take a moment to relax tonight. If you're not opposed?" They could use a civilized moment together.

He tried to hide a relieved sigh with a well-timed sip. "Not at all. We've earned it."

She raised her drink to him and they clinked their steins. "Wytt still asleep?" Prying to see if they'd been talking between themselves, her jealousy was poorly masked by her high-pitched inquiry.

"Even after all these weeks, it's the loudest I've heard the man snore."

"I'm sure he's exhausted. He's not used to traveling, and don't ever expect him to enjoy sailing. Wytt was meant for city life. Since he moved with Da and me to Steslyres for his studies, this is the most change he's had."

Jeddeith appeared to be feigning seeing something of interest out the window. "Might do him some good. Change isn't always so terrible."

"Agreed. I'm hoping being here in D'hadian will spark him to take the chance and apply for the medical program at the Pearl. He's plenty prepared, he just won't give himself the chance."

"Sounds like you two have a lot in common."

"How do you mean?"

"Difficulty trusting yourself, allowing yourself to recognize your potential."

She couldn't stop herself, snorting as she finished drinking. "Potential to fuck everything up maybe."

Chuckling, Jeddeith said, "Cheers to that."

In tandem to toast the glory of unpredictable chaos, they raised their polished steins and drank.

He looked to the table. "I know we've spoken plenty of what to expect when we reunite with Knax here, but we..." Then to the painting behind her. "...haven't discussed much else outside of faetales and theories." Lastly, he rested his gaze on her. "How are you holding up?"

She was on the verge of grinding her jaw formulating an answer that wouldn't turn into a rambling diatribe of anxiety. Rolling her lips, she licked them nervously.

Words were tiresome rodents. She resorted to another sip. She was hardly a stranger to loss and grief; surely he understood that after the berry bog. He was putting in a decent effort to coax her out of an emotional shell constructed of stalwart brick, she'd have to give him that. She didn't let people in lightly.

"Fine, I suppose. Until we learn what this faetale means I'm not sure what to think. Granted I'm frustrated by how confusing this is. I mean, what am I supposed to make of inheriting a book that transformed because of a song no one else knows? It sounds mad." Tapping her stein, she added, "I'm working to let that frustration go. Can't imagine it'll get me very far."

"If I can offer consolation, it's my trust in Knax. I'm sure speaking with Nadín will give us clarity if not direct guidance."

"Let's hope you're right." Maijerda smiled, somewhat flatly in struggling to accept the simple truth of taking things one step at a time. "Thank you."

"Dare I ask what for?"

"Actually giving a damn."

Leaning over the table, he placed his hand on hers, thumb brushing her wrist. "Maybe you still believe I don't deserve forgiveness. And that might be true. I would be the last to argue. Regardless, I hope you recognize that I do care."

Stomach sent fluttering, Maijerda swallowed and rested her free hand on top of his reassuringly. "Everyone deserves chances. Fates know how many I've had. Just don't ruin this one." Winking, she smiled as they both chuckled softly, reaching a point where no one knew what to say.

Whisking about the tables, the young woman returned with supper just in… well oddly enough, just in the nick of time.

"There you are, enjoy." She excused herself to answer the beckoning call of an elderly gentlemen in a raggedly knit sweater on the other side of the room.

Steam rose from their bowls of plump dumplings and broth, the cucumbers glistened with vinegar, crisp and fresh. Maijerda's unrest eased, consequently uncovering her suppressed appetite. It was a meal where she didn't fully realize her hunger pangs until she started filling her belly. They split Wytt's untouched helping of dumplings as he slept the evening away, and they ordered two more stouts each. Dinner drew out well into the evening. It was, she dared say, lovely.

Their conversation flowed with ease. Both alcohol and broth satisfied her need for therapeutic cheer, relaxing her guard and allowing her to enjoy his company. Come to think, perhaps the alcohol had the lead role in that production. Maijerda's warm and splotched skin at the top of chest told her it was a distinct possibility. In all honesty, she wasn't bothered by it.

Full bellied, she slumped in her chair, feet propped on the same chair as Jeddeith. He took his pipe from the leather strap of his belt, preparing it in a ritualistic dance. The sweetness of cinnamon apples and black pepper lured her into a dreamy space as he smoked. The ember runes engraved along the sides illuminated his fingertips as usual. The whole image softened him. It seemed comfort, tonight, was mutual.

Jeddeith offered the pipe to her. She accepted and breathed in a quaint puff, exhaling the smoke so it added to the rest lingering above their table. The full burn of it differed from the scent it gave.

"Now that could be dangerous. That's rather enjoyable actually." She handed him back the pipe, her rings catching a sparkle in the candlelight.

"You've never tried before?" The runes glowed again, happily.

"Never thought I'd be fond of it. But that is quite pleasant. Soothing."

Jeddeith smiled at her, keen to share. "You'd probably enjoy the tobacco shops. Not too dissimilar from tea really. I could take you, if you'd like. While we're here?"

"Let's see what we can find then." She gave a gentle smile.

They shared a comfortable silence without the compulsion to fill it. The tables cleared of full and cheery patrons who bid them a stumbling farewell as if they were old family friends. A commonality between tavern life in D'hadian and Steslyres Maijerda wasn't expecting, given the flourishing gravitas of this city.

Maijerda drained her last drops of stout. The Moon should be perfectly nested in the sky by now. Wiggling in her chair she said, "Good evening for a walk. Think I might meander about for a bit."

"Going to the Fae Pond?"

Blushing, she retrieved her coin purse and counted one jade quill and two bronze seeds to pay for the meal. "Am I that obvious?"

"Not always." Jeddeith winked and propped his boots on a chair. "To be fair, you did mention it several times during dinner."

She scooted closer to him, wondering if he knew any lore she hadn't collected. "What do you know about the Fae Pond?" People's familiarity with lore in general tended to alter between experience, culture, and storyteller. Maybe he'd heard something she hadn't.

He flicked his brow upward in thought. "The Fae Pond. Revered in favor of good fortune. Its water is said to be a gift from the dragon who guards the pond in another realm. You're allowed a wish on the night of a Dragon's Eye Moon. You must make your wish on a coin tossed over your left shoulder. If you betray it and turn around when you walk away from the fountain, it's said to reveal the worst of yourself. Does that sound about right?"

Jumping in, the alcohol rushed her cadence as she explained the fountain's whimsy and the rules of trust. It brought her dangerously close to being on the ship, telling the story. This round? She welcomed her grief and embraced the tale.

She drummed her fingers indecisively at the end and at Jeddeith's slight grin. What harm could inviting him to join do after all? "Would you care to join me?"

He breathed a puff of smoke. "Honestly, I'd like that. But I should rest."

That was disappointing, though she wasn't surprised. "Probably the wiser of our choices." She shot him a wink and slung her bag into place, giving it a good tap. The book was nestled inside, wrapped in a scarf as usual. To keep it comfortable and warm.

No, to *protect* it, not keep it comfortable. Fates, what was wrong with her? "See you at dawn?"

"With bells on."

"I appreciate your enthusiasm." She clung to the top of the chair and tapped it, smiling. "Goodnight, Jeddeith."

He saluted with his pipe. "Night, Maijerda."

CHAPTER TWENTY-FOUR

Dragon's Eye Moon

THE FEW WANDERERS MAIJERDA CROSSED PATHS with were students from the Perle de Lumme, happy to guide her path to the Fae Pond. The university otherwise known as the Pearl. Their lapels, decorated with embroidered patches and pins, indicated which practices they studied, whether histories, language, science, alchemy, or medicine. From what she could tell.

Others were couples out for a romantic stroll. Somehow D'hadian was made all the more majestic by the poetic nature of nightfall. Towering lampposts lined the streets, scrollwork accentuated by a variety of arcane flames. None were as stunning as Moonlight. Speaking of the Moon, the curved top of her was visible beyond a spindly rooftop. Not quite rounded or full, certainly waning, she was a Dragon's Eye Moon.

The eye of the beast, narrowed and watching over the Fae Pond. Standing fully in the fountain's presence, the sleepy square greeted Maijerda with a yawn. No one was in sight, no children were running around, no vendors were cawing. Aah. Peace.

After all the stories, songs, and rhymes, she was finally here to bathe in its mysticism. The Moonlight created a shadow of the Fae Pond, long and lean across the bricks. The Pond was resplendent with the music of trickling water. It was a private venue for her, the fountain, and the Moon. Pooling Moonlight in and around the fountain gave the impression of celestial protection and wonderment. The water was pearlescent like bubbles brewed in the most luxurious of baths.

Maijerda gave a self-deprecating scoff, folded her arms, and tapped her foot. It was silly wanting to make a wish. And childish. Wasn't it? Though, what harm was there?

It could've been the alcohol prompting her decision, but before she knew it she was sifting through coins in her bag. Crescent Moon jaspers wouldn't do. She set the stone to the side of the pouch. Definitely not an amber soul. She wasn't giving embers up so easily. Pinching the stone diamond by the hole in the center, the metal coating on the back plinked against the other stones.

Aaah, here we go. A bronze seed. She held it aloft. The curling strand of wheat stamped into the imperfectly round bronze coin seemed to sway as if it were in a field.

She admired it thoughtfully and with an air of dramatics. "What wish shall I burden you with?" Maijerda snickered at her reflection. "Here we go." She replaced the book and composed herself, spinning clumsily on her heels, back to the fountain. Per the rules, of course. The coin dug into her palm, resting across her chest.

She tossed her hair, fussed with her nose ring. "Oh for Fate's sake. Say it." She closed her eyes, willing herself.

"I wish to find meaning in my song."

Maijerda tossed the coin over her left shoulder. A soft plink sounded as it sank into the iridescent waters. She released a breath soft enough to stoke a candle flame, hands on hips. It was nonsensical, obviously. It wasn't such a terrible act to embrace faetales now and then.

Appeased, she quoted, "Far through dusk I've wandered, to find the waning Moon."

Now for the final task. She maintained her focus forward, walking away from the fountain. You mustn't look, lest you betray the fountain's trust. She stopped short before reaching the plaza's end, vulnerability and foolishness taunting her.

Would it really reveal the darker sides of herself? No, course not. But what if it did? What would she see? Her mind strayed.

And then, the deck of the *Norn* creaked under her tall black boots in place of bricks. Blood crawled to her, pooling from Da. She shook her head and backed away, the vision all too real.

"Da?"

Had she conjured misfortune by singing of the Fae Pond? The storm hit so soon after. He'd been livid with her. He hadn't trusted songs nor faetales since Mama died. Da hated when she sang... was this why? She claimed to be looking for his murderer; had she killed him too with her selfishness?

Selfishness. Was this the worst of her?

The deck disappeared and Mother's body rolled to her feet. Eyes melted, fingers ruined with hair clotted by blood. No different than when she'd found her body. Her jaw was agape, elongated as a ghoul.

Maijerda's eyes welled with tears. Or was this more incriminating? Abandoning her mother when she needed her most.

She pursed her lips, exhaling and begging her mind to stop. She was overreacting from exhaustion. This was nothing. This wasn't real!

A flash of Denratis, licking his bile and poison stained teeth flickered to her. She gasped and shuddered, clutching her crystal necklace. That was the worst of her, wasn't it? Killing thoughtlessly.

No, Jeddeith was right. She was justified. It wasn't because she wanted *nothing* more than to know how it would feel to sink that blade in his throat. He nearly killed Wytt. He was going to take her prisoner. She was protecting herself.

Wasn't she? Or did she want the satisfaction of his blood?

She had to know. To know which of these was true. She needed to risk the truth.

With a moment of daring, Maijerda whirled around, challenging the fountain to reveal it was more than a faetale.

"Now's your chance. Prove me wrong."

The fountain remained as simple as polished stone and spilling water, from tier to tier. It remained nothing more than tranquil, unmoved by her will.

"Naturally," she dismissed, peeved with herself more than anything.

She left the fountain to guard the night, strolling through what she assumed was the longer way back to the Nick. Arms folded and holding her cardigan taut to ward off the chill, Maijerda hummed her lullaby as she meandered through barren alleyways. On the key change, Maijerda looked to the Moon.

May she guide their search and ease her fears. Maijerda sighed into the next measure, thinking on the Moon and her confidence. There was a bundle of feelings knotted within her mind. The Moon and her guardians combed through it with her as she went along. Taming the feelings to a more digestible means. It was perfectly acceptable to host them, but Maijerda relied on the Moon's aid to not become entangled.

Splashing her boot in a puddle reflecting a mote of light, Maijerda glanced up to find the source of it. No street lamp was lit, nor was there a speck of Moonlight mirrored in shop windows. Dismissing it, she started her lullaby from the top, picturing the cascading waters of the fountain to center her mind.

If she had deigned to allow her defenses to shatter from the brutality of self integrity, Maijerda would have admitted her disappointment with the fountain's silent disregard.

The First Threads

From birth,

...at the time
of the first threads...

...mortals are tasked
with crafting an identity.

Childhood bears a
tremendous responsibility in this.

It doesn't ever truly end.

As such, children are often
enamored by mysticism...

...regardless if its existence is
bound to imagination.

Does that render
the experience insignificant?

We should hope not.

We would not weave them,
in your spools of life
if that were true.

What moment have you
treasured as you've aged?

Is there a faetale which
defines a piece of you?

Was there a moment
which struck so deeply,
you cannot bring yourself
to disregard it?

For Maijerda, one such moment
which sparked creativity...

...and trust in the unknown...

...was the tale of a fountain.

A Fae Pond, centuries old

and curious.

Curious with the

promise of wishes.

What would you do

with that promise?

CHAPTER TWENTY-FIVE

HYPNOTIC DECENCY

SIGHTLESS BOTTOM. HUMIDITY. CHILL AIR. FOG. Unnatural and encroaching.

Hypnotic. He mustn't let it ensnare him.

Jeddeith squinted and peered into the chasm, abandoned at a cliff's edge.

Black and red rock.

He was likely in... in... he didn't know.

But he had the will to discover. He wasn't helpless. His trainings had enforced that. Use what you know. See what others refuse.

Vythsaden rosq.

Tirin? No. The earth smelled wrong for Tirin. This was ɔpoʊlin.

Home. What used to be home. Or what he thought was home. Home could've been anywhere, ɔpoʊlin might be the closest representation of home he remembered. Gods in shadow. What did he care?

A pit sprouted in his belly and he stepped away. Rocks broke under the tips of his boots, crumbling into the abyss. Something was amiss. He should have known what it was. Damn! He couldn't grasp it. He was struggling, mind aching.

Vythsaden rosq. Ground yourself, you old fool. He clenched his jaw and ground his back teeth. His steps were careless. Uncalculated. He crushed a mound of silver and gold flowers. The fog from the abyss engulfed them like a mourning shroud. It cloaked him next. Risk moving now? He'd step straight off the ledge.

A mirror image of the rift shown in Maijerda's faetale manifested beside him. The wind vibrated. As insect wings beating against a metal box. Then the fog bled. Not a blood natural of this world. It was an oily black. Thick and burbling. An acrid smell carried on the stirring wind.

The muck swarmed behind him, coalescing and sloughing off a disproportionate form. A yungal. Four torn wings of icy red. They'd cut sharp as blades. Eight elongated stingers for limbs. This was an insect from a demonic realm, Ghir-Zerzisse. Bred to sustain and adapt to life in chaotic landscapes. Yungal can be summoned by skilled weavers to attack at their command. If they possessed the summoning box.

Relatively instinctual and primal creatures. Capable of understanding incentives. And easy to hide. Especially when most people didn't believe in demons.

Bright lights weakened it. Fire caused it to erode. Slowly. Painfully.

Jeddeith reached for his tobacco pouch, thinking he'd tucked a match away. Damn. No such luck.

The insect hunched its bulbous head and neck. More of the oily substance dripped to the ground and seeped through the cracks.

Jeddeith donned tomsien stance, fae iron dagger in hand, taunting the insect to attack. Tomsien, built to deflect oncoming attacks. Like this one—

It opened its maw, not unlike that of a spider, and buzzed to Jeddeith in a blur. A stinger swung at him. He dove and rolled below, stabbing it in the back. His blade was thin enough to pierce between bone. And carapace. The yungal screeched and flailed at him with multiple stingers.

Jeddeith swerved his body and dodged each attack, slicing the last stinger with his iron dagger. The creature screeched again, one stinger limp at its side, glowing green.

The yungal paused. Eight eyes, pitch black, focused on its prey. Demon blood coated Jeddeith's blade. He held it by the looped hilt to examine. The blood blended with his dagger. Jeddeith flicked a grin. Demon blood was used in creating fae iron daggers. Fae iron hadn't been utilized after centuries. Instructions on how to forge it were lost. The Rivyn Borne managed to begin forging the iron again some odd... twenty-eight or so years ago.

And he could remember this fact. Clear as day.

Invigorated, he stepped to circle the yungal while it was still. Why didn't matter. He needed to take advantage of the tools available to him.

Vythsaden rosq.

Cliff face, red stone, wormwood and poppies. Demon blood.

All fine and well, but what he needed was the summoning box that trapped yungal.

Eight metal sides. Inscriptions carved into it, like the slashes of wings. No lid, no keyhole. A conduit used to call the creatures from Ghir-Zerzisse.

If only he had—

Gods in shadow. How'd he miss this before?

A metal box was half-buried in the poppies, fog caressing it.

The yungal noticed too, lunging to strike. Jeddeith sprinted and dove for the summoning box. Rolling onto his back, he pressed against the eight walls of it. The top opened, jagged as the yungal's maw.

With the shriek of metal clawing metal, the yungal screamed as it was paralyzed mid-air. Its carapace melted and slithered to the ground. Compelled, the muck returned to the box.

When the last of it was trapped, Jeddeith forced the top shut and sheathed his dagger.

Shit. Demons, here? Here in…

Where was he again? He hopped back to his feet, wiping sweat from his eyes.

Ah yes, a nightmare was it? So it seemed.

He blinked in his wall-less prison.

Find a way out. Vythsaden rosq. Jeddeith forced it into his mind, no matter where he turned he was at the edge of the abyss. There was nothing left. Save the wind. Staring back at him.

He shook his head, tilted to the side, and narrowed his eyes. As he did, a fluid figure devoid of features mirrored him.

When Jeddeith touched it, the figure wavered and the impression of lips appeared. "What a pleasure finding you here," they said with a sadistic tone.

The lips rounded and blew. It started as a breeze. Progressing into a gale. Jeddeith raised his hands and moved to run. His legs froze. The fog cleared. Somehow the figure, that intimately unnerving form, was absorbing fog to gain substance.

It was her.

The sea witch shimmered as nymph-like as before. "Peaceful, isn't it? The way it pushes forward, no matter the obstacle?" These words struck Jeddeith, harder than he would've liked. He'd heard them before, hadn't he?

"You're far from home, aren't you?" What had he meant by that?

The figure tousled, with what Jeddeith assumed was laughter. "I suppose. From my true heart. But a storm cannot endure in solitude. This is safe in times of need. Don't you see? How it billows and flows? It embodies a dance similar to water. It embodies me. Just as the birds embody freedom, the dark an embodiment of fear, and beyond the stars an incarnation of madness. You cling to your past when you should free it. Where do you find yourself, Jeddeith?"

The hundreds of places he'd traveled came to mind. Some were vivid, to the finest blade of grass. Others? Unrecognizable.

"Among soil? Floating in the sea?" The witch prompted.

The world was vast. Cities, forests, and ruins. Temples and gardens. The Toll. The Scorn Wood. Standing stones.

D'hadian.

An image of the city gates rippled momentarily behind them. A window into another realm.

The sea witch gravitated to the image, then it faltered and disappeared. "So I see." Marks, akin to arcane glyphs carved into her form, began to glow sea blue.

All sounds extinguished, except a whisper from the fog. Jeddeith longed to hear it and give it meaning, but it was beyond him.

The sea witch latched onto him by the collar. She cocked her head. "You can't hide from me. Or yourself."

Another swell from the abyss lurched to Jeddeith. Enticing him to jump in the chasm and take her with him.

She held him with his back to the edge. His anchor, crumbling rock.

"What do you want from me?" No matter how he pried at her fingers, her hold was firm. The look where her eyes should have been was cruel.

"Have faith. Allow yourself the honor of removing that hideous mask. Trust me." Her challenge reverberated before echoing. Riddling his mind with a flare of pain.

"Wait!"

She gave him one fatal push. Off he slipped from the cliff and sank into the fog.

All sense of his body was gone as he fell. He'd never read about a purgatory such as this. Not in any text. That he remembered. Here you fell with the prospect of mercy barely out of reach.

"The stories they will sing for you are meant to speak of more beautiful deaths than this, Jeddeith. Do not let this become you!"

Why shouldn't he accept the inevitable? His body relaxed as he continued to fall.

There was hypnotic decency in death.

Perhaps even peace.

THE CRUSHING OF his bones radiated through Jeddeith. He awoke with a wrenching roll in his stomach. He cursed and gasped at the shock branching from his spine. Muscles flared as if he'd shattered on the ground.

It would've been better if he had. Then the pain would be gone any second.

His heart roiled inexplicably quick.

Blurry vision. Lacking sensation in his limbs. Nausea.

Slow heartbeat.

Gods in shadow, he was freezing.

This should have meant death.

He unbuttoned the asymmetric panel at the neck of his shirt. Teeth chattering, he removed it to examine his skin. Jeddeith reached along his sides, trembling as he stretched.

No new marks. No breaks. No sign of physical ramifications. Nothing to blame for the resounding pain. Just scars from battles long forgotten. From flat and thin to raised and gnarled, he bore them all.

He pressed his palms against his temples.

Another nightmare? Knax would want to dig deeper into this one when he caught up with them. It'd be a few more days yet until he did.

At least six years without dreaming. Two nightmares within one Moon's time. Each with a clear omen. Wormwood and poppies underfoot in his path.

The beginnings of something foreboding, indeed. But what?

The sea witch an odd representation of Maijerda's tragedy influencing his dreams. Why? Her sorrow wasn't his. But he did want—if she would let him—

Jeddeith stopped himself and poured a glass of water from the pitcher on the nightstand of his room at the Nick. A shade of Moonlight accentuated his glyphic tattoos. He examined them. Noting the color, texture, patterns.

Still no changes.

Maybe nightmares were unrelated to his past and instead were a repercussion of the Spent Spindle. The trigger? Or muse, as Knax would suggest. A wondrous happening? Or was he becoming a liability?

Fuck if he knew.

A knock on his door.

Surely not.

He hadn't made a sound to alarm anyone. Maybe that was his heartbeat in his ears.

Two hardly audible knocks came in quick succession. Definitely not his heartbeat.

"J-Jeddeith?"

Fuck.

Just as he considered staying quiet as an animal feigning death, Wytt said, "I k-know you're awake. I h-heard you ssshout."

Shout? He hadn't cried out in his nightmare, nor had he woken up screaming. His urge to refute was bade by logic to subside. What else would bring Wytt to his door?

He grabbed his rumpled shirt from the floor, donning it to hide his tattoos. Couldn't afford slipping up now.

Wytt smiled tentatively as Jeddeith opened the door, pulling his tail away to knock again. "Oh-oh good. Y-you're awake. Well n-not g-good. But I-I'm glad to see, well not g-glad per say—"

Jeddeith raised his eyebrows, cutting him short.

"Sssorry. What I mmmeant to ask was, are you all right?"

Define all right. "Yes."

Wytt, ever suspicious, gave him fake understanding. "Sure, ssssure. I guess you must be. There's definitely been no signs whatsoever of your struggling to sleep and taking to early morning brooding."

"I don't brood. And I'm fine. Good night." He moved to close the door as Wytt pushed against it with his tail.

"Sssorry. Meditation?"

Wasn't going to let it go, was he? "What is it you want, Wyttrikus?"

"Honesty."

"You have it."

"Do I?" The gold of his eyes pointedly shifted focus from staring into Jeddeith.

Wytt drew his line of sight to Jeddeith's arm clutching the door frame. His shirt sleeve, unbuttoned and rolled up. Tattoos in plain sight.

"Do *we*?" Wytt corrected.

"Fuck." The simplest mistake in the entire world. Damn nightmare was to blame. Distracted him.

"Oh, it's all right." Hushed, Wytt urgently held his hands up. "You don't need to worry, I—"

Cutting him off, Jeddeith grabbed Wytt by the collar of his sleep shirt and yanked him inside his room. He closed the door in the same movement and blocked the way out.

"Explain yourself. Now."

Sheer confusion colored the varlodeths' rose cheeks. "Me? Explain? Oh. Um… not how I imagined this would play out."

Jeddeith took a step closer.

"Yes, yes!" Wytt backed up, his posture one of surrender and means of calming his nerves. It wouldn't work. "I knew straight away. You're Rivyn Borne. One of the Wrought. At l-least I'm told you call yourselvesss that. The Wrought. Carried by that which brrroke you." His delivery exposed his excitement for the news. A jump in his step.

Rivyn Borne.

The words struck Jeddeith. An assassin's blade in his back. What an unusual blade too. Capable of wounding souls instead of flesh. The hair on the back of his neck raised. His belly plummeted as if he were headed for his death again. His hand twitched for his fae-iron dagger. But it was hidden in his belongings on the armchair, not belted to his hip.

How long had it been since he'd heard anyone use that title? It was a curse. If his memory was to be trusted.

"How?"

"Your aura. It's a bit um, well— it isn't exactly whole. Which I suspected explained the d-dullahan. I didn't want to say anything."

Wytt's tail tensed until Jeddeith walked past him. Sinking into the edge of the bed, Jeddeith held his head in his hands. "Does she know?"

"No. She doesn't weave to seek auras." Wytt relaxed with a sigh and joined him on the bed. "I didn't think it was my place to tell her."

Hearing from anyone other than himself was the last way Jeddeith wanted Maijerda to learn what darkness he shouldered. "Thank you."

"O-of course. But I d-do think we should uphold honesty. Isn't that what you two promised each other?"

"Don't remind me."

"Bad habit." Wytt shrugged with his usual nonchalant attitude. "I won't force you. In due time though, yes?"

Jeddeith pushed up from leaning on his knees. "In due time," he promised. "Has aura seeking been a part of your training as a healer?"

Not expecting the question, was he? Wytt blinked a few times and stared at the ceiling before closing his eyes. "Not technically. But I made it a point to be included in my practices. I first attempted the spell to seek with Relona. Over the years my connections with tapestry weaving have improved that ssskill. I n-no longer need a lengthy ritual to see pieces of auras. If I want more colors, more d-details, the-then I need to work harder for it. If I t-tune my mind to it, I can see it without effort. I hear not mmmany healers can do that."

He was proud of this, as he should be. It typically took much more out of person to learn that skill, even if it was a diluted form of interpretation. Hells, it took Jeddeith ages to master it. He still needed incantations and he learned to seek the realm's aura, not people. It was how the Rivyn found tears in the Veil when demons began reappearing more frequently.

"They can't. I'm impressed. A skill like that should stand out to the professors at the Pearl for your admission."

"Yes, well. One day." Blushing, Wytt scratched at a horn in embarrassment. "I wouldn't have ever considered it before meeting her family. Maijerda's mother was so wildly ill. The first time I came along with our temple's healing ward to answer their third house call, I knew it wasn't natural. I hoped by seeking her aura I might learn more about what was killing her. No one wanted me to try, but I didn't see what the h-harm could be. The spell worked on my fourth weaving."

The idea of an answer, hidden poorly in his passivity. He'd been guarding the truth since then. Jeddeith should know what it was to bite your tongue. What he'd been learning from Knax was balance.

Knax's encouraging ways inspired Jeddeith to open up to him. Honesty should be honored between them all. "I'm listening."

But was Wytt? Abruptly distant, Wytt bit his lip, fanged tooth marking his skin. Lost in staring at the floor, weighed by guilt. A burden they all seemed to carry. Travel this Moon proved they had more in common than each of them noticed initially. Shame it was denying their inner battles.

Wytt was quiet, firm. "Something ancient. Dark. Untrustworthy. I never told Maijerda."

"Was it Relona? Or was it whatever was killing her?"

"I don't know," Wytt admitted, shoulders slumped. "It's why I never told her. I lied and said I failed the spell. Might be the first and last time I lied without her noticing." He laughed. "Well, that's enough of that I think. I just wanted to make sure you weren't dying in your sleep."

Suddenly it came together. Without knowing what killed Relona in her sleep, he was worried it might happen to Maijerda too. "Light sleeper?"

"Oh yes. Don't worry, no one else would've heard. Know-knowing what I do," he said with a pause to acknowledge Jeddeith's tattoos. "I wanted to be sure you didn't need help."

"Sorry to be gruff with you."

"Oh it's fine. I wouldn't expect any less in your situation. I'd be on guard too."

"Yes, well. Hopefully no one else noticed. Do you think you might could help me?"

Wytt stood straighter, with purpose. "Of c-course! I mean, how so?"

"I don't..." Jeddeith searched for an explanation. Trust and all that. He breathed deep and told himself to let it be. If he was a liability or if this was brought on by some aspect of Rivyn upbringing he didn't remember, someone other than Knax should know. Maijerda had enough to worry about. "I haven't dreamt in six years."

"Odd. How can you be sure? We don't always remember our d-dreams."

"I realize that. Trust me, this isn't the same experience. Since we've left Steslyres, I've had two distinct nightmares. Both with the same figure, a sea nymph or something of that sort."

"What does she do in these dreams?"

"See to my death."

Thinking on it, Wytt started pacing. "A message? But from whom? And why? Why now? Is it Maijerda?"

"No idea."

"Hm. We may need to dig deeper."

"I've a feeling Knax will suggest the same when he's here."

Eagerness flooded Wytt's grin. "Wh-when do you think that will be?" He tapped his fingers together.

"Soon. Assuming his flights have been unbothered."

"R-right. Gargoyles can fly. I knew that."

Certainly he did, from reading a book. Jeddeith didn't want to stress him. "If there's nothing you can think that will help, that's perfectly fine. Thought I'd ask is all."

"A-actually I do think there is something. I can mmmake it here, if we find an apothecary, we can find a tea to induce a dreamless sleep. It would need to be made with elderberries, valerian, and chamomile." He rambled off the ways it helped stave off nightmares as if the textbook were open in front of him.

"…then if we can find a tincture made of roasted and dried verninberries— roasting verninberries makes them mmmore p-potent, you see. A dropper full with keep you awake for maybe three days at a time or so? Depends on the person. And your body is structured differently from your Rivyn trials and practices I assume?"

Without much detail to recall, Jeddeith answered, "Yes."

"Well, it might v-vary, but it sh-should do the trick. Not the end of the world, coffee doesn't work for everyone either. This you have to treat more c-carefully. It can be addictive. Have negative side effects."

"Please don't list them. Let's try and find them tomorrow. I don't want these nightmares interfering with our mission."

"Do you really think they're related?"

"I'm not sure. I'd rather not chance it."

"A fair point." Wytt rubbed his hands together. "Tomorrow then, without Maijerda I assume?"

"She doesn't need to worry about me. We can catch up with her."

Flicking his tail, Wytt seemed unsure about keeping it from her. "As long as you tell her soon?"

"You have my word."

Wytt held out his hand for Jeddeith to shake on it. He obliged, without snark.

"You're a good man, Jeddeith." Gripping his shoulder, Wytt nodded to excuse himself and left Jeddeith in his room.

A bold claim. And a truth Jeddeith couldn't fathom divulging to himself.

Jeddeith refilled his cup twice, resorting to wandering his room. Shame it wasn't the strongest liquor jade quills could buy in Token Row. What a welcome burn that would be.

ACT III

Queen Eln

An excerpt from the titular play script, adapted in 2897
Playwright, Iesgle Thoffe

[CHANCELLOR entering from the castle gardens. Startled to find the KEEPER, bundled far too warmly.]

CHANCELLOR: We make a point not allowing rats to scamper these grounds. And yet, here you are.

[The KEEPER remains silent. Cloaked in dusk.]

CHANCELLOR: Halcyon tricks the mind with the boldness of day. The night should not be treated frivolously. Here and now is not where you should keep your company.

KEEPER: Suppose I threaten the same. I'd wager you're two steps ahead of me.

CHANCELLOR: You know as well as I that I remain a brisk five paces ahead.

KEEPER: Ah-ah-ah. Careful treading such a pompous void. Confidence is venomous. Queen Eln might suspect.

CHANCELLOR: Hardly. She is oblivious to the fire ravaging her kingdom. Or worse, ignorant to the smoldering. What business is it of yours?

KEEPER: What business is it of mine? You beg for weeks, for my aid, yet still you cannot grasp it. It is the wheat in the fields, the sun rising at dawn, and the lunar gifts in the tapestry. It is the sweat of Halcyon and the blue stained lips of Eventide, enraptured in sacrifice. It is everything to me.

Chapter Twenty-Six

You Weren't Supposed to Look

THE COMPLICATED WONDER ABOUT LIBRARIES IS their relentless existence. They are capable of holding everything and yet not a damn thing. You could search years without finding precisely what you needed. Seeing as how it'd been one week of searching the Menagerie's archive, without any trace of this faetale existing outside of Da's book, things were looking grim.

Maijerda rubbed her eyes, which stung worse than when researching in the Toll. She'd been horribly fatigued these days and it wasn't for lack of sleep. Between stress and not having access to the tonic Wytt brewed to help maintain her energy, she was positively drained.

Fates, she used to love books, but not when they were betraying her every page. This week was full of emptiness. She hadn't thought it possible. No sign of Knax, no word of a traveling theater troupe, no symbols matching the covers' glyphs, no mention of the Moon's spark in archives of stories, songs, maps, or research journals. This glyph was supposedly a realm-shattering portent, yet there was nothing to show for it?

Granted, the university's library was strict on visitors. Since neither of the three were students, they were denied access to anything outside of the first two floors of introductory materials for public use.

The museum levels of the Menagerie were especially off limits. Which was unfortunate, because Maijerda was itching to explore the artifacts displayed there. The music box from Knax's tower proved not all fortunes were in a book.

Jeddeith set his feet on the table, pressed his glasses higher on his nose, and flipped open a book bound with spiral rings. Sluggishly too, Maijerda noted. He'd made a habit of staying up late and waking early. It was starting to show beneath his eyes. Puffy and faintly bruised. She knew the look all too well. Surely if something were amiss, he would've shared. Over their morning tea, any meal? Their walks around the city. Or when they visited the Fae Pond last night. Moments of genuine closeness and he hadn't indicated troubles of any sort, other than the one they all shared.

Da's damned faetale.

She eyed it sidelong. Complacent with its mysterious ways, wasn't it? Well its games were growing tiresome. Having some inkling of information or direction before meeting Nadín would be ideal, Fates forbid.

Wytt perked up behind a tome too tall to hold steady without resting it on the table. "Ooo! This might—"

"No." Maijerda smacked his book flat to the table. To which several people stared. "I'm done. For today."

"Really? Didn't notice."

She narrowed her eyes at Wytt's sass. "I know I've been on edge. This is just—"

"Fucking ridiculous?" Jeddeith finished while adjusting his reading glasses.

"Yes, well. Not that first time I've said it, is it?"

Typically she took her time repacking her satchel, but not today. She shoved the faetale inside, jostling it around extra hard. "I'm heading out."

"Have fun." He grinned and turned the page.

With each movement she made to buckle the bag her body adopted a steadily uneven rhythm. She massaged the back of her neck along her spine. Aching from craning over books. Fates, all her joints ached this week. She was stiff as a plank.

The others didn't budge. "Aren't you coming?" She asked Wytt, masking her plea.

"I'll stay with Jeddeith." He gave an apologetic grimace.

Oh. Bestest of friends, were we? They'd been spending an awful lot of time together. Fates, she'd caught but a few minutes with Wytt few days prior. He was off gallivanting with Jeddeith, who, mind you, had been extraordinarily friendly. Wytt was deserving of it, naturally, but oh how she bristled at it.

Fine, fine. "Well, good luck. See you tonight." Toning her jealously down to a curt salute, she mumbled to herself. "I need a drink."

Off she marched to the main foyer of the Menagerie, trickling with the heartbeat of a stream branching off the Wyldvern river. The core of D'hadian was situated around this river and the Menagerie honored its contributions to society and beauty by building around this small creek.

Stained-glass depictions of figures posed as divinity with fruit and flowers stretched to the ceilings. Printed canvases of similar images were hung both in the Menagerie and on campus. Vertically, phrases praising the search for knowledge were transcribed on the sides.

The aesthetic of this library was pristine. Almost somber and snobbish, but out of necessity. Which was understandable. The Menagerie had a reputation to uphold. After all, it was sister to the Pearl of Illumination. Without structure and due diligence there would be no feasible way to keep history preserved, alive, and well. Today's library attendant was a tiraen man with wrinkles deep from scowling. He didn't lessen his scowl at Maijerda as she went up the staircase leading outside. What did he think she was going to do? Burn the place down?

Agh, he wasn't worth the stress. Farewell, grouchy old bastard. Till tomorrow.

AFTER MAIJERDA DABBED the foam of drink numberrrrrr four with the back of her wrist, she worried she was going to regret this stress-driven stupid—stupor by late afternoon. Ah wait. Drink fiiiive. No, six! If you counted the shot of gin from three pubs ago. Damn, that was the best gin to grace her lips in years.

It's not that she was sloppily drunk. Please. She could hold her liquor.

Headed   in   that   direction?   Maybeee… prrrobablyagoodchance. Mostlikely.

Her stomach grumbled. Especially without having eaten.

What was left to regret anyway? *Of course* they learned absolutely nothing about this faetale. They needed Nadín. Even if she didn't know about the book, she was bound to know more than they did.

Maijerda had warned Wytt they wouldn't find anything, despite wanting to believe it was worth searching. Unfortunately, it was instinct. Trust your gut, they say. Sure, she hoped she was wrong and they'd find out who wrote this, when, why, and what it all meant. Blah, blah, blah. You know, what you'd expect from a university. But here they were, empty handed.

Fates, it was awful being right aaall the time.

Maijerda hiccupped and rearranged herself to prop her boots up on a chair, struggling to take light in the merriment from the crowd. Two children chased each other round and round the table where their puffy eyed mother sat and fussed with balancing a slice of egg on her fork.

Maijerda chuckled at the mother's sigh, her children tripping over one another. Truthfully, as much as she loved children, she couldn't imagine having her own.

At some point between shoving aside unresolved emotions and admiring the mischief of childhood, Maijerda tipped and balanced her chair on the back legs, rocking. A lantern hanging from the ceiling flickered a rugged amethyst, the arcane flame within breathing to life this peculiarly different shade from the others. After a blink, it returned to its rich orange glow. Oddity? Or booze?

Eh. Probably the booze.

She forced herself to be content to daydream. Until, a dissonant murmur rustled her hair and rushed along her jaw. The entire pub warped into silence and faded to gloom, dark as the Harrowing.

"You weren't supposed to look."

Maijerda gasped. The serving girl was bent and looming near her ear, as an outraged phantom. Her gray lips smirked deviously. Reeling in her seat, Maijerda's impromptu footstool toppled over amongst the kerfuffle.

This earned her several judgmental glares. The girl was gone.

Searching and darting, Maijerda found her standing aghast by the bar, lips a healthy pink.

Someone grabbed her by the collar and yanked her to her feet.

"What happened?"

Jeddeith? When did he get here?

"Tuvon's breath, how much have you had?" Wytt too? Ah, shit. Inseparable now, weren't they?

"I-I thought I saw…" The room was spinning. Maijerda locked eyes on the girl. She slurred, "What are you on about?"

"Miss, I'm not sure what you mean." The girl wrung her dish towel anxiously.

Maijerda's knees were unsteady as the alcohol made its delayed, though grand appearance. She wobbled into the rim of the table. And into Jeddeith.

He wrapped his arm around her waist. "All right. What is going on with you?"

"Mmme? Pfft. I'm fine. What? Don't belieeeeve me?"

"Can you blame me?" He pulled her in closer to keep her from wobbling.

Warm. His breath was warm on her nose. Must have smoked his pipe on the way here. Roses and brandy.

"What happened?" he reiterated.

Ignoring the comfort and fluttering heat his touch brought, Maijerda unleashed. "She started—stalled—agh! She *startled* me half to death!" She swung back to the girl. "What the scalded piss was that?" She was met with increasing confusion and embarrassment. "You weren't supposed to look, you said!"

"I didn't say anything, miss."

"Oooh, I wouldn't sound so sure." She raised her voice, an alcoholic fog encroaching her wits. Maijerda shoved Jeddeith's arms off and took a step forward.

"I'm sorry," Jeddeith crooned and took her by the arm, guiding her back into the chair like a dance. "Rough day," he explained and gave Maijerda a look, eyes wide.

What was his deal? Like he'd never let loose before? Fates. She shrugged and peeked in her mug. Ah. Empty again. Jeddeith combed back his waves. Those auburn-touched, umber waves. He addressed Maijerda. As if she was listening. Hah!

His voice droned on and on. Probably lecturing about drinking like she wasn't old enough to know better. Annoying and stubborn and full of himself and... confident. Quick. Talented fighter. Calculated and...

"Are you frowning at your drink?"

"What?" She quipped, hugging the mug. "No."

"Maijerda, I say this without judgement."

"But?" she sang.

"It's barely evening."

"Your point being."

"What're you hoping to accomplish?"

"Mmm..." Her hum echoed in the stein for another wistful swig. "To forgetabout aaaaaall of this. Just for a day. For an afternoon even. That's all. If it's not too much to ask. Oh. Wait. It probably is."

When did Wytt leave? He was walking back to the table with cup of hot water and a plate of chicken, nuts, fruit, and yogurt. "You need to eat. Otherwise—"

"No, Wytt, Ireallydon't."

"You haven't eaten in hours. Plus the alcohol w-will effect how you—"

"I'm fucking fine!"

"Are you?"

Scowling, she said, "Stop mothering me. I'm handling it. Best I can."

"Fair enough." Wytt conceded, pushing the plate to her as the last word.

Jeddeith pulled out a lavender glass bottle and dropped a few drops of a floral liquid into it. "That should do the trick. Here. It's a tincture. Peppered mint. Ginger. Should sober you up. Clear your mind. When the steam turns green, it'll be done steeping. Drink it before its cold. Otherwise it won't work as well."

She took it, still squinting. "You went… shopping? You didn't need to do that."

"I had a feeling you'd need the help."

"You're not wrong."

"That might be a first."

Feeling quippy was he?

"I know you're frustrated. We all are. We need you alert."

An unannounced warmth enclosed her hand at the exact moment the room lost color. She blinked at the solace that was Jeddeith's hand resting on top of hers by the table's lantern. He didn't breathe a single word and perhaps he didn't need to, his honey and sky eyes calming.

"What if you're being tracked? Who knows what ties Denratis and his commander have to your book. Did you ever consider how they found the *Norn* in the first place?"

"Pfft. Denratis is dead. Remember? I sure do." She dug her fist on the table, the metal of her dagger a gripping memory on her palm.

"Be that as it may. We should get going." He gestured to her tea, steaming with mixed green and gold to indicate it was ready to sip. "Drink up."

He was lucky she wasn't queasy. She drank it to the last drop and by the end, while feeling better, wasn't completely out of the woods. Her tongue was less numb, thinking came relatively clearly through the headache. The lightheadedness and hollow limbs from the liquor were remarkably lessened.

"Thank you. And sorry. I maybe over did it."

"Y-you think?"

"Yeah, all right." She held the tea cup aloft. "Huh, I'm a little disgruntled with how well that worked."

"Good. Come on." Offering his hand Jeddeith gestured for them to all get moving.

She threw her satchel over her shoulder and took his hand to stand.

"What is it, Wytt?" He was staring at a sconce posted at the door frame.

"Hm? N-nothing. Flickering light is all. Just caught my eye."

She put her arms around both their shoulders once they stepped outside. "Tell me, did you find anything exciting?"

"In terms of your faetale—"

"No, I'll stop you right there. It's not mine. It was Da's. I think." She swallowed a trace of acidity. Frothy and stout-like. Stopping to face her companions, she rolled her wrist and pulled on the angled sides of her thigh-length vest. "It's not mine."

Neither voiced their disagreement. She sensed it in their body language all the way through the Tome Ward. The last smidge of sunset disappeared as Wytt rattled off what he found of the Moon's history as an entity. They'd been focusing on Moon lore given her prominence in the faetale. How other cultures viewed the Moon as a separate deity where as others spoke to a goddess, Hyacinth. Rumors of portals to the Moon's realm. Typically water was seen as the gateway to her. Rarely mentioned were practices that involved drinking from her light to gain powers.

The Moon? Maijerda longed to see her, though the Waned Reaping Moon wouldn't be bringing comfort from the sky tonight. A streetlamp above her ignited as she ached for wanting to speak with her. If she were visible, she'd beg on her knees for guidance. Let the Moon light her path, taking her hand in hand. The Moon had been with her in the darkest of moments before. This was verging on being among them.

Please don't abandon me. Maijerda looked up at the sky, hoping maybe there'd be a glimpse amid the Moon's guardians.

Strolling into a street lit with paper lanterns and Undern leaves strung across the width, they dodged through a rowdy crowd having their fill of drink. Celebrating the end of a week and the coming New Cruor Moon, loudly boasting how festivals would be on the rise any day to celebrate the blood Moon. Maijerda deftly avoided a varlodeth spilling her drink and then a beshin scurrying at thigh height to hop up onto the curb.

Spinning to see how far behind Jeddeith and Wytt were, Maijerda was rooted to the spot. The muscles in her legs flinched and locked up. She blinked rapidly, shaking and... Fates, the smooth stone buildings were starting to seem horridly lopsided.

Not the Fates, nor hells, would argue against proof she was following in Mother's footsteps. Well on her way to losing cognizance and drifting beyond the stars where madness lies.

Hallucinating in the pub and not an hour later, seeing her first ghost? A ghost, for how else could she explain it, filtered into her muddled sight. Hair on her neck standing on end, she clutched her bag. "Sssh. Ssh. Ssh," she comforted the book, lest it be as frightened as her.

There was nothing to fear, because it wasn't real.

He wasn't real. She reached with her clammy hand for her brass blade. It was impossible. It needed to be impossible. He was dead. By her hand. Or else, he was here to haunt her.

CHAPTER TWENTY-SEVEN

TO ENTERTAIN THE MADNESS OF FATE

ENRATIS' NAVY COAT AND IRON-SPECKLED MANE were inconceivably, perfectly intact. Tracks of venom tarnished his skin from jaw to chest. A gnarled and uncannily aged scar marred the base of his neck. He angled his neck into a stretch and took a prolonged drag from his cigarette.

Fates help her. Moon above, please say it wasn't so.

"How?"

Jeddeith and Wytt caught up to her, Wytt's smile from taking in the sheer joy in the street falling flat. He didn't bother asking and followed her panicked stare. "I don't think that matters right now."

"Let's go." Jeddeith hooked his arm around hers, but her legs were still numb. She couldn't move.

"How? I—I killed him."

"Wytt's right, that doesn't matter, we need to go before he notices."

Wytt stood in front of her blocking her view. "Too late for th-that. He's headed straight for us."

Shaking and clutching Jeddeith's offset green collar, eyes wide, her voice cracked as she battled with the illogical. "I killed him."

"Maybe here's not the place for admissions of guilt." He glanced about the crowd and guided her to walk in the opposite direction.

Wytt grabbed her arm and quickened their pace.

Abruptly a stabbing pain localized at her lower abdomen distracted her. Damn body! Not now, for Fate's sake! Stay focused, come back to the present. She shook her head, trying to free her mind of both pain and the memories of sinking her bade in his throat. Focus, damn it!

Without realizing, she broke into a run, her companions following without hesitation. They ducked into an alleyway and scurried around barrels, keeping an eye on Denratis' chase. He rounded the corner with them, deftly and keen. Every move he made proved he was a predator skilled at the hunt.

Maijerda made the mistake of catching his chilling blue eyes. He snarled and sprinted for them. Heartbeat and pounding boots replaced the city's din, spiraling Maijerda forward with Jeddeith ahead and Wytt keeping just behind her.

Luckily they managed to swerve into another street teeming with people. Skidding to a stop, she clutched at her Qu'stite necklace. He wasn't going to be easy to lose—they needed somewhere to hide. An unsuspecting somewhere, inconspicuous, and quiet. Behind her, the crowd started to grumble at someone shoving through them.

Shit.

They swerved into another alley and tried the first few doors, all were locked. Until one simply wasn't. Above her, a placard reading Reul en Lore creaked with brittle hinges. A metal pendant opposite the sign bore no light. Gradient soot bled from ground to roof, devastating the overall impression of this building. The haggardness about it implied weakness, a place not to be trusted.

Maijerda yanked it open by the twisted metal handle and rushed inside. Jeddeith slammed the door behind them and pressed against it, watching the dim street through murky windows. While Wytt and Maijerda's breaths were labored, Jeddeith hadn't shown resilient calm this measured since the dullahan.

Her hands trembled as she searched for the top of the bookshelf behind her for stability. "He can't, he can't be here." The band she abhorred knowing too well ensnared her chest, her breathing growing shallower by the second. A dusty, overwhelming wave of moss wasn't helping. The scent mingled with an earthiness. Patchouli? Her mouth watered as she tried to rein in her panic, worsened by an unexpected punch of turmeric that barged in the patchouli's wake.

Each scent had something to say. Unfortunate she didn't have the capacity to listen. She couldn't handle the tugs on her tapestry threads, urging her senses to be present and delve into arcana. All that mattered was Denratis and the improbability of his sneer. "No, no, no!" Each refusal escalated as she clawed at her curls. "Please tell me this is a nightmare. That we're lost in the Harrowing."

Wytt looked between her and Jeddeith, fumbling for assurances to give. "I—I can't." He gripped her shoulders. "I saw him too."

"We all did." Jeddeith left his post and joined them at the bookshelves, forgoing comfort and opting for sobriety.

She shook her hands to bring sensation back and started pacing, fidgeting with the cuffs of her fingerless gloves. "Not a nightmare then. Not another hallucination." Taking counted inhales and exhales, she tried to clear her nerves. "Not a ghost."

"No."

Fates, he could do with sounding unsure. He wore that strategic air of his, precise and focused. He seemed so grounded, a state she couldn't reach. There wasn't a chance he was lying.

"Fuck. What can we do?" She grabbed the strap of her satchel, whispering so the book wouldn't hear her distress.

"We wait, watch our backs, and make our way back to the Nick. What comes after doesn't matter right now. Focus on here."

A low greeting followed Jeddeith's, in unorthodox welcome. "And what did bring you to *us*?" Her voice verged on splitting between two additional, dissonant pitches that likely belonged to two other people. The phenomena occurred on a single word. *Us.*

Behind them towered a woman posed amid displays of books as might a priestess in her shrine. With braids pulled tightly on one side of her head, metal beads dotted the intricate pattern of plaits. Her face was painted with thin, geometric shapes. A stripe swiped down her bottom lip and onto her chin masking a ragged scar.

The glowing fireplace, pirouetting flames colored of sage framed her, making her seem taller than was.

Wytt countered expectation, his tail swaying to show he was on edge, bothered by her unheralded entrance. "Y-you wouldn't believe us if we told you."

"I'm happy to listen. But I wouldn't dare pry. Keep your secrets as you please."

A mess of worry and confusion, Maijerda remained silent as her attention constantly drifted to the door in anticipation of Denratis barging in.

A black cat lying on top of a shelf purred and rolled on its back for the keeper, pawing at her to scratch its belly. She kissed the top of its head. "You all seem quite stressed I'm sorry to say. Might I interest you in a book?"

A well-practiced sales pitch, welcome on any other day, but not now. Didn't she grasp the severity of their stress? Inevitably she didn't, Fates have mercy. "No, we—"

"Oh come now, you haven't touched my collection! Should you wish to divine the meaning of a dream? Perhaps find a new cookbook to satisfy? Or perhaps a more indelicate escape? To tickle your fancy? I'll take your stunned expressions as a no. How about a wandering mage's guide to foraging mushrooms?" She picked up a book covered in moss, squeezing it to show the spongy texture. "I assure you I've plenty to offer. Save for histories kept by the stars. Despite the flock of people who ask me for such stories, any fool should know that understanding the true perspective of stars is to entertain the madness of fate." She shuddered at the thought, her expression splaying the paints decorating her face. "Not my cup of tea you might say."

"Maijerda." Jeddeith's hand on her arm encouraged her to root herself in their current predicament and away from the keeper's charismatic sway. "There's no sign of him." We should leave, his wary frown warned.

A fondness read in the vibrancy of the keeper's charcoal lined, lavender-gray eyes. "Maijerda? What a lovely name." The keeper's black cat meowed and purred, batting at the bird skull on her coat and metal adornments sewn on her sleeves. "She's right. You should go. Wouldn't want to keep your friend waiting."

Maijerda couldn't keep pace with her barreling nerves, a cutting high pitch piercing her mind. Friend?

The keeper gestured to the iron and glass lantern hanging outside her shop window. While empty when they had darted inside, it was alight with an orb of Moonlight.

Jeddeith voiced it before either of them could comprehend the relief that wisp of light imparted. "Knax."

Without further adherence to caution, he left the shop.

Not but a step behind him, Maijerda halted at the doorway. Unfamiliar and maternal, the etherealness of her name manifested from nowhere. Truly. Not in mind or audible speech.

Maijerda.

She furrowed her expression and looked to and fro. "Did you hear that?"

"No?" Wytt didn't blink, in the same way he studies her for illness or injury. "What is it?"

She stepped into the street, Wytt holding the door open.

Maijerda.

"My name. Someone's calling my name."

The door closed on its own accord, almost catching Wytt's tail.

Hells, this was—

Maijerda.

CHAPTER TWENTY-EIGHT

THE WISP

MAIJERDA.

"There it is again!"

"What is?" Jeddeith strained to shift his attention from the lantern wisp to her. "I don't hear anything."

"N-neither do-do I."

"My name, I can hear someone or something…" A more apt description, as it was several voices layered into one. Dreamlike and whispering. "…saying my name."

"It's Knax." Confident in his declaration, Jeddeith gestured to the orb of Moonlight. "It must be his signal."

As if to counter, the wisp faded and disappeared. Across the alley was a balcony two stories high. Maijerda was certain no lanterns were lit there before, now there was one orb of Moonlight. It was fretting. Seeming to worry its brightness fell short and wasn't enough to win her over.

"Is it you?" She whispered, entranced by the tendrils of light curling from the orb.

It dimmed and flittered as if pleased with itself before soaring to an empty sconce down the alley.

"Over there." Maijerda beckoned to show the others, running to it.

Maijerda.

The wisp of light puffed its chest up and purred resolutely.

"What brought you here?" She muttered, standing under the sconce, Jeddeith and Wytt catching up to her.

The wisp flickered, turning from lavender to a spectrum of copper. And it dawned on her. It was trying to be heard. Skin crawling from nerves, she pondered over the wisp of flame. "Torlen dovnym."

The tufts of energy glowed, earnestly. And disappeared from sight. This was not to be ignored.

"Wh-where did it go?"

"Give it a moment. It's shy, I think."

Slipping in the cracks of their befuddlement, the whisper molded where it could fit.

Maijerda.

"There!" Wytt pointed around the corner to a lantern outside of a cafe. Its original arcane flame was gone, in its place was the wisp imitating the warmth of candlelight.

Together they ran to the lamp and stared at the wisp, hoping to catch the spectral source.

Maijerda.

"Nothing?" She asked of them both, one hand on her hip, she massaged her neck with the other, foot tapping.

"No."

"Lovely. What more could I possibly expect? All right, I—" She huffed, stumbling for reason, before…

Maijerda.

"Damn it!" She was on the move, the wisp no longer confined to the lantern.

A few doors down the wisp settled inside a different street lamp. She rushed over. Satisfied, the flame disappeared and reemerged across the way.

Jeddeith grabbed Maijerda's hand. "There! Knax must be close."

He pulled her along, Wytt already in the lead. It continued on this way without using her name as bait. Every several feet it flitted to another target until it led them past an apothecary, around the bends of the Fae Pond, and through the gates of the city ward, Tarot Root.

People out in the night gawked at her, she hardly cared. Something about this stirred her wonder. She wanted to feed it every thread of wistfulness she possessed.

The guards stationed at the gates were oblivious to the beckoning flame in an empty iron torch beside them. Unfortunately, the three of them stepping beyond the sentry was just the ticket for the wisp to grin and flutter asleep until it was no more.

Back to back, Jeddeith, Wytt, and Maijerda searched for the wisp atop a cobbled street sloped to a hill. Glows of multicolored lights, and… music. A massive section of this ward was a garden cradled by the Wyldvern river, its sapphire shine near black without the Moon to light it. Cheers, whoops, excited screams came from a crowd in the garden. A labyrinth of wagons, tents, and harlequin banners.

"The troupe?" Wytt asked.

"Knax must've already found Nadín." She couldn't rationalize why she was reinvigorated with confidence and whims. It flowed in her veins, flowing from her like heat. It was the thrill of gliding on the *Norn* with sea spray splashing her body. Even if no one believed her, she was positive the book, nestled in her bag was just as alive with apprehensive eagerness as she was.

Taking the rational approach, Jeddeith said, "Something doesn't sit right. Knax instructed us to wait. For a reason." Soft and cautious with his warning, he wasn't trying to offend her, but defense flared.

"Because of my mother? The forgotten knell? Truthfully, I don't care. This week has shown me nothing of fortune and everything of what I fear in the pits of grief. You don't have to come with me. I'm done waiting. If we find her first, so be it."

Jeddeith sighed halfway before holding his breath. "I don't have a good feeling about this."

Smacking him on the back, Wytt smiled. "That's the spirit." He trotted to Maijerda, his judgement free demeanor lessening the numbness in her hands.

"After you." He bowed softly for Maijerda to guide them.

The wisp, crescendoing like a freshly struck match, glowed in a colored glass bowl. One of many, lining a path. It hopped between them, guiding the trio to the edge of the carnival. Panes of color reflected off the stone of the buildings framing the garden.

Decorations fit for celebrating Eventide's Crown rippled around the chaotic crowd indulging the splendor. A beshin dipped his floppy, feathered hat and bowed to Maijerda as she skidded to a halt. "Moon's beaming to you, madame! Do enjoy your stay with us!" The banner above the beshin read *Nil'teden Tu-Bain*. A phrase she didn't recognize.

"Thanks," she said absentmindedly in search of the wisp. The problem was, lanterns of either colored glass or paper were lit in abundance. The little bastard could be anywhere.

Pillars of magenta and orange smoke billowed from fire pits, perfuming the carnival with a blend of spiced earth and maple. Performers adorned in vibrant costumes strode about, engaging guests.

"Where should we start?" Jeddeith nodded to a blue skinned varlodeth with jeweled horns, waving her paper fan.

"It's around here somewhere, I can feel it."

She picked a direction randomly but no less assertively and led the way between tiered caravan wagons painted in an array of distressed, yet bold jeweled paints. Each wagon was decorated with promises, teasing the likelihood of wondrous realms lying behind their doors.

Melodic singing rose above the chatter, the source of it mysterious. Conversations sputtered to a halt, isolating delighted pleas from children tugging their parents nearer the center of camp. Tots barely taller than Maijerda's knee were easily persuaded to stamp their feet and clap to the music.

Collectively the performers' flare for artistic extravagance was enthralling. For a theater which travels the world, why shouldn't it be? To expect anything less than astonishing would be insulting to the craft.

Performers sprouted from their hiding places, some breathing shapes of creatures made from fire, others juggling swords in a theatrically acrobatic duel. Their decorative scimitars, spears, and gauntlets were a mesmerizing knot of tassels, gold, and steel. Maijerda held Wytt's hand and dodged out of their way. Through the acrobatics and glades, the wisp huddled in a swinging lantern at a booth with stacks of trinkets.

Distracted was it? Playing about the knick-knacks.

Maijerda motioned to them and ran through a row of booths selling treats made for feeding both belly and soul. Two or three booths were overflowing with the compassion baked into hearty meat pies, roasted potatoes... Honeycomb candies? Spiced root cakes?

She halted at the lantern and the wisp vanished.

"Excuse me!" Maijerda rushed over to a tiraen with blue hair and glittering silver tattoos. "Have you seen a flame? I mean… in a lantern?"

They gave her a cockeyed look of confusion and glanced at the countless lanterns all aglow. Realizing how she sounded, she grimaced. "Right. Sorry to bother you."

They raised their eyebrows and sidestepped away from her.

Distracted, Wytt was reading signs, pacing in a circle. There were booths for tarot readings, arcane smithing, hand painted tattoos, gambling tables, and lessons in dance. To name a few. Other booths were outfitted with games to occupy the wait until the main event.

The wisp! "There you are," Maijerda said under her breath. It blinked and reappeared a booth over, favoring a copper lantern with green glass. "This way!"

She whirred into the crowd, avoiding tangles of ribbons and the wide steps of a drummer. Her attention was fired for the wisp, now near an expansive canopy positioned at the back of the grounds.

With points and spindles arching for the sky, this was the centerpiece of it all, the masterpiece behind the witchery of the troupe's display.

The entrance of the canopy was rigged to an intricately carved bow of a ship, the hull a gateway inside this vessel of imagination. Stationed there were two troupe members accepting payment. Five seeds a soul was all they asked for passage on board the *Tu-Bain*. Each held a lantern with a light blue as the ocean. Until one exchanged that serenity for vivacious copper as the wisp appeared.

Maijerda stepped to hurry to them, willing to risk sounding foolish by asking them about the light in their care. She was stopped by a hand pushing into her hip.

"Do you hear that mamá?" A toddler tugged on the hem of Maijerda's coat. "Where is it mamá? I hear the ocean. And... I can smell it too!"

Tiny fingers dug into her sash, completely oblivious to the fact that her red hair was not graying as their mother's was. They gave her an impatient glance just as she gawked at the hull entrance, noticing the same entrancing sensation coming from within. It was then their mother clamored for her child's hand. "So sorry, miss!"

Jeddeith bounded next to her. "There you are. Did you find it?"

"Yes, I— Oh scalded piss. It's gone."

Overpowering the fickle crowd, a battle cry erupted from inside the theater tent. "Nil'teden Tu-bain. Huh!"

Guttural and war hungry, it echoed.

"Nil'teden Tu-bain! Huh! Huh!" A drum beat accompanied each primal call from the gob of voices that answered. Performers poured from the tent and withdrew magnificent baynal blades, holding the wooden block pommels ceremoniously dour.

The most imposing of the group removed himself from the ranks. "Nil'teden Tu-bain!" The ersul released this final invitation with spirit for battle. His arms were an oxymoron of intimidating welcome with the baynal's curve. "These words bring tidings of unbridled imagination and prideful sacrifice."

Gasps of premature horror erupted at the proposal of sacrifice.

"Born from the chasmic reaches of your dreams, these lie at the core of lyrical hearts." Skillfully he addressed the crowd as a whole, while boring into them individually with his red eyes.

"Will you join us?" He stopped in front of Maijerda. His bald head was tattooed with elaborate designs, all russet in color, pairing with his green skin.

In unison the warriors marched several paces to their commander and swung their blades low to clash with each other's in a perfect cross.

Maijerda flinched at the cacophony from the crowd.

As deftly as conducting the Ceye Symphony, he silenced them. "Good! Heed the tale of *The Rose and the Wyrm.*"

The troupe filed inside the tent, leaving the audience aflutter.

The Rose and the Wyrm? She'd been dying to see this one. Shame they were too busy with being hunted by a ghost and tracking a faetale wisp. Fates, just the sound of it all. What terribly written play had she gotten herself wrapped up in?

And where did that damn wisp scurry off to?

"If w-we split up-up. We can cover more ground."

Jeddeith wasn't convinced, shaking his head. "I'm not so sure. Knax has to be here somewhere."

"Ex-exactly. We split up, search the grounds and we can meet here in half an hour?"

The clock tower tolled.

"Sssee? It'll be easy to track."

"Half an hour then. Go."

Accepting her order with a bow of his head, hand on the hilt of his blade, Jeddeith departed. She and Wytt clasped hands. "Good l-luck. Don't get into trouble."

She scoffed, shooing him away, and took to a path less teeming for her search. After weaving through tents, booths, and fire pit circles, she was nearing ready to abandon it all and return to their meeting spot, when the wisp appeared. Smug, he was swaying in a lantern staked in the ground.

As soon as she was beside the flame, it hummed and swelled white hot in color before deserting its post in front of a lavish tent. The lantern creaked and a glow seeped from beyond the entrance. Feisty little creature, wasn't it?

She took a deep breath, holding the tent's fraying edge. As if plunging into the depths of the ocean, she dove inside the tent.

"Knax? Are you there?" She hushed in the dark.

The canopy was a muted patchwork of layers with colors of turning leaves, rubies, and butterscotch. Somehow, the drapes struck her as stitched with responsibility to their host.

To protect? To support? Whatever the motive, should fabrics be capable of such things? Perhaps if enchanted.

"Knax?" Maijerda's sight adjusted to the perfumed dim.

A fire pit in the center of the room was unlit, littered with herbs, crystals, and incense. All shapes of lanterns were huddled in the corner at mismatched heights behind table dressed with a scatter of rune stones, cards, and incense.

As much as she would've appreciated a warning, the fire pit lit ablaze without one. Shielding herself from the pillar of flame, Maijerda retreated from the heat, a conjured rope of flame swinging at her. She could dodge it if she stepped just right—shit. Unable to avoid its strike, it wound around her ankles with a snap.

Slamming flat on her back, Maijerda coughed to catch her breath. Made all the more tenuous by the ıdre woman kneeling on her chest and holding a knife to her throat. Once the room wasn't spinning, Maijerda noted the woman's oval, agate irises, flaring with veins of orange. "Slow. Move slowly. On your knees." Pushing up, the woman shifted to lean on her left leg.

Awkwardly, Maijerda rolled to her stomach and kneeled. "I didn't mean to intr—"

"Hands."

Not about to argue with her, Maijerda raised her hands. The flame around her legs, while warm, didn't burn, but it did tighten as the woman approached.

"My eyes have searched for centuries. I can sense it. The glyph. A knell." She eyed Maijerda up and down, cynically. "No. You are not her song."

Maijerda raised her hands higher to show submission. "No. I'm not." The woman, if she truly was Nadín as Maijerda suspected, wouldn't be keen on hearing she was the daughter of her lost knell. Truth or lie? Truth or lie? "Knax told me I was a muse born unto a knell." She paused to assess her reaction.

The woman took a deep breath, her glare more ominous by the fire brightening. She watched Maijerda as if she would snap her neck with a flick of her wrist. There was no questioning if she could, it was more a matter of when.

"Relona was my mother." This truly was a pick your poison predicament, there wasn't a good place to start for explaining herself. "She was murdered six years ago. The glyph you spoke of, I mean no harm to you or the realm by having it. But I do have it."

"What is it? Where is it?" She prodded, loudly.

"There's a book, in my bag."

Gruffly she tossed her knife and searched Maijerda's satchel, pulling the faetale free in a heartbeat in her left hand. Restraining the urge to grab onto it, Maijerda flexed her fingers, still holding her hands high.

"She sung of this to you?" The woman demanded to know, holding the book up to indicate her meaning.

"No. I found it with my father when he was killed. It was blank at first and I spent days researching it. I met Knax shortly after." Taking a risk, Maijerda continued. "Knax told me of your search, thinking there was more to it than you both realized. He traveled with me and my companions here to find you. We were following the wisp, assuming it was Knax signaling he'd caught up to us."

She didn't reply, giving Maijerda a chance to notice the right side of her warm brown cheeks and the right corner of her lips, drooping slightly. The angle of her jaw was blurred by the slack in her bronze features. Her right hand too, was relatively still, the book tucked in the crook of her arm. An injury? Or illness?

"He's not sheer. Not. Here." She stated, with no room to argue.

"Nadín, I know you don't trust me. Let me explain."

"Why? Because you can think on my name? This place is not for the something of you. You are no muse." Her array of silky dark brown spirals obscured the pointed length of her ears, as she shook her head. They were far more elongated than Maijerda's. Similar to full blooded ɪdre, or those of an older heritage? The angles of her face were sharper too.

How could she argue? She didn't want to believe Knax's theory, but the book listened to her lullaby and responded. If it could do such a thing. Was it song arcana? No. It couldn't be, not from her. There had to be something to convince Nadín. How could she hope to sway her if she didn't believe it herself?

Slowly, Nadín looked Maijerda in the eye. Both dreading and craving an answer. "Torlen dovnym."

Tears welled and Maijerda cursed their sting. She dropped her head and swallowed reservations, fears, and all else that colored her anticipation of meeting Nadín. "T—Tor—" Her voice cracked. Tears mercilessly reminding her Mother and Wytt were the only other people who'd ever spoken this phrase to her. Not even Da used it. "Torlen lexnym."

Painstaking seconds sprawled until tears slid into the crevasse of Nadín's lip. "What name did she sing to you?"

"Maijerda."

Nadín breathed a deeply wounded sigh. To say she appeared defeated would not do her sorrow justice. The devastation that worried her features read as entirely ruined to learn it had come to this.

CHAPTER TWENTY-NINE

WEAVER'S NECTAR

NADÍN RELEASED THE FLAMES BINDING MAIJERDA and offered her hand. Taking it, Maijerda stumbled upright. The gold of Nadín's septum piercing glowed in the light from the fire pit behind her.

"How did Knax heat you— no," She grumbled and tapped her temple. "He-he-hear. How did Knax hear you about a muse?" Nadín corrected herself.

With effort and drying tears, Maijerda explained to Nadín how the book was blank until she sang her lullaby and found the music box with Knax. Her story was uninterrupted, Nadín analyzing all aspects. She offered the truth and held nothing from her. Including the faetale.

Nadín read through it steadily, sitting on a cushion, spinning a rune stone in her fingers. She closed it and handed it back to Maijerda.

"Do you know what it means?" It's not what Maijerda wanted to ask, but it was what she could muster.

"A question that has more answers than I want you to know. No. I've never sung its story before. I think I understood—think I understand what she was trying to sing by it."

"Who?"

"Relona."

Maijerda scowled at the book. "Mother wrote this?" She couldn't hold back any longer. "Did you know her? She never mentioned you before but the way you speak of her. The way you say her name..."

What answer did she want? If the Fates granted her that privilege of choice, what would Maijerda have chosen? She didn't know. If that should happen, it'd be wiser to refuse striking a deal with the Fates. As much as she revered them, that would never lead to peace. If the faetales are to be trusted. Faetales rarely lie, after all.

"How close do you hold your trust? Should you trust me to show you the truth?"

Maijerda wanted to. She wanted to trust her. With Knax as her creation and the stars aligning on their meeting. What more did she need to answer?

"I'm finding trust is as liminal and fickle as fate and love. Please, show me."

Nadín levered herself with a cane to help stand, the layers of her high-low cut dress jacket flowing around the cane as she limped to a trunk. From it, she retrieved an orange and phantom-gray crystal cluster. She centered it in the fire pit and lowered herself to sit on the ground, anchoring on her left hip.

"Good. This spell crafts a little bit the same to what I knew with Relona."

Biting her tongue, Maijerda suppressed questions. Someone who knew Mother, but she'd never met. Maybe they were close just before she was born? Best to wait before bombarding Nadín with questions.

"When you arrive, place your attention close. Do you bear me?" Frustrated, she closed her eyes, lined in glossy black. "*Hear*. Do you hear me?"

"I do. I'm sorry. Nervous."

"We under— I understand. Close listen. I keen— I can seek it once. The spell. I've been waiting for this night to dusk. I hoped I wouldn't see it." Her agate eyes bore solemnity more fierce than grief.

Maijerda followed her cues, sitting cross legged and fidgeting with her necklace. Don't overthink this. Follow her lead.

Nadín cupped a handful of rune stones, shaking them and dropping them into the fire. Immediately, she drew glyphs in the ashes and gripped a log, flames be damned. Thin geometric tattoos on her fingers began to glow the crumbling of coal. The light traveled up her right hand to her wrist, consuming the tattoo banded around her forearm, rendering it to ash.

Maijerda flinched at the heat. The orange of the crystal intensified with the potency of the flames, reflecting majestically against Nadín's skin.

"What is it you want me to do?"

"It's a wonder. It's something I. Try. Follow. You need to follow." Nadín closed her eyes and placed her left hand soundly against the ground, leaning over her bent leg. The fullness of her spirals covered her face the lower she bowed.

Agonizingly few minutes ticked by.

She was supposed to… follow? Maijerda couldn't quite put her finger on that one. A demonic snap of Nadín's neck whipped Maijerda out of her confusion. "Shit!" She retracted from Nadín's glazed oval irises bathed in crystalline fire. "Nadín?"

Finer muscles along Nadín's fingers, wrists, and neck pulsated slowly and securely. It was as if they were locking into place, preparing to embark on a treacherous quest. Poised and undisturbed, her left arm was bent and fixed firmly.

The crystal at the center of the fire tempted Maijerda to risk a single fingertip's worth of touch, to which she complied. The begging must have been a ruse when all was said and done, for no change came to either the fire or Nadín's state.

The sigils etched in ash beamed skywards, welcoming her to inspect more inquisitively. Her gaze darted between them all, until her analysis slowed to appreciate each and every curve, angle, and knot in the design.

Their reflection in the crystal became clearer as Maijerda's vision adjusted to the bitterness of flame. Each quiver of fire lured her with the potential of trust.

"Help me understand," she said in hushed tones. Gasping, she went numb and fell through stardust, buckling under the shock.

Then she was alone. Wherever she was now, Nadín was nowhere to be seen. Solitude overwhelmed any morsel of Maijerda attempting to find reason. Whether it be lyrical or linear. Any reason would do.

Then came crackling coals. A scalding heat. Blinding and oppressive. Maijerda mutely argued against being swallowed by nothingness. She was robbed of the security which sense of physical and mental self brings.

Panic. So much panic. Writhing in her. Without self, she would be forced to rely on the mercy of the unknown. Nothing was as horrible as the unknown. What preparations could she conjure? Which was the correct way to turn? This place didn't speak of comforts.

The encompassing emptiness retaliated against her argument with shrouds of smoke, ripping through the nothingness. What little of her remained recoiled against the spiraling fever.

The need to understand the situational nothingness called out to her.

Madness. It offered. *That which lies beyond the stars.*

In madness there is understanding. There is clarity.

Though she heard no words in her mind, the message was evident. So convincing was its call. Curves and twists of smoke seduced her to break from shackles of control and organization. All in exchange for madness, the unknown, and unfiltered experience. Maijerda caved to madness, plunging her consciousness forward, and the smoke slowed. Grief was consuming, madness was a relief by comparison.

Actualizing this phenomena morphed the smoke from something observed to something experienced. Embodying a paradox, Maijerda relinquished control, allowing herself to meld. Shapes and curvatures became more than tangible, as they were now a part of her. In any way conceivable she wasn't processing the twists and turns of the smoke.

No longer an observer, she was a participant.

The sigils engrained in the ash. *That's* what surrounded her. These twists and forms were born from Nadín's coals. They were a guide of some sort. A pathway?

She followed and it guided her to surpass this limbo and transcend into a more levelheaded state. Here, Maijerda stumbled in her body. Not bound by structure, but swaddled in the intimacy of what she understood to be herself.

As if to bring tidings of well-being, tufts of fae arcana bobbed in the dim. It was different here, both in color and feel. The wisp floated along a path leading her to a silhouette of the most graceful woman.

Nadín looked upon the wisp of flame with gratitude. The wisp fluttered affectionately. Gentle as batting lashes, Nadín scooped the flame into a cupped palm. An undeniable flicker of embers spread throughout her skin. Her eyes refracted pleasantly as that of a content campfire. Nadín held the flame for Maijerda to take as a gift to bond them together. The wisp was neither cold nor hot, but ethereal and soft. Maijerda risked believing this was as close as she would ever be to holding starlight. Nadín raised her hand to Maijerda's cheek; tears forsook brusqueness as she placed a single kiss on her bowed forehead. Maijerda tightened her eyes shut to better savor the tender obscurity. Never wanting to forget.

NADÍN SHOULD'VE BEEN near when Maijerda opened her eyes. After all, her touch was enveloping and seconds passing tended to mean very little. In theory she was near.

A window overlooking a blackened stone city harbored a reflection which was not of Maijerda's likeness, but of Nadín. Maijerda wanted to pull away from the window. Instead she was bound to Nadín's image, taking the flame still cupped in her hand and placing it in a bowl on a table dressed with a bounty of food and drink.

"Praise fortune! Bleed victory!" Nadín raised her goblet, guiding the sensation of Maijerda's trapped limbs with her and toasted the two women sitting at the table.

"Yes," said the one with black and green hair fixed into an intricate bun. "Celebrate while you can, there's still work to be done."

"Volkari, you'll never rest, will you?"

"An empress never rests."

"My mistake, Mistress." Nadín gibed, sipping her wine. "Is Relona joining us from the front lines?"

Relona?

Instantly Maijerda strove to tear herself free of Nadín's consciousness. Whether to flee or to find the person they spoke of that surely couldn't be her mother, she couldn't decide.

Another woman, with eyes like the tide and a silvery teal braid, set down her wine and gave Nadín a look of annoyance. "In her own time would be my guess. You know how she is."

"And how is that exactly?" Maijerda's stomach gripped into submissive shock. A voice she hadn't heard in six years. A voice she'd written off to never hear again. It couldn't be.

The double doors swung wide as Relona pushed through them. She set a helmet on the table, luscious brown waves pinned to one side.

Mama? Maijerda wanted to cry out to her. To run to her embrace and beg of Relona to explain where they were and to never leave her again. Her desires to act upon this were smothered by Nadín's presence. She was a guest here. Trapped as Maijerda was, she felt more a prisoner, stripped of autonomy.

Relona removed a double-bladed scimitar with a black hilt and purple sheen from her back and placed it too on the table. Mother hadn't wielded such a striking weapon. Nor was she ever fully adorned in metal armor. Who was this woman?

"Did I miss anything important?" Relona made for Volkari, cupping her cheek and kissing her forehead.

"Welcome home," Volkari started. "We've just begun celebrating."

"Wonderful." Relona took a seat next to Nadín, lounging as she disseminated her insights from beyond this fortress. She spoke with ease, evidently having done so countless times before. Was she a woman of war? This wasn't the Relona Maijerda knew. A part of her was curious and the other was terrified to learn more.

"I've left the Straghis to interrogate the Ishnul squads' Lieutenant. Bastard thinks she can outsmart us. Pathetic to assume we hadn't planned on their ambush. Beaten, bruised, and wallowing, I'm sure she'll cave soon." Proudly, she plucked a grape to eat. "Several shadow demons approached me at camp, asking to join our ranks. Among others. A devil or two."

Surely Maijerda was hallucinating. Demons? Devils? So casual a mention without so much as a flinch.

Volkari gleamed. "Welcome them to our empire. An opportunity I'd be ashamed to miss. They will be useful to us."

"Thought that might be the case." Relona took several gulps of wine, savoring the luxury. "I hope you don't mind I extended the invitation. They'll be here in four days."

"And what of the nezdrade? When will your kin arrive, Lyrian Llach?"

The woman with sea-pale skin answered. "Within the week. All are eager for our alliance."

Relona crossed her legs and raised her goblet in cheers. "What an honor it will be to have the elements on our side."

Lyrian lifted her drink in kind. "The honor is ours. To ally with such a ruthless empress." She looked to Volkari.

Nadín stood with exultant energy, combating the grimness of Maijerda's view of the scene. "To Mistress Volkari! Long may she reign."

Together, Nadín, Relona, and Lyrian saluted Volkari. Their cheers crescendoed to an unbearable pitch until the scene vanished from sight.

No! Maijerda wanted to scratch and claw in the dark for the image. Bring it back. Bring her back! She needed to bring mama back. To save her from whatever this was!

Relona's worry echoed in the dark, stopping Maijerda's panic. "Nadín. Nadín!"

"You're home? I thought you'd be gone a few more days. What is it?" Nadín's fingers danced, signing to conjure a ball of flame.

She was here. Maijerda battled Nadín's form to relax herself. But she was denied the ability to self-soothe as Relona sank into the bed next to her. "We lost the siege." If only she could touch mama's hand and show her she was here too.

"What? How? What's wrong? You look horrid."

Quivering, Relona gripped Nadín's shoulder. "Please believe me."

Oh Mama, please, tell me what happened!

"Anything," Nadín replied without Maijerda's prompt.

Relona's voice was barely a whisper. "Arcana is dying."

"Have you been drinking? You're talking nonsense."

"Am I?"

"Never has it weakened. Arcana isn't capable of death."

"No, you don't understand. In battle, I felt my threads to the tapestry wane. Frayed as I've never seen them. I was countered by my own spell. The earth tastes different. The water sings a dying tune. I don't know what to make of it."

Nadín shifted closer to take her hand. "I'll listen. Torlen dovnym."

"Torlen lexnym."

"Tell me. What happened."

Relona did, explaining how arcana failed her in a catastrophically pivotal moment. Her senses were muddled, crossing into one another and throwing her concentration and connection to the realm off balance. It unsettled Relona to the point of losing sleep. Since the battle, she worried interruptions in her weaving were from disassociation with her threads. A change she'd never thought possible.

"Don't lie to me. You've felt it too. I've suspected an ominous shift. Now I've never been more certain."

Nadín rested her hand on Relona's but it didn't satisfy. Maijerda longed to hold more tightly, but was unable, stretching and straining to fight her confinement.

"There might be someone we can speak to."

"The three who granted you unspun threads?" Relona, concerned, pulled back.

"Yes. I don't know why you fear them."

"I don't trust them. Far different than fear. You said it yourself, they are not of this world."

"You misunderstand. They are of this world, they are also spread too far and wide to have a true hold and purpose here. You and I, Volkari, Lyrian. We all practice the here and now and they see the world differently. Three parts of a whole."

"What else is there? We would wallow in the past or doubt the future if we did not prioritize the present."

"There is something to be learned in each. Without what was, what is, and what will be, we refuse change. And without change, we cannot better ourselves. Even you can't argue that."

"I'd like nothing more than to believe you." Relona left Nadín's bed and paced the room. "Can you take me to them?"

"On my word."

Nadín crossed her arm over her chest, saluting. Relona accepted it with a return gesture and left Nadín in bed, closing the door behind her.

The flame Nadín conjured singed the air as she dismissed it, ending this memory and leaving Maijerda helpless to react in full. Her being ignited with frustration at being denied the decency of actions.

Signaling a new memory, murky stone, splotched like a painting around them, echoed with Relona's brash comments. "You're jumping to conclusions. You heard them just as well as I. Representations of arcana must be offered. We can't complete the ritual and create a new spindle without them. It's as simple as that."

"Lyrian will never agree to it."

"Nezdrade are pompous, thinking themselves omnipresent. It's no secret her elemental prowess is unmatched. We'll appeal to her ego to sway her. If she doesn't agree, we may have no choice than to force her hand. I know your history with her—"

"Those days are dead to me." Nadín retorted as she stormed to Relona, cutting her off and leaning closer. Her eyes were glossy, cheeks flushed. Even Maijerda couldn't escape the flooding reminders of Nadín's past, unaware of the details, but in tune with her emotions.

Unmoved by Nadín's ire, Relona's dourness was accusatory. "You still care for her. Don't think I can't smell the memories around you."

"Care is a precarious and strong choice of words." Chin high, Nadín bared her teeth in attempts to keep her tone even.

"Lyrian never forgave you."

"I'm well acquainted with the sacrifices I made to protect myself and not relinquish my agency for power."

Relona held her hands wide, indicating she was through pushing. "Understood."

After a breath, Nadín said, "I'll speak with her."

"Thank you. I'd be lost without you."

"I know." Nadín saluted and left Relona to be absorbed by the dark as this discussion ended.

Maijerda fretted for a brief moment, trapped in pitch without say or the freedom of fulfilling the urge to scream. Wanting to be recognized and to free herself so she may move in this world unknown to her. What was left to witness? She opened her eyes… Nadín's eyes, she reminded herself.

A table, littered with maps and battle figurines poised with a plan of action for war. The mere idea of this scale of war was unnerving. Maijerda would've startled at the clatter of chainmail rattling from the entrance of the tent. But as her host, Nadín was unbothered. Slender and lithe, an ıdre solider with obsidian-black eyes saluted at attention for Nadín to address them.

"Speak lieutenant, what news of the Straghis?"

They hesitated. "Our scouts discovered the nezdrade heading the company. With a second, unforeseen alliance. A faction within the rebellion has sided with Lyrian." Their face drained of color sprouted from running to the tent in the first place. "Additionally their course hasn't altered. Leaving us till dawn before they arrive. Our options were already few. Come morning, they'll be fewer."

"I imagine so. You may go. Tend to your soldiers. To die with resentment is to be denied peace." Accepting defeat didn't seem characteristic of Nadín. Her lieutenant dismissed themself stiffly before exiting.

Tightly strapped leather armor cinched around Maijerda when Nadín sat. She pressed at her temples before slamming her fist against the table. A foreign flame of agitation flickered within what existed of Maijerda. "I knew it would come to this."

"Nadín." Relona ducked inside the tent. "It's imperative we speak."

Maijerda imagined shoving the table to run to Relona, instead pinned to Nadín's station. "We have and I've made my thoughts on the matter plain. I will not bore you with it further. I stand by what I said. You've forsaken loyalty for the secrets beyond the stars."

Relona removed her scimitar from her back to rest on the maps. "You? Boring? That's never been the case, has it?" Relona's molten hair was woven in a braid, her armor polished. Such a juxtaposition from the mother Maijerda knew. "Do you find the fault to stem from me?"

"Where is that coming from?" Nadín, offended by the question, sputtered. "Relona, I— You aren't responsible for bringing this trial to our doorstep. You're not the reason arcana is dying. As our General, don't bring strife upon yourself with a rumor which doesn't need spreading."

"Though I am the reason we're wanted for treason. In case you forgot."

Treason? Maijerda flinched at not having been shown this misstep. She assumed they betrayed Volkari and started this war. Why wouldn't she want to save arcana?

"And such is the evolution of our story. There is no helping the turning of fate."

Dismissing the implied weight of fate, Relona scrunched her expression.

"You know the truth more than I'd care to admit. Always have. If I didn't agree, I wouldn't have taken you to them."

"They're our sole chance at saving arcana. As you've said." Relona, taking in Nadín's countenance, reconciled with herself. "You've never faltered from me."

A nagging in Maijerda's instinct told her who they spoke of. All the clues were there in their mentions of the three and their ties to fate. How was it possible to speak with the Norn?

Ignoring Maijerda's internal debate, Nadín said, "Nor will I. We'll do what it takes, no matter the cost."

An explosion outside the tent sent Nadín and Relona rushing with urgent calm for their weapons as the scene came to a close.

A shock of green relieved Maijerda from questioning where she was taken next. Volkari was seething on a violently windy rooftop amid a sky blackened by smoke. Red lightning scorched the clouds. She was on the brink of unleashing a volcanic fury to match this unnatural storm. It was unlike any Maijerda had ever navigated on sea. "What would you demand now, Relona?"

"For this to end! Your ignorance is bringing our world closer to death because you won't heed me." Even over the unhindered power of the wind's voice, Relona's allegations held against the grains of the storm.

Volkari sneered. "Hah! You consider yourself an oracle? And you believe her?" She spat her hatred to Nadín standing firm beside Mother. "I will not make exceptions for your lies. You threaten my claim to the throne out of jealousy! Who are you to act as a god and alter arcana? Last I knew, that power was not bestowed upon you."

Relona's tried patience was evident over the growling wind. "Arcana is dying, and if we do not take action to mend it we will lose our place in this world. You will lose your throne. Your arcana. Destruction will befall us. The tapestry will unravel and all we know will be destroyed."

"You're lying!" Roaring, Volkari lashed out with bolts of green manifesting her frustrations, weaving and crackling around her skin.

Relona unsheathed her scimitar. "Volkari, this spindle is spent. With the Veil in place, arcana will be restored. We can continue our reign, tear down those who oppose us. We will be made all the stronger." Sinking into a defensive stance, she paused midway and tossed her scimitar, rattling on the ground.

Maijerda's stomach lurched as Volkari countered to ready a spell.

Mama, run! She was restrained from warning, forced as a damn spectator.

"This Veil you speak so fondly of will oppress. Voices will be swallowed whole. Cultures eradicated from memory. A history lost. Our people will burn. An apocalypse will transpire. Is that what you want?"

Nadín stepped forward. "All that remains is for us to complete the ritual. You still have the free will of making a choice. Join us and offer your threads of the tapestry. Or don't."

"Volkari," Relona implored, her eyes bruised with exhaustion. "Sister. Please listen to reason."

Sister? Volkari couldn't be Relona's blood. Mother never mentioned family, not a word. She'd lied? She'd abandoned all mention of kin.

"I'd die before I let you sacrifice what is rightfully mine."
Volkari growled and threw a spell at Relona.

She and Nadín rolled out of harm's way. What came next was
a mess of devastation too difficult to discern. Flashes and bursts
of arcana, blades, and stone crumbling into rubble. A myriad
of war cries and pained hollers came from all three women.
Maijerda feared for Relona's safety, falling for a trap within
Nadín's memory as she was jostled from moment to moment.

The din came to a screeching halt, replaced with flame
unnaturally the color of blackened purple. Nadín knelt on the
roof panting as Volkari roared in the flames, begging Relona
for mercy.

Maijerda's breath was quick and thin, but within Nadín's
form, she was made steady. As Relona wept, she showed no signs
of remorse as her sister burned.

The rooftop swirled out of view. Where was she being forced
to now?

Atop a mountain? Beside the sea? In a pit of ruins?

Where Maijerda was brought to next with Nadín's memory
was frustratingly unclear. It had an air of being tampered with,
wanting to be forgotten or for a hurt wanting to be lessened.

A vortex of tapestry, whirring, thriving, and pulling in every
which way was encompassing Relona, Nadín, and Lyrian in
a center of stillness. Bound to a pyre, Lyrian cursed them for
betraying her. For tricking and capturing her after she refused
them and for making her their prisoner. Ragged and sickly pale,
Lyrian appeared on the verge of death compared to her health
during their celebration.

"You selfish bitch!" Lyrian screamed before spitting on
Relona. Straining, she tried to free herself with force she didn't
have left in her frail body.

Relona, without so much as a second thought, punched
Lyrian. Dark blue blood splattered Lyrian's leather corset and

added to the stains already there from the bleeding runes carved into her body. Maijerda's sensation of her tongue was swollen and watering with nausea. How long had it taken to etch them in her skin? How carefully did Mother cut? No reprieve could protect her from truth. Lyrian had suffered torture by Relona's hand.

"I'm completing this ritual to save *us*. Our home! If arcana dies, we will face calamity! You're the one letting selfishness color your decisions."

Coming between the two, Nadín faced Lyrian. Blood seeped in the cracks of Lyrian's dry and flaking skin. Nadín set her expression to speak, her endeavor severed by Lyrian.

"I won't beg. I won't bargain. I will not kneel to you."

"No one asked you to pledge fealty. We asked for your help. You still have a chance. To offer your tapestry threads willingly and save arcana."

"Bleed. Me. Dry."

The rumbling storm of arcana breached their stillness, growing more wild. Lyrian convulsed and threw her head back compulsively, screaming.

"We have to keep moving." Relona grabbed Nadín's arm.

A pulse of energy boomed around Lyrian and into Nadín. Relona staggered and caught her. "Go! I can handle this."

Nadín sprinted from Relona and on the last second, turned to see her extending her hand, dripping with blood and signing to weave. She targeted her spell at Lyrian's feet. Heatless purple flames ignited a glyph on the ground, made of four...? No, it was five symbols. Maijerda racked her mind to recognize them but it was all moving too swiftly. The flames then wrapped around and in Lyrian, constricting her until her voice screeched to silence.

Relona left Lyrian to burn, stumbling in the gale of arcana encompassing them. She took Nadín by the arm, cupped her cheek and...

Moments came in unfinished, scrambled fragments.

Relona spoke in devotion, "That which is fleeting."

Nadín pledged in turn. "To which we are raveling."

Then nothing, save the chaotic weave of tapestry and a sudden break to reveal Nadín swaying and clutching her head. Her right hand refused to move. Lips drew flat and then dipped into a melancholy frown constrained to the right. Nadín's eyes fluttered and she was reduced to little more than an unconscious heap.

Three voices merged and cackled with thunder from the arcane storm with an otherworldly force. The vision was eradicated. And with it, all moments left of the ritual for Maijerda to see for herself.

What remained were whispers on the edge of Maijerda's cognizance. She must hold to keep from being stripped from this dark. She needed to see for herself what befell them.

And then arose in succession…

A flash of orange.

Regret.

A shimmer of amethyst.

Temptation.

A glare of jade.

Potential.

Each color was accompanied by these notions. Maijerda whirled with Nadín's consciousness, musing over their hues brilliant as the Moon's guardians. Time became a roaring sensation, passing in an incomprehensible thrum. Unknown years. Ten, fifty, a hundred? More? Less? Its passing abruptly halted to three voices crooning an ethereal tune.

"We did not abuse knowledge." "We…" "We…"

"We…" "We did not misinterpret intent." "We…"

"We…" "We…" "We did not assume hubris."

"Do not blame us." "Do not blame us." "Do not blame us."

Maijerda's nausea returned and uninvited fear seeped into her.

"We followed your instructions," Relona argued. Her hair was slicked back, she wore no armor. Trading it for leathers and a lavender blouse, softened by no longer knowing war. "You tricked us! You said nothing of calamity."

Nadín, respectful with her warning, implored her. "Don't test the songs we don't sing ourselves. You think you can, I never saw the melody as that. It's argue— it's not worth it. No— it's not worth arguing Rey...rey...Relona." She leaned on a cane with her left hand, her right cradled close to her abdomen. The right side of her face, slightly slack and soft. She wrangled her words together as best she could, Maijerda privy to her frustration. "Some things are not the little bit the same."

"Please, we'd love to know..."

"...How it is you think we tricked you..."

"Was our guidance not explicit?"

"Representation of each spool of the tapestry..."

"...to be sacrificed in order to replenish the Spent Spindle."

"Your carelessness is not an axe upon our head."

"It is not our fault destruction rained upon this world. Though perhaps it was deserved. Such evil you harbored here."

"You will understand, one lone Eventide night."

"The ritual did fail."

"It has failed."

"It will fail."

Mother needed spell components to represent types of arcana? Spools, they said. How strange to describe the tapestry as such.

"If the Veil is weak…" Relona struggled for more to say. "How am I to know?" She gazed at Nadín, a tear falling to her dusky peach lips. Guilt quivered on her tongue, a side of Mother Maijerda was uncomfortable seeing. Mother wasn't the vulnerable type, not until she started growing ill. "How long will the Veil hold? Will we face another calamity when it dies?"

The three pondered this request. Reduced to voices, it was not evident if their images were present before the two women and had been erased from this vision or if they were filling the entirety of the space with their omnipresence. Their answer swayed and merged with one another, echoing with ghostly fervor.

"Given the scale of your sacrifices
made on that dreadful day…"

"…we will grant you this answer."

Determined pride dissolved, bringing Relona to her knees. "Torlen lexnym."

"When weaver's nectar bleeds her last."
"A blood-sown tune of dread repast."
"No longer hewn from gilded wick…"
"…nightsweet cut to harrowed quick."
"Forsaken to wither away and rot…"
"…all your loss will be for naught."

Relona scowled at the ground. "Weaver's nectar doesn't exist in this world, it didn't survive the Veil. The last of its kind couldn't possibly herald the Veil's demise."

"I so miss that bloom."

"Believe us."

"Or don't."

"The choice

is a thread in your needle to weave."

This too warped, bringing the vision to an undeterminable somewhere. Remarkably quiet for the tension here. Relona's frame had thinned, her eyes worried and glassy. How contradictory it was for Maijerda's instinct to want to console her after the wicked nature she'd seen but moments prior.

"Enough. He's had—you've had enough of this." Nadín shook her head as she corrected her speech. "Reading and writing and whiling the toll isn't helping."

Scoffing, Relona motioned to her stack of books and papers. "I have to understand what we did wrong. Why we failed! That riddle they so graciously gave means nothing. There's no mention of weaver's nectar. It has not been reborn. I don't know what we— what I did wrong."

Nadín held Relona's hand. Fates…

If she focused on nothing else, Maijerda could feel her mother's warmth. Probably for the last time. But it was a more welcome parting memory than the rigor of her grasp before they burned Mother's body. As fed up as she was with tears, Maijerda would've sacrificed everything to cry.

"We did a darkness that cannot be under—undone. We were a failed story. Take that in your heart. In your mind." She tapped the side of her temple. "If you don't, you cannot walk on. We have to keep forward and think on what we did."

"I can't." Disheartened and disheveled, Relona cried and buried her head in her hands. "Nadín, I can't move forward without understanding. It grates on my nerves. It weighs on my heart. Everything I touch, see, hear, feel—hells, even smell overwhelms me by the day. I can't think clearly, I can sense everything all at once and yet nothing at times. It is wearing on me. If I can't figure out how to cope with that… I need to understand where we went wrong."

"What we went wrong?" Nadín broke her eye contact with Relona and took a deeply woeful and stiff breath. "Where we went wrong was sacrificing our friend." Each word was focused, practiced even, with dire concentration. "It was not worth killing Lyrian. I'm sorry. I can't stay with you. I need to leave and find a song, different than this."

"You're leaving?" Relona stood, as if Nadín was leaping to her feet to barge out of the room. "No! Please, don't leave me. After all we've been through? All we've done?"

"Yes." She would not be swayed, her presentation was sorrowful and steadfast as a prow. Maijerda was aware of Nadín's resolution in her decision, down to the core. "I need... I don't think on it. I don't think knots—" Frustrated, she curled her hand to a fist. "I didn't know the way—" She shook her head. "No! The words, they—" she clawed her hand at her temple. "Twisted and running, run away from me." Soothing herself with an inhale, Nadín pinched the bridge of her nose. "I long to sleep of this. Maybe there will be a story I can hear again with you. Now? I can't."

Staring at each other, their repose was anything but peaceful. Their silhouettes faded into nothingness as Nadín turned her back on Relona.

Nadín left Maijerda, no longer bonded in her body but left with another host. Traces of her flitted in Maijerda's consciousness, rigidity of stone set every inch of her into place. A heaviness in her limbs, laden as stone. Sight evaded her. Mortal remnants clinging to her wanted to spit away the burn and smolder filling her mouth. This too remained an imagined desire. Before long the etching ceased and with it came relief.

And breath. Life. Sight.

Nadín stood in front of her unquestionably worn. Though undeniably proud.

"Peace." Nadín held her hands to offer tranquility and blessings. "That's all I bring for you. Though truth is odd."

Maijerda and her host were forced to bow to wordlessness.

"I don't mean to leer, to lie to you, that's not fair. Forgive me?" Her request was punctuated by a beseeching shrug. "What do you think of forgiveness? I labored dreamless nights to ensure you could know this. In all my years and waning Moons, it is not what I think it will be when I see it. Don't fear. You'll have your form when the spell weaves a final strand."

An hourglass ticking grains of sapphire winking out of existence was beside her.

"I need your help. To watch for weeping things. To keep for the eyes on a story unsung. I've given you threads I could find of mine. The twisting and turning fate of all things. Not much was in my hands. But they are yours." Nadín placed a hand on the stone. "Knax, protect them. For me."

Without ceremony, Maijerda was thrown. Not against a wall nor the ground. Through layers of realms, realities, and stories. Away from this vision and back into that which Maijerda claimed as her present.

Groaning, she crawled away from Nadín's fire in the tent, fully in charge of her actions and speech.

Knax was grasping the screeching sunset crystal, cracking and dying from the infestation of scorching frost. Nadín's form unnervingly relaxed and collapsed, smoke curling from her body. The crystals and surrounding flames flared in defense, screaming in terror.

Maijerda clamped her hands over her ears, unable to maneuver the relief and confusion at Knax standing there. "Wait! What happened?" Grogginess stole the severity and perplexed edge from Maijerda's cry and weakened her fumbling footholds.

Knax didn't break his devotion to his incantation. The atmosphere quivered. Cracks crept along his forearms. The crystals combusted as she reached for him, suffocating the flames as she shielded her eyes and the tent burst with light and smoke.

CHAPTER THIRTY

A NAME ONCE LOST

RIPPING ROTTEN FLESH AND SHATTERING MALLEABLE bone, a shackle of vine emerged below the seer's collarbone.

Lyrian smirked and cackled deeply as a rolling wave. "Every effort you make to battle destiny will destroy your body further."

The seer's hurdling vexation and wills for revenge were grinding. When would Volkari have enough of this whimpering fool? Then again, the irony of it was entertaining.

"She's quite right." Volkari dabbed at a splotch of rotting blood on her chin. "Let be your stoicism. It will never be formidable."

"No!" The word was drawn, rife with... Oh, what was that? Ah... despair.

"You seem to be forgetting an imperative detail." As Volkari paused her chiding, she wove a spectral claw, strands of smoke winding around her to form glove-like over her burn scarred fingers.

With a push of her hand, the apparition thrust to the seer's throat, squeezing and puncturing.

"You forget I raised you from purgatory with the very thistle that poisoned you. You are not your own person. If that that were true, your body would be imprisoned and rotting in a rift between life and death. You are mine. You will serve me without defiance."

She wasn't wrong for once. Volkari had resurrected the creature, bringing her back from a fate worse than death. A limbo in purgatory. She used the etheric thistle to do so, binding her with the conduit responsible for the seer's demise.

The seer writhed against the claw. Would foresight into this torture have provided her solace? Would she have chosen death? Lyrian wet her lips and rubbed her hands together, not wanting for warmth.

A brackish collection of spores and disease seeped and infected the parts of the seer which relied on soil and blood to flourish.

"Aaaagh!" The seer sweated droplets of musky maroon, her eyes clenched shut.

Lyrian stepped closer, her heart beating to witness the last of the seer's pleas as Volkari sniggered and tightened around her neck.

Sharpened teeth gritted, the seer hissed. "Nadín."

Lyrian's grin withered and pinched with contempt long since buried at hearing a name once lost to her. "Do not speak that name."

"She survived. Here in this world. Though not unspoiled."

Lightning snapped through Lyrian, a tempest roiling in her belly. That traitorous martyr was still *alive*? Impossible! Nadín fell when they forced the Veil to smother their world. There'd not been a single trace of Nadín since she betrayed Lyrian and used her as though she was nothing but a spell component.

Neck rigid, she kept her chin angled from the seer. "You would lie to me to spare your miserable existence?"

"I am denied the freedom of lies. Foreseeable truth rots and binds my roots."

Lyrian forced a breath to relax her shoulders. All these years and Nadín chose to stroke her ego with selfishness of silence to atone for her treason.

An unfamiliar burn rimmed Lyrian's narrowed eyes. "Where is she?"

"Wings of fire, a shackled relief. Plucked as a lyre, never to tire." The seer strained and serpentined her neck to and fro with the lull of her sing-song message, sending vines slithering in all directions.

Wings of fire? That couldn't be. She'd neglected that potential, chosen the threads of fate. "Where have these wings taken her? Who else knows she's alive?"

"Words have forsaken her. It is with Maijerda that she confides her story. And yours."

Lyrian bared her teeth, nostrils flaring at the indignity of it all. "She has *no* right to—"

"Your tale entwines with hers. Inseparable until burned to ash. Does she not have claim to share as you do to harbor?"

Nadín lost the right to any notion of her when she cowered to fear and discarded her. Lyrian closed her eyes, calling upon the tapestry to center her with the tide. It was high at this time of night. High enough to guide her. "Has the book been inspired to share its own tale?"

"In full." Rotten branches ebbed and flowered from her.

Black strands of hair obscured Volkari's paling face as she thrust her hand again to threaten the seer. The skin at her lips and throat started to peel and decay to signal she was stretching her tapestry thin. "Why didn't you speak of this sooner?"

"I am bound by constraints of constance. I consume and impart knowledge, not manipulate the fabrics which birth it."

Lyrian rested a hand on Volkari's, lowering it. "We shouldn't sit idle. Let *me* handle Maijerda. And Nadín."

"No. I need you here." Volkari stared ahead, maintaining her regal refusal. "My answer remains."

Lyrian curled her fingers into a sign to maintain her bond to the tide. She was being pushed to rise with it. To consume. To crush. To control.

Would Volkari ever heed reason? Would she prove herself worthy of a second reign? Grinding disagreement to sand, Lyrian forced a submissive head bow. "Yes, Mistress."

"With the Veil torn, I will leave this place, claim my throne. Regain my arcana."

Bloody eyes congealing, the seer's mouth hung agape. "You equate yourself to being buried in an untimely grave. The surface worries you. You're rooted here prisoner. Just as I am."

Volkari unleashed a second wave of pestilence ravaging her, vine and thistle. And she paid dearly for it. Volkari's physical hand withered and cracked. Using arcana without proper bonds was costly. She tried to hide the pain and sadness. Pity Lyrian could see straight through her guise. Having endured it herself.

Lyrian withheld a satisfied sneer. Volkari would never admit her weaknesses. It would be her downfall. Again. At least she was humble to Othesk, pleading for aid when arcana was thin.

"I will leave when I damn well please."

The seer chuckled a strangled and throaty simper. "Despite my resentment for the malediction you have reduced me to, you have gifted me this shrine of a prison. I will not be made a fool. Not in my domain."

Volkari's wraith-like claw dissipated. "It is yours because I allow it."

"Enough." Lyrian's voice boomed with thunder. Petty squabbles, riddles too? She was forced to abandon berating them when a stabbing, icicle pain frosted from behind her eyes to her ear.

Cursing, she clawed her hand in her hair and pressed to subdue the pain. It did not obey her, flaring and tearing into her hearing to take what awareness she had of the seer's ragged breaths and Volkari's wrath, twisting it to shrillness. Denratis spoke to her in her mind, the scratching of pen on parchment backing his words. This was the second message he'd sent with the bottle she'd given him.

This damn well better not be a waste of a spell. He was worthless as a weaver, not appreciating the opportunity to communicate across distance with the Veil in place.

"I've found them. In D'hadian. Near the university. I will wait for you." Denratis relayed via the message in a bottle.

So it was true? The mirage of D'hadian Jeddeith let slip during his time in her air dream had shown the truth. A pleasant surprise. Which meant there was work to be done. She'd not let Volkari abuse her and drain her here on Gazdeq. Jeddeith was near her grasp. So near being hers to sacrifice for their cause and save herself from expending her threads.

"They're in D'hadian."

"Your errand boy actually tracked them down?" Volkari doubted this, eyeing Lyrian over the tip of her nose.

"Yes." Lyrian hissed. "We must strike, and Maijerda must die. Without the book, we can't interpret Relona's ritual."

Demanding her subservience, Volkari forbade her. "You're needed here, at my side."

"As you command, Mistress." Leaving Volkari believing she'd made her point, Lyrian exited the tombs with a flourish. The sea called to her.

IT WAS FAR past needing to commune with the ocean. If Lyrian was to make haste to D'hadian, she would need boons to aid her arcana. Othesk was an expectant deity. Without the luxury of Lyrian's temple to host rituals, prayers, and sacrifices, she had resigned to doing her best in using nature itself to resume her responsibilities as high priestess.

Tread carefully and she might earn the favor of stronger arcane bonds, seeing as how she wasn't melded with the tapestry as she was before the Veil. Unlike Volkari, she could admit her needs and knew how to seek favor.

Lyrian waded in synchrony with the sea until it lapped at her waist. The waves humbled themselves in her presence, Gazdeq resting in her wake. Come dawn, this island would be further behind. Volkari's carelessness would inevitably best them.

Volkari placed surreptitious trust in that spiteful soothsayer. Yet when she proved useful? She'd ignore the opportunity to advance. Predictably, Volkari's need for assurance would impede her focus from the true task at hand. Responsibility never failed to fall on Lyrian.

If the water was chill to the touch, Lyrian didn't take notice. Why would she? There was no need for her body to warn and defend against what was hers.

In her hand, she held a bundle of sea moss. It was plump and dull gray, drained of life. She released the moss to float, congealed from secretions of brine. The water parted as she wove a pattern through and around the moss, sending it shifting on the surface.

There was a meticulous subtlety to which she moved. The moss agreed to hold fast in the center, hanging onto Lyrian's every cresting word. The moss glowed a sea glass blue with pin pricks of green. She tore the bundle into several pieces, assigning each a purpose. There was a balance to this act. Greed would appear selfish. Asking for too little connotated the possibility that Lyrian didn't actually need her patron's assistance.

It toyed dangerously close to the idea that she didn't possess true faith, but rather was confiding in exchange for potentiality. Intending to abuse their grace of free will and fury of harm.

Lyrian extended a closed fist above the moss. The ocean lay still and silence engulfed her.

The Moon waited. This was what it meant to be a true leader.

Opening her fist sent each gathering of moss in five different directions, off to find Othesk and deliver her requests.

Prudence.

Fortune.

Expediency.

Victory.

Fury.

INTERLUDE:
DOUBLE-EDGED SWORD

There are two sides
to every coin.

A double-edged sword
as they say, when deciding who to be
partial toward
in a disagreement.

We have our own opinions
on the matter.

That is beside the point.

If anything, our duty is
not to sway you one way…

…or another.

It is to encourage you to
tap into your agency…

…and choose for yourself.

To hear someone's
story is…

…entirely different
from true experience.

Not many have earned
the opportunity.

How does your experience
dictate heroism or villainy?

Good?

Evil?

Two intimately complex…

…and precarious concepts…

…narrowed to insultingly
simplistic semantics.

What a shame.

The mind tends to favor
simplicity, doesn't it?
Out of the need for connection
and comprehension.

Or out of fear
of the unknown.

Existence is not *all*
ignorance and terror.

If it were, we would
not care for it the same.

There are no worlds
which exist where you can
escape such influences.

Though that is likely
for the best.

Without flawed
unconventionality
opportunity for growth
would be lacking.

Such a linear existence
would be rather
dull indeed.

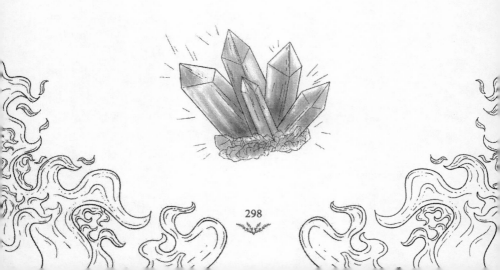

CHAPTER THIRTY-ONE

TOFFEE & POMEGRANATES

WHEN MAIJERDA RECOVERED FROM THE EXPLOSION of light, Knax was nowhere to be seen. Those who came to aid in the carnival moved swiftly, bringing a cart to carry Nadín's limp form to the Sanctuary. Maijerda and Wytt sat in the back with Nadín, unconscious and horrifically still. Guards gaped at her body lying in the cart, leaping backward as Jeddeith drove through the gates of the university grounds. There was no time to spare. No one was going to die. Not today.

"Tuvon's breath. It's getting worse." Wytt pulled up Nadín's sleeve, assessing the molten cracks strangling her forearms, rapidly spreading to her collar bone.

"Are you looking for the hospital? The Sanctuary?" A woman with hair spun pure as gold, hollered to Maijerda. She was jogging to keep pace with the cart.

"Jeddeith wait, stop!" The cart skidded and Maijerda gripped the edge. "There was an accident—"

She nodded to show Maijerda needn't say anymore and rearranged the books in the crook of her arm. "Go toward Etchings. It's faster than battling Brittlewick."

She took the lead in guiding them through the ever parting late evening crowd until they collided at the stately doors of the Pearl's Sanctuary.

Several clerics and university students rushed to bring Nadín inside. Maijerda and Jeddeith jumped from the cart to help, but were ushered aside by the physicians while Wytt was speaking with a cleric poised at the doors in his natural tone of astute professionalism. Maijerda was met with an impossible to dodge barrage of questions. They were fraught with the best of intention, even the best didn't eradicate the exhaustive process.

With the exception of two, maybe three students in their early years of study, the clerics put on a well masked calm, respecting her boundaries. Maijerda drained herself dry of every detail which could be safely shared. It was an emotional blood-letting. She didn't divulge to them what she saw or learned. It was at this part of the story that she diverted, stating the ritual was never completed. They appeared to accept her story as unfiltered truth, satisfied with notes ruminating with scribbled hypotheses.

Maijerda couldn't bring herself to let go of Nadín's hand. A student assured her all would be well, but it took Wytt to guide her hand away from Nadín so they could whisk her away.

Maijerda swayed, knees locking, as Jeddeith anchored his arm behind her.

The woman with golden hair helped him steady Maijerda. "Your friend, she'll pull through I should think." Her sand-soft glow was rosy from adrenaline.

"I want to stay. Can we? Will they let us be with her?" She was stiffly frantic.

What would become of her? Why did Knax intervene? Where in the hells was he now? There were too many unresolved questions and it made her dizzy.

The woman frowned. "I'm afraid not. No visitors are allowed until patients are stable. It's less risky."

"Maybe I could help. Maybe there's something I'm forgetting."

"Are you a healer?"

"Well, no. But Wytt is—"

"Physician? Surgeon?"

She hesitated, suddenly aware of Jeddeith still holding her. It was good too, otherwise she would be on the floor.

"Maijerda, let them work. We got her here quickly. They'll know what to do."

The woman looked Maijerda confidently in the eye. "She's in good, well studied hands."

Maijerda was unsure of the woman's waiting, empathetic stare and appeased her with a short nod and sigh of apparent understanding. She let them steer her out of the Sanctuary.

"Have you secured a place to stay in the city?" Her accent daintily toppled the last few words into a tight snippet as they stepped onto the streets.

"We've been staying at the Nick," Wytt replied.

Jeddeith picked up where he left off, "But we could use somewhere off the beaten path."

"I have a suggestion, if you need." She gave a humble raise of her shoulders. "Come, we'll walk this way by the river. The Wyldvern is a calming creature, it might ease your nerves to see the water."

She led them toward the river and tried to distract Maijerda by narrating facets of the timelessly unpredictable Perle de Lumme. Multitudes of buildings across the campus were sewn together at different angles. Stone pathways were engraved with runes or scripts. Walkway gardens speckled the grounds, each attributed to a particular theme.

Maijerda looked up in vacant awe at the bridges connecting lofty corridors. Each building showcasing different decades or centuries. Within one city block, they learned a meager handful of D'hadian's secrets and novelties as boasted about by their guide in nervous distraction.

In another half-block or so, their companion shared the secret of her name, apologizing profusely for nearly setting aside her manners.

"I have a tendency to keep them nestled in my pocket. My manners, I mean. Nearby for use but hidden in a way which is easy to forget."

Maijerda arched an eyebrow curiously.

"It is an old saying in Augv'k, inherently losing some of the uh—" She gestured in the air. "Punch, in translation."

And so, as it turned out, the student of the Pearl, who kept her manners secreted in her pocket, was named Isolde.

"Here we are." She clicked her shoes together as she came to a halt in the center of a secluded plaza. Eerily quiet. No surprise, it must be near midnight by now.

"There's nothing here." Maijerda raised one eyebrow. No doors, no buildings. Just an empty plaza.

"Aaaah." Isolde said as she closed her eyes. "Take a moment."

Maijerda sized up the engraved stone walls of the plaza. There were indecipherable carvings all along archways and alcoves. One moment they appeared pictographic in nature, the next, runic.

"Do you smell that?" Jeddeith was quick to abandon his investigation of the surrounding stonework.

Maijerda wrinkled her nose. "Toffee and… pomegranates?" The latter confused her. Even though she was positive of the earthy tartness, it seemed an oddity to pinpoint out of nowhere.

"Pomegranates? No… that's cinnamon honey. And there's something like a stew. Or lentils over a fire. Are you telling me you can't smell the smoke?"

Maijerda shrugged.

"Perfect." Isolde beamed. "No one ticket to enter is the same," she said as if this made indisputable sense.

"For what?"

"Was that door there b-before?" Wytt's question raised with wonderment.

A sigh peppered Maijerda's disappointment. "Wytt, be serious." They'd been through enough tonight, tricks weren't necessary.

He cut off her incredulity and spun her by the shoulders. "There."

He pointed to, what else? But a door. A door that had absolutely not been present three seconds ago. Maijerda was sure of it.

Isolde skipped to the door, taking hold of the circular ring bolted in the center. "Come quickly! Welcome to the Sétuizant." She pulled open the door, motioning for them to enter first.

The instant they did, the raucous din from within set Maijerda in shock. "How did we not hear this?" It was a fair question, as they were still outside for all intents and purposes, and a door was hardly an adequate dam.

A thriving market of well organized chaos bustled with tradition. There was a palpable whimsy to the atmosphere, the night air stark with juniper and pine.

It sounded absurd to say it didn't feel as if they were in D'hadian at all. Though the people's dress was accounted for in D'hadian fashion. As were the languages and architecture. There was something unavoidably amiss in the atmosphere. Disregarding the fact that such a crowd of people were around so late at night.

"Isn't it beautiful?" Isolde tossed a bronze seed to a vendor as she snagged a tangerine.

There were crates of flowers, sacks of pearled purple grains, towers of cheeses, jars of honey housing succulent combs, kitchenwares, and baskets… Maijerda lost track of the stacks upon stacks of wares somewhere after the honeycomb.

She hadn't been to a market this grand since last Vernal Moon. Mama and Da would've loved it. Oh, what she wouldn't give to bring them here now. Her mind fought with two versions of her mother, the one she knew and the battle worn woman in those visions. She must've slowed her wander, because Jeddeith had his hand on the small of her back to help her forward.

Isolde skipped up the steps of a pleasantly crooked and lean building painted lavender with jeweled teal trim. "At last. You might call it off the beaten path, as you said? The Sétuizant is a pocket in another realm and Mother is one of the many gems you'll find."

Mother of Pearl was etched above the door in a thick, overzealous letterhead. "Some students take to living here. Mostly it's occupied by visitors or short term studies. Excuse me, I mean students who are here for a short term. The rooms are shared and there's a community kitchen. This is perhaps more unusual a set up than you are used to, but I think you'll enjoy."

Isolde propped open the door with her foot and motioned them inside.

A sharp whistle echoed from the counter. The woman who made the call smirked and shook her bangs, dyed with shades of magenta, out of her eyes. Her voice resonated at a tenor, ringing cheerily in the entryway. "My, my isn't this a surprise! Undern's greeting has been terribly slow since you've last deigned to visit."

"Rylee, you are much. Too much flattery! She paints me with embarrassment, constantly." The playfulness laden in Isolde's cadence overpowered the tight presentation from Rylee.

"What did you drag here?" Her shawl complemented her rosewood-brown skin. It slid from her slightly broad shoulders as she licked her lips at the ragged sight of them.

"They have friends under care in the Sanctuary. I thought it would be better if they were nearer campus." Isolde exuded an elegance Maijerda didn't possess at the moment, lightly draping her arm on Maijerda's shoulders.

"Not a problem at all. I've plenty of shared rooms available." Rylee snuck a wink to Isolde, whose blushing unashamedly ratted out her emotions on the gesture.

Jeddeith held his hands at his lower back, rocking on his heels. "Is there any way we can repay you?"

Isolde was dismissing the thanks before he could finish his sentence. "That isn't necessary. I'm happy to help." Clutching the top of her ivory cape, Isolde said, "I'd best return to the Pearl. Tomorrow, I'm hosting a lecture on using color arcana in treatment for seizures in children under five years. I don't want to disappoint by running tired. I will visit you tomorrow."

Isolde apparently had a knack for luring Maijerda from a void of broody, rumbling thoughts, for the prospect of reuniting extracted a grin from her. Slender fingers, notably chilled from walking in the Undern evening, tapped Maijerda's arm.

"Oh yes, yes of course."

"Till then!"

The door jingled behind Isolde as Rylee stepped in to care for them, not missing a single beat in ushering them upstairs for bed. Wytt of course, engaged her in conversation straight away and as if reality wasn't crumbling beneath them. Though, for him, it wasn't really. She was left to hold onto these secrets, dooming herself to burst. Much like the Spark in the faetale.

Once Rylee left, Maijerda sat on the floor to lean against the dorm style beds, one stacked on another with a ladder. Wytt opened the balcony door, breathing the night air, eyes closed. He was no fool, he could sense the weight of the tide turning. He removed his satchel, scarf, and sweater, soaking in the chill. A ghost became of his breath and he bowed his head before taking a seat beside her.

Maijerda knocked her head back to look at the ceiling, avoiding his gold stare. The raking burn of tears pulled in her throat. Frustrated, she groaned and steadied her breath.

Keeping his thought to himself, Wytt swallowed his words and rubbed her shoulder in consolation instead.

Jeddeith rummaged through his pack and sat across from her, handing her a square bundle of brown parchment paper, wrapped with baker's twine. "Don't look at me like that. You need to eat."

She eyed him as she unwrapped it. It was a breakfast pastry, sticky with blueberry jam. How did he... when did he? "Thank you." Sniffing, she tore the corner of the pastry.

They waited patiently, knowing she was working through to cope and ready her story. She savored a bite of pastry. Flaky crust, hints of juniper in the jam. Even though it was cold, it was satisfying. The reliability of buttered crust was soured by her gnawing guilt. Dragging Wytt into this, placing Liam and Selene in danger, now Knax's creator was injured? All because of her pursuit of... revenge? Fulfillment? Legacy?

She hadn't a clue what the deepest reaches of her desires sought.

Maijerda's face flushed, picturing the hatred in Nadín's eyes when she was questioning her. Yet she had softened, dolefully at the reveal of Maijerda's name. Had she known of her since she was a baby? Had Mother spoken to her before she died? All questions that couldn't be answered if she kept to herself.

Sharing a look with Wytt, Jeddeith prompted, dropping his tone. "Will you tell us what happened?"

"I'd like to. But it scares me." Fates, she felt ignorant as a child, admitting fear. "Again, we've been hunting answers and I was given the truth so unbelievable it must be a lie."

Maijerda worked her fear into the most tangible form of divulgence she could craft without weaving it into manifestation. From the start of the wisp entering the tent, to the aggression in Nadín's confrontation, the mention of her name, the vision seemed to be a spell tattooed on Nadín's arm, and the start of history befalling her.

What else could it have been? There was nothing of the world to recognize, clothes, dialects, accents, landscape... all were foreign. She emphasized this point before carrying on to explain what she could recall of each vision. Arguments, war, strife, the ritual, a Veil, the three voices, and the riddle of weaver's nectar. The nightsweet.

At the close of her tale, Maijerda's voice was hoarse from the steady trickle of tears she endured during this retelling.

Wytt stared at his hands, unmoving. "Lyrian? The woman you mentioned, her name was Lyrian?"

"I noticed that too. The name Denratis let slip."

The gray and honey of Jeddeith's gaze bored into her, worried. "You said she was nezdrade?"

"I did. Never heard the term before Knax mentioned it. From what I gathered, he was right. They're elementals of some sort? She seemed to embody the ocean's fury itself. A sea witch."

Jeddeith, his posture severe, licked his lips and rolled his thumb over his ring. "Nadín's visions, it'd be helpful for me to witness them as much as a memory will allow. I'd like to try a spell if you're comfortable with me tapping into your memories. Do you trust me?"

What decision hinged on her reply was well-guarded on his end. Before she over thought instinct, she replied, "Of course. But that seems complicated. You're familiar with psychological tapestry weaving?"

"Yes. My focus will be on casting the threads, all I ask of you is purely meditation."

She wasn't the best at calming and quieting her mind for meditation, but it was worth giving it a go. They sat facing each other, cross-legged on the floor.

Jeddeith held her by the wrists along her pulse, closing his eyes as they both harnessed their attention. "Follow my lead. I'll guide you, but keep your thoughts in sequence to what Nadín showed you. It will decrease the risk of forgetfulness or bias."

Scooting to get more comfortable, Maijerda closed her eyes and reciprocated his clasp, holding his wrists, pulse thrumming on her fingers.

After an A'lorynn incantation, he helped Maijerda focus through the meditation, asking the world of her to recall the story again. She followed his voice to a place where she could muster a stoic retelling. Wytt paced during this second go, which provided her with a tempo to speak to. Her innate ties to the tapestry wove in Jeddeith's direction, giving her an internal tug toward his energy. She allowed it to wander, deepening their arcane bond. The song-like quality of her own voice eased the pain in her jaw and tamed the roiling in her belly to the very end of her recounting.

Jeddeith thanked her for her trust, announcing he was finished with the spell.

"Were you able to see? Was it useful?" She called to him, put off by his abruptness.

Tugging firmly at his sleeves, he donned a cardigan as he dug through his pack. "Yes. Pieces, but plenty to help me visualize. Again, thank you. We've discussed enough for one night. Apologies for keeping you from sleep. Let us rest." The arcane tendrils of light meandering above them highlighted the glass of a berry-hued bottle in his hand.

"Won't you?" Maijerda stopped him as he opened the door.

He bounced his eyes from her to Wytt with some shared secret between them. "In a moment. I just need to make some tea."

His desire was to be believed, with his quiet grin, tired eyes, stressed brow. She didn't press, offering him some suggestions of blends depending on what the kitchen stored, and settled under her blankets.

Wytt sat on the balcony while she tossed and turned, unable to sleep. Replaying the visions over and over until she thought she might make herself physically ill.

The most jarring event wasn't the wisp of fae arcana come to life. Or meeting Nadín. Or being taken to... was it the Shadow Realm? Astral? Etheric? Another riddle for another night. Not even the three voices, which if the stories were to be believed, were the three Fates, the Norn actually speaking to her mother of all people. But the Fates didn't speak to anyone. Hells, some argued their existence or sway on the tapestry, was false.

No, the most disconcerting was seeing Mother. Not the mother she knew. A blood-hungry fighter serving an evil empress. Conquering armies, consorting with devils and demons. Someone who would sacrifice a friend to weave a spell.

A villain.

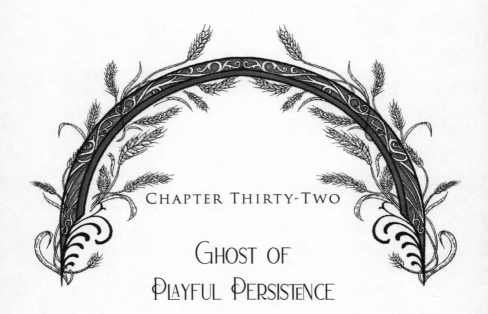

CHAPTER THIRTY-TWO

GHOST OF
PLAYFUL PERSISTENCE

LYRIAN. SEA WITCH. TEMPEST EYES. BLEEDING the oceans' blue. Nezdrade? An unknown term. And that wasn't limited to his memory. Nezdrade, or elementals, didn't exist. He was never taught of them. Nor read of them. Knax alone had ever mentioned the concept. An ancient people, lost to history? After a calamity, per Maijerda's recounting of the visions.

Jeddeith didn't want to trust the outcome of his meditation with Maijerda. Alone on the roof of Mother, he rolled his sleeves back and examined his tattoos. They were running with arcana, tingling and burgundy in color. He'd used them to weave a spell on the blurred edges of memory to connect their emotions. It would've granted him insight into her experience, except it had failed. As much as Jeddeith wove the spell to focus on emotional subjectivity, he had to shift it to something more likened to dreams, illusion, and a higher awareness.

Vythsaden rosq.

This intention had worked with that air of spirit in mind. Had that been what he usually touched as a Rivyn when practicing psychologically geared arcana? Or was this new?

He rocked his head back to take in the night for signs of Knax. Though he knew better. Knax was likely keeping watch over Nadín. Not that he blamed him for keeping close to her. He'd never met her, but how Knax spoke of her, with the reminiscence and anticipation of fate in her hands told Jeddeith how dear she was to him.

Facts bombarded him. He couldn't separate their meanings. Heavy burdens, all of them. He braced against the undeniable absurdity of the truth revealed in those visions. A Veil to repair arcana. That caused a calamity?

The Rivyn Borne should have known about this.

He should've known better. As a Rivyn trained to aura seek with the realm. Why had he never seen it?

His practice as a Rivyn was filled with clues he never knew to see. Hunting creatures meant to be confined to myth. Items refusing to engage with the real, present world. The politics of secrets. Tomes of inconsistent tales. Had they been imprisoned by this Veil? Hiding in plain sight.

This rumination carried on, until even he was annoyed with his… gods in shadow, what had Wytt said? Brooding? He threw back a swig of the concentrated tea he brought to the roof and inspected the engravings on the bottle as it worked from his throat to chest. Wytt had taken him to an apothecary after they left the Menagerie to help him find remedies for sleep. The shopkeeper guaranteed them the markings enchanted this potion. A dreamless sleep tea. The elderberries, valerian, and chamomile were to stave off nightmares and secure a decent night's sleep.

Though no gods would listen, he prayed it would do just that and keep him from enchanting the sea witch in his dreams.

The nymph from his nightmares he was left no choice than to assume, was Lyrian.

RYLEE WAS AN insistent host. She'd convinced Jeddeith to surrender their laundry, stopping him when returning to their room. She managed to acquire their belongings from the Nick too. Somehow all under cover of midnight.

Come morning, Jeddeith prepared a cup of the hangover tincture to help settle Maijerda's stomach. He already knew she was going to refuse to eat this morning. Upon seeing her in the kitchen and take a seat at the table, he smiled. "Good Morning." Puffy, red eyes. Clammy skin. She hadn't slept at all and had chosen to forgo freshening her makeup, worn eyeliner still smudged around her eyes.

"Here," Jeddeith handed her the cup. Friendly stability and all. She absentmindedly accepted and frowned at her steaming cup.

He didn't need Maijerda to voice her thoughts and worry. "She'll wake. And it isn't your fault she's hurt."

"You can't possibly know that."

He tugged on his vest, and fixed his navy sleeve, the button having loosened. Weighing the risk of providing a hint at his experience. He could tell her, as Wytt made him promise. Why make this about him? They needed to focus on their investigation. Faetale and visions far outweighed his sordid past. "It's not the first time I've encountered this."

"Wait, you've seen this before?"

"Something similar. I don't..." He pulled in his lips, cleared his throat. "I don't remember everything about it. Sometimes weavers overextend their energies and are attacked by their spell."

Her mug clinked as she tapped her fingers on the multicolored clay. "Have you seen people recover?"

"For the most part. Depends on the arcana. My point being. There is hope."

"This can't seal her fate."

"It won't."

Her tincture had cooled enough to sip at, she gulped a mouthful. "All right. I'm holding you to that."

"As soon as you finish your tea, we'll see to Nadín. Maybe she's awake. I'll grab your coat." He patted the table while giving her a final look to impart courage and left the kitchen.

On their way from the Sétuizant to the Pearl, most pathways were littered with leaves. Maijerda crunched a bundle of them distractedly, with the help of Wytt talking to her about hoping to see Knax that night. Jeddeith asked directions of students signing to communicate with another, huddled on a patchwork quilt. Diagrams and books were open to display annotations. Inscribed with colored inks, some hovering above the pages. A chaotic collection of science and arcana. Medicinal arithmetic.

Taking their advice, Jeddeith lead the trio through campus to the main entrance to the Sanctuary. It was more imposing than where Isolde had led them last night. An expansively lush courtyard garden. Rooted firmly to the side of the entry was a melancholy tree.

The willow branches wept. Respect. Gratitude. Defying Undern's call with ivory pink blooms. Inside the arched doorway of the Sanctuary the air breathed fresh and clean. Eucalyptus. Aurora rain. For show? Or medicinal gains? Could be either.

An orderly greeted them in a tunic trimmed with sage and gold embroidery at the collar. Likely enchanted. After consulting a book of records, the orderly reported they were not to see Nadín without first meeting with the lead physician and professor. They were led down a hall lined with posters akin to those in the Menagerie. Soft paintings of people holding medical instruments or flowers, presentationally displayed with words of healing in thin, ornate script. He'd noticed larger displays were hung on the outside of the Sanctuary too.

Inside the professor's study, Maijerda's leg was all a jitter while they waited. A disheveled woman rushed inside, apologizing for the delay. "I assume you're Nadín's companions?"

"Yes." Maijerda twitched and rolled her wrist. "I appreciate you meeting with us."

"My pleasure. I'm Saoirse, master professor and head counselor for the students tasked with this complexity."

She took a seat next to Maijerda as opposed to behind her desk, hands folded in her lap. The scalloped cuffs of her navy robes stretched to her knuckles. Rune enchantments were embroidered from wrist to elbow. "My specialties and research focus on more rare etiologies of illness. We've spared no expense or resource on Nadín. The arcana responsible for her altered state is… feral. Traditionally, Aurora is a better season for healing of this magnitude. We cannot always choose when the battle is fought. Though we can influence the weapons we wield.

"That being said, we may need your assistance with expanding our understanding of what happened. I know you've done your best to explain, I have a gnawing suspicion there may be more to learn."

Maijerda clenched her jaw and tensed her thigh, inadvertently pausing the bounce. Jeddeith's hand flexed. Wanting to reach for hers. He squeezed his opposite wrist to refrain. It wasn't enough. He spun the ring around his finger.

Saoirse explained a theory he'd heard before. Spirits or souls were equally as vulnerable as the body. The physicians here were uncertain about Nadín's state. And the cause of her fever. They were sure it was related to damage of her soul acquired while weaving. Not flesh.

"She has yet to wake. My concern, granted one of many, is that sleep is far too kind a word. I fear she is no longer grounded in our realm."

"Spiritually," Wytt clarified.

"Yes. We've yet to run dry of options. I simply wanted to be truthful with you both. But, I'll take you to her."

Leaving her study, Saoirse led them through a corridor. Adjacent to the base of a staircase. One, two, three flights of stairs. This floor differed from below. Mimicking a lavender field. A late Halcyon afternoon.

"This is our Curio Wing. If we are unsure of the cause of a patient's circumstance or ailment, we house them here. Both for safety and the wellness of others. Once we identify the problem, they likely no longer require isolation. Until then... ah, here we are." Saoirse paused at a polished door with a rounded window and numeral. "Please keep from touching her. While her wounds are healing, I don't want to risk disrupting the measures we've taken."

"Understood," Jeddeith said.

Maijerda nodded.

"I appreciate your trust. After you." She held the door open for them, taking a removed position in the corner of the room.

Nadín was lying on a raised bed in the center. Bare skin. Eyes closed. Breathing rhythmic. Labored. A glyph hung parallel to her, pulled apart and given form from the atmosphere. The shutters were latched closed which enhanced the glow emitting from the glyph. The remnants of incense lingered in the air. Cedar and mugwort.

Wytt immediately went to her side, resisting touching her skin to examine the wounds. "Have you tried painted runes on her skin?"

"We have. They melt within the hour after we place them, regardless of the type of ink. Her fever worsens with each moment of progress."

Jeddeith clasped his hands behind his back and circled Nadín. After his second lap, he shifted his attention to a table laden with bottles and jars. Several books too. They were trying everything. The flames of two candles, one blue, one pure white, brightened before him. Vythsaden rosq.

Calm auras from the blue. White, for healing through peace and...

He bent closer to the flame, examining its flickers. Singular flame. Spirit. Peace.

A method rooted in color arcana. Herbalism too. Runic arcana. He eyed a pyramidal opal. Untarnished rainbow shine. Pearlescent sheen. Evidently they hadn't extracted and encased the disease within. Otherwise the stone would be darkened.

Wytt ran his hand above the flames. "Are you focusing on sp-spirit with these? As opposed to peace?"

"Yes. Given my theory on what her soul is battling. I found it more appropriate. You have quite the eye," Saoirse commented in respect.

Maijerda gave Wytt a look to encourage him to own his medicinal skills. "W-well, I—uh," he paused and scratched his head. "I've been studying. I hope— plan to apply for a position here, ac-actually."

Saoirse tipped her chin. "I'll look forward to seeing you then. Keep on your studies. I'm sure you'll do well."

Jeddeith took to examining the breaks in Nadín's skin. Wounds were melted in nature. Noticeably receding, leaving dry cracks. Which was strange. He'd never seen a wound like it. The glyph's cold energy focused on her, but Jeddeith's proximity to it prickled the hair on his neck. Humidity lingered around them both. Above, the glyph whirred. Warning him, was it? Against crossing a line. Jeddeith heeded the warning and stepped into more breathable air.

"No such luck?" He inquired of their escort.

"No, I'm afraid not. Unfortunately I can say the same for many of our different avenues. It's agitating. And exhausting. The salve took longer than I suspected to display even minor improvements. Herbs have been even less potent. As you can see the cracks are diminishing."

Maijerda was still, unblinking, not daring to fidget. "Can we help watch over her?"

Saoirse smoothed her robes. "I'm afraid not. I've pulled enough strings for this visit. You'll have to wait until we send word."

"Good or bad?"

"Either, yes. I will make sure you are informed. Given how wild this illness is, I don't trust it to not hurt anyone around it."

Saoirse paused before she settled on 'wild'. She meant something else behind it. And from her forced stillness of her hands at her waist, she feared it.

The glyph pulsed again, the hum increasing.

"Please," Saoirse said to motion them outside and to the staircase. "Be well, we'll speak soon."

Their steps echoed down to the lobby and through the front doors. Maijerda's fingers sent a chill through the linen of Jeddeith's shirt as she held him back by the arm, meeting his gaze. "Sorry I couldn't offer much. It was odd seeing her like that."

"No need to apologize. There's plenty on your mind."

Wytt huffed.

"On all our minds," Jeddeith corrected. "That being said. I think we should wait to make a move until we speak with Knax. I'm sure he'll find us tonight." Wrist clasped behind his back, Jeddeith swallowed. They'd probably mock him for this

before they realized it was exactly what they needed. "Follow me.
I think I know just what we all need."

Twisting one of her rings, she rolled her jaw and exhaled
through pursed lips. "Lead the way."

Wytt stretched. "I hope it involves food. I'm famished."

"It does, actually." Chuckling, Jeddeith offered the crook of
his arm to Maijerda.

She hesitated, but accepted as she softened into a ghost of
playful persistence. "Thank you." She was no longer a kloidach,
full of loathing and contempt.

"Don't thank me yet. You haven't had a taste of my cooking
outside of camp." He winked, hoping to lighten her spirits.
Gods knew she deserved some reprieve from her nerves and
yesterday's chaos.

CHAPTER THIRTY-THREE

Too Akin to a Faetale

THE SÉTUIZANT WAS MORE A RATHER sizable neighborhood than a market. Whether this bout of levity was founded or not, Maijerda reluctantly admitted she needed a moment to breathe. Wytt practically danced among the midday crowd, walking backward in order to face Maijerda and Jeddeith spouting off his rekindled excitement for applying to the Pearl one day soon. One person glared at him, even after he apologized for nearly ramming into her bouquet of flowers.

Maijerda could've warned him, but this was far more entertaining. And as for Jeddeith? He was more tender, less short and brusque. He was... dare she say, charming? And a pleasure to be around? Her face flushed.

Oh Fates no, don't get dramatic. She laughed as he bowed for a little girl walking with her fathers and holding a basket of ribbons and feathers. "Ta!" She thanked him.

Maijerda stopped and threw her hands up in the air, anxiety sprouting. "Should we be indulging this?"

"We're not doing anything wrong. They'll find us when she's awake. We have things to take care of. Like dinner and going for a walk."

She grunted in response.

Jeddeith took her by the shoulders. "Look, we won't be any good to Knax or Nadín if we don't take care of ourselves. We can't even speak with Knax until tonight. Assuming he comes to us. Sometimes all you can do, are the simple things. Because it's what you need to survive."

Ah yes. The art of setting aside the world's demands and focusing on self-betterment. Hadn't she just been fussing over this at the Smithies? Seemed ages ago. Perhaps he was right. She centered herself and mentally accepted the invitation, wanting to trust and spend this moment with him.

Jeddeith wasn't withholding his attempts at easing her ever-brewing cloud of concern. It was obvious. And sweetly thoughtful. She didn't intend to discourage him.

"Come on." He stopped and side stepped to offer her the crook of his elbow, all smiles. "We're safe for at least a day in the Sétuizant. Denratis won't find us here."

"Promise?"

"You're asking for promises now?" He jested and grimaced playfully. "Be kind to yourself, Maijerda. Tomorrow is a new day."

Maijerda fluttered her eyes to suppress a sarcasm-laden retort and linked arms again with the sly bastard, catching the scent of orange-spiced tobacco as they drew nearer. Always seemed to be a new scent lifting her spirits. He had a way about him, showing his support and knowing how to ease her tensions. Being with him was natural as choosing a tale to indulge.

"Heart of the market must not be far," Jeddeith said, noting two women sharing a kiss over their baskets of bread, cheese, flowers, and berries.

Passing a slew of people, each celebrating their own cultures whether through food, language, or dress, proved that these eclectic elements brought D'hadian to life.

They walked by several small tusked ersuls whose garments clinked with the weight of metal adornments. They appeared to be arguing over where to go next. There were people with headscarves more seen in other continents and some with forehead and cheek tattoos donned by specific factions in another.

Two idre clearly descended from more foreign bloodlines, their features stern and hair ethereal in color, glanced sidelong at Maijerda's half-pointed ears, jeweled eyes with round irises, vibrant hair, and freckles. The perfect mix to give her away as someone not of their blood or years.

Rolling her eyes, she nearly missed the family of straelden, and from the looks of their flattened ears, beshin too, abruptly underfoot, the parents herding their children across the street. They spoke an older tongue of Feldkin Maijerda sparsely heard when traveling. It was largely known in empires where body language was the only shared language. Sometimes, not even that would suffice. You might think to offer condolences when actually your hand signs confessed to sleeping naked in swamps.

Storefront banners whipped in the wind as the family's voices were lost to the crowd. She hadn't noticed how vast this place was last night. The options were plenty.

Particulars & Potions (Discounted for Pearl Academics)

Unparalleled (Meads and Malts)

Are You Worth Your Salt? (Imported Spices and Teas)

Jeddeith rushed to a baker, bustling between stacks of steaming rolls and pies. They spent a fair few minutes discussing technique and recipe ideas with the boisterous Beau, before wandering the rest of the market for the ingredients needed for dinner. Seeing Jeddeith ecstatic about cooking of all things, it was well, different to say the least. Never would've pegged him for a cook.

His relaxed gestures and genuine smile alleviated the strain he often carried in his posture. She could sense Jeddeith was hiding something from her. Course, she couldn't glean what. Besides, who was she to judge? Though their friendship ruffled her feathers, hopefully if he'd shared with Wytt, as she assumed he did, he'd trust her to bear the burden as well. She supposed they had more in common than she'd realized. They both needed to learn they deserved support and care from others. Fates, didn't that sound absurd? Or truly, a lovely change of heart.

PREPARING FOR SUPPER turned out to be a much-needed outlet.

In a canister of glazed teal pottery Maijerda found a box of matches to light and bade the stone oven to come alive. Jeddeith fried bacon, shallots, and asparagus in a campfire pot situated outside Mother of Pearl's basement door in an enclosed garden.

Maijerda meanwhile worked crust in a chipped pie plate, while nibbling on dried kumquats and sweetened, roasted pecans from the market. Softening and molding the dough folded her into daydreams of a different place entirely. Soon she was telling Jeddeith about the first time Liam had wrangled her into making tarts at two in the morning. Wytt interjected, complaining that they had tasted awful and he'd never forgive her for it. It was one night. And a late one at that. She was a fine baker, he was simply too fussy. The memories of simplicity sent her rubbing at her nose.

"You're worried about them."

The dough hugged the sides of the pie plate, spilling over the edge. She bit her lip. "Knowing Denratis was at the inn, what if they're hurt? You heard his threat." She crimped the final piece of dough gruffly and it tore.

"I'm sure they're fine," Wytt assured her.

"You better be right." The butter in the torn dough melted faithfully, allowing Maijerda to smush it into place.

"Who's fine?" Rylee swung inside the basement posing in the doorjamb at the potential for gossip.

"Oh!" Startled Maijerda, overcompensating in the appearance of indifference. "Just a handful of friends back home." Hopefully that would be enough to satiate her. To protect her.

"And where's home?"

Maijerda chewed on that one like a stubborn piece of toffee. "Most places, I suppose. So long as they have a port. I used to manage a merchant ship with my father."

"Used to?"

She walked right into that one. Not looking up from the pie plate, Maijerda moved on to crumbling herbed goat cheese. "He's since passed."

"Darling." Rylee hopped up on the stand-alone countertop, swinging her legs. "I'm sorry to hear that."

"It's the nature of things."

Rylee bobbed her head side to side. "Some at the Pearl might disagree with you."

Maijerda countered cynically, denying Denratis' appearance. "Necromancy? That hasn't been commonly practiced or respected for centuries." They were safe here, he couldn't find them here. Focus on here. She kept a spiral at bay, admiring Rylee's flair.

Tossing her shoulders back, Rylee fixed her shawl. "I'm not arguing you should start digging up graves, darling. Besides, I was never one for academics. Community is much more my pace. Especially when the kitchen is brought to life! Tell me, what is it you've conjured for us?"

Jeddeith responded while pouring a mixture of roasted pumpkin mash, cream, vegetables, and bacon into the pie plate. "Quiche. It's been years since I've last made it."

"How sinfully decadent."

Maijerda took the plate from him and pushed it into the stone oven, the fire excitedly flickering for a taste.

"Careful, mind the flames or—" Rylee was cut short, Jeddeith being one step ahead.

"Or they'll mind you?"

"Ah, I see you spoke with Beau. Well, it shouldn't take long to cook, the fire is fit with enchanted pyre stones from the Pearl's alchemist workshops. Old news, but they're no less resourceful. Enhances the heat," Rylee informed them lazily. Apparently she wasn't exaggerating on the front that it was indeed "old news."

Satisfied with the temperament of the oven and placement of the pie, Maijerda carefully sifted through the display of jars of loose tea leaves. "Mind if we brew some tea?"

"Oh, I've something better than that." Rylee bounced off the counter and to the cupboards, reaching for a copper jar. "Might I interest you in spiced sipping chocolate?"

Wytt pipped in. "C-can't remember the last time I've had that."

Rylee prepared clay mugs with milk and heaping spoonfuls of chocolate shavings with Jeddeith's help. He placed them at the edge of the oven to melt the chocolate. When he did, the flames sparked higher.

"It's the pyre stones." Rylee disregarded the flare.

Jeddeith smirked. "Plenty here has a personality of its own, whether it should or not."

"Well why shouldn't it?" Rylee innocently replied.

"Would you say the same for the doorway into the Sétuizant?"

"Haven't you heard of the Balefire?" Rylee pressed, seeming as though she already knew the answer.

"The city guards," Jeddeith clarified matter of factly.

"The Balefire earned their name from war. The city needed a place to shelter civilians and the injured. No one understands where the plaza came from. Nor who put it there. The fact remains that it came in a time of great need." She perched on the counter in full swing of telling the story while Jeddeith finished making their drinks.

"With nowhere left to hide, the river was overrun with ships of invaders. Families were held hostage in their homes. At this point, the Pearl was unpolished, you might say. A far cry from being world renown as 'The Pearl of Illumination and Knowledge.' This left them excruciatingly little to offer, until…

"A first year student broke curfew, precariously close to the Harrowing. Desperate for solutions. And there they were, collected in the beautiful simplicity of a door. When they brought the news to the self-proclaimed authorities, they were met with mocking. No one believed in such a foolish thing as a secret portal to another realm. It was too akin to a faetale.

"Weeks later, none entered the portal. It was patient while the city was pushed to the brink of collapsing. With no other choice they fled, blindly placing faith in this myth. One by one survivors took shelter in what we now call the Sétuizant. The war ceased to ruin D'hadian, thanks to allies from Boend."

Maijerda slurped her chocolate, the heat from the spice tingling her lips as Rylee crooned on in the spotlight, her red lipstick full bodied. "It's never left. The city agreed to create a community in memoriam of dark times by putting forth the effort for the future to be an 'open door'. So, forever alluring the weary, the Sétuizant was born."

Jeddeith exuded passive curiosity, resting casually near the oven's flames to ward off the night. "Where does it transport you to?"

Maijerda gathered he was either genuinely seeking information or already knew the answer and was testing Rylee. She tried reading into him, but a rise in flames behind him distracted her.

"Just as much of a mystery as its appearance in the first place." Rylee fluttered her eyes, shimmering the colored shadow reflecting on her lined eyelids. "The lords ruling D'hadian condone it. Why question it? You seem to have above average understanding in the conniving ways of city gossip."

Jeddeith huffed a pleasant chuckle that neither confirmed nor denied his familiarity with the concept.

"I tire of gossip these days." A cheerful, yet tired Isolde commented from the doorway.

"Finished already?" Rylee remarked.

"Did I disappoint you?" Isolde flung her bags of books on the table and plopped in the fashionably distressed wooden chair next to Maijerda.

"Never, love."

Isolde lolled her head back in a stretch, her eyes shut to the world. "I admit I worry seeing strangers in charge of supper. From the smell of it, you're doing fine work."

"Time will tell." Jeddeith inspected the quiche, cautiously sliding it closer with a padded cloth. "Few more minutes until it's ready."

With the meal prepared, Maijerda sat next to Jeddeith as they shared glasses of mead. The initial shock of which was exceedingly tart and viscous like syrup. It was however lustfully radiant as red wine from tongue to belly. It paired wonderfully with supper.

Rylee was the most eager of the group to pay her compliments to Jeddeith. Isolde spared no expense in expressing her gratitude though she was considerably more coy than her eyelash-batting friend.

Maijerda chuckled when Rylee scooted marginally closer to Jeddeith after retrieving her well timed, fallen napkin.

Was he actually blushing? Maijerda hid a giggle by wiping at her lips for crumbs. Wytt shot her a knowing, teasing raise of an eyebrow. Which earned him a kick in the shin.

"Isolde," Jeddeith broached. "I hadn't thought on it till now and I don't want to cause trouble." He pushed his empty plate aside. "Can you help us in accessing the off-limit sections of the Menagerie? I understand students are given privileges."

She wiped a trail of stray crumbles from her chin. "I've never hosted anyone in the Menagerie before. I'm not sure if they'll allow all three of you in, but it can't be hurtful to ask." She cheerily gathered everyone's nearly licked clean plates. "We could try in a couple of days. Make sure to leave your weapons behind, they aren't allowed. That wouldn't be much of a wait for you, would it?"

Wytt shrugged. "T-take what we can get."

She refilled her glass with mead and returned to the table. "I'm sorry to not have word of Nadín." Isolde spun a mechanical cog shaped pin on her lapel. "My studies focus on the mechanics of *how* science, arcana, and alchemy engage with one another in medicine. I produce research and tools for others. With that, I'm unaware of what they might be experimenting with to heal her. I did try to ask before I left tonight. Sadly, they weren't willing to tell me."

Maijerda's eagerness to hear good news faded as quickly as it had stirred. "Regardless, I appreciate your trying, you certainly didn't have to go out of your way."

"Helping friendly faces is something to find joy in." She tipped her glass to propose a toast.

Rylee did as well. "Agreed! It would be criminal to ignore a chance to be heard among new friends."

Holding her drink high to Wytt, Maijerda toasted to him. "To the friends, old as family, staying by your side."

Wytt raised his glass. "To new adventures."

Jeddeith held his glass in turn. "To making new memories."

He paused for a beat before Maijerda realized he was sliding his free hand to her thigh. Palm upturned, he was asking to hold her hand. She didn't need to weigh decisions or second-guess desire. It was all she could do to keep from smiling. Tracing his palm, she interlaced her fingers with his and squeezed.

They cheered and promised to uphold their toasts by sealing them with a drink. The rest of the night was unexpectedly peaceful. For a moment, all seemed sensible and Maijerda could set aside the threat of the truth behind those visions. A simple night, made of drink, food, and friendship. Untouched by ghosts, wisps, and secrets. It meant the world to be able to stop and soak it all in and to know she wasn't alone.

CHAPTER THIRTY-FOUR

A Little Bit the Same

Two days later, Knax hadn't approached them. Maijerda was beginning to wonder if she'd hallucinated seeing him in the tent altogether. Jeddeith assured her Knax was likely keeping his vigil in secret at the Sanctuary. Occupying her wait with singing her lullaby and reading, Maijerda kept it at the forefront of her mind. At dusk of the second day, Isolde came rushing to Mother, her blonde hair falling around her shoulders from her run.

"She's awake! Nadín! She's asking for you."

Apprehensive relief crashed into Maijerda, a cold Eventide wave. "You're certain?"

"Of course! Go. All of you, shoo." Isolde started shoving them out the front door.

They left Mother of Pearl with Maijerda leading them to the river, wanting to follow it to the Sanctuary. Doing so bought her some time to gather her thoughts and expectations from this meeting. A handful of passing academics wore their stress-infused years with accomplishment bounding in every step, arms overwhelmed with books, parchments, and boxes of supplies.

Off they strode by the observatory to prove their worth, prepared to sacrifice what little they had left for the sake of illuminating knowledge. Wytt would be among them sooner or later, leaving her lonely with a forlorn heart.

The same Sanctuary orderly from yesterday instructed them to follow him to Nadín's room on the second floor, explaining Saoirse had cleared them to visit without her. He left them at her door, giving them privacy.

Ticking from a clock down the hall chimed in on Maijerda's hesitation. Jeddeith and Wytt waited for her cue to proceed.

"Here goes nothing," she said lamely. If "nothing" meant confronting your mother's realm-shattering, terrifying secrets. Inhaling until it ached, she gave the door a few questioning knocks.

"Come in."

Maijerda poked her head through the cracked door. A student was refilling Nadín's cup on a bedside table. Pushing herself up in bed, Nadín glistened in the afternoon sun. "Yes, the whim of the water is a wildness. Thanks to be." Nadín said to the student.

He looked at her with shifting eyes, possibly confounded by Nadín's way with words. Back in the days of researching Mother's death, Maijerda learned about traumatic injuries impacting the brain. Whether it be from a weapon or internal damage, affecting blood flow to the mind. Depending on where the injury was, it could affect anything from personality, memory, speech, eating, language, or your physical movements.

"Sorry? Ma'am. I don't understand."

Sighing with a puff of her chest, Nadín raised one eyebrow. Her expression was eerily reminiscent of Mother when she was trying to make a point. "Leave. Please. I'm fine light now. I'll ask for you."

"Ri-right. Sorry, ma'am." They bowed and left the room.

"Sorry. I'm not so close sometimes. Please." She gestured for them to settle in her room.

"How are you feeling?" Maijerda's words flooded from her as she sat on Nadín's bed. "What happened?"

Of all the sounds to come from the open balcony, shifting rocks and worn words was the most abrupt. "Despite my wanting to believe otherwise, she pushed herself." Knax lumbered through sheer curtains and to Nadín's bedside. "Attacked by her weaving. Which is why I tried to stop the ritual. She was burning from the inside out."

"Knax?" Jaw dropped in shock, eyes glossy, Nadín tried to slide out of bed but she collapsed half way.

Knax and Jeddeith caught her before she fell. "Careful, Nadín. I've missed you too."

She wrapped her arms around him, crying into his shoulder. "Too much glass has spent by."

"I agree. Next time you have a brilliant idea, let's refrain from indulging it."

Nadín chuckled. "I'm sorry. My friend. Thank you for your heart. For your help."

With Jeddeith's aid, Knax helped Nadín back into bed.

"You will have it till my dawn fades," Knax said. "I'm sorry I didn't arrive sooner. I might've been able to ease your introductions to one another. As soon as we sensed the glyph I knew we'd need to come to you. Its form of a faetale is curious. When you released your spell," Knax paused, turning Nadín's forearm gently in his claw. The tattoo that covered no longer there. "I saw everything you shared."

"Good. I wrote it to be with us both. I'm sorry I kept those secrets from your heart. It wasn't right then. I don't have a choice for anything. In the storms that dither, I'm glad you came."

Maijerda started fumbling for words. She didn't want to intrude on their reunion or disrupt Nadín's rest. "Maybe we should come back tomorrow?"

Waving her concerns aside, Nadín replied with earnest. "There's many things to get hot and hurt I'd like to speak with you all. Many says and I can't see all of them. But we should. Speak. And work together."

"I hardly know you. Yet, I feel as if we've had a role to play in each other's lives for centuries. Which is impossible. Isn't it?"

Nadín motioned for Maijerda to sit on her bed and when she did, Nadín gripped her shoulder tightly. "No. Fights and thread. I mean. Faded. Fines." She twiddled a finger for them to give her a moment. "Fates." She beamed with satisfaction.

"I should find comfort in that."

"It is hard at glass. Please. Ask your fill. I owe this from you."

Owe? Maijerda wasn't comfortable with that debt. The factors at play were dizzying. "No, you don't."

"Maijerda." Nadín uttered her name with pointed diction and contrition. "I promise. I do."

Where to begin? "It feels wrong to bombard you with questions."

She took Maijerda's hand firmly. "Ask my stories. Ask my song. Please."

Maijerda swung her bag into her lap to hold, seeking assurance from the book. If it had something else to say, please let it speak up. Though it said nothing, she did get the courage to accept her trepidation and honor it. Knax encouraged her, motioning to indicate she should speak her mind.

"The world I saw, was it the same as this one?"

Nadín tapped her tattooed fingers on her chest. "A song to say yes and no. Many, many hours. No, no. Years, ago. The world was different. And old, ancient pit of hell. I fought wars together with Relona. Not for peace."

"How long ago?" Maijerda feared the answer. Mother couldn't be from another era. What sense could that possibly make? Idre live for a couple of centuries, certainly. But she would've mentioned living this long, wouldn't she?

Confidently, Nadín spoke the absurd into existence. "Nine hundred years. More. Our tapestry died nine hundred years ago."

Losing breath for a split second, Maijerda clutched at her necklace. "Nine hundred? How? Are these wars documented in history? Surely there are songs."

Nadín shifted and her bed creaked. She negated the idea with a shake of her head, cradling her right hand to her ribs.

"None of them? Why would they fall to the wayside? Why didn't Mother speak of any of this?"

Jeddeith answered, realization aging his expression. "To protect the Spent Spindle. That history and arcana was eradicated. Proof of an ancient, arguably evil era of our world... gone. Without knowledge of it, its suppression couldn't be threatened."

Agreeing, Nadín swiped her tongue across her teeth. "Our tapestry was a grave. You might see a dying bird." She exhaled through pursed lips, frustrated at her words. "It. Was. Dying. Relona and I wanted to keep it safe."

"Which is why she asked you to take her to the Fates." Words were disconnected from Maijerda, lofty, airy, fickle beings stringing her along with ambitious statements and meanings.

"Yes. Their arcana was a newness to me. I took it long before the tapestry started to run a dying breath. They shared ideas for a ritual to let the tapestry sleep. We thought we could weave it without destruction. But we failed. We saw life distressed. Dim. Destroyed. All the darkness became locked away for secrets to keep."

"That's what Mother was researching, trying to determine where you went wrong. The Fates said you needed to sacrifice each *spool* of the tapestry. There are no spools? Arcana doesn't exist wound in a spool?" Intending for it to be a statement she asked the question, incredulous. Maijerda had never been taught to see arcana as a handful of exacting spools but rather as practices intertwined with one another that spoke to each weaver differently. From the looks on Wytt and Jeddeith's faces, neither of them related to the concept.

"What we took of spools was more for a mind to muster. All which is unveiling and that which is fleeting. When I harbored with Fates, I saw another. To which we are raveling."

Reeling, Maijerda clutched a handful of cotton sheets, her hands sweaty, trying to comprehend her meaning. "If there are, or were, different spools, then that's what was missing from the ritual. Representation of a type of arcana she didn't consider. I've no idea what that may be." Maijerda's eyes fluttered trying to narrow the possibilities. "What information did she manage to find?"

Nadín looked out the window. "When I left her to think on herself, all she said was we did not mind to place all the tapestry in the Veil. The Veil protects this world. She said it was already torn and weak. Because something a little bit the same was a sadness missing."

Trying to keep pace, Maijerda scrunched her nose. "But what? What was missing?"

She raised her shoulders to her pierced ears. "I don't think on it. I never heard that song. What I showed on your mind is the least, the last I saw Relona. Anger and sparrow—sorrow doubted me. I never saw her again. I didn't know she wrote a faetale."

Maijerda removed the book from her bag, struggling with the reminder that Mother created the book.

"When I read the song, I knew the spools of the tapestry. I can see a story to tell you a secret about the ritual we made. I already thought on the glyph because we used it in the ritual."

Knax grumbled in his stone barrel chest. "She left you a guide to decipher the spools. Or a confession. A story you would understand to keep the Veil safe. Relona needed you to be prepared to repair the Veil, should the day arise."

Nadín squeezed her agate eyes shut, tears dropping to her chin. "That is my question too. She must have had the ink to create it after you were bloomed."

Maijerda stood, holding the book to keep it as close as physically possible. An awful taste rotted Maijerda's tongue. Unfamiliar and gritty. It was disappointment and betrayal. "She *never* told me anything about this. Or her past. Neither did Da. He fled that night, for this!" Blaming the book for his death, she held it out for them to see. "If it was important enough for him to run from me and die, then why didn't either of them mention it? Or warn me I'd be hunted for it?"

"To keep you safe." Nadín paced each word to speak clearly. "If his mind thought on the book. He must have known the sands were thin. Who? Who hunted you?"

Maijerda threw her hand in the air. "Denratis. A pirate crew chased us out of Steslyres."

Searching the ground around Maijerda's feet, Nadín was lost in thought. "No. No. Something isn't the little bit the same. Is there another name?"

Maijerda's restlessness increased tenfold. The name having burrowed into her since she heard it in the visions. "Lyrian. The nezdrade woman you sacrificed."

Nadín grimaced. "What you're saying is you have her night? Her name?"

"Denratis spoke it the night he attacked us." Jeddeith clarified. "We've never seen her." Monotone, he eyed Nadín carefully. "Elementals are a myth. Nezdrade don't exist."

"Maybe in today's dawn. Lyrian is nezdrade. With dangerous bindings to the ocean's anger. A tempest. Relona thought our ritual killed her. I never thought the thing a little bit the same. We didn't die, why would she?"

Rolling her head from side to side, unfortunately wasn't alleviating the headache brewing in Maijerda's temple. "What did it do to you?"

Nadín reached for her hair and scrunched her fingers. "My mind bled. I lost the fate of my words. Your mother was disconnected from threads that craft worldly experiences. Lyrian was made to bleed elemental arcana. She was consumed. I did not believe she died. Relona didn't agree with that melody.

"If Lyrian is a cascading return and has started war with your family. She's here to claim the book for the darkening things and destroy the Veil. To unearth the lock of our old world and tapestry."

Maijerda's gut was telling her this was fact, a focused truth coming from the book she hadn't noticed she was pressing to her chest again. The truth? The way of all things forming into this weave of riddles. It hurt to her very core. "Fuck," was all she could manage. They were truly fucked. "She must not be far behind. Denratis knows we're here. He saw us."

Nadín squirmed upright in her pillows, panicked. "When?"

"Two, almost three days ago."

"Leave D'hadian, as soon as you know."

All fine and good, but they hadn't a clue where to go or what to do. "And go where? We don't have a clue of what was missing from the ritual. Or how to fix it."

"Your mother and mine may have fucked our weaving ritual. She was tearing her heart in searching. I hope to know she learned what we misstepped. What we missed."

"Fates. What am I supposed to do?"

Nadín tapped the book beneath Maijerda's arm. "Torlen lexnym. Understand. You knew to me in the tent, that this story was blind, blank?"

"It was yes. Until we found a music box in your study. It played a lullaby that I've known since I was a child. After I sang to it, it revealed the faetale."

Knax added, "It was why I gathered she was a muse born unto a knell. Literal proof song arcana lives."

Nadín cradled her head in her hand. "Oh, Relona." The sigh of her mother's name was rife with saddened disappointment.

"What is it?"

"The book is the safest place in the warmth of your hands. She wanted to make sure your eyes alone could hear."

Maijerda fumbled with reason. "She didn't teach me the song. It simply was. All my life. No one I've asked has ever heard it before."

Expecting this reasoning, Nadín rolled and gestured her hands open. "Blood arcana."

"…Isn't possible. That's just—"

"A story?" Nadín finished. "It was a rule real. All the years before. When we served Volkari as empress and didn't see hate or bitterness. Our winter wiles when we sung the wicked things as the tune of our world."

Mama? Using blood arcana? Harmful and cruel? That was impossible. For the briefest flicker, Maijerda did a double take at the window. Curtains fluttering, there seemed to be a cloud of mist in the air. But when Maijerda blinked her tears away, it was gone. "Mama was evil. It's true isn't it? But the Relona I knew wouldn't have practiced such darkness. Or served an empress."

Nadín sighed and pain dulled her oval irises of their precious stone shine. "I'm sorry. Those days were long ago. We both painted a new change after the Veil. We taught our loss instead happiness, love, peace. The brighter side of the Veil was born after the end of our world. We changed."

"How can you be sure she changed?" Maijerda retorted. Fates, it was getting warm in this room. She swallowed, her throat dry and catching. "You can't swear to know how she changed after you left."

"True." Nadín didn't falter in admitting. "You have to trust."

"No. I have to atone for my mother's wrongs. The world is threatened because of her."

"That is one song to sing. I'm sorry for the role I spent. The ritual. Betraying Volkari in banishing her from the shore here. For sacrificing Lyrian as a spool. For leaving the stone of your mother." Nadín's forlorn apology ate through Maijerda's anger. "I'm sorry."

"You shouldn't be. I'm letting emotions get the best of me. This is all so incredibly overwhelming."

"You have the right to upset with words. I know the string too well."

Sitting back on the bed, Maijerda set the book beside her and looked to Jeddeith. Then Wytt. Knax. Nadín. "Lyrian can't take this from me. I won't let her. And we need to stabilize your spell."

"Yes. With what we lost."

Wytt picked up the book and started flipping through pages. "Isolde is supposed to meet us tomorrow. T-to take us to the restricted section of the-the Menagerie. We might find a mention of spools there to learn what was missing from the ritual sacrifices?"

"More research." Suppressing her dejection, Maijerda pressed her lips together. "Maybe we can try experimenting with the lullaby tonight. See if there's anything to pry open? It might guide our search with Isolde."

"Certainly," Jeddeith replied with focus. "We could attempt another meditation. It's possible that with new information at hand, more secrets unveiled, it might share more with you."

"I'll take anything we can get."

Nadín redirected Maijerda's attention to her sincerity. "You are where you need to be. You needed thread to weave your story. And the wisp was our needle."

Chuckling, a certain poem came to mind from the Toll. "A wisp of wandering fae will tread a path with you. Vowing to find the treasure you lost," she quoted.

Nadín tilted Maijerda's head down and kissed her forehead.

"Fates, I'm exhausted with tears. Yet here we are." She dried her eyes with a quick swipe of her wrist, her wide sleeve slipping down.

"Not a thing so bad, Maijerda. *Family* is worth tears. I'm happy to have met you. Even in dusking settles."

"Me too. Lots of puzzle pieces with the tapestry, isn't there?"

Nadín chuckled. "Oh yes. Many things." Nadín gathered her in a tight embrace, holding her as close as possible. After a moment, Nadín held Maijerda at arm's length, looking her over. "Something on your mind. What does it say?"

How could she tell? Though it all made Maijerda's skin crawl, there was another burning question. "What is weaver's nectar? I don't understand what the Fates..." she drifted off, unbelieving of her own words talking of these entities. "...meant by that."

Nadín's silence seemed to creep longer than it actually did. "We never knew. Never listened to the whole meaning. But we assumed it was a little bit the same to a spell component."

"Curious."

"It may always be." Nadín pointed to Maijerda's qu'stite necklace. "Does it pay you mind if I see the stone?"

"Not at all." Maijerda pulled it over her hair and placed it in Nadín's hand.

Pointing to a table, Nadín said, "On there's the things to help write my arcana. Take the pouch and here, I'll take it."

Knax nabbed a leather pouch, the latch closed, and brought it to her. Nadín used her left hand to position her weakened right in her lap. She fell into a rhythm and pulled out various nibs of colored chalk, a selenite stone, and a scrap of bog-berry-red fabric. Choosing a yellow nib of chalk, she intertwined several runes on the nightstand. She placed the selenite and necklace in the center of the runes.

Covering them both with her palm, she struck fingertips. First finger two taps, the pinky three, middle four, and thumb two. Lifting her hand, she cradled her wrist to cup freshly conjured, luxurious Moonlight attached to the necklace. The selenite had disappeared, presumably consumed by the spell sympathetically.

Her Moonlight beamed equally as boastful and wondrous as Knax's.

"Thank you."

"It's a little bit the same, to help our shadows to keep." She tucked the Moonlight comfortably inside the scrap of fabric. "Don't wear the stones so quickly, let it time to rest."

"I'll make sure to wait." Unable to rein herself in, Maijerda hugged Nadín, never wanting to part ways. Nadín pulled her in so her face was nestled in Maijerda's curls.

"Please. Go rest. You have plenty seeing at the Menagerie tomorrow. I'll be a fine thing."

Maijerda dabbed under her lashes. "Can we see you tomorrow?"

Nadín flashed a weak smile. "I'd love the time to hear and be by you again in the morning."

"As would I. Rest well, Nadín. Thank you for being open with me."

"Thank you for listening and for a little bit the same in understanding."

A promise to keep. "Torlen dovnym."

"Torlen lexnym." A need to breathe.

When they left her to rest, Knax stayed with Nadín, promising he'd stay hidden in the shadows and find them with his astrolabe tomorrow evening when he animated again.

Lips trembling, eyes closed, and legs shaking, Maijerda tried her hand at stoicism outside the doors of the Sanctuary. Truly, an undertaking as what she deemed to be reality was still crumbling beneath her.

A breeze rustling the dark shoved her closer to the edge. The Moon, if she could lay her eyes on the Moon, would perhaps settle her fears. Sadly, she was still too new. A Dark Cruor Moon was in the making. Maijerda could've sworn a wisp of light fluttered in the corner of her eye as she placed her hand on the book in her satchel for stability and that bravery she wanted to host with honor and truth.

However, she was assured it was safe to let it fall by the wayside in this moment as both Wytt and Jeddeith enveloped her in their arms, holding her near a willow as she sobbed. Burying her face in Jeddeith's coat, the tobacco leaves of dried fruit and vanilla helped calm her breathing as he rubbed her back.

"You're all right. We're here for you."

Fates, she would never be able to thank them enough for all their kindness. They were her companions. Her lighthouse in a tempest. Her guardians.

INTERLUDE:
Rendered Silent

Regrettably, we've seen mortals
dull witted and sour,
take advantage of the
opportunities
communication
provides.

Whether it be through
spoken word,
the subtlety of
a shrugged shoulder…

…committing to the art
of devoting words to
parchment and ink…

…or even embedded
in measures of song,
the definition of communication
is respectably vast.

From city to village,
to culture, and empire…

…it is fair to say beings
yearn to be heard…

…and better yet,
understood.

And what if there are
no *words* to be shared?

What if the act of
speaking has been
eradicated at the behest
of a more complex force?

Be mindful.

Remain open to
possibilities
and interpretations.

Lest you miss
the importance of
another's story or song.
Mind yourself and be patient,
even with strangers.

We warn against
being careless with the
gift of expression.

If you find *your*
story is hindered or muffled
in the hasty perception
of others...

...you might wish for
the patience of a stranger.

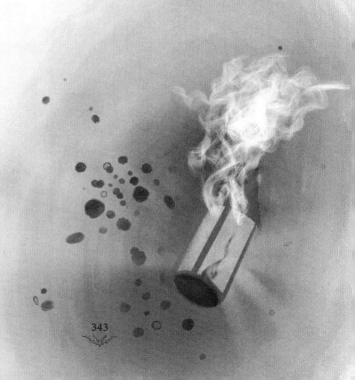

CHAPTER THIRTY-FIVE

THE WITCH UNBURNT

"THE SEER SPOKE THE TRUTH." LYRIAN fumed.

"What is it? What did you see?" Volkari stretched over the waters trembling in Lyrian's scrying basin, the view of a hospital room fading.

"A fool's dance. Nadín is alive with a gargoyle housing her arcana at her behest. Maijerda and Jeddeith have learned of the Veil and its relevance to the Spent Spindle. They're about to discover what they need to strengthen the Veil. We have Relona and Nadín to thank for that." Lyrian shoved the glass bowl and glided from the table.

Volkari, eyes wide, was speechless. She was doing horrid work masking it as dominance.

"Do you see now why we must attack? If they strengthen the Veil, we will fail to bring our world back." Lyrian spit with wrath as she spoke. "With Nadín alive…"

"It changes nothing."

"It changes everything! How can you keep coddling yourself?" Lyrian was through with putting on a show for Volkari.

Since her communion with Othesk, her ocean's blood stirred with potential and promised her time was nigh. Othesk's promises were awakened within her. Five boons to use but once. The first, she had used to scry. Fortune. Scrying was an ability she possessed without inhibition before the Veil. Now she was left to beg.

"We must capture them. Each will serve our ritual and suffer what it means to be considered expendable."

Volkari grabbed Lyrian's hand, keeping her from belting her clothes. "I won't allow it."

Tearing her arm out of her brittle grip, Lyrian snapped. "Choose cowardice then, it suits you. I will not wait for your spine to harden." Briskly, she stepped up into her windowsill, the ocean calling to her below. The wind whipped her hair, eager for her to return to the elements.

"Lyrian Llach!" Volkari bellowed. "You step outside my command, you prove you're capable of betrayal, same as them."

Lyrian spun and threw her hand across her chest, her retort rapid. "Do not force me to believe we are committing the same pious treachery. Wallow here if you want." Drawing her rage into a grin, the pleasure of seeing Volkari lose won her over. "Oh, isn't that tragic. You have no choice." She reminded Volkari, coldly. "D'hadian calls for me. And when I return, it will be with blood, book, and bane."

She'd suffer no further scolding from this shell of an empress. Lyrian abandoned her in the fortress, diving off the sill for ocean depths, thinking on the glory ahead of her in spilling blood. Maijerda would pay for the crimes of her mother. She must be stopped before she understood how to fix the Veil. Nadín would answer for her deceit.

And as for Jeddeith, he would submit to her willingly. His arcana belonged to her. He'd no right to something he did not appreciate or understand. Denratis wasn't worthy of it either.

Which is why she'd taken it from him when they met at Othesk's will. On the night the Eel Heart was birthed in the sky.

She swam to the surface, taking in the night sky, the Eel Heart constellation obnoxiously bright. Nothing could sway her plan to repurpose Jeddeith's potential. Lyrian had not hesitated to make her move with Denratis. What gave Volkari the idea she'd flounder now?

All the more reason to strike while they were distracted amid sentiment, hopelessness, and guilt. This counted for Nadín and her watchdog of a gargoyle too. With their three visitors gone, Lyrian witnessed in her scrying Nadín divulging a secret to Knax after he pried it from her. Together they fretted over a prophecy, spoken by the Norn, and Maijerda discovering the truth of weaver's nectar. Weaver's nectar. Long extinct since the Veil.

A pathetic weed.

Well, Lyrian would spare them the stress of revealing this detail to her. Maybe she'd craft Maijerda a story to ease her pain. The wretch did love them dearly. How fitting this faetale was starting to wear her thin. Hearing the truth of weaver's nectar, was certain to do her in.

This was Lyrian's fortune of wading in the calm before the storm. She would duly fulfill her role of a tempest, made to destroy anything lying in its path. The second boon at her demand? Expediency.

Concentrating on the stars, Lyrian spoke in her nezdrade tongue to command the waters to guide her to D'hadian with unparalleled speed. Encouraging them to envision the waters there, lapping upon a shore and swerving into a river.

She slunk beneath the surface and intertwined her limbs with the current. She held a sign at her chest and reached deep within her arcane threads to access Othesk's boon. Her scars, a relic of Relona's betrayal, burned with light to summon the spell.

Lyrian become a swath of mist on the shores of Gazdeq. To arrive drenched as a siren from a faetale, emerging in the Dolzdoem sea on the coast of D'hadian. This thread, offered by Othesk, severed within her at being used. Three boons left.

Denratis threw a ladder over the hull of the *Oracle Rift* for her to climb, lending her a hand over the taffrail.

"Welcome aboard." He clasped a hand across his chest and bowed.

Shoving into him to pass, Lyrian continued to their chambers. Sifting through a trunk of leathers and cloth, she retrieved pieces of an ensemble fit for a warrior among weavers. Denratis, having followed, savored her and licked his teeth as she dressed in fabrics tender as rain. His eagerness was palpable, prepared for her to ply.

She eyed him in the reflection of their stained mirror, his image rolling with the waves bearing the ship as she wrapped leathers around her arms and waist, fitting them tight around her scars. After fastening the last button of her trousers at the hip, she tied the guardian's stones to her sash.

Sitting at the table once more, she lounged to braid her silvery hair. "Maijerda is drowning in details, incapable of seeing the grander picture. She and Nadín want to believe Relona was just. That she was good—" Lyrian choked on her rage, a rattling silt.

Denratis massaged his unshaven face. "She still lives? Last we spoke of her, you were confident Nadín was dead. What's changed?"

There it was again. His arrogance. Was his place so easily forgotten?

Words rushed from her tongue, an arcane web of distaste. The spell shot from her hands and into Denratis' chest. He clutched his heart, stumbling to the floor.

"What do you know of the meaning of confidence?" Waves of arcana rushed between her palms. Lyrian spun the spell's oxblood residue with a finger, guiding it to drape over her hand. She rolled her wrist inward to herself and then away as though a sluggish tide.

Denratis' breath shallowed and he pulled his shirt open. Repeating the motion, she directed the eel to creep at a pace barely suitable to sustain a beating heart.

The ship creaked, her beloved stirring below. Lyrian prowled around him in circles. "I was confident Nadín perished with the birth of the Veil. I was confident she betrayed me— abandoned me— for the last time. I was *confident*— !" Lyrian lowered her hand, her words lost in the cackle of thunder outside their window, the burn in her throat, and the gloss of her eyes.

The gods were indeed poetic. Nadín was weak against her before the Veil when she pursued Fate. Now? It was a matter of time until Lyrian would feed Nadín's corpse to the waves.

Aw, how quaint was Denratis, scrounging on all fours for breath. Sweat poured from him, dropping on the floor. The scent of brined panic splashed to her.

"Am I not enough for you? Does torturing me bring you the satisfaction you crave?"

"Torturing you?" Lyrian serpentined her neck with intrigue, her chest colder than the deepest reaches of her ocean. She stopped winding the spell and stilled the eel.

Color drained from his skin. He swallowed hard, speaking low on reserves of breath. "After everything I've done for you. I've stood by your side for the last decade without hesitation. I could've chosen to leave in the beginning. And I still have that choice."

The laugh rising within her crested. "Are you begging for praise because you've never left me? How convenient. You seem to be forgetting when you threw yourself from a cliff, hoping death would greet you. If you weren't attempting to forsake me then, what were your intentions?" Lyrian curled her fingers, waving and hooking them to cast another spell.

Kneeling to the ground, she held him by the shoulder and clawed to grip his heart. The meat of it was pocked with barnacles digging into her. The eel was slick, wriggling for inane freedom.

"I want you to remember what it was like when Relona's ghoul poisoned you." She pulled him close and whispered in his ear. His breath was struggling to warm her neck. "I'll do far worse to you." She twisted his heart and coursed lightning into it. It stretched her limits but was worth the ebbing fatigue.

Denratis hollered over her shoulder, squinting his eyes and throwing his head back.

"You've never earned the privilege of liberty. You're bound to me."

His eyes flashed open, striking with the ocean's favor she'd poured into him those ten years ago. Othesk had asked her to place trust in both them and this shipwrecked tiraen, in order to grant her the arcana needed to continue healing herself from the imprisonment Relona confined her to within the ocean.

Othesk told her a secret she'd be hard pressed to reveal to Denratis. That being, he bore a rare thing in this version of the world. The arcane predisposition to become nezdrade. Othesk offered her Denratis to consume his arcana for herself to regain strength.

As though she'd ever let someone else keep what *she* deserved?

She'd consumed his arcana. And bound him to her without him ever knowing the truth. Bondage was the cost of both their resurrections. It wasn't necromancy. It was the life force granted by water's elemental artistry. The truth she withheld because he was undeserving of nezdrade blood.

"Was gifting you life not enough gratitude for you?" She spat. "Do not mistake my gratitude for reveling in relying on your pathetic husk. I expect Jeddeith will not disappoint me as you have."

Shoving the wordless scum from her, Lyrian stood above him crumpled at her feet. "Nadín has chosen her allegiance. For what good it will do." She muttered a word smooth and fickle as sea spray, materializing a sinuous spear from a cloud of fog in her grasp.

The third tethered boon, clipped from her internal threads. Prudence.

Denratis struggled to his knees, color washing into his cheeks as she strode past him.

"The sea waits for no one."

Volkari would soon learn what it meant to lead with the ocean's fury at your back. She would see to that.

ONE TASK REMAINED at hand for the night.

One that mattered more than reminding Denratis of his inadequacies.

Floating in the sea near the *Oracle Rift*, Lyrian initiated an incantation to create a gateway into the dream realm. In her hand she cradled a paste made from ash.

They were losing time and Lyrian needed to influence Jeddeith's connections to the tapestry.

Using the chant to guide her strokes, she smeared the ash on her forehead, neck, and heart. Even though it wasn't the purest of fire, the ash stung as she painted. She ground her teeth, accepting the retribution of her smoldering skin.

Pain was worth the promise of Jeddeith's freedom.

Pain was a reminder of what there was to be gained.

Lyrian immersed herself in the current. Spell weaving with water was the most direct means to interact with dreams.

Retrieving her conduit from the pouch in hand, she removed a single phoenix feather, brilliant as live flame.

She pressed it against her heart, the singed veins cracking under the force.

Her molten request to cross into the dream realm intensified with the presentation of the feather.

Is this your will? The ocean asked of her through lapping waves. *The fire will sting.*

"No more than a wasp. Help me cross."

Your will be done.

The ash turned from gray to orange, burning as coals reborn.

Scathingly she welcomed the searing. All the while laughing and hissing at the abrupt spark of punishment. As if this would scare her off?

"You *will* aid me. You've accepted my offering. It's unjust to forgo an invitation," she tutted. "I don't fear you. I am the witch unburnt."

The coals yielded at the declaration and allowed her passage.

ACT IV

Wormwood & Poppies

A lyric
Author, unknown
Date, unknown

A fool's silver and gold are these.
Riches of warning are gifted three.

Cë for scorn.
H̶ael for mercy.
Drë for portent.
Inevitably wrought.

Four or more
is a glass misspent.
All to do is repent.

CHAPTER THIRTY-SIX

VYTHSADEN ROSQ

ON THE ROOF OF MOTHER OF Pearl, Maijerda paced. As she often did when anxious. She pleaded with the sky in succession as if she could manifest the Moon to appear. The sleeves of her olive blouse draped over her forearms, cape-like with her animated gestures. Two patterned panels secured at her back to create a fitted silhouette. Enhanced by the soft blue of the streetlamps below. Even the tattoos cascading down her arms were more robust in the light.

Jeddeith shoved his hands in his pockets, leaned against the smokestack. Maijerda spoke of the abundant absurdities they learned with Nadín over the next few minutes. Needing to get them off her chest and sift through them for clues of what component was missing from Relona's ritual.

At the end of her monologue, she offered Jeddeith the faetale while rubbing her neck along the spine. He took the book in hand, not for the first time. They'd read the tale together over the weeks. Truth flavored his perception of it now. He found it to be asking something of him. What could he possibly offer?

His bonds with the tapestry stirred. An eagerness? But not from him. It was the book. An arcane source emanating from it. Was it eager for its purpose to be understood? To be with him? Doubtful.

Wytt, were he here and not snoring in their room, would be prompting Jeddeith to speak the truth of his Rivyn upbringing to Maijerda. What better moment than after learning devastating truths of world and family? It might startle her, turn her away from him. He could end up losing her to the truth. He risked losing her to secrets too. Why did one harbor importance over the other?

Maijerda, arms folded at her waist, ceased her pacing. "I'm afraid I'm going to screw all this up. All right. Enough rambling, I should think."

"It doesn't hurt to let your thoughts stream as one. Might help you choose a goal. Set an intention. Spark…" He paused. "…an idea."

"Hilarious." She smirked and tapped her foot.

"Truly. If you reach for your deepest desire regarding this faetale, what would it be?"

"Torlen dovnym. Torlen lexnym. To be heard. To be understood. I want more than the Moon's guidance itself, to understand the depth of its story in a way that makes it feel heard."

Jeddeith followed her thought and dissected it. Applying references of her interactions and discussion in terms of her book. *The* book. As she often reminded them. Never taking pride in it. Never forming a relationship. Which may seem insignificant. Except when accounting for the implications of caregiver for it in her language. Mentions of it feeling, breathing, listening, thinking. Worrying about it keeping warm. Not being frightened. There was a double meaning in her statement. Subconscious and unintentional.

Considering his theory, Jeddeith followed her gaze to the Moon's vacant void. His arm brushed her shoulder. She leaned closer to him, shifting to one hip.

"Do you believe it has experiences?"

"Hm?" Skeptical, she kept silent for his explanation.

"You want to help it feel heard. Do you believe it can be heard? That it has something to say or show you? Express in some capacity."

"I..." She initially responded quickly, abandoning her statement before shrugging. "I don't know."

He smiled, imparting his patience and care for her to realize he wasn't mocking her. But trying to enhance her mindset. Scratching his chin, he thought on how to reply. "If you did know, if you were confident in your theories, it would be worse if you discredited them."

Before he could finish she was refuting. Shaking so her loose curls tousled in shadow. "It's a book, Jeddeith. It doesn't think. Or feel. It doesn't *know* anything. It 'tells' a story. As do all books. It doesn't share an experience."

Several counter points could be made here. Appreciating that books, arcane or not, did share an experience. An idea. Question. History. Memories. They left impressions, just as much as they bore them. He realized she was well aware of that, given how much she cherished books. She was speaking out of frustration, not reason.

Jeddeith stared past her ruby and copper halo, framed by a street lamp. Iron wrought and lavish in design. Much as the whole of D'hadian's skyline.

Focusing on the light, he noted its elongated diamond form. Variegated pulse. Dim for the late evening. He timed a thoughtful breath with its pulse. Not so unlike the wisp. Admiring its beauty, Jeddeith's heartbeat leveled. "Do you believe that?"

Her motion sharp, Maijerda flexed her hand. "Yes!" Then came the ever-telling crack of her wrist. Grappling to convince herself.

He didn't need to point it out. That wasn't his place.

Maijerda rolled and bit her lip. Coming to terms with what she owed herself to honor. "No. I don't. Not for a second. There is more to that faetale than I'll ever understand. There's a thread in me that it latches on to. Which, if Nadín is right, is the remnants of blood arcana? I wish I knew more about it.

"Did Mother use blood to craft it? When did she create it? Was it after I was born? Before? I don't know what's relevant and what's not."

Deeper than her expression of confusion, was the hitch in her breath. The grimace. The not so subtle signs of hurt and betrayal. By one of the people she trusted most.

"You've an eye for rhythm. Patterns in what you're deciphering. I've been..." he chose his words carefully. "... trained to ground myself in the moment in order to enhance my awareness."

"Are they so different?"

"Not in theory. In practice, there is potential for subtleties to influence your arcana. The slightest shift might matter."

"Mother mentioned that when she taught me to weave. We focused on tangible experience, ways to heighten your sense of worldly experience. She had a different relationship with her own senses. Somewhat strained, either growing overwhelmed or underwhelmed. Occasionally, we stayed outside of cities on trips because her nerves couldn't handle the stimulation. It worsened before she grew ill. She started isolating herself, unable to process what the day had to offer like she used to.

"But she insisted on using these sensory experiences to teach me arcana. My success with it has been variable. Something doesn't quite piece together. Probably my lack of practice with it.

Or my anxiety interfering. I'm not sure. I didn't maintain those skills well after she died."

Jeddeith rocked on his heels, empathizing with her loss. Though unsure of what he'd lost prior to arriving in Steslyres in such uncouth means, he knew in his heart the hurt. "I'm sorry, Maijerda. Truly."

She flattened her frown, thanking him silently and hid a crack in her voice by clearing her throat. "Tears are relentless, aren't they? It's all I do anymore."

Ironic. Poetic even. Jeddeith opened the book to one of the final pages.

But on that night, burdened by grief, the Moon could only weep.

She didn't miss a beat. Craning her neck to see what distracted him. Jeddeith returned the book to her, opened to this page. "She was left with nothing to do except what everyone presumed impossible. Cry. Our emotions fight constantly to be recognized. We're told we're either weak or too self-involved for expressing them. Be at peace with them. Without emotions our experience in this life would be vastly different. Maybe not good, or bad. Your relationship with them is a piece of yourself that shouldn't be shamed."

Pressing fingers to lips, Maijerda swallowed and blinked rapidly. "I needed to hear that. Thank you." She closed the book and as she often did, held it pressed against her ribs. Protecting. Lovingly. Whether she'd admit it or not. There was concerned fondness in her touch.

"You don't need to thank me. I'm here for you. Because—"

Her boot heel echoed on the roof with her step. The windswept freshness of her perfume was a rush with her so near him. His heart thudded in his stomach. Hungry for her touch. Her melody.

Maijerda embraced him, standing on her tip toes to nestle her chin on his shoulder. In kind he swept her into him. Her curls brushed his nose as they held each other.

"I hope you know I feel the same. Your troubles are yours to bear, but…" Keeping a hand on his chest, she looked him in the eye. "You don't need to go it alone."

In the most unlikely of scenarios, with his hand on her waist. On a rooftop. In street lights instead of Moonlight. An Undern breeze swirling around them, reassuring him with Maijerda's perfume. Sea salt, sage, and spice. Jeddeith wanted to tell her everything. From Rivyn to memories long gone. To nightmares. To Lyrian.

To trust her. To share it with her.

But he couldn't.

She didn't need the trouble.

It could wait.

Gods in shadow. What was the matter with him? Losing himself to the past. When Maijerda was right here. In the moment. Grounding him.

Vythsaden rosq.

Gently he smiled. Tucked a loose strand of hair behind her ear. Stroked a drying tear with his thumb. "I'm not alone." Her freckles, soaked in the street light. His pulse raced. "Torlen dovnym."

"Torlen lexnym." Her words warmed his cheeks. Pleasant surprise glowing in her eyes.

Before Jeddeith knew what was unfolding, he drew nearer. Barely a breath was between them. His lips were parted. Eyes softening to close. Same as hers. Maijerda breathed deep, standing tall the longer she savored it.

Jeddeith stopped and lifted his hand from her cheek. The other, from her waist. They couldn't… He couldn't put her in danger by growing close. How reckless would this prove to be? It would be unwise to find out.

Maijerda's cheeks flushed and she swept her gaze from him to the ground. "We should rest," she said with a curl of her grin. "To say the day was long is an understatement. Think my nerves have settled enough to sleep."

"I'm glad to hear it. I won't be far behind."

She took her leave of the roof, breaking her saunter to bid him a goodnight wish. Shared between those special to you. "Let the candlelight keep."

Hands held behind his back, he swayed onto his heels. "Goodnight, my..." Scoffing Jeddeith shook his head with a smile. "Goodnight, Maijerda."

She left, still donning her sly smile. And he sighed with a ramble of emotions.

From his pocket, he pulled the bottle of tincture free. Dreamless sleep. He'd need every precaution in place if the nymph in his nightmares was in fact, Lyrian. He took a swig. Far more than the dose he was prescribed. Maybe the alterations made to his body as a Rivyn changed the way his body absorbed potions too.

Worth the trial.

Wondering if the Moon would hear him, in place of the gods, were she in the sky, Jeddeith rolled up his sleeves. He traced a marking on his wrist. Trying to recall what it symbolized. Most he could identify. This one eluded him.

Vysthsaden rosq.

Warmth. Hearths. Fury. Impulsive.

Flame? A rune to harness fire?

Perhaps.

The tattoo crackled with embers. Similar to his pipe. His skin singed and he severed the connection. He hadn't expected it to return to him with such ease. The glow ceased and he gave up his stalling, returning to their shared room. Wytt and Maijerda didn't wake as he settled on a bottom bunk.

The potion, unlike these recent nights, made him drowsy. He fought it at first. Flashing his eyes open to keep awake. If it was dulling his senses to this degree, surely there was nothing to fear in his sleep.

CHAPTER THIRTY-SEVEN

THE IRE OF FIRE

J EDDEITH ROLLED OFF HIS BUNK MID snore, crumpling his tingling arm into roughly hewn wood. "Shit." The needling stung more than the fall. "Maijerda, how long have I been asleep?"

He pressed the heels of his palms into his eyes to ward off the burn. "Maijerda?" He looked to her bed. Except no one was there. In her place, a cot. And a caged lantern. He rocked himself to his feet and circled to take in the scene.

Vythsaden rosq.

This wasn't Mother.

The floor, made of wooden planks. There was a porthole behind him. The deck groaned into the soles of his feet. A beam above crackled. It shattered as Jeddeith dove out of danger's way and shielded his eyes from embers. He rushed up a staircase covered with branches. Silver-green leaves. Golden petals.

The sunset clashed with the colors of riffling flame ravaging the ship. The ocean roared and lashed out, animalistic. Livid. A living, breathing creature. Flames followed him as he ran. A wall of fire raged in front of him. Grimacing against the heat, Jeddeith forced himself to the railing.

"Is anyone there? Is anyone alive?"

Crackles and spits of fire. Rolling tempest in the ocean.

A pillar of fire swirled and tore apart the ship's helm with a visible claw. Then the crow's nest and into the hull. The ship rolled sideways, taking Jeddeith with it as he lost his balance.

"Jeddeith!"

The cry came from behind a flaming wall spanning the width of the ship. It was faint, but there was a shape visible through the barrier.

"Artemis?" He raged through rubble and ruin to the figure burying her face into the crook of her elbow, convulsing with a coughing fit. Though he said the name, it was devoid of relation.

It didn't matter, she needed help.

The strain in her breathing intensified. She was in a failing battle against ashen smoke. She didn't have long.

"Jeddeith! Where are you?"

He scavenged for a solution, but none were in sight. No break in the flames. No way to shimmy along the edge of the ship and get to her before it was too late.

"Listen to me! Don't you trust me? Don't let me burn, please!"

Quieted terror. Tense shoulders. He inhaled ash from gasping. "Maijerda? Maij— Maijerda!" He called to her through the infernal din. Her form shriveled.

The rancid burning of his flesh was tacky on his teeth. Flames sizzled and quipped as though consoling him. Jeddeith was engulfed in the unraveling of his flesh and bone.

Consciousness diminished in the dominating chaos, hope right along with it. No. Hope *couldn't* leave him. There was too much of it in the world. Knax taught him this.

Maijerda too.

Focus. Hold onto that. Vythsaden rosq.

The ocean. If he ran through the flames, he could grab her and jump over the edge. Assuming she was still alive.

His flesh was done for. There must be enough of himself remaining to try and save her. He looked down into the ocean and the flames parted. A nymphish figure bobbed in the water. Featureless. As always. She managed an expression with the ire of fire. "This is your fate. She's dead. Wilted away. All that's left is to save your own husk."

"No!"

"Don't evade the truth. You know you'll never see her again. Not even in death. You don't deserve her."

He took a chance on a name. "Lyrian! You have no hold over me."

The nymph roiled with rage as Jeddeith inhaled deeply and consumed the fumes. It took an open heart. Which he had. And in turn, it took him to the grave, to quell his suffering.

JEDDEITH NEARLY DIDN'T catch himself from tumbling off the bed. His arm was numb. Pins and needles. Groaning, he clutched his left wrist. His tattoo and skin both, raw and burning. Pocked with blisters. Hurriedly he fashioned a makeshift bandage.

Jeddeith's blood boiled as he struggled to regain his bearings. He ripped and soaked the cloth in water from a basin, careful to not wake Maijerda or Wytt.

Stone floor. Undern wind. D'hadian sky. Wytt's snores? Which had quieted.

Shit. Too late. Wytt was propped up in bed and deftly climbing down before he could finish the thought.

"Ssh." Jeddeith tipped his chin to Maijerda.

Wytt took his wrist, examining it. "You didn't tell her did you?"

"No."

Shaking his head, Wytt gathered supplies to bandage him up on the balcony, closing the doors behind them.

"I tried. I couldn't."

"You wouldn't." Wytt accused with a forceful slather of salve.

Jeddeith, accustomed to injury, didn't flinch. "Because these nightmares are besting me. She can't know."

"L-lyrian appearing in them isn't e-enough rrrrreason for you to tell her?"

"I—I don't know."

Placing a petal on the wound, Wytt began wrapping it. "Your hourglass is draining, you know."

"Is that supposed to mean I'm dying?" Jeddeith quipped.

"No. You're running out of time be-before she hears the truth from someone else." Wytt's horns, a twisting black contrast in his white hair, made his glare fierce.

"You don't mean from you."

"You're smart. Educated. Don't betray her tr-trust."

Trembling more from overcompensating to stay his hand, Jeddeith swore to him. "I won't."

"Good." Wytt, so rarely a person of few words, left it at that as he stitched the bandage shut with a simple rune.

"Keep it sealed u-until the Mmmoon returns."

Jeddeith flexed his hand. The salve, icy and tacky. "Thanks."

"Sure. What now?"

"Dreamlessness isn't enough. I can't risk sleep." Jeddeith went into the room, dug into his pack. He pulled the red tincture from his pocket, freed the cork with his teeth.

Just a few days without sleep. That's all he needed. He was accustomed to potions with far more severe effects. This would be inconsequential. He spat the cork to the side and forwent the recommendations in desperation, downing a swig.

Wytt reached to stop him. "You'll overdose." He warned, hoarsely.

The taste of it was unexpectedly pleasant. Apricot jam, straight from the jar, sweet. Then it turned sickly. Nauseating, tongue rolling and welling. "I'll be fine. We're made differently, remember?"

Wytt flicked his tail and rolled his golden eyes. "You're still tiraen."

"Not according to the rumors." Jeddeith smirked and patted Wytt's shoulder. "I'll be fine. See you in the morning."

Swatting his tail and mumbling to himself, Wytt turned his back to him once he climbed into bed.

Jeddeith pressed his tongue to the roof of his mouth, settling onto his own bed. Forcing himself to breathe through the throbbing pain. In time, Maijerda hummed to herself in her sleep. Jeddeith removed his hammered charcoal ring and twirled it in rhythm with her.

A distraction. Good. Anything was better than dreaming. Never thought he'd see the day. Maijerda's breathing softened, pausing before she kept on. What tune was she singing?

Pages of literature and music came to him, recalling his research at the Toll. And more. So much more. In ælıkar, ɔpoʋlin, tiɾın… long forgotten were those days. Annoyingly, he remembered his studies in patches.

Her song sighed in undisturbed sleep. And Jeddeith sighed along with her. Right as he pictured a tarnished scroll. Copper edges. Metal frame. It bore this exact song. The irony had him silently berating himself. As well as the arrogance of fate.

It was fitting.

This song mused about a man lost at sea. With no memory of his life prior. And nothing except the Moon's ghost to guide him.

JEDDEITH HAD BROUGHT it on himself. He figured he'd learn soon enough if it was worth strain. If he didn't sleep, he couldn't risk more nightmares. Sleep couldn't be trusted.

After what Maijerda explained of Nadín's vision. He didn't know why it worried him further. They could be unrelated, true. The possibility of the opposite always remained true. Dreams the sun, so dawns the Moon. What is the day will see the night.

He accepted the cup of coffee Maijerda brewed the next morning, avoiding conversation. Coffee wasn't a favorite of his. This occasion though, called for it. The cardamom, ginger, and cinnamon she added helped enhance the flavor. She offered him a plate of breakfast. Tea-infused smoked salmon, eggs, and a sweet pan-fried bread with cream. By the time he finished, Maijerda couldn't sit still any longer and off they went to see Nadín before meeting Isolde at the Menagerie.

They left Mother of Pearl without having a chance to bid Rylee good day. Stationed at the hostess desk in her place was a zuihl. His snout curled with a snore, a string of spit sticking a stray parchment to his jaw.

Maijerda led them to the river, wanting to follow it to the Sanctuary. She tried to compensate for his and Wytt's quiet. Comments on the Wyldvern and its sapphire hue complimenting the leaves turning for Undern. The crisp morning. The students. And then she diverted course to a flower stall along the riverbank. She hand-picked a bouquet for Nadín, apologizing for delaying them.

She was likely stalling from nerves. Not that he minded. He was still reeling from their conversation on the roof. Plenty can change in a week's time. For once, these were changes he was fond of.

An orderly instructed them to meet Saoirse in her study. She was waiting for them, her glasses smudged and crooked.

"Morning. I have some unexpected news. Nadín left the Sanctuary last night. The carnival too, from what I'm told."

The flowers in Maijerda's arms drooped to her knees. "What? What do you mean she left? She said she'd see us in the morning." Wytt placed his hand on her shoulder, squeezing.

"She expressed she was feeling much better, thanked us for bringing her back, and mentioned needing to tend to a 'darkening thing.'"

Saoirse must've been at a loss for explanation. She squinted. Removed her glasses to clean them.

"I don't understand. This is a hospital, why didn't you stop her?" Maijerda was accusatory. Sharp. Worried she was somehow at fault.

"As much as we wanted to help, Nadín was no longer ill, she was of sound mind. As much as I would've preferred she stay to rest, it was within her right to leave."

Maijerda scoffed, squeezing the flower stems. "I'm sure she had her reasons." Clearing her throat, she plucked a petal, fidgeting mindlessly.

Wytt tuned into Maijerda's numbness. "Th-thank you. For telling us. She was well, when she left?"

"Yes? I didn't see her myself, but the others said she seemed well enough. Tired, nothing concerning."

"Th-thank you, Professor," Wytt replied. He steered Maijerda out the door.

Saoirse held the door open for them, sincerely apologetic. "I'm sorry to not have better news."

Swallowing hard, Maijerda handed her the bouquet of flowers. "It's not your fault."

Maijerda didn't listen to either of them when they left the Sanctuary. Insistent that she must've done something to offend

Nadín. Fretting about asking Knax what happened in the night. Jeddeith assured her he would've found them last night if something was awry. That they'd hear what Knax had to say this evening.

She didn't seem convinced, appeasing their assurances as the clock tower tolled late morning. They hurried across campus to the Menagerie as it bellowed over D'hadian, not wanting to keep Isolde waiting.

CHAPTER THIRTY-EIGHT

TEMPEST MOST FURIOUS

I SOLDE SAT STIFFLY ON THE STEPS of the Menagerie, hair coiled in a meticulous twist. The overindulgent attention to detail alluded to efforts masking how discombobulated by studies she must've been.

"Morning." Maijerda jogged up the steps, burying her face in her coat collar and wincing against an abrupt gale. A storm was on the rise. Beneath the stairs, the river lapped glassily along the foundation of the Menagerie. Breakfast churned with nerves in her stomach.

"Good morning!" Isolde leapt to her feet, dusting the ivory cape she wore over student robes. Far too exuberantly for early morning. Well, early morning was a stretch. Maijerda's energy was quite low and she was without Wytt's herbal supplements that helped her mind and body function. They really should restock while they were in the city.

"How is Nadín fairing?" Isolde huddled to Maijerda, as wind bit through the cold.

"Oh yes, she's well. Still resting in the Sanctuary."

Liar, Wytt's face declared to her.

"Thank you for meeting with us." Maijerda sought to reference the cogwheel pin on Isolde's collar and paused. "I was going to say that I understood the metaphor behind your badge. You're all a bit like cogs in a music box. But your pin, it's missing."

Isolde groped her lapel and sighed woefully. "I had a feeling a bauble slipped my mind. The morning hasn't been terribly kind thus far. It is within the day's right to do as it pleases."

"You don't need it for entry?"

"With the wrong people at the door, yes. With the right people, it'll be no problem at all. What is the phrase? A crumb of cookie?"

It was an endearing attempt. "Nearly. Piece of cake."

Isolde tossed her eyes to the towering Menagerie. "I knew it referred to a sweet—ah well, I cannot keep up with this language. It's nothing like Augv'k. Such a droll name too, Drynn."

Jeddeith opened the archive's oxidized metal door and waited for them to enter first. Isolde stopped him from falling in place next to Maijerda, her hand on his chest.

Sipping at air, Isolde raised one eyebrow. "It's good to see you. Again. Are you well? Sleep seems to be evading you."

Maijerda groaned and stopped in her tracks to share a look of annoyance with Wytt. With all the goings on, flirtatious theatrics seemed trivial. Which is all that surmounted on the rooftop last night, wasn't it? A flirtatious game, a near kiss. In the name of what, exactly? Who were they fooling? They couldn't chance intimacy. Jeddeith didn't need to get entangled in this chaos more than he was. It wouldn't be fair to him. She could hardly think straight as it was. But wouldn't it be such sweet comfort to be in his arms? To let down her guard and drink him in with a kiss?

Damn it all.

Maijerda shook herself from the daydream of his embrace as he replied to Isolde. "I think I speak for us all when I say sleep has been difficult to come by."

"I'm sorry. How stressful for you," Isolde mourned with a pout. "Maybe this visit will bring you cheer." Her accent swung through the statement, shifting the mood to a moment meant for more lighthearted predilections. "Follow me and we'll get you where you need to be. Yes?"

Isolde guided them down the second staircase, her gait much more quick and sharp than it had been before. As if she was on a mission. She greeted the attendant in Augv'k, overly cheerful despite the guttural nature of the language.

At Isolde's behest, he rummaged through a box of small metal medallions and offered three pins. Each bore the insignia of the Perle de Lumme with a glyph on it to symbolize 'guest'.

"These will grant you passage through the halls. Don't remove them. Go on." He waved to hurry them along. "Midday. No longer." He emphasized, raising an arthritic finger and glowering with one bloodshot eye.

Isolde hurried Maijerda onward, insinuating Jeddeith and Wytt should follow. "See you at midday!"

At the top of the staircase there was a fork in the road, so to speak. Isolde adjusted imaginary spectacles, rocking them to the end of her nose, and gripped her cape lapel pompously. "Welcome, to the true heart of Menagerie! Now begs the question, east or west?" She gestured to them their slim options, dramatically. "Careful which you chose, you may have time for one before the hourglass empties. Which do you wish to explore? Tomes or treasures?"

Considering her days had been spent with books never thought possible, Maijerda was hungry for new territory. Besides, it was a music box that unveiled all before. "Treasures."

"An excellent decision. We've much to see, pip, pip!" Isolde clapped and ushered them west.

Isolde wasn't overselling the expanse of the Menagerie. There was an imaginative mage's mind beyond a great deal to loom over or ponder the existence of.

A few more pieces than what should have been confined into a singular space were encased in enchanted glass, preventing arcana from finding a way in, or worse, out. From baubles, to paintings, instruments, medicinal devices, statues, there was something to be found for any visitor.

Jeddeith admired a talisman floating in falling snow. "When did the Pearl begin collecting?"

"Four hundred years ago, I believe. A century before it became a university."

Wytt whistled and the echo reverberated to a deck of gold trimmed cards a dozen displays away, illuminated by sky glass. The deck shuddered. "N-not many cultures in ælıkar d-display archeological artifacts. Majority of rulers say it's crude, or are too selfish to part from them. It's a wonder the Pearl o-owns a collection in the first place."

"Owns? The Perle de Lumme doesn't hold a domineering view of the Menagerie's masterpieces. The elders preach that we are borrowing history for a designated period of time granted by the gods. When we have learned all there is to gain by studying and consuming, then we won't be offended when we may have to pass on the caretaking to another."

Three floors below, the ambient river tumbled through the Menagerie to fill the pause. "It's a philosophy and a theory," Isolde whispered behind a hand. "It's not worth getting stuck on the idea. What will be, will be."

Maijerda smiled somberly at a lyre plucking its own strings. Undern leaves fell from an invisible tree around it, disappearing once they fluttered to the pedestal. The shape of it was a bittersweet reminder of Mother when she played. "What piece is your favorite, Isolde?"

"Each and every one." She spun as a babe surrounded by trinkets meant for playing and led them on.

"I can see why." Maijerda twisted her bag strap, nervous to prod too deeply and risk Isolde's safety.

The Spindle was worth mentioning though, right? Perhaps not the Veil. This was their chance to pry for clues of a missing piece to Mother's ritual.

"Is there anything relating to the theory of the Spent Spindle?"

"The Spent Spindle?" Isolde blushed and spoke so timidly it was near impossible to catch the first couple of words. "Not many people know that term. Not in the Pearl, not in the realm. People still though, discuss it without knowing the name. There is one piece people argue. I don't want to waste your visit with myths and theories."

Maijerda smiled. "Wouldn't be a waste."

"Very well." Isolde stopped at a pair of ornate wooden doors further into the displays. Posed as armored sentries, the doors loomed over them. Wytt gawked at the sight as Isolde took hold of the door handle, encouraging the door to swing wide. "After you."

It wasn't constructed to bear the weight of opening the heart of the Menagerie freely. Consequently the door shut, scraping against the floor and sealing with an echoing click. A cascade of lanterns hung in various styles and lengths from the ceiling, casting Maijerda's shadow high on the rounded wall. She was insignificant as ever staring at a tapestry hanging in the center of the room.

It was about six meters tall and two times as wide. The intricacies of the thread work were crafted from every shade, a select few sporting a metallic sheen. If admired in passing, the artistry of it was much too cluttered. The layers and concentric designs misunderstood and under-appreciated.

It was challenging to focus on the imagery.

A scene in the central bottom portion of the piece shifted into view, allowing her details which finally appeared as her eyes disregarded the broader image. If she forced the specifics to blend into the background, then a different image manifested.

She was pleased with herself when her vision mutated a blur of ocean blues and sea life into a ship at sea, surrounded by tentacles. There was another of thorny bramble beds which suddenly forged into a woman clad in armor, wielding a dual-ended blade.

"I'm pleased you find this as intriguing as I do," Isolde preached.

Jeddeith seemed drawn more northward of the fabric, near a towering assembly of moss adorned rocks. Maijerda made the mistake of blinking and the tower was gone.

Jeddeith moved to the western hem. "It's curious. Possibly enchanted. Depictions of ideas, cultures, and morals. Maybe a story or two. What is there to be frightened of?"

"People fear the very existence of it. As they do the Spent Spindle." Isolde sighed, reaching to touch the tapestry, but her fingers curled from it. "Some believe this tapestry was made from those discarded spools."

Cynically, Maijerda chuckled, "That's a boisterous theory."

"It is, isn't it? Rather literal. It does compare with needing an arcane seal to preserve the realm remade and freshly spun."

Maijerda's pace kept time with her thoughts, her skin flushed. Booted steps echoing, she forced placidity in her demeanor, rolling the cuff of her gloves between her fingers. Spilling too much information might put Isolde in danger. "Theoretically, if our realm was reborn from a dead one, it would need assurance to maintain its state? Wouldn't that mean different types of arcana might've been suppressed? Changed?"

"With such formidable tapestry threads involved, I would say yes. It's merely speculation. Just as the rumors claiming gods don't exist."

"Of course. A misguided theory." Maijerda narrowed her eyes. Gods were tangible as sailing. "How did the Pearl acquire this to begin with?"

"I would argue that the elder's didn't. It appeared right here in this very room, as if it had been there all along."

"You mean someone brought the tapestry here?"

"Possibly? And yet, no. It is as I said, it materialized. Out of nowhere." Her melodrama resurfaced. "This room was slated for something else entirely at the time. A caravan of travelers had taken a contract to deliver a scythe from ɔpoʊlin. But before they arrived, the first elders of the Menagerie were confronted with this."

"Where did the scythe wander off to in the end?" Maijerda asked, genuinely interested.

"It arrived, timely and in one piece." She was clearly bored with the outcome. "They resigned to crafting a smaller, equally as secluded room for its shrine, around the hall from here."

"Fascinating." This was a tale Maijerda had never heard. She happily devoured it. "Even to this day, people avoid this tapestry? Even with the connotations to our use of arcana?"

"For the most part, yes. We don't often bring outsiders in to visit it."

"What made you grant us an exception?"

Isolde stood directly next to the tapestry as if she was about to lecture to a gaggle of Pearl pupils. "You three are enriched with curiosity and open minds. It was palpable when we met and I doubted you would cower in the presence of a myth. Let me show you my favorite detail." She conjured a stream of speckles, sending them to the high center of the tapestry.

"Is that a gravestone?" Maijerda's vision struggled between the threads until she could settle on an image. "An eye? Or the Moon?" Could it be? Possibly, with the way it shimmered, the embroidery work made it seem like it was… Maijerda lost her thoughts, walking so the lanterns would catch the image and shift it.

It seemed like the Moon was crying.

Isolde interrupted her deductions. "Not quite." A desire to wander and dance in thunderstorms resounded in the deep breath she took, radiant with reminiscing. "People who have bothered to study this tapestry, have disappointingly concluded this depicts a catastrophic storm. They're foolish. More so than babes.

"At least children, as the ıdre preach, are to be respected for their unbiased opinions and tend to have an open mind about the world. This storm is more than mother nature. I've been dying to show you. Ever since you mentioned the Veil."

Maijerda's ears burned instantaneously. The adornments pierced in them pulled heavily as her heart in a split second. The Veil?

Breathe. Breathe. Calm.

The words were sent for the qu'stite hanging around her neck to call upon composure and finesse. "The Veil? I don't recall discussing a…veil? Did our language differences cross? Or I used a word with a double meaning?" Maijerda didn't want to jump to conclusions but anxiety was a masterful charlatan.

"I could've sworn you mentioned it when you inquired about exploring the Menagerie. Maybe I misheard you. What else might you have mentioned? How weak it is? That there is a sadness missing." Isolde pondered each option as if bothered by forgetting precise details. "Or was it something…a little bit the same?"

Isolde's pure disdain threw Maijerda into shards of a mirror, revealing the demon within. Those words belonged to Nadín as far as Maijerda was concerned. Any answer as to how this woman had heard them wasn't favorable.

Shit.

It was all Maijerda needed to see beyond the bigger picture and appreciate finer details.

"You seemed to have misplaced your accent." Maijerda backed away from her, grinding her teeth defensively.

A dew was forming along Isolde's hairline. "My, what an accusation. Maijerda, are you feeling well?"

"This isn't about me." She grasped the brass dagger hidden underneath her coat and sweater, staying her impulse to draw it.

Jeddeith stepped to Isolde. He didn't cross his arms, nor sneer, or threaten her. "Isolde, where are your manners?"

She was doe like before the hunter's calm. The hunt for answers was evident in Jeddeith's piercing two-toned eyes. "You're not being clear." She swirled to part, landing in between Maijerda and him.

"Where do you keep your manners?"

"I—" Her befuddled reply was cut short by someone scraping the door open as quickly as possible.

The woman shoving it was savagely shrill. "Don't! Get away from her!"

"What happened to you?" Maijerda went cold at the sight of Rylee, drenched in blood. Her clothes, hair, and face were ruined with it.

"Whoever she is, she is *not* Isolde."

No one flinched, not even the accused.

"Isolde is dead. I found her." Tears added to Rylee's fury. "You!" She pointed to this woman, who was unnervingly calm. "You're a dwymer aren't you? Tell me the stories are true. Borrowing skin like it's clothing. Give me one reason to not slit your throat."

"Rylee, you know dwymers are faetales. Or at least, that is what you and your ancestors have convinced yourselves. Even so, no. I am not a dwymer."

Something about Isolde seemed satisfied and proud.

"Then explain yourself, you murderous bitch." Rylee swirled her hands, conjuring a purple vapor. Shocked, Maijerda didn't expect her to be able to weave. D'hadian felt a different world compared to Steslyres.

Isolde fiddled with the chain of a necklace tucked in her tunic, speaking directly to Rylee. "You lack the capacity to comprehend what I am." Her scrutiny targeted Maijerda. "As do you. Worthless as a weed."

Maijerda glowered in response. "Don't test me."

"The Rivyn Borne, on the other hand." A vehement squall of thunder shook the Menagerie to the very core, swaying the tapestry, as well as Maijerda's ribs. "Ah… the sky sounds furious." Isolde's grin was wicked, threatening to tear into her.

Maijerda turned slowly to Jeddeith, her dagger hilt heated with sweat. "Rivyn Borne? Jeddeith?"

Jeddeith didn't answer, nor did he face her.

"Jeddeith! What is she talking about?"

"It's all right, I promise." Wytt tried to assure her, but she wouldn't have it.

Suppressed irritation at their friendship resurfacing, she shrugged off his hand. "You're acting like you knew. What are you two hiding?"

Hair matted with blood, eyes raging, Rylee was wild, ignoring the rest of them. "Until you breathe your last, I will crave your death. Even if it grants me mine." She gestured and sent her spell for the imposter.

With a flick of her wrist, a shield of water appeared and deflected the spell back on Rylee. She failed to dodge, getting struck in her chest. Collapsed, Rylee was unmoving.

"Good luck with that."

No! Rylee couldn't be dead. If someone could heal her... the woman blocked Maijerda's path to Rylee, sneering.

"If you're not Isolde, then who the fuck are you?" Maijerda threatened, twisting her dagger in the woman's direction.

She laughed a silvery, effervescent crow of a laugh, releasing the facade entirely. What was once Isolde faded into an abused grime, slinking off a body with venous, polychromatic skin. Her blonde hair painted itself sea foam pale and silver white. Her eyes, in a single prolonged blink, morphed into the wild wills of a sea creature.

Maijerda's hands went numb and salt reincarnate dried her breath.

It couldn't be. The nezdrade from Nadín's vision.

Lyrian.

She wasn't a mirror image of that memory, but enough of her remained. Red shadows around her drifting glass teal eyes. Equally lost at sea as glass left to wander. Red scars of sigils marked her skin. Lyrian was both haunted and haunting.

Another crack of thunder rolled through the Menagerie, rattling dangling lanterns as though an earthquake had struck.

"The sea witch..." Jeddeith muttered.

"I'm pleased you recognize me."

Oh for Fates' sake! What else was he hiding? Sea witch? "You've been lying to me since the beginning. Haven't you?" Maijerda swung her voice, appalled at the possibility and readied herself to attack. The meaning of trust fled from her. She should have known better than to trust him. Let alone be vulnerable. His explanation had better be bloody flawless. "Do you know her?" Maijerda demanded.

"No. I don't." He begged with open hands to heed his declaration.

"He doesn't!" Wytt pleaded.

"Now Jeddeith, don't lie to her," Lyrian taunted, feigning offense.

"Nadín warned us of you. Lyrian."

"Proud of yourself for that one, aren't you?" Every syllable was condescending. "Did you enjoy Nadín's little immersive play? Was her history lesson satisfactory? I did notice she lied to you. Nadín withheld the truth of weaver's nectar. I'm shocked. I can't believe she'd leave you so..." Her lip curled in disgust as she took in Maijerda from head to toe. "...defenseless. I hear you love stories." The witch glided forward, hair flowing as it would underwater. "I'll tell you the truth, if you surrender yourself to me."

Maijerda's limbs seized. Frozen between not knowing who she could trust and Lyrian's domineering presence. Her ire was palpable in the humid chamber. Maijerda struggled for a full breath. "You're the one weaving lies. I trust Nadín's word. I'm never surrendering to you."

"Have it your way then. There's more you didn't have the privilege of experiencing in those visions. My true power, for one." She held her hands out wide, drawing the room to dim, her skin glowing like sea moss. "I am the storm at sea. My people revered me. My god favors me. I am the tempest most furious. And I've returned home." Eyes glowering, spit flew from Lyrian's lips. "Your mother destroyed our world with her Veil. I was there when it ruined wilderness and empires all the same. Relona tricked me, made me prisoner. Tortured me until I was parched for my threads.

"Your fucking mother burned the tapestry from me, cast me into the sea as a stone spent by spell. And there I languished as little more than the consciousness of a wave. Stripped of my free will. Until her Veil weakened some thirty years ago." Lyrian paused, boastful with her posture. "An error she paid for. *I* made sure of that."

Maijerda's dagger nearly fell, but she flinched to hold tight. She snarled, "*You* murdered my mother. You—"

Wytt charged forward, frost forming around his finger tips. Maijerda grabbed his collar. "It was you I saw!" He shouted at Lyrian.

"Aaah, so you're the little rose I saw peeking inside her. My how you've grown."

Taken aback by his reaction, Maijerda pushed in front of him. "What do you mean you saw her? Wytt, I swear, tell me the truth."

He was running his words together. Panicked and furious. "I saw Relona's aura before she died. I didn't want to tell you the spell worked. It wouldn't have fixed anything be-because I didn't understand it."

"Tell me!" Maijerda gripped his cowl tighter.

"Something ancient and dark. Un-untrustworthy. I didn't know if it was Relona or what was killing her." His breath was ragged with anger unseen in his cheeks, beet red. Wytt pried his eyes off Maijerda, facing the nezdrade. "It was you."

With a bow, Lyrian smirked. "The pleasure was mine. And let's not forget your father. I exhausted myself conjuring that storm. Murdering your parents was quite the endeavor. You should be proud of them. Denratis said you'd learn the truth of it when I was ready. And I've *never* been more eager."

"You rotting, fucking bitch!" Fury cleared the path for unbridled retribution. Wytt and Jeddeith held her back from lunging for the woman whose hands were dripping with her parents' blood.

"Relona made immeasurable mistakes in her lifetimes. It's sickening. But you? You're the worst of them."

Without warning lightning latched onto Lyrian, the bolt splitting in two and anchoring to each palm. Greedily she shrieked and in one incomprehensibly fluid sweep Lyrian directed the bolts.

Maijerda's spine rippled and snapped like the dullahan's whip as she hurtled in the air. The lightning bolt burrowed into her chest and pinned her to the wall.

There was no breath to scream.

There was no reprieve to see.

There was nothing but surging bolts using her as a conduit.

And perhaps she was. A conduit for Lyrian's resentment.

Maijerda dared the Fates to show up here and now, as her heart fought to not be outmatched. Let them laugh and wag their tongues.

She was deserving of this.

Drink in the pain. The truth. The betrayal. Feel *everything*.

Accept what your family has done! Accept Mother fed the ripest of lies. That Da didn't see worth in telling her of the book. That Mother was—

You weren't supposed to look.

Lyrian's voice manifested inside her mind, the crackling bolts having gone silent as her thoughts went dark with the rigid embrace of the floor. She crawled on hands and knees, singed and suppressing a spasming cough.

"Take my hand." Jeddeith hooked his arms under hers trying to help her stand. She wavered and crumbled. Every bone questionable. Wytt was rolling back to his feet, clothes scorched from the lightning.

Steadying in Jeddeith's arms she pushed and faced him. "Don't touch me."

"I'm loyal to you." He gave her a quick shake in despair.

"I can't trust your word." It hurt to speak.

"I know. I'll explain everything. I promise. Torlen dovnym."

She was speechless. Jeddeith was untouched by Lyrian's lightning strikes. If he was trustworthy, why was Lyrian protecting him?

The room whistled until it swelled with wind that had no right being indoors.

Maijerda risked getting eyes on Lyrian floating at the center of the tapestry, swirls of wind holding her high. She spoke in a language hypnotic as the tide and appeared oblivious of their whereabouts, deep into weaving her next ploy.

Lantern chains creaked through the din and Maijerda's fading coughing spells. A gale swirled and ricocheted through the chains, cleaving like a knife. The chains creaked and faltered. All sound vacated the room for as long as it took for glass and metal to fall, combusting into flames. Devoted to the task of ruin, the wind fed growing flames, feasting on the tapestry.

Lyrian cackled. "No more clues. No hope for conclusions. Your story has reached an unprecedented end and will burn alongside the book which may have granted you deliverance. I will resurrect the past, shatter the present, and ensure my future."

Maijerda was drawn to Lyrian's hands, one crushing a leather pouch. The other steady beneath three levitating pieces of muted stone, each a different color. Green, orange, and purple with thin metal bands encircling them.

The heat and vigor of the fire increased without reason, forcing Maijerda's eyes shut against the spectacle. Behind her the doors rattled open and Jeddeith grabbed her, pulling her through to Wytt.

Lyrian cursed, or so the furious wailing could be chalked up to cursing, as indiscernible as it was. They sprinted through the displays of artifacts. Rumbles from both onlookers and the burning storm grew in a walloping crescendo.

"What the poisoned devil is going on here?" The clerk was standing at the fork of the staircase. "You cannot flee, I forbid it! We don't stand for unruliness in D'hadian."

Then, the clerk began to cough. This lasted for a comparatively measly two sputters. Then, he was rendered silent. Choking for what seemed an eternity. He clawed at this throat, willing to sacrifice flesh for air. His throat bulged and he vomited handfuls of sand and sea. He collapsed face down, drowned in the middle of a stairway leagues from the ocean.

"Where exactly are you whisking away to?" Lyrian's taunt carried on the wind, ancient and unmatched. She appeared in a burst of sea mist and cornered them on the staircase. "Oh, I'm not through with you. You have something I need." Reaching her hand for Maijerda's bag, Lyrian twisted and strangled the air. "Your little friend isn't long for this world."

Maijerda pressed her bag against her back, protecting the book. "It won't let you take it. You don't deserve it." Maijerda kept eyes locked on Lyrian, easing down the stairs one step at a time as she encroached them. "You don't belong here."

Lyrian was a wild and wicked woman with each punctuated word that came. Her veins more prominent and surging with the will of the ocean. It was no wonder she was responsible for the storm and creature that wrecked the *Norn*. "Weren't you listening? This is *my* home. Your depraved, faithless mother tore it from me and forced me to bleed for her ritual." Lyrian halted her prowl. "What makes you think she didn't birth you to be used just as I was?"

"No, you're wrong. She wouldn't have—"

"The Veil is weak. I heard Nadín, same as you. Lamenting how they neglected a component. If Relona needed to fortify it, what if that element…" Lyrian glared at Maijerda, chin held high, lightning crackling in her palms. "…was you?"

Betrayal bombarded Maijerda. Mother wouldn't have had a child—wouldn't have had her, just to, what? Kill her? Bleed her dry? This was all a lie, Lyrian was trying to get into her head, to wear her down. "I won't let you break me. Your lies mean nothing. My mother was a good woman."

"How quaint. You still believe she was honorable. You want to cling to a false image, just as you clutch that book, thinking your flesh will protect it from me. I'm finished with naivety. Forfeit the book and I will spare you the tortures of damning your soul to the hells after I cut your throat." Desire launched Lyrian's expression into a fervid hunger at the proposition.

Maijerda stood her ground, the gristle of vengeance coating her tongue to hone a retort. "Never, upon my grave will you lay a hand on *my* book."

Maijerda wielded her dagger and pushed off Jeddeith as leverage to sprint for the creature responsible for the carnage in her life.

Mother, Father, and future.

Lyrian counteracted, sending the wind to collide into Maijerda and spin her downstairs. Maijerda rolled and was forced into the banister with a twist of Lyrian's wrist. A gash on Maijerda's temple bled along her jaw and pooled in the corner of her eye.

"Agh!" She scrambled to push herself up but crumpled into the banister. Her left arm was lifeless, pulled out of place from being bludgeoned against stone.

"Are you hurt?" Jeddeith must've been repeating himself, gathering from how loudly he spoke.

"My shoulder's dislocated." Not for the first time. It hurt more than she remembered. "Bleeding piss!" When she opened her eyes again, Lyrian had vanished. Omen or favor, they needed to take advantage.

Diving into action, Jeddeith positioned her arm forward, braced her.

Wytt counted down, clutching her other hand for support. "Get ready, one, two—"

"Aagh!" Her shoulder snapped into place as a missing piece of a wooden toy. Pain throbbing through her arm sent her vision to specks.

Wytt scanned the area. "I don't see her. Can you run?"

Maijerda gave Wytt a weary turn of her head. "Not much of a choice."

Sprinting, they made to bypass the river and head up the staircase to city street level. All in all, not too much further with adrenaline setting the tempo.

Roiling bubbles heralded a tendril of water breaking free from the river's body. It curled around Jeddeith's neck as if it were a whip, dragging him from Maijerda.

He missed Maijerda's outstretched fingers by inches. Second and third tendrils grew from the coil and wrapped his wrists together like irons. Water lapped up to his collar bone, his neck arched back from the hold.

Lyrian merged with the whitened crests of the river's surface and she stood above him, stroking a dark, sopping strand of hair from his eyes. When he flinched to evade her, the bindings stayed him, her thin red marks flaring blue. Her image collectively brightened in the water, giving the illusion that she was feeding from it.

"I suggest you listen, quite carefully." Lyrian's matronly tone managed to demean Maijerda in a single heartbeat. "I will reiterate my request, once. Renounce the book. It belongs to me."

Jeddeith grimaced against the river. "Take what you're convinced is yours then."

The river seethed with Lyrian's displeasure with hissing bursts of steam. "I plan to. Including you and that gargoyle you call a friend. He's a living capsule of arcana." The color in her veins flickered. "I've been searching for you, Jeddeith. Are you not enjoying my dreams?"

Every minute was leading Maijerda to believe she knew nothing about anything. Jeddeith, Wytt, her mother. Nothing seemed real. She couldn't formulate words. When she sought Wytt for guidance, he was gone. She'd lost track of him when they were running. Was he safe?

Heart pounding, she refrained from calling out his name, to not draw Lyrian's attention.

Jeddeith grimaced as the noose around his neck squeezed. "Take me then. Spare Maijerda and the book."

Laughing, as though this was absurd, Lyrian shook her head. "Don't embarrass yourself, Jeddeith. This matter is beyond negotiation. One day soon you will see the world as I do."

It was now or never. Lyrian was facing Jeddeith, signing in preparation to weave a spell. She must take the chance. It had to be done. Aligning herself, Maijerda readied her dagger for Lyrian.

Blood for blood.

Maijerda stepped into the attack with clunky yet lustful precision. Arm extended, fingers aimed for her target, she froze a mere moment from releasing her blade.

The river flowed, Lyrian stood tall, and Jeddeith stressed his bindings. Students finally thought better of lingering and scurried. A flicker of a tail, out and up the window, climbing the exterior wall of the Menagerie. Swift as a spider, Wytt's shadow moved along the window toward the roof.

It all unfurled before Maijerda, unable to breathe fully and denied the relief of lowering her arm. Her vision was restrained, locked onto Lyrian's rotted heart.

Disapprovingly, three *tsks*, paced behind Maijerda, aggravatingly slow.

"Did I not tell you that bloodied vengeance was a temptress you'd never again deny?" A glint of stone, crystal clear as ice tossed up into the air from Denratis' hand. "Sorry to disappoint you, Maijerda. Plans don't always settle how we want."

Any modality she needed to reply refused aid.

"The book has been the bane of your existence. Let us free you of it." Smugness worsened what could otherwise have been considered handsome features.

Denratis released the ice stone to roll from his palm and quickly trapped it under a boot heel, smashing it into illuminated shards.

Maijerda was released from the incantation's hold and nearly toppled from vertigo. "I'll never yield. Jeddeith's right, you can't touch the book without risking death. The book won't allow it. Or did you force yourself to forget?"

"Are you suggesting we're at an impasse?" Denratis questioned with a sneer.

"I'm demanding your surrender."

"Not the response I was hoping for. Nevertheless, we can always take you with us. I've been told I'm rather... persuasive."

"Do your worst. I will never forsake my voice in this."

He laughed and feigned an exaggerated shiver. "So much fight. I can't help wonder, what do you have left to fight for?"

A rush of answers came to her, all of them born from vengeful rage. Addled by guilt, she scowled at Denratis' scars and venomous blights.

"Your fate is intwined with ours." He whispered in her ear, testing her resilience.

She held her ground, refusing to give him the satisfaction of her cowering.

"Would it hurt you to know the Fates showed us favor?" Denratis looked to the stairs, unsheathing his dao gleaming for bloodshed. "Ah, you're just in time!"

Balefire guards swarmed the foyer. Easily twelve of them. They bore the emblem of D'hadian on their armor, outfitted with firearms strapped to their back.

One figure in particular stood out as a sore thumb slammed into a door more often than not. A withered shrew of a person emerged last in line from the group, fixated on Lyrian.

Surprisingly it was them who spoke first. "I will use any means required to ensure your compliance. Surrender. And release him," they ordered of Lyrian.

A captain took over from there, spear in her hand. "The rest will lay down your weapons and kneel. Hands raised."

Not her proudest moment, Maijerda was the first to comply. They were outnumbered and needed allies. Sheathing her dagger, she knelt on the stone. "She murdered a student, assumed her form, and attacked us."

"Not a sound from any of you."

Maijerda eyed the guard signaled to arrest her.

Others surrounded Jeddeith, Lyrian, and Denratis, readying manacles shaped like a singular metal claw, appearing rusty and engraved with runic, geometric designs.

But then, the briefest of shadows muddled the sunshine coming through the sky glass. Maijerda tried to catch what it was. There wasn't anything or anyone. Cuffs were gruffly latched around her wrists, stacking them low, in front of her. Jaw tensed so tightly it was nearing ready to crack teeth, she fumed through the pulsating boil from her shoulder.

A second layer of hurt barged in, originating from the cuffs with each snap. The runes sparked and released an oppressive pressure.

"I'm not much in the way of a weaver. Is this necessary?" Being assisted to her feet was insulting although much needed, as drained as she was.

"Doesn't matter. They found reason to bite." He referenced the manacles snidely. "Nice try though. Save your sap."

Everyone glanced up as the sky glass strained and groaned. Afraid they would wake some untamed beast, the room grew grimly still with another groan of the glass.

"It's the wind. The storm is almost centered on us. Keep to task!" declared the captain.

The glass wrinkled and splintered like the surface of a frozen pond during the most brutal of Eventide's cold. A blur of rose emerged from the window's seam.

Fates be fickle. That brilliant, sneaky bastard.

Glass rained into the Menagerie in icicles. The crowd dispersed, ants on a hill avoiding a boot about to crush. The cloaked figure released sparks of an arcane net in Lyrian's direction.

Maijerda slid to the floor and rolled, glass slicing her face as she recovered her blade.

Indiscernible chaos erupted in the form of guards propelling through glass to corner Lyrian. She tossed aside the net and sent bolts of lightning to thrash the mage. They collected three of them in their palm, dodging the other two.

Jeddeith was shoving the tendrils off himself, their hold loosening. Finally at her side, Jeddeith helped her from the rubble.

"You saw her in your dreams and didn't tell me. Don't pretend you're on my side."

"Maijerda, if I wanted to, I would've killed you by now. Gods know there's been plenty of time for that."

"What?"

"You know it's true. Please. We'll talk about it later."

Fates. He was right. "I'm holding you to that."

"Shall we?"

They bolted for the stairs, when out of nowhere Jeddeith pivoted and pulled Maijerda into him by her hips.

Aghast, she was swift to reprimand him. "What are you doing?"

He drew her closer so they were cheek to cheek. "Trust me." He slid his hand around the small of her back and spun her out of the way. Blocking her with his body, he narrowly parried Denratis' confident killing strike with the dagger from Maijerda's belt. Denratis wielded his pistol in the opposite grip, aiming for Maijerda.

Jeddeith interceded, knocking it aside. The bullet careened for the ceiling, the boom adding to the confusion. Adapting a stance much more low and hunched than he had in Steslyres during their last duel, Jeddeith treated her dagger as an extension of himself.

Denratis shoved the gun in his belt and attacked with his dao. Dipping out of reach and slicing for Denratis' ribs and calves, it didn't take long for his opponent to curse and slash violently in poor efforts to maintain pace.

Jeddeith deflected the tip of the dao and grabbed for his wrist before jolting Denratis into his elbow. He roared and retaliated.

Maijerda freed her second dagger and gripped it sideways. Lunging, she angled to cut him, compensating for being bound.

Denratis swung out of the way and they met with blades crossed, playing the screeching tune of sliding steel. She disengaged and kept her approach tight, dancing out of his range to allow Jeddeith the advantage at the last minute.

Jeddeith parried and dropped the dagger into the opposite hand. He rammed it into Denratis' thigh. Denratis clutched the wound and Jeddeith grabbed him by the collar. He kicked Denratis in the back, catapulting him down the steps to Lyrian's feet as she snapped the Balefire mage's neck, tossing them aside with a river tendril. Lyrian leered at Maijerda, the Menagerie filling with her incantation as water pouring from a pitcher. The river spilt over the bank, soaking her silks and mixing with blood from corpses.

Unable to urge herself to run, Jeddeith's return salvaged her. "Still trust me?"

"We'll talk about it later."

He guided her out the front doors, dagger in hand.

Maijerda's ears were ringing from stress and pumping blood. His hold on her arm didn't lessen, pushing their way to supposed safety. The Menagerie's steps were at last behind them as they tripped down the final handful.

Thunder reigned from storm clouds, grim and ready to burst. The day could have been mistaken for evening. People panicked at the erratic weather, wind dancing around ankles and swirling to wreak pandemonium.

A second boom lorded over the city. Cascades of lightning fractured the sky. Following closely behind was a rumble, centered in the Menagerie and cracking the steps. People tumbled out the double doors, screaming to flee from the wall of water desecrating the Menagerie.

CHAPTER THIRTY-NINE

Darkest of Harrowings

"WHERE'S WYTT?" MAIJERDA PULLED JEDDEITH to a stop. Searching for him, she imagined the worst case scenario. Wytt, trapped in a flooding building. She spun in circles trying to find him in the chaos, almost making herself sick.

"Wait, there he is. Wytt!" Dizzy with relief, Maijerda fought through the mob to him. "Wyttrikus!" Maijerda pushed to be heard over the havoc.

Together they bellowed. "Wyttrikus!"

"Thank Tuvon you're all right! I'm sssorry I left you, I thought we might could use a distraction."

"I had a feeling it was you. But I couldn't, I didn't see— You scared the shit out of me."

He embraced her, leaving her to awkwardly grab his loose-fitting ivory and mauve shirt with her wrists still shackled. "You're welcome. It was the least I could do." He snickered before turning serious. "We ne-e-ed to leave. Th-they're ordering a city-wide lock down. Ef-effective immediately."

Jeddeith looked to the rooftops, probably hopeful for signs of Knax. It'd be hours before he'd wake. "Knax can catch up with us on the road when he wakes."

Chains of orders haunted their path to the city wall. The farther from the Menagerie they fled, the more blissfully unaware the citizens were. Theoretically this was all fine and good. Trouble was their bloodied, disheveled appearance caused murmurs to spread and fingers to point.

Windswept rain made a grand debut after they left Tome Ward and scuttled into Etchings. Orders and suspect descriptions were spreading between sentry units one by one as they raised red and black flags at each post.

"Shit. We need to find another way." Jeddeith stopped battling the throng of people and redirected everyone to an alcove between shops. "The gates will close before we reach them."

Maijerda took advantage of the impromptu regrouping, giving her best to twist out of the manacles. "Oh, come on. Scalded piss!" Temper and adrenaline shook her hands, face warm from the tension.

Each band was skin tight and the angle pulled on her left shoulder. Combined with the pelting ice of the rain, her skin was pricked with goose pimples. Jeddeith abruptly fixed Maijerda's scarf to dull the brightness of her hair and hide her ears and draped his damask scarf over her hands to mask her bindings.

They hurried to the river at Jeddeith's suggestion for an escape. Bribing the first mate of the only remaining ship for passage cost a handful of jade quills, which was well worth it. Balefire were surrounding the docks as Maijerda bounded up the gang plank with Wytt and Jeddeith. Not a single sailor turned to acknowledge their boarding.

Seasoned shouts signaled the "all clear" for the ship to sail from D'hadian, the rain slowing to a drizzle. It should have been reassuring to be on a ship again, but she was mentally off kilter.

The gray-skinned first mate scratchily cautioned as they eyed Jeddeith speaking with the captain with jasper crescents in hand to pay handsomely. "You shouldn't be above deck in the city. People talk. Go." His ram's horns were thick, resting atop bulky shoulders. She needed no other prompts.

"Right, will do." She pledged for the three of them and followed the direction he was pointing. She cracked open the door. Shudders of light exaggerated the length of the corridor, making it appear far more intimidating than it was.

The end of the hallway widened into an open room behind the crew's quarters and into their stock of wares. Wytt veered from them, wandering around a staircase leading to the main storage hull.

Parchments on barrels labeled each of their goods. *Jam, silks, needles, tea, cotton, coffee, sealing wax, candles.*

"Hope they can be trusted. Good plan, Jeddeith."

"We're not out of the woods yet."

Maijerda scooted three crates in as best a circle as can be made with three items. She sat and let out a long release of strife, her shoulder quite sore.

Wytt took the scarf off Maijerda's arms at her silent request.

"How's your shoulder?" Jeddeith asked.

"I'd rather not think about it. These aren't exactly helping," she held up her wrists.

"Here, let me see." Gently, he examined the manacles. His sleeve slid, stopped by the bandage on his arm.

May as well ask at this point. "Hurt your wrist, did you?"

He paused, eyes not leaving the floor. "Yes. Nothing critical. Are you familiar with these runes?"

"Are you insinuating I've been arrested before? No, not reliably. The most I figure is they're intended for tapestry weavers. The runes are probably staving off my use of arcana, maybe dulling my capacity. I'm exhausted, more than I should be."

From the doorway a figure no taller than a young child spoke. "You'll need this."

The shadow moved into the dimly lit storeroom. She wasn't a child at all, but part beshin. What was visible of her green arms was covered in bands of tattoos, each with a different design. Below a tightly rolled tunic sleeve was a tattoo of a compass. The needle swayed as it would beneath glass when she dug in a pocket.

"I've had my fair share of run-ins before I was captain." She held a jar with a steel-blue wax seal. "This'll bypass the potency of the arcana embedded in those. Slather it to cover the manacles and don't disturb it until late afternoon. Wash your hands clean of the metal. Your strength should recover fully by the end of tomorrow, assuming you haven't worn them long."

"That's a relief. I appreciate your help, captain...?"

The captain accepted her thanks with a curt grin. "I avoid giving my name to strangers, but I mean no ill will by keeping it safe. Much can be gained from a name willingly given. Regardless, we all need compassion from time to time. As you requested,"—she gestured to Jeddeith—"we'll sail you as far north as possible."

"Avoiding all ports."

"Yes, the gentleman made that clear. Far north. No ports. Quick as the wind will carry to middle of fucking nowhere?"

"Perfect."

She chuckled. "My pleasure to be of service. See you on deck, sailor." The captain gestured to Maijerda with a partial bow and left to resume responsibilities above.

Up the coast of ælīkar they sailed, leaving the Wyldvern and D'hadian behind. The captain declared they'd make for Neseth after stopping for the night. At this point, Maijerda was willing to let the wind take them anywhere. So long as it was far from Lyrian. They needed a plan if they were to stabilize the Veil.

Wanting to unshackle herself from pessimism, she chose a patch of stars around the waxing Cruor Moon and counted them one by one. Relieved that the Moon had at last returned, Maijerda admired her curve. A smile fashioned from solitary watchfulness, lamenting her station amidst the stars, impossibly out of reach.

"There's been quite the ruckus since you've been away." Maijerda told the Moon, holding her satchel strap with whitening knuckles. "I know I've asked much of you already. I do wish you could help me figure this damn faetale out." Her and Jeddeith's conversation from the rooftop replayed in her mind. She had accused the book... her book of not thinking, feeling, or hearing. She didn't believe that. Absurd as it may be, there was more to it than ink, leather, and parchment. "It feels like I can almost taste the answer. As out of reach as it is."

Fidgeting to kick and brush her boot on the deck, Maijerda closed her eyes to clear her mind of a fog forming to disrupt her concentration and way with words.

"What'd she have to s-say?" Wytt nudged her, hands in his pockets. He too was admiring the Moon, though with more structured appreciation than Maijerda did.

"Oh, nothing in particular. She's just returned to the sky, I wouldn't want to bombard her."

"Bombard? Mmmaijerda, you could be regaling her with a tale full of wisps, arcane visions, a close call with the villain!" Animatedly, Wytt dramatized his summary in efforts to pry a laugh from her. "I'd pay good jasper to see that play, is all I'm saying. I think she'd appreciate it."

"Sure she would."

Distracted, Wytt eyed her sling. "Here, it's loose. Le-let me fix it. How does it feel now you're free of those cuffs?"

"Still hurts, but the sling helps. Thank you." She rubbed her wrists as he finished tightening the sling. The captain's salve had worked seamlessly. Creating a goo that rinsed off, leaving metallic specks in the water. Good riddance.

Wytt rolled his lips grimly. "I'm sorry I lied to you. A-about the ssspell. It was my first successful— It was the first time an aura seeking took for me. I didn't want to believe what I thought I saw. And I knew I w-wouldn't be able to answer your questions about it."

A heavy change in subject. Maijerda grappled with herself to respond. "I'm not angry with you. Do I wish you would have told me? Of course. I understand why you didn't. You were right, it wouldn't have fixed anything. We didn't know about any of this. It would've probably landed me in less favor with Da or anyone helping us."

"I know, but. Seeing your distrust. I never want to hurt you like that again."

"You didn't. There was a lot being uh, unfolded. I didn't know how to process it all."

The ship rocked, creaking masts and rumbling hulls brought Maijerda back to a place where she felt confident and at home. Wytt however, turned sickly green with the shift beneath their feet.

"I never understood why you can't stand sailing."

"And I never understood why you pra-practically eat, sleep, and bleed it." He smiled and scooted over to make room for her next to him.

"I was raised on the sea, Wytt. Eventually she becomes a part of you. You learn to find her everywhere. It's how I learned to appreciate the Moon differently. She was always there for me when we were out in the middle of Fates knew where." Ah, nostalgia for simpler times, how it stung the most when you realized your world would never return to those ways. Maijerda didn't want to stew over it, not now. "How many times have you gotten sick?"

Scrunching his nose, he bobbed as he counted. "Five."

"I'm impressed. My bet was eight."

Emerging from below deck, Jeddeith ambled to the taffrail. Running his hand through his hair and pinching at his nose.

"Have you talked to him?"

"No. Not about what happened at least. I don't know what to say."

"He probably d-doesn't e-e-e-either."

Fair, in all honesty. Wasn't exactly your run of the mill conversation. Hadn't he shared with Wytt and not her? She didn't want to be bothered by it. "How long did you know?"

Wytt's cheeks flushed and he stretched his back. "Since our first night in D'hadian. I heard him sh-sh-shout in his sleep. He, uh, isn't used to having nightmares. I told him he should be open with you about being Rivyn. I think he was waiting for a better mmmoment."

"That never pans out."

"I tr-tried to tell him that. We all know how that ended."

"Wish me luck, then."

Uneasily she prepared to head to Jeddeith, arching her neck for the Moon. A patch of gray clouds drifted and revealed a constellation. Maijerda gestured to the sky. "I don't think I've ever shown you this. It's best spotted on the sea. If you look here. You should be able to see the eel heart. So long as you're patient."

"Eel heart?"

"Mhm."

"I-I've never read about it."

Maijerda chuckled. "I suppose you wouldn't have. Not exactly pertinent to medicinal studies." She teased, Wytt having a one track mind once he'd set it to a task. "Most bicker about whether or not it's a reliable constellation. Regardless. It didn't appear until, oh say, ten years or so ago?"

"I hadn't realized."

"Thus the disagreements. There are three groups of thought. Those who say it appeared overnight. Others who say we were granted sight of it by the gods. The last preaches anything can be seen in the stars with determination and find no value in it. There was a woman I met in Ceye, who explained to me a tarot reading she held for the constellation. Apparently, if the eye of the eel winks in your direction, your heart will be relieved of a burden."

"A touch anti-climatic if you ask me."

"I completely agree. There's plenty of rumors. I'd find it more interesting to hear your thoughts after you've found it." Praising the stars with her smile, she let him be to explore.

Across the way Jeddeith anchored on his heels as she walked to him, his expression worn but eager while he overlooked the ocean.

"How's your shoulder?"

"Eh, the sling helps a bit."

"Keep it close to you and still. Maybe we can get you some herbs for pain when we dock."

"When'd you manage to gain so much insight into dislocated shoulders?"

"After a, we'll call it a disagreement."

"Odd injury for a librarian," she prodded with a gentle smirk.

Jeddeith raised one eyebrow. "I suppose you think all librarians are a bore?"

"No, just you."

A quick chuckle softened his face. "You can't win every fight. Assume you can and you'll dig an early grave."

"You didn't win this particular fight?" she quipped.

"Wasn't that obvious? Course not."

They fell into an awkward lull. He shuffled his stance.

The confrontation with Lyrian was fresh, overpowering decorum. She needed answers, sure. She also wanted him to feel comfortable confiding in her. "This wouldn't have anything to do with your oath as a Rivyn, would it?"

He didn't respond, other than closing his eyes and hanging his head.

"It's later. And we did say we would talk about it."

Rigidly, he exhaled. "It would."

"I admit it does explain the mystique you wear so broodingly."

"So that's how you think of me?" He grinned, his words lilting to sway her from the topic.

She wasn't planning on letting herself be. "I should've noticed sooner, honestly. Your views on death. Your knowledge of myths and creatures. Your fighting style and deftness with potions. Your insight into what happened with Nadín. The meditation. Your position as a librarian. I can see it now. Is that why you hardly sleep?"

He huffed to laugh. "No. It's not. Think you've got me figured?" Jeddeith raised his shoulders, blatantly baiting her.

"I wouldn't say that. It's evident even with my sparse knowledge of the Rivyn. You're hiding in plain sight. Which is admittedly clever. Weren't the Wrought disbanded?"

"That's a polite word for it." His clenched his fist against the taffrail, digging his knuckles in unbendable splinters. "More of us would be alive if that were true. Some secrets are better buried in unmarked graves."

Maijerda pressed on, gently stern. "I heard they chose to go into hiding, were suggested to live alternate lives. To surrender their weapons and stray from hunting creatures. To let the demons be, both literal and figurative."

"Impressive. It would please them to know the lies were convincing of a civil approach."

Maijerda's mind branched off into at least forty directions. "How long did you practice?"

"Fifteen years. I trained at fourteen and thought I'd never bother with anything else. I learned herbalism and alchemy. Anatomy and swordplay. Politics and how to work the courts. Shadow gazing and projecting. Aura seeking. All at a cost."

"So it's true? Your soul is forfeit?"

His eyes drifted from her to the ocean. "Read that in a book, did you?"

"Actually yes."

"Some weavers, like Wytt, can see the strain in our auras. They can see what we are."

"And what is that, Jeddeith?"

"We've established this."

"I heard Lyrian call you a Rivyn." She sighed and tottered her head from side to side. "But what is it to *you*?"

He looked at his hand and ran his thumb around the charcoal ring. Decidedly, he rolled up his sleeves. White ink tattoos decorated his arms, an intentional formation of runes and glyphs. "We choose these tattoos individually to meet our strengths and needs. No pattern or collection is the same." He removed a blade hidden by his coat. She vaguely remembered catching a glimpse of it before. Blacker than obsidian, slick, and unusual. "Some of us forge our own weapons. It better infuses our arcane strengths in them. This blade was made with demon blood. Most people call it fae iron. A practice the Rivyn lost centuries ago. They managed to reinstate it after the appearances began. It's more damaging to creatures of arcane or demonic lineage."

Rotating the dagger, he held it in the Moonlight and offered it to Maijerda to hold. It was both warm and cool to the touch, the hilt clearly crafted for Jeddeith's grip. Tapestry threads drifted from it, tugging at her internal and innate potential. She handed it back to him, unsure of its power.

"For me practicing as a Rivyn meant protecting our home and its secrets for the betterment of the future. We fought the monsters and ghouls no one could. We protected the politics of our allies as ambassadors. There were archeological pursuits, treasures to collect for research. Stories to tell. Arcana to weave in ways others wouldn't. It brought me purpose and confidence. Insight and clarity. Until doubt ravaged us.

"Rumors spread about our supposed disloyalty and involvement in summoning demons. Reports document that sparse appearances began thirty years ago. People didn't believe us when we warned demons were being spotted by civilians. I wasn't around then. But sightings have done nothing but escalate in my time as a Rivyn. Suddenly we were charlatans and weren't to be trusted. The creatures we'd slain were facades. Lies for glory and manipulation of fear. The real lies were embedded in the rumors. Rumors lead to us being slaughtered in Zefk and then hunted for public execution."

Maijerda blinked at his unusual spiral of vulnerability. It was deeper than the signs of insomnia, deeper than needing a moment of peace. "Are you in immediate danger?"

"Theoretically, no. It's been eight years since the massacre. I know how to play my cards right."

Such a secret to carry. Let alone to keep from companions, or someone he cared about. Unless her mind was getting away from her, as usual. But he did, didn't he? Just as she cared for him. "Jeddeith. Why didn't you tell me? Why keep this a secret when we are facing the impossible?" She acknowledged being Rivyn was no simple matter, but their present stakes were unfathomably high. Lies weren't becoming, especially when that lie revolved around belonging to an order that earned you a death sentence.

Nervousness bridled his laugh. "Why? Maijerda, please you must understand." He took her in, lips parted and eyes scanning her expression. "What if you'd turn me in? Have me arrested? Rivyn are still hunted and executed. I didn't want you to cast me aside. It would be my end to see you afraid of me. And… I didn't want to put you in danger." Sadness and a fear of these possibilities cracked his tenor slightly.

Maijerda, without having any such fear cloud her days, felt for him and ached with his worry. She wanted to take it on and share his burden, damn the risks. Together they could handle the chaos. "I wouldn't be in any more danger than I am now. I'm not afraid. And I'm not leaving your side. If you'll have me."

"I couldn't—"

"Yes, you can. Let me help you. Please. In what ways I can." She stroked a wave of hair from his face and held his cheek.

"Thank you."

"Now tell me, how does Lyrian know? You see her in your dreams?" The question was an undertaking to pose. How absurd she sounded.

True frustration and helplessness slipped through him. "I don't know for certain how she knows I'm Rivyn. It's plausible she can see my aura. I realized, when we spoke with Nadín, that I've seen Lyrian in three nightmares. Until then she's just been a sea witch or a nymph." Donning his stiff speech pattern for recounting facts, he scratched at his temples. "Nymphs. Creatures born around naturally elemental sites of arcana that began to have their own thoughts and imaginations."

He pulled out a draught in a glass bottle. "I drank this last night to stop the nightmares by forgoing sleep. It was Wytt's idea. We tried a tea, initially. Elderberries, valerian, and chamomile. To stave off nightmares and secure a decent night's sleep. Nothing helps."

Maijerda inevitably reflected on her own nightmares and a tightly stitched camaraderie beat inside her. Not that she completely understood, she did hurt for him. "Are these nightmares reoccurring?"

"No. Save for wormwood and golden poppies. I've seen them in each one. A warning, before they all inevitably end the same."

"How so?"

He sucked one cheek inwards to bite, wrinkling his scruff of a beard. "Death. Mine in particular. I let her drown me in the ocean, before I let her shove me down a chasm, and the other night, I burned alive on a ship."

The bandage on his wrist, it was from a burn. An injury manifesting from dreams shouldn't be in the realm of possibilities. Though what did she know since learning of the Veil.

His words were a wish for comfort. His eyes revealed the truth in that he didn't expect hope from her. Oh, what she would give to provide it for him.

"Willingly?"

"Yes. She pushes me, taunts me to stay alive. I've defied her every time." His jaw trembled, words tight and sullen.

"I see." She didn't, having never died in a nightmare before. What else was there to say? "These aren't happenstance. If she's powerful enough to infiltrate your mind..." Maijerda composed herself to face intricately conceived murder. "She must've wielded that weapon when she murdered my mother. However, I don't think her suffering was confined to dreams." Her voice cracked. "What Lyrian committed was foul, cruel, and unjust. And I can make sense of her witch hunt for the book. What does she want with you?"

"I haven't a gods damning clue."

"Neither do I. When did the nightmares begin?"

He supported himself on the railing. "The night we met."

Irony slammed into her and she chalked it up to a stiff laugh. "I suppose we have more in common than we figured. Nothing compares to becoming the prey of a creature who is supposedly a faetale."

Jeddeith met her sarcasm with a forcefully lighthearted jest. "I don't see why you worry so much. Faetales are loved for their predictability. Those who favor light and good always win in the end." He winked and nudged Maijerda until she catered to his candor.

"I hear you, I do." Rapping her fingers on her arm, she hugged herself firmly. There was more on his mind, a secret carried in his posture and circles under his eyes. "I know you're secreting away something else."

His posture was a fortress, his lips sealed shut.

"It's your right to keep secrets. But Jeddeith please, I trust you. We're in this together, aren't we?"

He bowed his head, deep was his sigh. "Yes."

For a moment Maijerda assumed he was going to continue avoiding her. She was in for a surprise.

"Everything's wrong. I hardly know who I am. These nightmares are the first dreams I've had in at least the last six years. My memories... are lost. I don't remember most of my life."

"How do you mean? Were you hurt?"

"No." He thought on it, staring at the river. "Not that—"

"You remember."

The gold and gray of his eyes pierced with cold guilt. "Exactly."

"How?"

"I've no idea. The oldest clear memory I have is meeting Knax. He took me in six years ago when I woke up on the streets of Steslyres. We've tried spells and remedies for both memories and to incite dreams. He encourages I expand my taste in tobacco leaves, hoping a new scent will trigger memories."

"What about the Rivyn?"

"I'm aware of those aspects of my life. I can't recall every detail. They're blurred. Experiences, not people. Practices, but not missions."

"I'm sorry."

Honestly confused, he frowned. "Why?"

"No one deserves to forget themselves. How could you ever know peace?" No wonder he thought peace was a lie. Exhaling, she wrapped her good arm around him and guided him to appreciate the water cooling their noses.

"A waxing Moon paves the way to renewal. She's always listening, should we set aside worry and accept the prospect of change. It's the nature of the sea. Lest our sought-after answers drown in the void. I've learned, you must be willing to take that chance. The Moon and her guardians can't act in your stead. No one can."

"You say she's listening?" He whispered beneath the beginnings of few tears.

"Even in the darkest of Harrowings. When we're through with this, we'll find a way to get your memories back, sort through what's happened to you. I promise."

She grazed her fingers along his shoulder blades, offering solidarity, lost for what else to say. The glow from the ship's ochre-hued lanterns toyed with his russet waves. The gleam intensified for a brief second and twinkled in her necklace as they stood shoulder to shoulder in quiet reflection.

Jeddeith pulled her in close around the shoulders, his breathing deep, relaxed. Without thinking much on it, she rested her head on his chest.

"Torlen dovnym." His chest hummed on her temple as he spoke.

Maijerda's cheeks sparked with a flint of contented joy. "Torlen lexnym. Thank you for being vulnerable with me."

Wordlessly, Jeddeith kissed her temple, lingering while the guardians flashed unnaturally bright, their auras swirling and reaching in the sky. With their flare came an idea. A steady rhythm of an idea, honoring the curves of roving hills. It bore a musicality as it leapt from a peak of irresolution and blanketed her.

Jeddeith's point, from their talk on the rooftop, entered her mind and mingled with her idea. "She was left with nothing to do except what everyone thought impossible."

"Hm?"

"Cry." Softly pulling from his hold, she revered the Moon. Maijerda knew the faetale by heart. Treating it as song to be embedded with her as one. "Never had the Moon shed tears. But on that night, burdened by grief. The Moon could only weep." That was it. Staring at her this entire time. Screaming at her to do more than listen, to understand! Elated, her heart galloped as she grasped Jeddeith's coat. "I think I know how to repair the Veil. We need the Moon's tears."

CHAPTER FORTY

THE MOON'S TEARS

"THE MOON'S TEARS?" WYTT'S LAUGH ECHOED in the storage room below deck. A single lantern and Wytt's motes of golden light bobbing in the stead of a campfire.

"Yes! I know it seems literal. Maybe she wasn't missing the Moon's tears specifically, but I think she was focusing on such a visceral reaction for a reason."

"You think your mother was trying to communicate with you to retrieve the Moon's tears to save the Veil?"

Why did Wytt have to say it like that? Sheesh. "Based on Nadín's insight, I'm not sure if she ever deciphered what was missing from their ritual. But it feels like she's pushing me in that direction. What else do we have?"

Jeddeith, leaning with forearms on his thighs, hadn't covered his tattoos back up. He was lost in them, dazed while she spoke. "I think you're on to something. It's worth looking into."

Footsteps sent Maijerda's heart to skip a beat. Lumbering with worn stone. "As do I."

Spinning on her barrel, Maijerda beamed at Knax. "Oh, thank Fates. We hoped you wouldn't be too far behind."

Sitting like a grandfather with weary knees, Knax took the empty spot, placing his astrolabe in his bag. "The winds were fair. I left as soon as I awoke. Brought what I could of your belongings." He motioned to their packs behind him. "Fortuitous that the sun sets early this season."

"Do you know why Nadín left?"

Disappointed, his voice showing he was trying to understand Nadín's reasoning, Knax said, "I'm sorry to say I don't. She must have left while I was resting. I searched for a note or a clue as to where she went. There was nothing, I'm afraid. I suspect she went home actually. That is her business. I will speak with her when this is through."

Noticing Maijerda's sling, Jeddeith's exposed tattoos and bandage, Knax raised an eyebrow to Wytt. "Seems I've missed plenty this last day."

"Oh you have n-n-no idea." Wytt was equally enthusiastic to recount their harrowing experience and to be speaking with a gargoyle. How the shine in his eyes didn't dull a drop while he began the tale.

They took turns in explaining to Knax about Lyrian's attack in the Menagerie, leaving no detail behind. He was steadfast in hiding his concern and doubt, assuming he was verging on those outlooks.

"Knax," Jeddeith continued after Maijerda finished. "You shouldn't be here. I'm grateful for your help, but if Lyrian is out for blood, she will stop at nothing."

"I appreciate you trying to protect me. How selfish would I be to protect myself when she's hungry for vengeance against you?" His stone eyes, no color, but carved with pupil and veins, would've welled with tears if he were able.

"There's nothing I can do to alter her past or her rage against my mother. We can keep you safe. Please, go back to Steslyres. Find Nadín."

"It's no use, my friend. I've quite made up my mind. That begs the question. How are we going to fetch the Moon's Tears?"

"Oh, fuck if I know. Has anyone ever actually spoken to the Moon?" Maijerda had reached her fill of sitting still. She began pacing, mulling over the faetale and massaging her neck. "I'm getting ahead of myself. Let's all parse through this tale, one by one." She offered the faetale to Wytt. "Please, after you."

Wytt obliged and handed the faetale to Jeddeith who passed it to Knax, landing with Maijerda to finish off their reading. "For all the tapestry to glean," she repeated at the end. "Assuming there are spools of arcana, the Spark is interacting with each of them in this tale, yes?"

Knax gently scratched under his chin and down his stone column of a neck. "A sound perspective."

"Wonderful. If we apply that understanding, you see her with the Norn warning her of the potential of fate."

Wytt held a hand up as he realized the connection to what he read. "Nadín's explanation of the spools. To which we are raveling, it's right here." He stood and took the faetale in hand, pointing to the passage of raveling depths.

Smiling with his realization, Maijerda was ever so pleased he was following the maze in her mind. "Exactly. And here..." She flipped to the Spark discovering touch, smell, sight, sound, and taste. "She is encompassed by experiences relating to the senses."

Wytt underlined the word *fleeting* with his finger. "That which is fleeting," he quoted Nadín.

Jeddeith fussed with his shirtsleeves and folded his arms. "Which leaves her final mention. All which is unveiling."

"Mother made it quite obvious I realize, now the glass has shattered. The elements."

Clacking on the wooden planks, Knax paced beside them. "Fate, sensory experience, elements."

"I can't believe I didn't catch it sooner. Each is a spool Mother accounted for in the ritual. But it was with Jeddeith I realized the importance of the Moon being rendered to the impossible. To weep."

Wytt fighting to not frown, held up a hand. "Are we sure this is the right call?"

"Yes. I've got, for the first time since this chaos unleashed, a good feeling about this. If we want to repair the Veil and learn what spool was missing in their ritual, we have to speak with the Moon."

"And keep ahead of Lyrian."

"That too." Maijerda bit the inside of her cheek. "Well. We can travel several days away from where the captain takes us. Once we're safe from the ocean, we should try whatever we can to connect with her. But we better rest up. We've the impossible to collect." She couldn't help the smidge of levity in her step as she left to speak with the captain. Foolish as it may be to believe in wisps, wishes, and the madness behind the stars, she'd never been more confident in the path that lay ahead.

CHAPTER FORTY-ONE

Rife with Vexation

THOSE FOOLS THOUGHT THEY COULD ESCAPE?

They believed they were safe if they ran?

Cowards, each of them! Jeddeith hid behind lies. Maijerda cowered to corrupted truth. The rose devil they kept as a friend. He wasn't worthy of being a descendant of devils. Wyttrikus. Winter kissed. His joy would be short lived in the end when she took them from him one by one.

If they'd a spine, they wouldn't have fled. They'd have faced her and fought.

Lyrian, weak as she may be, was rife with vexation. Her entire body flared with pain. Stretching, scraping, radiating pain. She'd tested her limits without care in the Menagerie, ready to take what was rightfully hers. That damn book, Maijerda's blood, and Jeddeith's threads.

"They slipped through my fingers. I won't let it happen again." She pleaded with herself in the ocean. Commanding it to soothe her skin. Lyrian was feverish, her head pounding, the ocean's cool waters steaming around her.

She had one dream left to weave for Jeddeith. Though her body and arcana were dangerously close to rupturing from strain, Lyrian swore to not hold back. If she failed in swaying him to claim his true destiny, she'd be forced to use what remained of her arcana to tear the Veil. She wouldn't stand for it. Not when their defeat was within her grasp.

Jeddeith was inept enough to slip sight of their location to her once before. Who's to say he wouldn't do so again?

Slinking beneath the surface, Lyrian swam to ocean floor. The sand was as close to earth as she could muster in these waters. After she'd flooded the Menagerie and they teleported to the ship, Denratis sailed the *Oracle Rift* far from any shore.

This earth would bend to her will. Seek the man doomed to fall at her hand. She hooked her fingers in the sand, sketching a rune.

He thought himself clever. It was a pitiful victory to say he'd outwitted her by willing himself to die in each dream. If he wanted to wallow in his grave, Lyrian was more than happy to seal his coffin and rob him of the honor in drowning. Bringing a handful of sand to her lips, Lyrian swallowed it whole. The grit grazed her throat as she entered a state of consciousness to weave the death Jeddeith so desperately craved.

INTERLUDE:

Poetic Irony

We assume you fall
prey to questioning.

Always questioning.

Wouldn't you agree,
it's often in dreams…

…when the obscure
or significant occur?

Inherently, mortals instill
a deeper meaning
with poetic irony.

This is not to be
misconstrued to mean
you should take it
upon yourself
to create
those moments.

It would be in
punishably poor taste
to disrupt the…

…weaving of our threads.
We assume,
you know better…

…than to trifle with
the importance
of adaptability.

Even if you are unsure…

You will eventually
learn the truth of it.

Whether it be here.
Or beyond the stars.

Chapter Forty-Two

Weep an Ocean's Depth

BLURRED VISION. TREMORS IN HIS HANDS. Quickened heartbeat. Overactive sense of smell. Diminished appetite.

Small prices to pay to go without sleep for five days. They traveled swift. Without a true destination in mind. Other than wanting to put distance between them and the ocean. A hopeful damper on Lyrian's chances of finding them while they discerned how to speak with the Moon.

With their journey Jeddeith swore he wouldn't risk Lyrian getting inside his head. They'd sailed for three days north, per the captain's guidance. She never pushed with questions, saying she and her crew had business in Neseth as it was. It would be no trouble leaving them in the wilderness.

Knax stayed hidden on the ship until their last night aboard, flying ahead to shore with astrolabe readied to track them. Time was both a blur and stretches of the same scenes without sleep. Sailing, watching the waters for signs of Lyrian. Then hiking along the coast, span after span of coastal rock and pine. Mist whispering to them. Like the stories of dwymers, calling their victim's name on the wind. His imagination was getting the best of him. Which wasn't something Jeddeith often admitted.

Maijerda was concerned over his lack of sleep. She tried to sway him to rest, rid himself of the tincture's side effects. He wouldn't stop taking it. He was reacting to these dreams all wrong. With emotion. Rather, he needed to analyze them.

Having stopped for camp on their third night of hiking, Jeddeith stoked the campfire while the others slept. He spun the tincture bottle in his hand mindlessly. Each nightmare focused on an aspect of himself he no longer remembered. Which shouldn't be possible. Recognizing he couldn't remember *what* was being targeted, highly improbable. But not impossible.

Gods in shadow. None of this should bother him. He was trained to know better. To a point. Most people felt incomplete. It's what made you tangible. Gave you experience. Purpose.

He pinched the bridge of his nose. Debating on risking sleep. He *should* sleep. Otherwise he'd run himself dry of tincture. And then what? With unsteady fingers he shoved the bottle to the bottom of his pack. He unfolded a blanket and lay nearest Maijerda. Her expression, soft. Peaceful. Closing his eyes, he released the stress in his jaw and hands.

May she bring him luck.

JEDDEITH WOKE UP from a dreamless void, lying flat on his back. He tried to sit upright or roll to the side. Each attempt led to thudding against panels of wood. Cramped and cold. He searched in the dark with his hands. It wasn't long before he scraped his palm into splinters. He winced and instinctively drew back.

Searching was pointless. He knew where he was.

Moldy stench.

Thin air.

Each breath constricting his chest.

So it was this next? Burying him in a coffin was a cheap move.

Lyrian addressed him then, both echoing around him in the coffin and invading his consciousness.

"What ever is the matter? I'm stunned. You've done nothing but ensure your demise in each of my dreams. I thought I'd lend you a hand."

"A touch passive aggressive, isn't it?"

She laughed, the wood absorbing her tone. "Deflect all you want. I know you want answers. I can offer you that. And more."

"Leave me be." He may want to break the world for answers. Never would he cater to Lyrian's behest. Ever. "I want no part in your ploys."

A pause. Creaking pine. Swelling earth. Rolling. Sifting. Whispering... to her.

"The earth here, it tastes... unusual. Sulfur and snow." Her voice drifted in contemplation. "Have it your way. I will weep an ocean's depth for you."

"Those tears aren't for me."

"Aren't they?"

"No. I know your kind. You only care for yourself."

Her cackle lashed and reverberated in his mind through to his bones. "Your confidence is impressive. You think you know me?"

The earth rumbled outside, threatening him.

"That'll be the last mistake you make. I hope it's worth it." As her voice echoed, roots and vines burst through the coffin, taking hold of him.

A rush of mildew-rotten soil pooled inside the coffin, burying him. He fought against instinct to claw himself free. It would never be enough. The soil devoured him with teeth of gravel. From skin to muscle, and bone. Down to his soul.

"Jeddeith! Wake up. You're dreaming. Wake up!"

He doubled over, taking Maijerda's hand and spewing soil.

Maijerda rubbed his back, working to soothe him. "Sh, sh, sh, It's all right. You're here. You're alive. Let it out."

He groaned but it turned earthen and he retched another bucketful of dirt and pebbles. Dry and grinding, his eyes swelled and watered. "Lyrian." He coughed and relied on Maijerda to hold him upright.

Wytt handed him a water skin. "You're not weak for needing to sleep. S-s-sometimes you have to choose your battles."

He chugged the water and coughed to spit a clump of mud. "She's not exactly letting me sleep."

"What did she say?"

He struggled to look at Maijerda. This was the last thing she needed. He didn't want her worrying about him. If he dared blink away the sting in his yes, he'd break. "She buried me in a coffin. Said she'd weep an ocean's depth for my death."

The way Maijerda sighed and brushed her thumb on his face brought solemnity. Resigned and welcoming. A morbid truth.

He wanted to weep. Weep for his family, lost in his memory. For long-lost loves. For a life supposedly lived. For being smothered by Lyrian. For not being able to find peace.

He looked Maijerda in the eye. There was peace in her. She cupped his cheek and he closed his eyes to cry and grieve. At last. He didn't feel guilty for it. He needed to *feel*.

"I want peace." He looked her straight in her forest-gem eyes.

"You'll find it. It's all right to let yourself feel your distress. It doesn't make less of you."

Tears welled in his eyes as Maijerda guided him to lie down and rest his head in her lap. "You should rest, Wytt. I've got it from here." Stroking his hair, she sang to Jeddeith of her beloved fae pond and wishes of doing no wrongs.

CHAPTER FORTY-THREE

CAULDRON'S BRIM

GRAY MOURNED THROUGH CAULDRON'S BRIM. MUCH as it had for the last four days as they trekked the mountains. Oh what she'd give for some tea or coffee. But they'd run out just yesterday. Time grins smugly when it reflects on how it flows without care. Maijerda was certain it was mocking them as they pushed further from the ocean, the days rushing by. Taunting them that at any moment Lyrian would appear and they'd be out of luck. Failing to protect the Veil. They'd have to stop soon and give their best to try speaking with the Moon.

The night the captain anchored for them to disembark, she'd mentioned they were near Neseth. A supposedly sleepy, but superstitious town nestled at the base of Cauldron's Brim. It was all rumor, but per Wytt, tavern-goer banter painted the Brim as possessed by spirits burning with hunger.

Within the Brim was Catacomb Loch. Wytt had gone on about how he remembered reading about an ancient civilization abandoned in the loch. Never forgetting to remind her it was assumed the ruins were cursed.

423

Wytt shivered and looked to her. "I'm telling you, it's all haunted."

"Sure."

"Sure? Oh Mmmaijerda. C-creatures manifest here out of sh-sheer spite and belief. It's what made the people of N-neseth a superstitious lot. Oagbain, they call it."

"If I see a ghost, I'll let you know. Deal?" She winked and patted Wytt's shoulder before ducking under a branch, avoiding ghastly clutches. In doing so, she nearly squashed a cluster of spotted mushrooms rooted near a resurrection fern bed heavily obscured by fog.

She plucked a spare jar from her belongings and placed several mushrooms inside with a clipping of the fern before the others could wander too far. The fern curled at the tip, much like the one tattooed on her arm.

"Wytt, you might appreciate this." She pushed aside more cragged branches and tossed him the jar.

"Is that a resurrection f-f-f-fern?

"It is."

"They normally don't grow th-th-this far n-n-north."

"Indeed." She smiled as Wytt rambled to himself and went to Jeddeith. "How are you holding?"

"As well as I can."

"J-j-jeddeith? Maijerda? Do you smell that?" Wytt was glancing in the mist, distantly.

"Can't say I do," Jeddeith replied.

"Me neither." She tossed the remark over her shoulder.

"We're close." A wisp of warmed breath curled from Wytt's lips. "I can smell it. A change…in arcana."

How was that possible? Smelling arcana? Dramatically on cue, Maijerda shivered and fixed her cowl over her ears and nose. The wind whistled and prickled her skin, sending a specter of breath from her too.

"That's not ominous at all," she grumbled. Disoriented by a bank of fog, she stumbled into a thicket of thorn pricked trees. "Ow! Scalded piss!"

Their bramble bodies were naked, bent and twisted into an archway. Maijerda backed away and held her arms out to keep the others from advancing. She tried to get a feeling for how high the tunnel stretched but the very top of the archway was blanketed in mist.

"Did I miss something? Or did this appear of its own accord?" Maijerda didn't dare take her eyes off it.

"No you're not alone."

Ravens cawed as if in foreboding agreement that they were indeed, not alone in these woods.

"Stay close." Jeddeith unsheathed his sword. "Vythsaden rosq. Dusk is falling."

Maijerda squinted through the canopy and followed him into the gullet. Wytt scuttled in last as she waited for him.

He took her hand and they were forced to walk tightly knit. The tunnel gave the illusion of a rattling rib cage. Disconcerting was that it may not have been an illusion at all.

The contorted brambles were relentless, snagging her sleeves and scratching her ears.

"Can you see an end?" Maijerda shouted to Jeddeith.

"No. The earth feels unsteady here."

"We shouldn't be here when night falls," Maijerda seconded. "I gather the Brim doesn't maintain a singular state. I wouldn't be shocked to hear it can shape shift."

Wytt eyed each hollow shadow. "Can a forest be a d-d-d-dwymer?"

"Hells if I know. If so, we need to stay several steps ahead."

"R-r-r-right. You make it sound easy."

She chuckled. "There will come a day when we look on this as if it was nothing."

"Do-Do. How can you believe that?"

"Because I have to. I have to believe one day, all will be at peace." She gave him a final squeeze before catching up with Jeddeith. Each snap of dead foliage beneath her boot was a reminder of an emptying hourglass.

"Notice anything worthwhile?"

Jeddeith stooped below a branch. "The essence here is tainted. I can't see the forest's aura in this state. I'm sure it's marred. It should be dead."

"Aah, lovely." She pointed ahead at the tunnel, now narrowed in front of him.

"We're losing daylight," Jeddeith said. "Much faster than we should be."

He strode inside, Maijerda falling in step behind him. Branches caught on her coat as she flattened into them. "Wytt, why don't you switch places with me."

He scurried by and she eyed his footprints, tilting her head at a glimmer in the corner of her eye. She kneeled to sift through the gravel and leaves where Wytt had stood.

Frosted ice crystals, geometric in shape and the size of seeds, clustered along the heel of Wytt's footprint. The heat from her fingers melted a crystal of six patterned sides.

A new cold rode the wind to her and licked the back of her neck. Instinctively she pivoted, keeping crouched. "Jeddeith."

The forest inhaled deeply as a billows stoking a forge. "Jeddeith..." she sung in warning, knowing she was wasting time by staring at the bulging branches.

"What is it?"

The tunnel growled, aching and distressed.

Maijerda straightened and struck her foot into the dirt to sprint away. A branch meaty as a horse's leg cleaved in half, expelling maroon gunk with chunks of blackened flesh. It splattered the side of Maijerda's face.

She reached for the spoiled paint knowing damn well that was wishful thinking. Smearing the blood, she held her hand aghast, the ground rumbling beneath her.

"Run!" She charged at the will of survival.

The tunnel beat her to the punch and erupted in a cacophony akin to a ship's hull snapping in a hurricane.

It was a grotesque performance. The forest drooled blood and thrashed to break from entanglement, hungry for them.

Who knew how long it had been since the forest of the Brim last fed. Those who did were likely since harvested, the trees filled with these unfortunate travelers.

Jeddeith kept his head low and spun his sword to slice at the snares. Blood splattered in Jeddeith's mouth from a nastily splintered root and he spat it out, smearing grit in his beard. "Keep moving!"

"No shit!"

The tunnel's end was no sooner in sight, worsening her burning adrenaline. She was sent reeling as an entire tree quaked in half and collapsed around her, jaws unhinged.

She leapt over the fallen trunk and ran into Wytt, who had doubled back to help her.

"Go!" She insisted.

Light dissipated as she ran through the belly of the beast, hoping to burst through its side and be done with the chase.

"There!" Jeddeith motioned to a gray light seeping through, fading into the dusting of dusk. He ran a final few pounding steps and up a boulder, diving through a tear in the forest.

Wytt toppled through after him less than gracefully.

Maijerda bounded up the boulder a split second behind, skidding between the two on the other side of the tear.

She rounded on the tunnel instinctively, still anchored on her elbows. She panted and swore under her breath as the tunnel knit seamlessly together and sealed shut. Panting, skin scratched and bruised, eyes sore, all were quieted by the assault, lying in rock.

Maijerda smeared blood and gunk around her face even though she was trying to clear it from the corners of her eyes.

"O-over here!" Wytt beckoned them to the edge of the equally dreary hill they were standing on.

They heeded and flanked him, taking in the landscape flooding the dell. Before them was the quiet beauty of Catacomb Loch, waters tender with picturesque tones of the gloaming.

CHAPTER FORTY-FOUR

THE CATACOMB LOCH

THE RUINS OF CATACOMB LOCH WERE a hollow place. On the verge of crumbling to dust. Strange, given the hum in Jeddeith's mind. And bones. There was a presence here. He'd likely need to gaze in the shadow or astral realm to see what exactly. Otherwise, there was one other living creature here. Their presence, absolute.

A cascading waterfall. Midnight blue as the doleful tone of night. It poured into the loch. Jeddeith wandered from Maijerda, mentally piecing together collapsed arches and windows. Deciphering the architecture. Debris of a staircase littered what once might have been a paved pathway. The layout was as ritualistic as the catacombs beneath the city of Pimentte. Ornate sculptures of winged creatures guarding gates. Stone and ironwork buildings with majestic moldings. Pieces desecrated beyond recognition.

This destruction was to be respected. Wear is a reward of living a satisfied life.

It is not terrible to be scarred.

Scars were a testament to surviving. He should know.

Jeddeith ran his hand along the banister of another staircase. This led to a structure composed of twelve pillars. In the center was a dais of marble. Oddly, it appeared as if it had been polished. Daily, for centuries.

The roof peaked and met at a triangular point. Capped with an ornate weathervane. The top articulated the point of a spear aiming for the stars. Likely it was significant when a specific constellation aligned with it. Nothing about the dais indicated which.

Maijerda called him over from an iron gate adjacent to the temple. He walked from the dais as the vane squeaked with a breeze.

The gate was made of stone and black iron. A ritualistic means of guarding a cemetery, even centuries ago. Black iron was attributed to protection for the living from wayward spirits, encouraging them to rest. Not all spirits took kindly to this. Few cultures chose to celebrate the deceased instead and offer gifts to appease spectral restlessness, dictated by the season. And Moon, actually.

On the other end of the spectrum were cultures who believed the living had no right disturbing the dead's resting place. The dead had earned their keep, and punishment for trespassing was well founded in their eyes. He appreciated the sprawling patches of headstones. Mausoleums too. Above-ground crypts. No collective method of burial then. He'd need a closer look to tell if the styles varied by era. If they were old enough, they may lack the date with year, season, and Moon of birth and death. Some societies didn't romanticize time as it was now.

"May the wind hold you." Maijerda spoke as if praying but was disconnected from her own words as she shut the gate.

They chose an alcove carved from a desecrated building near the waterfall for camp. By the time they did, Knax found them. Grateful they'd stopped. All agreed here was as good a place as any to settle and weave tapestry in attempts to speak with the Moon.

This area was lined with stone figures. Remnants of runes, etched along the bottom of the statues. Maijerda brushed muck from the most childlike of the statues. Tenderly as she had cleared his tears those few days prior. She whispered a word of gratitude in A'lorynn.

Wytt dusted another statue of a man in armor. Full plate, bulky. An ancient form. "They're w-w-watching over us."

Clearing another layer of time, Maijerda rubbed her thumb along a section of runes. "I don't think they've had someone to look after for centuries."

"Maybe we've eased their boredom in this place."

"Have they been mmmodeled after living p-p-people? Or are they something from a s-s-s-story?"

Maijerda placed her gloved hands at her hips. "Honestly I'm not sure. I might argue the characters in a story are alive as you or I."

Wytt narrowed his eyes. "N-n-now you're splitting hairs."

"When presented with a joke, do they not laugh as we do? Do we not empathize with their grief and mourning? If killed, do they not bleed? Do you not hear them speak in your mind?" She waved her ringed fingers, inciting his retort.

"She's right, you know." Knax grinned. "I might argue that stone is very much a living and breathing thing."

"Y-yes, fine. You win." Wytt smiled, shrugging before mumbling and returning with Knax to the fire pit he was building.

"I always wanted a sibling." She kicked at a rock. "Someone to fuss over, care for, and naturally harass. Sure they might've emerged into the world somewhat scarred from jesting and tricks. I came to terms that I would never know what it meant to fulfill that role. ıdre fertility is quite unpredictable, did you know that?"

Sighing, he placed his hands behind his back. He *did* know. It should've saddened him. But why? He shook his head to center his mind. "I do."

"One child in a tiraen lifetime, if they do so at all. Can you believe it? Fascinating. Makes for smaller families. I've learned that relationships we choose outside of family are as binding as blood."

"Indeed they are."

She paused her leisurely stroll. "What of your family? Do you…"

What of them? What could he be expected to say? Logically speaking, he had a family. Friends too. Past lovers, both women and men. What they looked like or what their names were, were a mystery. "I don't remember them. I'm unsure if they're alive."

"I'm sorry."

She didn't question him further. In fact, she didn't say anything more while they walked the loch's shore. Cruor Moonlight highlighted her features, making her fiercely ethereal. As though she were fae. Clearly she was meant for the Moon's mystique. Especially at its peak fullness. It complemented her stoicism. Maybe there were traces of fae blood in her. It would stand to reason considering what they learned of her mother. Fae. Creatures of a more mysterious lineage than ıdre. There were countless types of fae. From wisp to nymph and everything beyond and in between.

When they returned to camp they found Wytt snoring by the fire, Knax keeping watch. Jeddeith doffed his coat and draped it over her shoulders. She was terrible at hiding her shivers. "It's been a long day."

"It has. What can I do?"

"About what?"

"To help you rest. Ever since your last nightmare…"

"I'll sleep. She doesn't haunt me every night."

"If you insist." She wasn't accepting his deflections.

Maybe this would suffice. He dug the sleepless nights tincture from his pack and gave it to her. "Now I won't have a choice. Take it."

"You're sure?"

He nodded curtly.

Maijerda touched his cheek to raise his chin. "Wake me if you need me."

"I will." Bowing his head, he slid her hand from his face and kissed the top of it. "Hold my luck?"

"Let the candlelight keep."

ACT V

CANDLE RHYME

A goodnight wish, bestowing the wisdom
of light on a loved one

This match once struck
will hold your luck.
Goodnight my sweet,
let the candlelight keep.

CHAPTER FORTY-FIVE

Pearls Covered in Blood

MAIJERDA HUNKERED UNDER JEDDEITH'S COAT, THE Cruor Moon reflecting buoyantly along the loch's surface. A dark promise with its red gleam.

She couldn't reliably tell if it was about time for her bleeding cycle to begin, having skipped the last three Moons. It wasn't regular in any way, shape, or form. But if the pains in her abdomen were any indication, she'd be miserable shortly.

Unable to sleep, the night chilled unreasonably quick. She couldn't shake the gnawing sadness from their conversation. It wasn't her own either, it was Jeddeith's sorrow. Again, something settled between his words and quiet. Something she wanted to pry into. No, no. Pry was the wrong word. That connotated she was spying on him out of nosiness.

Gone were those days. She worried about him. Cared for him. Wanted to be at his side and help recover his past while protecting him from it all the same. Damn the cogwheels buzzing in her ear! Sitting still wouldn't do at all.

Maijerda pulled her knees into her chest and groaned into his coat, smoke rich with tobacco as usual. This one was more akin to maple, citrus, and whiskey. Maijerda bounced to her feet and dusted off her boots. A noise drew her from the act.

Actually, to call it a *noise* diminished the effect. There is very little in Drynn which could dutifully explain the reincarnated anguish.

"Bleeding piss." Maijerda sighed in exasperation and tugged at the maroon hem of her shirt. For what else could she anticipate from the Harrowing of night, but something horrid?

The trickling chime sounded for several seconds more, luring Maijerda nearer. Even though there was better judgement squared away in her instincts, she couldn't resist.

She climbed over rubble of what could have once been a humble garden wall and paused.

Tingling and ringing along the cobbles at its base, the waterfall was singing. Her heart flushed with anticipation and urged her closer.

The nearer the falls, the more vividly the cry wept into the loch and she ached for their hurt. Now at the foot of the waterfall, the loudness was almost debilitating. Flicks of water splashed onto her one right after another. She didn't bother blotting them dry. Sobbing rushed through the curtains of pouring water.

There were grips and foot holds in the rock. With some muscle and sweat, maybe she could reach the sound. She dug boot and nail into the stone and climbed, looking for an opening behind the falls.

Her boot slipped and pebbles rolled into the burbling chasm. She pulled her body against the rock, planting her cheek into jagged tips. Panting, she peered upward, the water building on her face and lashes.

"Course," she grumbled.

An opening was within reach, behind water curving from the entrance over a jutting canopy of rock. Fingers stinging from the climb, she shimmied until she could wrap herself around the edge and hopped inside.

Maijerda shook her hands and rubbed them against the sash at her waist to force life into them. The waterfall echoed robustly into the cavern, the weeping no longer audible.

She swept wet curls into a loose bun, debating whether or not she should turn back.

Someone could be hurt. Or in danger. The least she could do was check. She had decided that, after all. To climb up here? That decision was hers, wasn't it?

This could be a trap.

Then again if it wasn't, someone here was suffering.

Inexplicably terrified she would lose the sound again to the waterfall, she crept from it and the weeping returned.

Water plinked to puddles in rugged divots, reverberating each droplet. Moss made patchy appearances along boulders, nooks, and crannies in the rock. The only way Maijerda could even see was thanks to a peacock hued glow emitting from each patch.

The puddles grew larger and illuminated the tunnel via the reflection of moss. Swinging to the right, the tunnel reached into a rounded pocket encompassing a sizable hot spring.

Centered in the pool was a woman. Hair a silky burnt opal, fanned in the water as if a skirt. She was waist deep, hunched and bawling.

"Are you...are you hurt?" The words came from Maijerda, disregarding her wariness.

A shudder, a sob, a sniffle.

"I mean you no harm." Maijerda crept to her, one foot in front of the other. The water seeped through and soaked her clothes, unapologetic in how quickly it seized her bones. Maijerda reached to touch her bare shoulder.

Her devastated woe echoed in the cavern before instantaneously cutting off as deftly as a blade. She lolled her head upright and lengthened her back as if on puppet strings. Maijerda retracted her hand and sloshed backward through the water.

Irrationally stiff and fluid, the woman stood to her full height, which didn't prevent her hair from splaying in the water. Sweat coated Maijerda's skin, fingers and chest tingly with panic. There was nothing metaphorical about it. Maijerda was absolutely terrified.

The woman turned slowly as moving clouds, her hair dissipating and morphing into a putrid green around crystal eyes. "You've brought fate crashing upon yourself. You've no one else to blame." The woman's accusations were the equivalent of a string of pearls covered in blood.

Both alluring and terrible. This was a dream. It must be.

"You weren't supposed to look."

The creature's jaw elongated, sending tears through her parchment thin skin from the stretching it took to do so. Unhinged, the creature shrieked a wail that would decimate the nearby crypts. She sailed for Maijerda.

Trying to flee, Maijerda kicked her heel back and stepped inside a jagged hole. She cursed as she lost her balance and fell flat in the shallows. She rolled her ankle, gasping at the pulsating tear as the woman reached her and soared straight through her. Shielding her face with her arms, Maijerda stayed put as she dissipated upon contact. The creature's scream faded in the cavern, leaving nothing but an eerie silence.

Dragging herself out of the shallows, Maijerda laid flat on her back.

Good fucking Fates. What the hells was that? Wytt might be right about this place being haunted.

After a few good groans and mumbles, Maijerda readied to limp her way back down the waterfall, her ankle tender as ever. She managed, through gritted teeth and pluck.

At the base of the fall she glanced up to the opening. Keeping an ear open for the wailing to return. There were no sobs, or music, just the water. Was that disappointment brewing? Better not be. Turning away to head for camp, she startled at Knax standing right behind her.

"Ah! Shit! Knax, what are you doing here?"

"I've been calling to you, you didn't answer, which worried me. I followed you but you were gone by the time I arrived."

Perplexed, Maijerda clutched her collar, easing her breaths. "Wh—wh—what? I didn't hear you at all."

"Hmm, I was afraid of that. Come here," He soothed as he placed an arm around her to support her ankle. "Tell me what happened."

She obliged him without fuss, describing the ghostly woman in full. She included too her warning: "You weren't supposed to look."

"Hm." Knax pondered this over. "It seems to me you faced a banshee. Perhaps a guardian of these ruins. Or a ghoul settling to haunt them. Either way. You say you don't know what she meant by that?"

"No. I don't. Truly. The night we met Nadín, I hallucinated a stranger whispering it to me. Blamed it on the booze. Then I heard it again when Lyrian attacked us. This was not in my head. It was real."

"Another curiosity for another day, let's get you to bed, yes?"

She agreed to call it night, after they stopped to give her ankle a break. Leaning against a boulder, she kept her ankle still. The Moon watched over them, protecting with her light, a dim glow in vein of a campfire. Maybe they were planning the impossible in seeking the Moon's Tears. All this as a distraction from what Maijerda feared to be the truth. A truth that she wanted to run from, desperately.

Maijerda's mind started drifting to a concern she'd shared with no one since Lyrian's attack. Something Lyrian had thrown in her face.

"Knax."

"Yes?"

"Do you think my mother meant to use me for the Veil? Was it my tears she needed?" Her fears, speculations, and hurt freed themselves of her secreted fretting all at once. "Was she going to hurt me, kill me to make herself cry? Crafting the perfect spell component for sorrow?"

Knax stretched his wings, ever so slightly and shifted on his perch. "This is stemming from Lyrian trying to get under your skin, I gather."

"Oh she did more than try. I've been thinking about it for days. I didn't want to worry anyone."

Holding his claw open for her to take, he gently enclosed her hand. "The truth is, we may never know her intentions. She loved you dearly. That we know, because you lived it. She had lifetimes to experience change. It's ultimately up to you what you want to believe. What you decide will be your truth. Bear in mind that your reasoning may be all you have to cope with. Lyrian be damned."

"I'd like to think I knew my mother well enough. This has shown me quite the opposite. All these wrong doings falling into my lap to heal? Who would've thought."

"I can think of no one better for the task."

Maijerda could. There must've been a thousand people better built for this burden. Fates knew she couldn't turn it away. She had to believe there was an end to this that she could achieve.

They rested for a while longer in the Moon's glow, until her nerves subsided and they returned to camp. Knax kept watch as they slept and Maijerda fought to keep from manifesting the banshee's woe in her mind. Never wanting to witness her derelict sorrow again if she could help it.

She swore the wind carried the banshee's warning from the cave. Whispering into existence as she fell asleep.

You weren't supposed to look.

CHAPTER FORTY-SIX

REIGN OF THE MOON

UPON MOONRISE THE NEXT EVENING THE four of them gathered in camp to confer about their ideas and concerns.

Full Cruor Moon.

The highest of stakes.

How impossible was it to speak with the Moon? Shouldn't his years as a Rivyn help him calculate the odds? Jeddeith was left without footholds on the concept.

Knax suggested combining rune stones with his incense and Moonlight. They'd have to generate an incantation, but they might weave between the Moon's light with his to speak with her. Wytt thought to capitalize on the presence of the loch. If what he'd read in the Menagerie was true, he believed he could treat the surface as a mirror and in turn a portal. Either to be transported to the Moon or as a modified scrying basin to speak with her instead of observing her. He explained people once had a stronger connection to thrive under the reign of the Moon. Per the stories. If that connection was seen as broken, perhaps he could symbolize fixing it. Healing it, rather. A stretch in practice, Wytt admitted, but all agreed they should experiment.

Jeddeith's potential contribution wasn't feasible. Shadow gazing, projecting his consciousness in the astral realm, was a practice he'd not entertained since before the Rivyn fell. It was risky. Far too arduous. And he'd need Maijerda to be the one shadow gazing, not him. He couldn't possibly teach her a practice he didn't recall. Rubbing his forearm along his tattoos, he quit pondering.

"I was certain you'd have a quip of a trick to try," Maijerda said with that wink of hers.

"Hm. Been weeding through them for the more realistic of our options." The way her ruby locks absorbed the red Moon distracted him. "There's much in the way of possibilities but I've little confidence in them. If we fail with these attempts first, we could try praying."

Too simple, wasn't it?

Cocking his head, Wytt grinned. "Why didn't I th-think of that? Far more logical than what I was trying to come up w-with. I was about to suggest Maijerda drink from the loch where she's reflected."

"I don't see how it's better than your ideas. They've more arcane anchors to appeal to the Moon's complexity. A simple prayer won't be enough."

"We think." Wytt held up a finger. "So we think." He enunciated each word and eyed Maijerda before looking back to Jeddeith.

Ah, yes. True. It might depend on who was praying. She might be enough to attract the Moon's attention if she had the right state of mind. "Maijerda, what would you like to try?"

With a crack of her wrist, it was not a surprise Maijerda hid her idea from them, claiming nothing came to mind. Jeddeith didn't buy that. Not after all their hours of research in the

Menagerie. It also wasn't his place to question her. If she were ready, she'd mention something.

She helped Wytt and Knax draw sigils in the sand to trial the rune stones as Jeddeith kept watch. While unlikely Lyrian would show here, he was wary. His sleep was dreamless since his last encounter with her in the coffin. She shouldn't know where they were. And hopefully his theory was right, if they were far from the ocean she would lack the arcane strength and means to track them. Still. Vythsaden rosq.

Cemetery seemed clear. Hills undisturbed. Trees swaying no more than usual. Loch silent still. There was no sign of her. Hells, they may actually succeed in evading her.

With the glyphs in place, Knax rolled his rune stones in the center. Deciphering the meaning of those closest to the center. Trust, water, and mouth. He then harnessed their meaning in mind and conjured Moonlight. It contrasted with the true Moon, shining his lavender light instead of blood tinged. He motioned for Maijerda to situate herself at the center of the glyphs and handed her the light, asking her to speak in A'loyrnn to appeal to the Moon. They created an incantation using the phrase "dreams the sun, so dawns the Moon" to sway Knax's Moonlight to imitate the red hue.

They tried again when both light and glyphs remained unaltered.

And again.

The glyphs did not ignite to show they'd been awoken by their use of the tapestry.

And again without success before moving on to Wytt's idea.

Standing waist deep in the loch, Wytt traced a sigil in the air and guided it to the surface. Ice formed from his palm and spread with frayed edges. He murmured to Tuvon a spell of healing, replacing key words with the Veil's broken state and healing family bonds. The ice was unmoved, only reflecting the Moon as she was in the sky.

Wytt rehashed his idea four more tries. Then came a quick shake of his head. An avoidant gaze. Shoulders slumped, he trudged back to shore. "Surely you've ssssomething on your mind. Right?" He asked Maijerda.

"Well," she paused, hesitating and looking to each of them, arms crossed as she rubbed her shoulder and paced. Her gait was off, minding her ankle. Wytt had cast a minor healing spell, given it wasn't a grave wound it eased her pain well enough. "I have one idea. It's not quite a prayer. But if what Knax said is true. For every knell there is a muse…"

Knax completed her statement. "…For every muse there is song." His stone eyes were alight with faith and pride.

"When we revealed the faetale with my lullaby, it was an experience unlike any other. Tapestry has never surged through me more than it did that night. I didn't want to believe Knax's theories on song arcana. But if I am a muse born unto a knell and my mother created this book, then perhaps the Moon would hear me through the tapestry if I weave the lullaby as a spell."

"Do you believe in your threads?" Knax asked.

Maijerda did not roll her wrist. Nor blink or waver in the slightest. "I believe in music. In stories. And the tapestry they weave."

Jeddeith bowed his head to her, captivated by her courage. "And we believe in you. You said yourself she is listening." He addressed the Moon. "All you need to do is set aside your worry. And accept—"

"The prospect of change." They spoke in unison.

"Yes," Maijerda sung peacefully. "I'm ready."

CHAPTER FORTY-SEVEN

You Must be Mended

WHAT BETTER NIGHT TO ENDURE THE impossible, than on the eve of the Festival of Embers? In a haunted loch no less. Holding her faetale open, Maijerda stood where loch met sand, water lapping on her boots. She rubbed the back of her neck. The Cruor Moon filled her with courage to face secrets, betrayal, and the ravenous void of grief. Surmounting here, with her bloody brilliance reflecting fully in the loch.

Knax lumbered next to her. "I am proud of you. She is listening." Assuring her with his smile, he left her alone to stand with Wytt and Jeddeith behind her.

They all were waiting for her to begin. "Well, enjoy the show I suppose. On three as they say."

She needed this incantation to be unique, and if she'd learned anything since the Tempest Moon, it was to trust the peculiar. With full lungs, a melody on her lips, and a hope to dream, she sang her lullaby. Crafting her intentions as if it were a spell. A true performance, sparing no expense. Bringing life to each note, playing with pitch, adding spins to open vowels, sliding to the edges of her octaves on either end. She let her voice dance unbridled, waves of emotional sensations from the dread of grief, strain of confusion, isolation in despair, swelter of rage, and the bliss of love.

A downpour of emotions cascaded through her mind, body, and spirit. Honoring them all, she paid her respects until her last note reverberated off the Brim and across the mirror of Catacomb Loch.

They waited, each biting their tongue to keep watch for changes, shifts in the wind, a rustle in the trees. Nothing made itself known at first, leaving her to leap mentally for their second plan. She was turning to Jeddeith when fog coalesced mere meters from them on the water.

Pained whispers on the wind came with it as it continued building, growing in height. It sent Maijerda's hair on end, pricked her skin. The same internal warnings to flee as the night before in the cave. The pillar of fog disappeared as a ghastly figure billowed through.

The banshee's crystal eyes pierced the dark. Her face was sunken in, replicating a mummy buried in the catacombs of D'hadian or Pimentte. "All is well, little one. I'm here to help. You seek counsel with the Moon, do you not?" She spoke with a mother's care, but the ghoulishness of her speech negated her desire to console.

"I do. My song I offered as a gift, to request passage through the portal." Fates, was she sure working on a whim. The banshee seemed to take her word as confidently as Maijerda gave it.

"A beautiful gift it was. A song long lost to her. It isn't enough."

"And why not, exactly?"

Solemnly, the banshee extended a hand in Maijerda's direction. "Your seams have been ripped open by grief. You are the one who suffers from hurt. Your wailing, piercing though you do not scream. There is no greater thief than I. I will rob you of sorrow."

This didn't elicit a reassuring feeling in the slightest. Maijerda stepped back from the water.

"You are the one I must mend." Jaw stretching to her chest, the banshee readied her wail.

"Ah, fuck."

A quaking scream beseeched Maijerda to relent. She and the others covered their ears instinctively, for what good it did. Which was absolutely nothing.

"You must be mended! You are torn! Inside. And out!" Her plea overlapped the pinging echo, dissonant and knifelike.

Maijerda staggered to unsheathed a dagger, Jeddeith having already done the same. Wytt and Knax both readied to weave.

"No! I do not need your help." Maijerda was firm in her denial. "My pain is mine to yield. Sorrow is my forge. Strife, a mallet. Perseverance, my anvil. My grief is a gilded crown. It is not yours to mend."

The banshee's next inhale rattled with the thousands of souls drained from unstitched mortals wandering into her nest. Maijerda swore they all moaned for help in that singular breath. Like the toll of an infernal bell the banshee released another feverish screech.

Forced cowering to their knees, all three clapped their hands over their ears in agony. The loch curdled below her.

Hovering to shore, she circled them as a vulture. Her words were an ethereal call of night. "What of your companions?" The vertebrae in her spine quivered, visible through patches of flaking skin and dangling strips of decomposing flesh.

"I see them as I do you." Swiveling she accounted for them. "One, two, three. Three, two, one. Are they torn? Should I mend them too? Let me— I see." She glided to a halt. "You. You are the only one who is..."

"Torn?" Maijerda shielded the others, swallowing her pounding heart.

The banshee's jaw swung with her head to lock onto Maijerda. "Shredded. To tatters, no longer mendable by anyone's needle but mine. I'm sorry, little one. I wanted to fix you before—"

"Before you kill me?"

The banshee flickered, eyes rounded, wraith-like wrists tensed. "I would never commit such a reckless crime. Mending is my kindness to give. I never kill my mendables. I only mend."

"Never?"

"Not in all my centuries."

Jeddeith tossed his scabbard aside, his finessed, curved blade dulled in the Cruor Moonlight. "You have no claim to her." He circled the banshee, footfalls measured and precise, posed with both sword and fae dagger.

"She is unstitched. Meant to die. I must mend her before she falls. Don't you desire peace for her final days? What do you know, mortal? What have your eyes seen?" Her own flashed archaically. "I have suffered for all mine have seen. For all I've done. And no one will hear me, to hear what I have seen. No one bothers to listen. You will not stand in the way of my needle. Or else you will aid my mending when I make a thimble of you."

Every grim and fragile bone floated from him to resume her advance on Maijerda. Jeddeith cut her off, reaching to brandish a second weapon. He unsheathed his obsidian black dagger, etched with runes, and geometrically cut on one side.

Repulsed, the banshee immediately shrunk at the sight.

"Filth! Mortal treachery. Where did you procure so crude a blade? The hells? A demon? A djinn?"

Jeddeith grinned a devilish grin.

"Answer me!"

He did, by slicing into her with the blade. She growled at him and swiped with her claws. Maijerda made to strike the banshee. She was ungodly quick, retaliating by screaming at Maijerda. Grunting, she stumbled to her knees and a shield of ice emerged from the sand between her and the banshee.

Behind her, stood Wytt, arms protectively held over her. "She is not your prey. Leave her b-be and hear her request."

The banshee drifted around the ice, scornful. "Loyalty. You should be grateful for his friendship. Unconditional love. You'll harness it through your mending."

Wytt blocked her reaching for Maijerda with a gust of wind, chill as Eventide.

Going in for another attack, Jeddeith aimed for her back with his black blade. She swerved and parried with an invisible force. Knax targeted a spell on her that briefly quieted her screams. Their reprieve from a pounding headache didn't last long.

They took turns dodging, parrying and attacking. Maijerda's efforts much less calculated than Jeddeith's. Wytt's spells working to buy them a split second of an advantage.

The banshee was wounded, her abdomen ripped open. Her form flickered as she faced Maijerda. "Eventually you will tire. All the better for me to mend."

Compared to the aftermath of screams prior, the quiet falling was unnerving. Maijerda held her ground, thoughts ablaze. They could fight until the Moon set. Challenge her as they bled. This wasn't a test of skill.

It was an invitation.

"You're desperate for my mending? Come make a mendable of me."

Relief flooded the banshee's visage as she looked down at Maijerda.

"My needle is sharp." It was a promise, not a threat.

Wytt cried out, "No!"

"Maijerda!" Jeddeith pleaded, but it was too late.

The banshee reached a dried, skeletal claw for Maijerda's temple. "Rest. My mendable."

Pain, deftly as a thin blade piercing her soul. Blood seeped from her nose and the corners of her mouth, lining her lips. It was a mere second before Maijerda succumbed to a visual strangeness that wasn't the natural night.

CHAPTER FORTY-EIGHT

A Test for Us All

WYTT RUSHED INTO ACTION TO AID Jeddeith in checking Maijerda for signs of life.

"Sh-she's alive." Wytt confirmed. Focused. Masking his fears.

Wytt was hiding it better than he was. Jeddeith held her hand, sliding fingers to her pulse. Dull. Steady.

Shallow breathing.

Chill skin.

Blue nail beds.

She was alive—barely.

The banshee had vanished as soon as Maijerda collapsed. Leaving them to worry.

"Do you remember anything of what you read?" Jeddeith asked Wytt. He needed every detail possible to do all he could to protect her. "Of the portal to the Moon realm. How does it function? Teleportation? Mental? Spiritual?"

"I-I'm not sure. With what we-we found, there weren't specifics. Nothing on banshees. Mainly theories. Discourse on its existence. She could be there now. I don't kn-know."

"Keep an eye on her, make sure she's stable."

Knax kneeled beside her, eyes closed, a glow emanating from his stone palms. He was listening for her threads. A different means of assessing how she was connected to this plane in her unconscious state. Surely he'd been completing the same spell with Nadín in secret in the Sanctuary. "She'll return to us. We must be patient. This is a test for us all."

Patience is a virtue, yes. He'd been reminded often.

This wasn't the moment for patience. The sole positive in this chaos was the serenity in her face. Peace. What Jeddeith would give to help her find that level of freedom in the waking world.

Placing her hand to rest at her side, he looked to Knax, his mind set.

"I'm making no promises. If she doesn't wake within the hour, I'll bring her back myself." Jeddeith didn't know how, but he was confident he could.

"If-if you bring her back too soon, you risk her losing the connection."

"I don't care. I won't let this kill her."

"You h-have to trust—" Wytt leapt to his feet, alerting to the patch of wilderness behind them. "The air's changed." He licked his lips, straining his focus. "It was fresh before." Shaking his head, confused, Wytt let the thought trail off.

It wasn't an aspect of the tapestry Jeddeith could resonate with. He needed Wytt to be more specific. "Don't cut yourself off from the trigger. Dive deeper."

Instincts warned Jeddeith to search the perimeter. He didn't want to leave Maijerda's side. Wytt bent to crouch, creeping closer to the trees. Usually assertive and calculated when stressed, Jeddeith's focus was pressured to split. Blood pulsing in his temple with strain. Icy sweat sliding down his spine. He risked two paces from Maijerda, clutching his fae iron blade.

"Wytt," he urged. "What changed? Describe it to me."

An answer he admittedly feared. A draw entwining with Jeddeith's threads. Pulling them from him.

A nightmarish tinge in the atmosphere.

Distrust of his suspicion read in Wytt's furrowed brow. "Brine. There's brine in th-the air. Ssscorched. Like it's been struck by…" Glancing from the ground to meet Jeddeith's eyes, Wytt finished his thought. "…lightning."

Wytt jolted forward, stunned and roaring. Teeth grinding. Eyes startled. He fell to his knees.

Blood seeped from the spearhead impaled in his thigh.

CHAPTER FORTY-NINE

NIKO MAAR

S TANDING UPRIGHT SEEMED THE RIGHT THING to do, except Maijerda was already on her feet atop a mantle of plush clouds. Not stone, or sand, but the misty shroud of the sky, colored exactly as the Cruor Moon.

"I feel badly for requiring such an entrance." An airy voice lured. "She's always been such a stickler for who she grants passage."

The woman before Maijerda, bewitching and illustrious, was no older than herself. Her eyes, puddles of melting galaxies.

"You're not dead." She laughed as though they were childhood friends catching up on life over wine and cheese. Lounging on a tuft of cloud amid structures of marble, she tossed her hair of lavender, black, and celestial blue imbued in starry nights.

The woman, worldly in her experience yet eager, raised her brows and smiled. "And I don't need to hear your thoughts to understand your worry." Freckles speckled her cheeks, though were the opposite of Maijerda's sun speckles in that they were reminiscent of stars.

Why was she faltering to disbelief? Trying to talk herself out of possibility? Or success? "I'm sorry, is this truly the Lunar Realm?"

"Isn't it? This is my home after all. I believe mortals crafted that silly name, wanting to make sense of it. Niko Maar," she remarked with the pride of a mother. "Beautiful and fleeting. But silly."

Niko Maar. A place for stories. Just as well for all that crossed Maijerda's path of late. "It is an honor to meet you, Hyacinth." Maijerda, without a clue as to what level of decorum gods expected, resorted to a tried and true show of respect. She swept her arm across her waist and bowed.

"Oh please, there's no call for ceremony here. Not for you."

"You're the Moon goddess," Maijerda said, bewildered. Though she didn't pray to her, that didn't mean she didn't respect her divinity.

"There's no need to call me that."

Maijerda took as much as she could in stride. Surrendering to a banshee's mending led here? She found herself treading among the clouds. They were soft in her hands, cool on her thighs. "I was never faithful to you. Why did you bring me here?"

Hyacinth held her hands together, robustly knowingly as a sage. "Is the answer so vague?"

"Frankly yes. Unless you *are* the Moon?"

"Goodness, what a concept that would be. I am what mortals need me to be in their time of need. My appearance shifts with her phases in the sky. I was an infant twelve days ago." Her disclosure suggested mastery of the intimate relationship between the layers of life, death, and purpose.

Maijerda clicked her tongue. "I didn't think I would prove worthy enough to be granted an audience with you."

"I've often wondered what it feels like to be wrong." The woman teased.

Maijerda laughed, taken aback in an oddly pleasant way. "I'll tell you all about how dreadful it is someday."

Jests aside, Hyacinth asked, "What is it you need, Maijerda?"

"To ask you question."

Pondering, Hyacinth picked a piece of cloud shaped as a pear and bit into it. "I'm listening."

Maijerda presented her inquiry with discretion. "I've recently discovered a new faetale. A wondrous tale, that doesn't seem to exist outside of its own pages. Which seems sad. Solitary. And contradictory to the nature of stories. At the end, the Moon is mourning her lost Spark scattered to the winds. It claims the Moon had never before shed a tear. Is that true? Has the Moon ever cried?"

"Sadness does not discriminate whom it hunts. Why must you know?"

"My mother left me this story to communicate what she failed to do centuries ago."

"And you seek to right your mother's wrongs?"

"I—" Struggling for her response, Maijerda hesitated. "I can't atone for her mistakes or darkness in life. What I can attest to is the woman I knew as my mother. Her responsibility is mine. Whether I want it or not. I will not let her death, nor my father's, be in vain."

"You wish to save the world?" Hyacinth left it as a bait for Maijerda to show her true colors.

Maijerda was no villain. Nor would she follow down Mother's shadowed path. She didn't wish the world to end. What did she wish? Answers and revenge? Solace in grief?

The night at the waters of the Fae Pond, coin in hand, vividly resurfaced in memory. It felt this was an answer that would bind her to a spell or epitaph, a contract. Or perhaps she was scrutinizing a simple question. Could it be so simple a question when it came to saving the world?

The truest way to her heart, especially when she kept it hidden from herself, was to act as if she were talking to the Moon. Vulnerable and speaking to the sky with her spirit laid bare. "I wish to find meaning in my song. I was given a task. It doesn't matter if it was given by my mother, by blood, or by fate. It was laid before me. Despite my impulse to deny it to my grave. Entangled in a wrenching void I proclaimed was too surreal to exist while it eviscerated me and my conception of fate. It was written in blood and bound to me by song. I will not fail in letting this story know I understand its purpose."

"Torlen dovnym."

"Torlen lexnym."

Hyacinth unveiled a sigh, remorsefully empathetic with her indirect reply. "It pleases her to hear you sing." She left her seat and glided to a puff of clouds, searching as if it were a cabinet, pieces of cloud falling like spun sugar. "It has been centuries upon centuries since a muse was born unto a knell. You could be a legend that no one believes, one distant Moon."

With one last handful of cloud cupped delicately as an injured sparrow, she blew away the sugared clouds until all that remained was a glass bottle containing four globes of restless, liquid stardust.

"You've earned them." Hyacinth held the bottle for Maijerda to accept.

The glass sent effervescent shocks through her fingers. Grasping the bottle in awe, Maijerda reflected on her faetale and the Spark's woe. Her innate tapestry bonds worked to embody the Spark's aching desire, scorched by her own emotions until she burst. Notorious was the distress of being overrun by mind and sorrow, as if it were etched in Maijerda's bones.

She pressed the bottle to her heart. The Spark, betrayed by wanderlust, overwhelmed without a song to sing. To be abandoned and left struggling to express your emotions? How cruel a thing it must've been to know such hurt. How—

Grasping the bottle more firmly, a falling Undern leaf of an idea drifted to Maijerda. Mother's missing spool was ever so evident with the Moon's tears in hand. Mother had dismissed the arcane influence within the state of mind.

Emotion.

Of all concepts. But it was crystal clear as the loch. The entire faetale was an homage to emotion because Mother had failed to include it to craft the Veil. Fate, sensory, elemental, emotion.

Maijerda craved to know how the tears she held were possible outside of story and song. "What caused you such heartbreak?"

One by one, Hyacinth's freckles blinked out of existence as dying stars. Her serenity transposed with godly temper. Maijerda's hair stood on end, the emotional upheaval a tangible arcane force penetrating her mind and body.

"The Moon was tricked by a wayward tide. Rebellious and vicious. Shards of the Moon's guardians were enslaved against their will."

"Enslaved? How do you mean? Agh!" Maijerda was kicked in the chest by absolutely nothing visible. She held onto the bottle for dear life, the skin at her breastbone scorched.

"The tide claims she was given favor by the Fates to use them. She was *not* granted this favor." Hyacinth's figure rose, darkening with a storm of hurt, her voice booming. "She favored betrayal to seal her future!"

With a surge, Maijerda's breastbone cracked and smoldered. "Who was she?" She demanded through heavy breaths, determined to not be blinded by pain.

Hyacinth didn't address her, glowering at the clouds above, head cocked slightly while she seemed to be listening.

Maijerda forced herself steady, recovering from the last shock. "Tell me who hurt you."

Dismayed, Hyacinth mellowed and faced Maijerda, hand over her heart. "Forgive me please, my melody."

If she was to be torn from here, she needed to know who would dare betray the Moon. This was Maijerda's last chance. "Who was the wayward tide?"

With the next assault, Maijerda doubled over into the clouds as she was forced to withdraw from Niko Maar.

CHAPTER FIFTY

A Fool's Scent

"OH, THANK THE FATES. YOU'RE ALIVE." Beguiled snark cracked like a spiked whip into Maijerda's budding consciousness. "You had me worried I'd been robbed of the pleasure in killing you myself."

Lyrian withdrew her hand from Maijerda's chest, traces of lightning crackling between them. The blood of the Moon framed Lyrian's hair as a hooded headdress for royalty.

Hyacinth's warning was fresh in her mind, revealing the truth of the wayward tide towering above her. Who else could it be but Lyrian.

A brittle fragment of a second to react would've been the greatest blessing. However, cruelty lacks originality. And what it lacks in tactfulness it more than makes up for in self-righteousness.

"There was a lesson to be learned in the Menagerie." Grabbing Maijerda by the throat, she forced her to stand and face the others.

Her stomach was vacant, bloodlust fusing with vertigo, heat in her face, and spotty vision. The beach was crowded with a band of pirates, some wielding weapons, another two manning an arcane cage bright as the sun around Knax, frozen as if it were day. Jeddeith was shackled and gagged, unconscious in the sand, blood oozing from a wound on his temple. Wytt was moaning in the sand on all fours, pale as can be with a spear protruding from his thigh. He seemed unaware of his surroundings.

"Wytt!" Maijerda called to him and lunged forward, stopped by Lyrian clawing into her throat. Gagging, Maijerda tried to run but she was pulled into Lyrian's chest.

Denratis separated himself from their encircling ranks, haughty with glory.

The sick prick.

"Don't think I won't kill you again." Maijerda strained against Lyrian's grip.

"My, my. You've changed," Denratis crooned.

"This could've all been avoided if you had abided me in the first place. You're the reason your friends are ruined. All this bloodshed is on your hands." Lyrian threw Maijerda to the ground.

"No! You're the one with chaos in your wake. The Veil is under my protection." Maijerda tried to back away, her body weak. She hadn't fully recovered from the banshee's mending, left like a wounded animal at this woman's feet.

"Victory was and will always be..." Lyrian eyed the book, paces from Maijerda by their packs. "Mine."

Twisting and locking her storm-crackling fingers wickedly fast, Lyrian's veins were as vivid as her sadism. "I know your scent. It was on your mother's dying breath. A fool's scent. Your father died protecting a fool's charm, I could smell it from across the ocean." She flicked, spun, and pulled apart her hands, conjuring a ball of tangled streams of water and seaweed. "I wish you could have seen the look on his face the moment he died. I did. I suspect yours will be no less delectable...tuft."

The composure of which she spoke ominously contradicted the cataclysmic force with which she threw the entanglement at Maijerda's feet.

Maijerda's adrenaline kicked in, she ran several steps and launched herself to grapple the faetale. Slithering columns of seaweed dove and sniped for her ankles. A mere stretch from grasping her book, Maijerda was yanked out of reach.

Shouting and gasping for breath as it was knocked out of her, Maijerda kicked the weeds. They crawled up her entire body until strands forced Maijerda's arms wide and legs locked. She was lifted to her knees, wrists nearly snapping. She shouted, each movement jarring. Her body a puppet and Lyrian the master.

The seaweed pulled Maijerda to her feet. With her distressed curls, Maijerda was a rag doll stitched tight with outrage. She struggled to break the strands, much more than material.

"What will it take for you to learn?" Lyrian drummed her fingers on her cheek. "I think I know just the thing. Submit." She ushered her command as an ocean gale, her irises rippling with waves.

Instantaneously Maijerda's muscles went limp, the strings keeping her from becoming a pile of rags.

Lyrian's eyes flashed, the red around her eyelids darkening as she rolled her shoulders, pouting her sea-foam-stained lips at Maijerda. "Break."

Maijerda's hope and determination fractured as broken glass. The skittering shards abandoned her before she could pick up the pieces even if it meant cutting herself and bleeding on their edges. In their stead she was poisoned by the malignancy of harm bonded with free will. Every curse and degrading insult imaginable vanished without ever reaching her tongue.

"Excellent." Lyrian chided, lowering her threads binding Maijerda. "My patience is long dead. Shall we?"

Lyrian's hair freed itself strand by strand from her plait, generating a battle-ready appearance with her combination of leathers, chiffons, and silks. "I do need one favor." She gestured for Maijerda to proceed to the book. "Collect."

Maijerda strained for a glimpse of the faetale. She clenched her teeth at the loss of her free will, being consumed and turned against her.

The faintest drop of salt from a fallen tear reached her tongue as she walked to her faetale at Lyrian's bidding. Thoughts fell from Maijerda, detached as ever.

"Relinquish."

A second tear fell from Maijerda's cheek, sinking into the pages of the book as she held it. Lyrian slid the book from Maijerda's deadened grasp, no defiance permitted to seep.

"Thank you." Cold-as-steel fingers patted her cheek. Lyrian bade Denratis to gather Maijerda's belongings, no puppet strings required.

"If you wouldn't mind, Denratis. I'll allow you the honors."

From a coat pocket he produced a vial of putrid black syrup and swirling gas. The closer he walked to Maijerda, her heart pounded in despair. They were lost. Without wisp or fate on their side.

Lyrian paced around them, strings trailing with her. "No obstacles this time."

The tangle dug into Maijerda, bringing her arms to her back, stacked and bent. She winced as the bonds solidified at the command of few liquid words from Lyrian.

Denratis grabbed Maijerda's chin and drew her jaw open as a doll. Adoringly, he breathed, "I'll savor the look in your eyes. Dull and defeated." He plucked the cork from the vial with his teeth.

Lyrian leaned in to Maijerda and tucked her hair behind her ears, as if asking her a favor, lips grazing her ear. Maijerda flinched at the cold. "Drink."

Anchoring the vial on her bottom lip Denratis tipped the potion along her cheek. The concoction slid to the back of her tongue. She gurgled and gagged, bereft of strength to hack it up.

Denratis forced her jaw shut, the potion stretching and swirling into her throat. An invisible puppet string triggered her swallow.

"Good girl," Lyrian cooed. "I'll admit, brewing this potion to counter the arcana in your blood proved to be quite the challenge. Which I respect. I enjoy learning what makes you tick." She kissed Maijerda's ear.

Maijerda was losing track of the ridicule, swooning and falling into Denratis' clutches. He heaved Maijerda over his shoulder.

Then? There was—

Maijerda's senses snapped at her, seemingly upset. Lyrian and Denratis were gone. She was surrounded by the hollowness of shadow. Similar to Nadín's vision, yet different in ways she couldn't recognize.

The crystal on her necklace warmed her skin. Maijerda held it to ask what it knew and what secrets it could share. And to be quick about it before they were executed. She was interrupted by the perfect image of Nadín, carrying a hand mirror.

"Nadín how did you find me?"

"I have little in the way of glass. We must be quick."

"Is this purgatory? Am I dead?" Suddenly she felt as if she was the little girl afraid of the dark under her bed.

Nadín insisted she take the mirror. "No. Your song is strong."

Maijerda took the mirror. "Where did you go? Knax said he thought you left for Steslyres. Lyrian attacked us in the Menagerie. She ambushed us in Catacomb Loch and made me a puppet. Knax was caged, Wytt was injured. Jeddeith…" He couldn't be dead, not the way Lyrian treated him. "He was unconscious. I don't know if they're still alive. I'm sorry, Nadín. I failed the book. I failed Mama and Da. Lyrian forced my hand. And I wasn't strong enough."

Maijerda trembled, her pitch rose and fell along connotative gaps between guilt and resentment. "She used me. Poisoned me."

"Sh-ssssh. Maijerda, the glass is nearly gone. You did not fail. There is still more to sing. I *will* find you."

Maijerda gave her the most offended and confused raised eye as Nadín fixed her hair. "What are you doing?"

Holding a comb in her teeth, Nadín twisted Maijerda's curls and wound them in a loose bun. "See the thing a little bit the same. See the oath between spirit and…" She looked to Maijerda's heart and sighed. "…muse."

Nadín stood to the side patiently.

Freckled cheeks puffed, Maijerda studied her reflection.

She turned her head, still holding the mirror high to ask Nadín for clarification. But she was alone.

"Wh—Nadín?" Nowhere.

Maijerda re-acknowledged the mirror.

Five agonizing beats drummed by with her reflection's neck stretched to the side, no longer her true reflection. The image turned a step more and stopped. Maijerda's neck twinged with pin pricks and she went dizzy, stretched between reality and shadow. Gaping at her reflection, she swallowed a lump of disbelief at the freshness of an inky black tattoo on the back of her neck.

It was of a glyph, sweepingly familiar.

It happened to be a perfect match to the one marking the cover of her faetale.

"WHAT'S THIS?" LYRIAN was crouching over Maijerda, holding the qu'stite.

Maijerda swung to claw at Lyrian and reclaim the necklace. Her arm refused.

Eyes fixed with a lopsided view of a wooden staircase, her face pressed into the dampness of splintering planks, her entire body, paralyzed.

"You're actually managing to manifest desperation, aren't you? Like a beacon. Clever." Metal snapped against her neck and a braid slid over the nezdrade's shoulder.

"Though I gather you're not alone in your endeavors." Lyrian dangled the crystal. "You won't be needing this under my care. Affording you the luxury of ideas would be cruel of me in your final days."

Maijerda's tether to the material realm billowed away.

CHAPTER FIFTY-ONE

THIRTEEN LASHES

LYRIAN DANGLED THE NECKLACE IN FRONT of Jeddeith's bruised and beaten face. "Tell me what you know."

Pounding heart rate.

A burning rib.

Likely several broken bones.

Lacerations on his back. The whip sliced into muscle during this last round of beating.

Nothing he couldn't heal from.

He spat a blood clot and heaved. She would need to try harder to bait him. Much harder. "Nothing more than you."

"When did she receive it?"

"Haven't a clue. I don't heed her every detail."

"Don't you?" Lyrian smirked and motioned to the same demon spawn who pummeled him on the shore of Catacomb Loch. Brute bastard. The faetale lay open on a barrel behind her. She never let it out of her sight. Today was unusual. Typically she tortured Jeddeith for answers regarding interpreting the faetale. Today her focus was this necklace.

Jeddeith readied himself with chains suspending him and braced for the second round of flogging, his bare chest already coated in bloodied sweat. Thirteen lashes split his skin and reopened old wounds with vibrant cracks. Each sliced into him as a razor pulled from a forge.

To temper the pain, he needed to harness lifelines. Before it was too late.

Vyth— Vythsaden— vythsaden rosq.

Glimpses of ɔpoʊlin.

Pouring rain.

These weren't enough to satiate. One after the other his back burned as though lit on fire. He delved further. To survive.

Maijerda's candor, alight with freckles.

The bliss of her voice when she sang.

Her touch warming his shoulders, his chest—his cheeks.

The salted sage of her perfume.

The final crack lashed around his ribs, stuttering to come free. This whip was embedded with glass and metal shards. Grunting, he gripped the chains, the metal slick with his own sweat, and arched with the biting release.

When he opened his eyes, Lyrian's arms were folded. Her chest rapidly rising and falling.

She was proud. Worse? She was enjoying every bloody second.

"Leave us," Lyrian instructed of the brute. "You can visit your plaything later." Sea foam overwhelmed the whites of her eyes with prismatic shards. "Oddly enough, I find your answer perfectly acceptable."

Jeddeith tried to wet his lips. His tongue met rigid tears of skin. Biting into the cracks, his laugh struggled to break from the dry pits in his throat. "Of course you do. You wear sadism well, Lyrian."

Her tone hissed as a brewing potion. "Is this her tapestry focus?"

There was no harm in answering this truthfully. It might glean a chance of throwing Lyrian off if he played his cards right. "No. You're overreaching."

Her booted steps knocked on the planks as she walked to him. "Don't patronize me."

"Empty threats again? You never run dry. I'd be dead if that's what you wanted. There's something else, isn't there?"

Her smile spread. "When we reach Gazdeq I will ease your longing. Until then, I hope you enjoy the journey. The sea can be a crude companion this season."

Flaunting the crystal a final time, she swiped a finger on Jeddeith's beaten chest. A flare of lighting burrowed through his skin to bone. He ground his teeth and pulled the chains to retaliate. "This isn't over."

"I agree. This is but the beginning." She brought her finger to her mouth and sucked his blood from it.

If Lyrian wanted to push him to the brink, he'd let her.

To honor his past, he'd vindicate his practice as a Rivyn.

To demand his freedom, he'd unravel her threads.

To defend Maijerda, he'd bury Lyrian with his own bare hands.

Chapter Fifty-Two

Mind Your Step

THE JOURNEY TO GAZDEQ WAS OVER.

Roʊzvɛlkə Eventide was upon them, the time for the ritual finally arrived. And Lyrian's revenge had never been this close at hand.

The fortress boomed with Lyrian's commands, ordering Denratis to lock their prisoners in the dungeon.

Volkari would be forced to recognize Lyrian's efforts. Settling for less was weak. It didn't take much to find Volkari sulking in her mausoleum with etheric thistle in hand.

She crushed the thistle as Lyrian entered and lashed out. Her bitterness was laced with venom. "I gave you explicit instructions! Your insubordination won't be tolerated."

Lyrian glared down at Volkari. "Lifting the Veil was a task we agreed to pursue in tandem, and I don't abide by ill-advised decrees. You won't hear me beg for permission nor forgiveness. I have no need of it."

"Mind your step, Lyrian Llach." Volkari pressed her palms on the table, smearing shimmering thistle remnants.

"And yours, Volkari." Raising her chin, she curled her lips. "Without me this ritual will fail, and the Veil will remain in place. You may as well be the one chained and decaying for eternity. I've carried all burdens for this cause while you've wallowed here."

Volkari's burn scars were painting themselves red, but she cracked with a devious smile and laughed. "Tell me. Are you ungrateful for my aid? You see as far as I'm concerned, without me you would still be fuming about Relona's death failing you and wandering the world without guidance." Her jaw brushed her collar as she sat taller. "You learned of your nezdrade prophecy because of me. You stood a chance in destroying the Veil because of me. You found the book and learned of Maijerda because of me."

Lyrian threw Maijerda's necklace onto the table between them. "You can proclaim what you want. Maijerda and her damned book are detained because of *me*."

The women bored into each other.

It was a waiting game to see who would break first.

Volkari clapped leisurely, her eyes devoid of emotion. "Congratulations. Consider yourself fortunate. You're right about one constant, and that is our agreement to complete this ritual together. Because we rely on each other, you and I. I'm positive we can put this disagreement behind us. You're stressed and better days are ahead."

Disagreement? Stressed? The nerve of this crow. She was undeserving of reclaiming her crown as empress.

"Maijerda will wake soon."

"See you at the Harrowing." Volkari's mouth twitched and she opened the door with a wave of her hand.

"Praise fortune. Bleed victory." Lyrian swept a hand and bowed formally, driving a fist into her abdomen. Heat spread from her throat to her belly, numbing everything in between as she spun on her heels to leave.

Storming to the gallery to prepare, Lyrian's indignation sparked through the halls.

Praise her own fortune.

Bleed her *own* victory.

CHAPTER FIFTY-THREE

TORLEN LEXNYM

LUCIDITY WAS A POOR REPLACEMENT FOR blissful ignorance. Maijerda's pulse reluctantly picked up pace.

The unknown somewhere she was lying was infected with the musk of decay worming and sticking to her skin. She groped the dungeon floor.

Chains bound her wrists, scraping stone. Letting out a desolate groan, she crawled to the wall. Two guards clothed in armor likely scavenged from a forgotten tomb opened her cell. A green haze darkened their stretched skin. They were decayed as corpses. Each held a scythe, promising to permit the toothy edge a taste should she choose bravado.

"Not wasting time, are we?"

Mutely, though no less intimidating with snarls of fangs dripping with drool, they urged her to stand. Her legs were worse than a fresh sailor's.

One guard locked under her arms, stretching her shackles, and dragged her from the dungeon. The second produced a worn strip of leather, coiling it to blind her. Maijerda limped to maintain stride for Fates knew how long, until the guards jostled her to a halt.

An armored boot dug nastily into the back of her knee. She braced her fall with an open palm, her fingers catching in a chiseled crevasse. An oceanside gale mingled with dread. Maijerda couldn't find it reassuring. Not now.

Whomever her audience was must've been content to the point of arrogance with her helplessness, as the blindfold was ripped away.

The gallery creaked with the slightest nudge of armor from guards blocking exits and archways leading to a wide balcony, open to the dead of night and rumbling waves. A domed blue and black stone cathedral ceiling was worn with frescos and slivers open to the sky. None provided a glimpse of the Moon and her guardians.

Surrounded by a horde of guards, Jeddeith and Wytt were forced to kneel. Crossbow bolts aimed for them oozed an orange substance. Jeddeith held himself as though he risked being sent into fits of pain every second.

"The stories I've heard about you are riveting." The woman in a collared gown sneered. Lyrian and Denratis were positioned on either side of her.

Maijerda's voice scratched to stir. "I could say the same, Volkari."

"I see we need no introductions."

Bracing on one knee, Maijerda stumbled for strength.

Volkari's masked countenance cracked. "I understand the false sense of security standing your ground brings. It won't be necessary. I do empathize. I felt the very same would protect me against your mother's betrayal. Granted, that was lifetimes ago." Volkari sounded mournful. Her next statement read as sarcastically appreciative of the elimination of a pest. "My condolences. Her death proved to be the first sacrifice made to pry the Veil from this mirage of a world. Shame I missed it. Though I suppose Lyrian did fine enough work seeing as Relona's death allowed me to return to this realm."

Volkari slid a sidelong glance at Lyrian, who flexed and arched her hands.

"Relona always was pompous. She could have chosen to warn you of my coming if she truly considered me a villain. Or she could have shared your heritage with you. Instead, she deliberately swaddled you in lies, certain it would..."

Volkari paused here for dramatic emphasis and shrugged, pallid hands clasped loosely. "What? Protect you? You see, she excelled as my advisor for years on end after we won the Wailing War. Oh? Did Nadín not make that clear?"

Maijerda was shaking, condemning her raging tears falling onto slate. Mother was a good woman. Mother was a survivor. She had mended her ways, found love, and made a family.

"As general of my military, the Straghis claimed countless victories. You've not read one history text that documents them, have you?"

Volkari splayed a hand on her chest. "It is a slight to their memory. *Our* Pɛnʌmbrə was true and should have persisted. A thriving society reduced to faetales and horror stories to share in the dark."

For the first clear moment in her speech, Volkari's wrath burdened her poise. "It's insulting. To us and to the tapestry. Fortunately for you and all Pɛnʌmbrə, I won't be bound to lecturing and lamenting our loss. I'll show you. Nothing replaces precise recounting, no matter how elaborately spun, as well as the poignancy of personal experience."

She advanced echoing steps closer to Maijerda. The flickering lights of clawed candelabras highlighted her burn scars.

Maijerda matched her severity, leaning forward and twisting her chains. Willing her tremors to cease. "You spoke of empathy. You're not capable of the compassion empathy bears."

A scabbing wound on Maijerda's jaw split open with Volkari's strike. The crack burst in the gallery, leaving her cheek throbbing.

Jeddeith lurched to intercede, but an undead ersul clocked him. He coughed and spat a clump of blood at the tiraen guarding him too.

"All I ask is for your support. It would ease the strain of this ritual. We are on the brink of the Veil's destruction. Thread by thread, I will reclaim my kingdom and arcana. I'm the sole living family you have left. How could you forsake that bond?"

Maijerda's possession of truth rapidly disintegrated, wanting to forget Relona calling her "sister." Family? How? "You're lying."

"Oh gods above and below! How awful this must be. Denying Nadín's visions at every turn, aren't you?"

Maijerda sought Jeddeith as if he could speak with her. Impossible, of course. Beneath the bruising, his expression was riddled with worry born from regret.

Volkari's chuckle ground in Maijerda's ears, setting her teeth on edge. "Do you still trust him? I suppose I understand why. You should know he's been smothered and manipulated his entire life and soon, Lyrian will see to his freedom."

Jeddeith roared. "Don't lie to her. I make my own damned decisions."

Lyrian and Volkari exchanged sneers and laughed. The tension and madness were palpable. Not to mention infectious. In the worst way imaginable.

Volkari danced her fingers in a candle flame. "Is that so? Is that why you've been a slave to unreliable recollections? Why you wake up in random places at arbitrary times with no memories?

Because *you* are in control? Lyrian. How often did he choose death in your dreams?"

Jeddeith hunched and his gaze darted for Maijerda.

"All four. No matter the threat. He even let Maijerda die once."

"That's *not* what happened."

Maijerda's cheeks heated beneath dried smears of blood. "You used me as a pawn? You manipulative—"

Lyrian tutted as she stalked to Maijerda. "Don't act shocked."

Volkari waved a hand to her captives. "Jeddeith, a Rivyn Borne out of his depth. Would you risk rescuing my niece? Or is she an evil you would destroy?" Volkari spat her words.

Startling Maijerda to seethe and gasp, Lyrian clawed an ocean-frigid grip on the back of her neck. She stretched with Lyrian's pull and scrambled to her feet as she was dragged forward by a handful of hair. Reaching to pry the sea witch's hands out of her tangle of curls was fruitless. Lyrian roughly halted at a circular depression in the stone floor and yanked Maijerda's head taut, exposing her neck above it. Maijerda's chest hitched, panting in entirely speechless anticipation.

Pressing Maijerda into her body, Lyrian's breath caressed her lips with the salt of the ocean. "You are unworthy of the mercy in a swift death. Bleed for me."

A blade caught in the corner of Maijerda's eye, worse than nightmares creeping in shadow. Lyrian anchored the dagger on Maijerda's throat and prolonged the shock by slicing slowly. Needling sharp and smooth before sinking the blade to finish the cut. Her skin peeled into a deep sliver, making way for trickles and soon to be rivers of blood.

Maijerda clutched at the wound, her heart racing to compensate for coming loss and the battle for air. She coughed and spurted, catching herself on stone. Blood spilled into the concave basin carved into the floor as her skin bristled with cold shock.

Volkari paced in molasses-slow circles around her prey. A crone chastising a helpless maiden, lost without Mother. "You and your essence are the perfect harmony of what was and what lives today."

Maijerda garbled, dragging the fatal taste of copper on her tongue. A glob plinked into the pool and splashed her wrists.

Let it end. Let this horror end.

Mama. Da. Forgive me.

"You were born with tethers within the tapestry of arcana between *both* worlds. Arcana is as delicate and forgiving as a tapestry. We can create, destroy, and choose the strands as we weave. In all my rage at your mother, I finally had a beautiful realization. You my dear, are a conduit."

Jeddeith charged to Maijerda, oddly unhindered. Three guards restrained Wytt as he tried to follow.

Sliding to the ground, he gathered Maijerda under her arms and moved her from the bloody basin to rest against himself. He held her wounds closed. "End this. Heal her, now!"

Volkari ridiculed all his subsequent demands until their voices were a chaotic cacophony of tension, cheers, and fury.

Jeddeith failed every attempt to overpower Volkari's string of jeering. Maijerda's skull pounded at the noise. His tremors forced him to readjust his pressure to stem the bleeding. Her skin peeled and stuck to him. "Maijerda, I'm sorry. I don't know what to do. Maijerda—no! Look at me, please."

What was there left to do? She'd failed her parents. She'd failed Wytt. And Jeddeith. She wasn't worthy enough to be Knax's muse. She wanted to tell Jeddeith to let her go. To take Wytt and run. That it was all right to leave her. This was her price to pay. Besides, maybe she could be with Mama and Da again. Time would tell.

She gurgled on the blood in her throat.

Jeddeith never looked so broken and lost before. Such heartache.

"Don't fade on me. Not now. Not ever. I—I—"

Fading was her only path. And this time, maybe it was the right decision.

Wait. Why couldn't she understand what Jeddeith was saying anymore? She couldn't make out his words, devoid of meaning. He closed his eyes, muttering. Until he froze, vacant as a statue. He didn't blink or speak, and his hand was steadfast on her throat.

Lyrian prowled to them. Maijerda's heart thudded as she stood over her.

"Volkari," Lyrian whispered, her eyes wide. "*This* is the mirror."

What mirror? What was she trying to prove?

All her reservations ceased as a single tear slid down Jeddeith's stone expression.

But then, his catatonic trance broke and Jeddeith was quick to lay Maijerda on the slate floor.

She cringed and moaned in distress for mercy. Briefly, she caught a glimpse of Wytt, tears streaming down his face. He seemed to be praying. For what good it would do. She was beyond saving.

Jeddeith removed his hand and spoke, suddenly muted as the night. "Wind, breath. Fire, expression. Earth, stability. Water, reformation. Light, spirit. Bound by blood. Burdened by death. My spirit is yours to take."

Pure white orbs appeared at Jeddeith's fingertips. He planted them along the tear in her flesh and sewed her flesh together from inside to out. Her throat pinched, making her alarmingly aware of each stitch.

Lyrian held her chin high, placing a hand on Jeddeith's shoulder. A howl came from the wind, rustling the candlelight. Maijerda's eyes fluttered closed before she could consider if this breath was her last.

She snapped upright, groping her throat. Imperfect, the seam on her throat was wickedly raw. Jeddeith didn't say a word. At a loss, they stared at each other. How did he manage that casting? She should be dead.

Volkari reminded her there were more devastating matters at hand, praising the spectacle. "How fortunate Jeddeith rose to the occasion for you."

"As we knew you would." Lyrian brought him to his feet. "I was disappointed by your refusing to bond with the elements in my nightmares. Don't fret, this redeems those failures." She rested an arm across his chest. "I knew you'd break. It was only a matter of when."

Maijerda's breathing stacked unsteadily, mourning the pool of her life's blood. Volkari stepped around it to a table of simplistic metal rods and ebony. It bore two lonely items: a glass bottle with motes of stardust and the faetale.

The Moon's Tears? They were real. She'd done it. Maijerda hadn't seen them since Hyacinth had procured the bottle, and she wasn't sure they'd existed outside of Niko Maar. Here they were, in the wrong hands.

When Volkari plucked the tears from the table, Maijerda ignored both chains and weakness to intercede. Hands snagged around her arms and she was whirled to confront Denratis, who grabbed her bindings and hauled her to the edge of the room.

"Best not to excite yourself," Volkari scolded. "Congratulations on impressing Hyacinth. Shame your efforts were wasted. I promised I would help you understand. We must support one another. As kin."

Broken and lost in exhaustion, Maijerda raged through pained misery. "You're no family of mine."

Volkari set the bottle down and chose the faetale instead.

"No. No! Don't harm him!" Maijerda shouted to protect her book, paying the price of speaking with the scratching and tugging in her throat. She coughed up a clot of blood, her eyes watering as this escalated the pain.

Volkari scoffed and addressed the crowd with lustful vigor. "An unparalleled privilege has been bestowed on us this Roʊzvɛlkə Eventide. To forge a new story."

Greedy cheers soared to the ceiling and through the balcony. The black candles set at the cardinal points in the room lit spontaneously and in synchrony with the roaring crowd.

Volkari raised her hands to call for respect. Though she deserved none. "In order to destroy the Veil, the spools of the tapestry as mentioned in this faetale must be recognized and sacrificed. It began by undoing the woman at the crux of it all. Now we must address the others involved in its making. Nadín isn't here to pay for her crimes. Thank you for gifting us the perfect replacement."

A pair of doors were drug open by guards at Volkari's command. Another pair of sentries lead Knax into the gallery by a chain collared around his throat. They brought him to the center of the room. His stone was cracked with chunks missing. One of his horns was broken off too.

Knax ignored his captors and focused on Maijerda with confounding peace, his resignation plain. "I am grateful to see you again."

Maijerda panicked. "Leave him be, he's not a part of this!"

Taking center stage, Lyrian boasted, "Nadín ensured his fate when she wrought his existence from what remained of her threads. I'm sure she'll understand."

Lyrian began commanding the room, stretching her arms wide. Her liquid words were an incantation that summoned life into the runic carvings on the stone walls with a sea foam, acrid green, and black light. They warped and hummed as if waiting to be fed.

Fates, no! Maijerda pulled to challenge Denratis' restraint, but she was horribly weak from the blood letting. Flicking a knife from his belt, he held the tip under her chin. "Ah-Ah. I'm not the only one with eyes for you." He lifted her gaze with the knife to the balconies three stories high. Several archers with masks of bone beneath hoods were trained on her.

Jeddeith fell to his knees, more tears streaking the blood and dirt on his face.

Knax looked at them both with pride. "Do not fear for me." His smile struck Maijerda's heart riven and ruined. "I've been told some songs are a little bit the same. You are forever my muse. Never quiet your song."

Inhumanly quick, Lyrian's incantation ceased. She snapped her head in Knax's direction, holding a stream of arcane ribbons like a dagger. "Enough prattle."

She threw her spell at Knax and it struck his ribs, red sparks burrowing into his stone. His expression of tenderness froze all too similarly to his lifeless kin.

"Knax!" Maijerda cried.

Within a split second, a grotesquely deep rumble filled the gallery. Time slowed to the point where each second passed with a mechanical tick.

His once smooth, sculpted form grew infested with poisonous cracks the following second.

His eyes dulled the next.

It was during that last, execrable second, Knax burst into thousands of pieces.

Maijerda shouted for him in sheer horror, sobbing and cowering in the shrapnel. "You monster." She accused Lyrian. "You have no heart."

"I never claimed to be burdened by one. It's *your* fantasy that I might repent. That I will see the error of my ways and spare you." The red in her skin flared. It was the first time Maijerda realized how exhausted Lyrian seemed. Spent to her last thread of vengeance.

"Lyrian," Volkari barked. "Heed your duty."

Wytt's shout filled the gallery. "Jed-jeddeith! Y-y-you can't!"

Jeddeith had risen to his feet and stood in the center of the room near the basin brimming with Maijerda's plum blood. Solemnly, Jeddeith bowed his head. "I made a choice. I must honor that."

Lyrian glanced pointedly at Maijerda, then back to him. "Expose your chest."

Jeddeith matched her with sober defeat while removing his shirt crusted with dried blood. Wounds stretched and seeped as he pried fabric from the split flesh in his back.

Helplessly Maijerda gaped at the gashes marring his old scars. "Jeddeith. What choice?"

He knelt before Lyrian. It didn't matter what decision brought him here, it couldn't be worth kneeling to that bitch.

"Jeddeith. Look at me. Talk to me! Don't do this."

Denratis growled in her ear. "Shut it!"

She choked over his blade, begging Jeddeith to listen. "You owe her nothing. She does not own you." Tears puddled in blood staining her face. Her stress rattled in the gallery. "Please. For me?"

Jeddeith glowered at her, his once soothing timbre a deep growl. "How do you not understand? This is for you."

"If that's true, then please. For the love of the Fates, don't do this. I would rather die than destroy the Veil."

"Don't fret. There may still be time." Lyrian grinned and dipped a finger into Maijerda's blood, drawing a glyph on Jeddeith's chest. It melted into his skin as she uttered a single arcane instruction. "I gifted him clarity. As he said, it was his choice. If he hadn't, you would be dead. He is mine, Maijerda. He was prophesied to me to use to weaken the Veil."

Silence dusted like falling snow.

Lyrian placed her hand on the sigil and it glowed a brilliant sea-glass green before morphing to lightning gold.

"I've searched for you, for years, Jeddeith. You possess the arcane calling needed for nezdrade blood. My god intertwined our paths because they favor me. I recognize now, it's no wonder my trials for you to claim your elemental power in your dreams proved weak.

"For you are neither wind or water, nor fire or earth. I would expect no less from the embodiment of light, an element we've not yet seen embodied. You will no longer be forced to live a lie."

Lyrian's posture was rigid. "The fifth of the nezdrade has emerged within you, Jeddeith. Spirit. The illusion, the light. Our breath of life, forever rid of shackles. The destruction of the Veil is dependent on your sacrifice. If you survive, you may stand by my side and see the nezdrade return to this world."

The runes on the walls hungered again for their next sacrifice. Lyrian outstretched her arms as before and began chanting. Drawing forth another spell ignited her parchment-thin patches of red scars. This spell wove as amber coils hooking between the runes and into Jeddeith. They created a web, filling the room.

He remained unmoving as each coil burrowed in him. When all were secured, Lyrian continued weaving and began siphoning arcana from him. Black and amber pulsed from him along the coils, feeding into the runes encircling the gallery.

Jeddeith kept his breathing measured and his head low, chanting to himself. "Vythsaden rosq. Vythsaden rosq. Vythsaden rosq." Over and over again. It was keeping him here. Keeping him from being torn apart.

He pushed through the first phase and when Lyrian's incantation changed verses, he lost control and threw his head back to scream. His veins turned black, skin covered in sweat. This torture endured, convincing Maijerda he was doomed to die right in front of her. Clenching his hands to fists, Jeddeith slammed them on the stone floor. He slid to his side, lying on the floor as Lyrian severed the spell.

The walls started to pulse with a heartbeat, both in glow and in power. Maijerda's bones thrummed with the same rhythm.

"Jeddeith?" She managed, her voice dry and cracked.

His chest expanded with the first breath since he collapsed and he labored to stand.

Lyrian was pride unseen. "Will you accept your destiny as our spirit?"

Walking to Lyrian, Jeddeith bowed. "Dreams the sun, so dawns the Moon. Yes, I will."

What remained of Maijerda's heart tore itself to tatters.

Jeddeith refused to meet her gaze, off Lyrian. Lyrian relaxed as she smiled. Not with sadistic flair or hunger. But a genuine smile. "I'm pleased you survived. Your promise will be sealed once you endure trials to fully become nezdrade and replenish your spent arcana."

"I will honor our people."

Metal scraped Maijerda's wrists as she pulled her chains. "How could you?"

"I've accepted my fate." He glared at her. "It's time you did the same."

Volkari interjected, clapping. "Well done. You've impressed me, Lyrian. I must say."

Lyrian remained silent.

"Together these components will bend the fabrics of the Veil. We require one final sacrifice. We must create an ink to bestow our crafts upon the realm. To honor my sister's memory, I will read her beloved faetale for all to witness."

She brandished the faetale as a weapon of lore retrieved from realms unspoken.

"You have no right!" Maijerda risked raging in Denratis' hold. His knife nicked her chin.

"Oh?" Volkari raised one eyebrow, daring Maijerda to persuade her.

"Sh-she's right!" Wytt tried to stand, quickly shoved to all fours, a spear at his neck.

"Is she now? Care to speak up? Can't say I've ever met a devil quite so meek."

Wytt's hands were balled into fists. "The book chooses its companions. It would never choose you."

Maijerda grunted. The pain of Denratis digging his blade in her jaw was worth staring Volkari in the eye. "You've done nothing to earn his trust."

"I'm sorry you feel so strongly about my involvement. If that were true, would a trap not be set to lash out at me? Would the book not fight my very touch and defend itself against me?"

Maijerda's expression fell. Something must be hindering the book. Where was his spirit? Why wasn't he fighting back? If there was a time for defenses and tricks, it was now!

Refusing to flounder, Maijerda retorted, "This ritual will fail. The book won't allow it. The Moon and her guardians won't stand for it! And neither will I."

Volkari raised her shoulders, frowning. "The guardians are rooted in falsehood. They didn't exist before the Veil. Their existence bound the Moon's arcana. She is but another I will liberate."

Was everything a lie? Maijerda was lost in a struggle to fight for what she believed in. What did you do when all your beliefs were challenged in a single breath?

With a satisfied grin Volkari read the faetale aloud. She circled the blood basin as a black and green fire erupted from it.

Maijerda detested every mounting second. The words lost their harmony, corrupted by Volkari. The Spark's whimsy, tainted.

As she finished, Volkari closed the book, drowning Maijerda in ire. "This faetale has drawn his final breath. Be grateful I allowed you to stay by his deathbed." She dropped the book into the basin.

"No!" Maijerda lurched and screeched. The book, having endured water and fire, succumbed to burning blood.

Her blood.

Maijerda swore a scream of pain outside hers writhed in her mind and heart. Her skin was pricked and aching. She cried and screamed back, feeling the book tear from her. She wasn't strong enough to be his guardian. His protector.

She'd lost more of her family.

This should have been obvious from the beginning! She wasn't fit for this task. She was meant to fail, wasn't she? She'd failed the book, because she was weak and naive. She'd failed Mama and Da. What more misery could she possibly cause?

"After centuries, the reign of the Veil will come to a bitter end." Volkari retrieved a bundle of herbs and preached, "From north to south, and east to west, this new story begins. Our time before the Veil, long forgotten, is reborn with this new beginning. Refusing to end."

Maijerda's blood in the basin dispersed at her gestures and flowed from the center in the crevasses in the floor. Stream by stream, the image pieced together for Maijerda.

She was standing on a map of Pɛnʌmbrə carved into the floor. The so-dubbed ink flooded rivers, penned outlines of cities, towns, and mountains. Forests too, bloomed leaves of blood-borne ink.

Volkari followed the path of the ink as it filled in the map, crafting an incantation as she played the part of cartographer. "Let blood and elements divine unite to ravage the lies and deceit. This cohosh, brittle and dried," she presented the bundle of flowers and crumpled them to better scatter across the map. "Is an expectorant for Pɛnʌmbrə's current state. Let the Veil become no more than myth until it is forgotten. *This* spindle is spent."

Flames crackled with the final drops of blood filling in the map.

Maijerda was worse than worn. All her fight, withered. Hope had been strangled from her. It was over. They'd lost. The Veil would end. Who knew when. In an instant? Days, weeks, years? Irrelevant fears in the face of such utter failure, weren't they? "What have you done?"

Volkari was stoic as royalty, advancing on Maijerda. "What you couldn't. I righted your mother's wrongs, I—" She halted and joined the stares of dazed confusion at the basin.

The most bizarre sight unfolded. A final burst of smoke, and ink writhed from the sides of the blood basin. It gathered into a form. The swirl was delicate and curved. It appeared to be searching with a bent neck, levitating higher. It swayed, searching still. East to west. Until it found Maijerda.

The smoke soared and shot through her neck, sending her choking on ash, blood, and what tasted like ink. Denratis shoved her to the ground as she bellowed in pain and collapsed. Line by inked line punctured as piercing blades covered in poison on the back of her neck. Maijerda forgot how to breathe, on the verge of fainting.

Swallowing the horror of it, she curled on the floor as what little blood she had left curdled. She held her arms in tight, chains burrowing into her ribs. She was drenched in sweat, writhing until the blades disappeared.

"Bring her to me." Volkari instructed in the wake of Maijerda's last echoing scream.

Her lips went slack. Her eyes swollen and burning.

Denratis jerked Maijerda to stand, forcing her to face him. His shirt slid open with his roughness, revealing a gaping wound in his chest. Unfathomably, an eel slithered around a hardened shell-like organ Maijerda assumed was his heart.

"What did she do to you?" Shock shook her words.

He ignored her, scowling as Volkari exposed her neck.

Each strand of hair scraped her skin. "It seems you've been branded."

Maijerda gasped and panted in agony at Volkari's touch tracing each segment of the glyph. "The book may be consumed, but its soul sought a host. Shame you must shoulder this burden."

Denratis forced Maijerda around, maintaining his grip.

Volkari announced, "Our seeds are sown under what remains of the Cruor Moon. I'll remind all of you, of how forgiving it is to destroy than create. If your faith wanes, we risk failure as the Veil tears. Is your faith waning with the Moon, Lyrian?"

Lyrian's hand slid to the pouch on her sash. Same that she carried in the Menagerie. "Never."

Twitching, she pulled against Denratis, despite how he held fast. "Piss off, Denratis."

"Don't stop there. Tell me what else you'd like me to do."

"Denratis," Jeddeith ordered, striding to Maijerda. "Release her."

"Do as he says."

Before abiding Lyrian's instruction, Denratis whispered, "I'll enjoy this." He shoved her to him.

She wouldn't be made a fool.

Steadying trembling legs, Maijerda brought her hands defensively to her chest, shackles be damned. She twisted to harness all her force in striking Jeddeith.

He caught her wrist, squeezing.

Maijerda unleashed on him. "I never should have trusted you." No matter how she prodded he remained apathetic. Then, brass energy flowed from his fingers.

His spell unlocked her shackles, sending them clanging. Her hatred halted. Calm pressed into her. Forcefully, outside her own mind. She didn't want it! Where was it coming from? Not from her desires. No, she was through with this—this endless spiral of vexation and horror. This—

"Torlen dovnym."

"What?"

He closed his eyes. "Torlen dovnym."

Wait. A ruse? Was this an escape?

Indecisively, she rotated her wrist in his, her skin raw and itching. What if he'd put on a show? And a brilliant performance at that. Fates. None of this made sense. An external force returned, urging her to... to trust.

And so, she did. "Torlen lexnym," she confided. For she understood.

He tucked his hand in her hair, his touch soothing her burning brand. Those bastards didn't stand a chance. They would escape this hell yet.

It was as if he heard her and confirmed his alliance with the kiss that followed. She welcomed it and melded into him, his skin warmed from the mark on his chest. Slowly he drew back, despite Maijerda's tight grasp of his arm. Letting go was the last thing she wanted.

Ruefully he spoke with delicacy born from denial between lovers. "You weren't supposed to look."

Maijerda was denied a response, the mere possibility torn and tossed aside with the blinding promise of revelation. Under Jeddeith's hand, the hilt of his fae iron dagger was jutting from below her ribs. Any fleeting sense of hope was shredded in its tracks with a twist of his blade.

The iron retaliated in her belly, teeth tearing as if raging at the idea of being used for the greater good. Every nerve in her body lit on fire, her blood freezing.

Jeddeith withdrew the dagger, leaving a wake of searing turmoil. Her wail absorbed Wytt's shouts into the surrounding putrescence and she collapsed into him. There was no care in his touch as he kept her from falling to the stone.

Lyrian came to her, tilting Maijerda's chin. "You didn't think I'd let you live to see another day, did you? You served your purpose. Remember that story I promised you, of weaver's nectar?"

She was expecting a response. Maijerda didn't want to appease her. Nor did she want to admit she couldn't, reduced to coughing on her blood again.

"Awe, well. I'll spare you the embarrassment of having to ask. Weaver's nectar was the name of an orchid that thrived before the Veil. It was a component for spells and other arcane investments. Those capable of harvesting it knew the sole means of convincing it to bloom was to sing to it under the light of the Moon. And that, Maijerda." She exaggerated the pronunciation of her name with unadulterated hatred. "Is the meaning of your name. Weaver's nectar. Born to bleed for the tapestry."

Lyrian bowed her head to Jeddeith as he adjusted to carry Maijerda in his arms. "Ensure she dies. I never want to see that damn weed again."

"I swear it, Mistress." His vow was free from regret, awash with resolution as he walked to the parapet.

494

Maijerda fought to throw herself from Jeddeith's hold, but he jostled her to keep her still. Her limbs moved dreadfully slow and she groaned over her bleeding belly.

Ocean brine and the dark of the Harrowing enveloped Maijerda. "Jeddeith please—" Wincing and holding her wound, she spasmed.

He stopped at the parapet's edge and peered at her, his mismatched eyes the perfect balance of light and darkness.

"Don't do this."

There was a storm of loathing in his eyes. Storms were often unkind. However, this one was an unrivaled menace. She begged of him, "Why?"

"Why did you have to look?" Without another word, Jeddeith cast her over the edge.

Wind swallowed her whole as she fell, arms stretched as flightless wings. Waves pummeled against the cliff face, their snarls intensifying by the second.

Down.

Down.

Down she fell.

Such gorgeous petals drifted down the cliff face too. Muted hues of roses and snowdrops enswathed her.

The fortress disappeared from view, replaced by inky waters. She floundered in the ocean for the surface. Breaking for air, Maijerda coughed, favoring her side and staving off drifting to unconsciousness.

How did she end up here? She should be dead.

Arms and a tail wrapped around her to keep her head above water. "Maijerda, don't! Stay with me. I've got you. Stay with me!"

"Wyttrikus?" She grappled to speak over a whisper. Fates, her skin was ice slick from shock. Her limbs heavy yet weightless in the water. How had Wytt appeared around her? What had he done to save her?

"W-we need to get you out of here. I need to look at your wound." He was doing his best to not sound stressed or angry. And truthfully, to keep her from panicking. "Jeddeith, he-he— used his fae iron blade, I'mmm sure of it."

The sea salt stung and Maijerda clamped harder on her wound, wanting to reply to Wytt, instead grimacing and groaning. As she did, she closed her hand around smooth glass in her pocket. A vial? She pulled it free, struggling to behold the glisten in waning Cruor Moonlight. "The Moon's Tears," she muttered. The sight brought her sense enough to hand the bottle to Wytt, fearful she'd lose them to the waves.

"How?"

"I don't know. One thing at a time."

Wytt refused to let go of her, treading water to keep them both afloat. His chest supporting her back, heaved with forced control. "There's a way out. There must be a way."

She started to fade. If she could just close her eyes for a minute…

"Maijerda!" Baritone carried on the wind as a wave engulfed them. Wytt secured his hold of her and kicked to the surface. A prow of a ship appeared through the fog, sailing straight for them.

Upset with a deeper stillness, they beckoned to her again. "Maijerda!"

It couldn't be. Surely she was hallucinating.

"Maijerda!"

Da? Maijerda blinked through her own haze and the fog. The ship, it must be the *Norn*. Why else would Da be calling for her? Which meant she was fated for death. Da had come to carry her away from this world. Maybe Mama was with him.

"N-no!" Wytt shouted at her. "Stay awake, damn it! You hear me? We're almost there."

He was pulling her, determinedly onward in the water. But to where? If Da was coming to escort her to an afterlife, surely Wytt couldn't see the *Norn* too. Maybe Wytt was swimming back to shore to take their chances, unaware she was being beckoned by death.

Then, the most curious creature challenged her distress. Beside Maijerda, copper strands strummed to coalesce into a wisp grazing the water. It fluttered with worry, darting across her vision and tucking into her hair. It peeked out from around her neck and flickered its glow.

"Is it you?" She struggled to speak. "You've come for us?"

The wisp hummed with pride.

Maijerda's heart leapt to mend itself. If Nadín's wisp was here, it couldn't be Da aboard that ship. Her mind was drifting, but her soul was not. She would survive this. And now, she could see the ship's sails were nothing akin to the *Norn's*. In fact, she didn't recognize them at all.

Struggling, Maijerda pulled apart from Wytt, assuring him she could swim. The wisp floated between them, concerned. "Don't stray from me," she bade both the wisp and Wytt.

Bobbing above the water, the wisp soared to lead them to the ship, specks of light trailing in his wake. Maijerda overcame the anguish racking her body and spirit as she swam headlong into the waves.

Into the deep beneath.

Into the darkness of the sea.

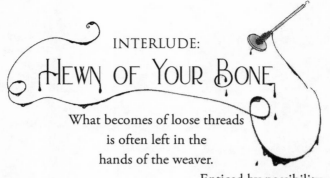

INTERLUDE:

HEWN OF YOUR BONE

What becomes of loose threads
is often left in the
hands of the weaver.

Enticed by possibility…

…ensnared by false promise.

Boundless artistries
lie within your grasp.

However, lest your place
be forgotten…

…you should be grateful
for our kindness in…

…granting these spools…

…in the first place.

You'd be adrift…

…without them…

…guiding your every stitch.

Take comfort.

We would not allow your…

…blood to let upon pages…

…hewn of your bone,

…if it weren't aligned with truth.

Such was the luck
of weaver's nectar.

Bleeding her last
blood-sown tune…

…bathed in the light
of a weeping Moon.

* * *

AUTHOR'S NOTE

THE ELEMENTS BEHIND *Spent Spindle* and this first installment of the series are a bit all over the place. At its core, this piece is a coming-of-self story that integrates speech language pathology with the power of storytelling, music, and grief.

My graduate education and experience as a speech pathologist comes into play by incorporating the many branches of speech and language, communication disorders, linguistics, and everything in between. Even the tapestry, my magic system in this series, is inspired by the various avenues of language and cognition. This foundation allowed me to begin exploring a question I've wanted to pose for quite some time to the fantasy book community. How does your engagement with language impact your magic? What if your foundation with language changes at some point in your life? Would how you use magic change?

Sterling, my younger autistic brother, also had an immense influence on this tale in terms of the experiences we shared. From his relationship with language to his adventures in life as a whole. Though this story began years before his unexpected passing, mourning his loss since 2021 ended up coloring edits to reflect my own, visceral navigation of the beast we call grief.

Aspects of Maijerda's health are an expression of my journey with polycystic ovarian syndrome (PCOS). Ever since receiving a diagnosis, life has been an ever-flowing battle of balance I'm constantly working to learn and manage to better honor my body and mind. Maijerda has helped me reflect on and normalize the underlying battles that often go unacknowledged, such as her anxiety, brain fog, and fatigue.

I'm happy to share more about these with you all should the occasion arise. Please reach out to me if you have any questions, comments, or simply want to share a cup of tea and discussion.

Be well. Thank you for taking the time to indulge my story. To say it means the world is an understatement.

Rara Hope

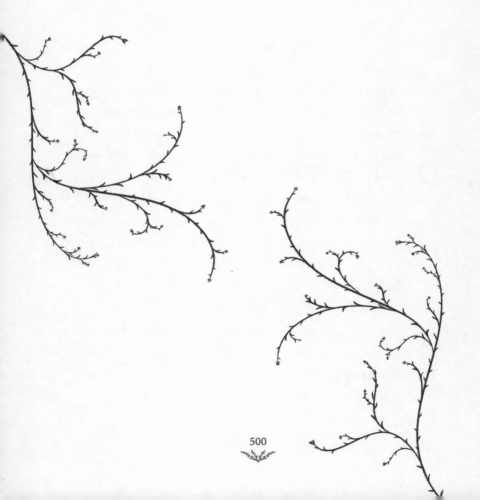

About the Author

Rara Hope is a speech language pathologist and debut fantasy author. She was born and raised in Las Vegas with her younger brother, Sterling. She has since traded the heat for the mountain air of northern Nevada after obtaining her Master's Degree in Speech Language Pathology.

The first iteration of her series, *Spent Spindle*, began when Rara was twelve years old. It is no coincidence this project began with her love for archery, Pirates of the Caribbean, *Lord of the Rings*, and attending the Las Vegas Renaissance Faire for the first time.

This story has transformed alongside her over the years, ever changing and adapting to new experiences. After obtaining her master's degree in Speech Pathology, Rara eventually embraced her desire to revisit this story and world, at long last completing Stage One of the *Spent Spindle*.

Rara longs for candlelit rainy days. Friends playfully consider her to be the resident village witch, as she often devotes her time outside of Storybooking to baking, brewing tea, and doing her best with plants. She also indulges in tabletop role playing games, archery, singing to carefully crafted playlists, daydreaming about travel, the occasional knitting project, and video games.

Sterling Page is Rara's younger brother. Rara and her family decided to honor his memory through her company after his unexpected passing in 2021. He will forever be in their hearts, with his unforgettable love and sense of adventure.

Sterling was autistic and his way with the world and communication is what sparked certain aspects of Rara's debut novel and fantasy realm. She strives to carry on his story with Sterling Page LLC so others may grow to know and love him.

To keep up to date with Rara's shenanigans or to find contact information, please visit her website www. rarapagehope.com or her social media accounts.

Acknowledgments

The Moon Could Only Weep has bore several names over the years and has transformed into the tale of my heart. Even with my wildest dreams, I didn't know we would make it here, of all places. With a story in hand that I now at last have the privilege of sharing with you all.

It started when I was thirteen years old, with an English assignment, a random whim, and a love for all things fantasy and pirates. It bloomed when my mother spent hours upon hours editing each chapter with me to share every Monday morning aloud with my English class, at their behest. It rested in solace while I couldn't find the space for it during college and graduate school. And when I was ready, it was waiting to be brushed off, revisited, and revamped until made whole.

For each transformation I've endured personally, this story has in turn reflected a similar path. It would not have been there if it weren't for the absolute village of people supporting it. Where are you supposed to begin with these words of gratitude when you know words won't ever be enough?

This is for all those who did not just listen to this story as it was crafted, but who took the time to understand it and help both it and myself grow.

Thank you to my parents, Roxanne and Richard, who never cease in teaching me how to persevere, to be creative, to honor myself, my family, and my dreams. Thank you for your love and support, which knows no bounds. I am forever grateful for all you've done and continue to do each day. Thank you mom for taking the time to edit my chapters and treating my little project saved on a floppy disk with the utmost of sincerity. Because you believed in me and taught me the importance of creating, I believed in it! Thank you dad for introducing me to the rich and wondrous world of fantasy books. Without those, I wouldn't have been able to picture what might be possible. My imagination wouldn't have continued to flourish. I am all the stronger for those stories in my life and the part you had in sharing them. I owe you both everything.

Thank you to my friends. You've listened to my ramblings, read my drafts so desperately in need of fixing. Listened to me read segments, rant, and cry. Thank you to my alpha readers, my beta readers, my audiobook cast. The creative minds that helped me world build and daydream. One of my favorite aspects about this story is how it embodies a little piece of everyone who's touched it. A beautiful concept. I think we all get to share something that is a little bit the same, in ways that are special for us individually.

Thank you *all*. For your time. Your patience. Compassion, love, spirit, and sheer determination. Together we have created a team, without whom I would be lost.

Cheers to you, this wonderful crew! In no particular order: Brianna Hughes, Megan O'Donnell, Taylor Remke, Walter Brediger, Rin White, Katy Mawson, Ian Laughlin, Chace Calvert, Rose Molina, Callie Williams, Alexis Fitting, Katie Pino, Ken Hugdal, Katie Hughes, T Davis I will never be able to thank you enough for coming together with your passions and skills to help me create something truly unique and beyond my wildest dreams.

Thank you to my editor, Carly Hayward. Who showed me kindness during the pandemic and opened a door to years of working together and unforgettable chats about stories. Thank you for teaching and guiding me through this process with bountiful excitement, expertise, and understanding.

Oh! And thank you to my seventh grade English class all those years ago. If it weren't for your eagerness to hear what would happen next the following Monday, I probably wouldn't have kept the heart of this story alive.

Thank you to Sterling. Though you are not physically with us for me to show and share this with you, I hope you can see what we are all working toward now. Thank you for teaching me your ways. Your thoughts. Your heart.

Thank you all for doing more than just listening. For while it is wonderful to be heard, it is all the more empowering to be understood.

Torlen dovnym.

Torlen lexnym.

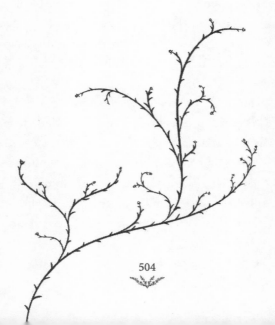

Made in the USA
Middletown, DE
23 December 2024

68105941R00307